SOFT SEDUCTION

It was dark; the full and black dark of night between Nocturn and Matins when a man's sleep was heavy and his soul most vulnerable. It was then that she came. It was then that she always came.

He watched her come to him, her movements graceful and light, her hair a dark veil that moved with her. As before, he could do nothing to stop her. It was the heart of his shame.

He could not resist her. She lay upon him, tucking her chill feet against his calves as her mouth opened damp upon his exposed throat. He had strong arms, warrior's arms, fit and long, yet he could not hold her off or keep her back. She lay atop him, a light and stirring weight of femininity, and defeated his resolve.

Her mouth moved slowly up the column of his throat toward his jaw; she traced the shape of it with the tip of one finger before pulling his mouth down to hers, giving him her wild and reckless heat. Dark hair spilled over her back to lay tangled on his arms and chest, cool and heavy like the night itself. They were not alone, but it did not matter. She had come for him, and he could not refuse her seduction.

Other *Leisure* books by Claudia Dain:

THE FALL
THE TEMPTATION
A KISS TO DIE FOR
THE WILLING WIFE
TO BURN
WISH LIST (Anthology)
THE HOLDING
TELL ME LIES

THE MARRIAGE BED

CLAUDIA DAIN

LEISURE BOOKS   NEW YORK CITY

In loving memory of my father, Richard,
who spoke little and loved much.

A LEISURE BOOK®

March 2008

Published by

Dorchester Publishing Co., Inc.
200 Madison Avenue
New York, NY 10016

ISBN 10: 0-8439-4933-3
ISBN 13: 978-0-8439-4933-9

The name "Leisure Books" and the stylized "L" with design are
trademarks of Dorchester Publishing Co., Inc.

Printed in the United States of America.

10 9 8 7 6 5 4 3 2

Visit us on the web at www.dorchesterpub.com.

THE
MARRIAGE
BED

Prologue

It was dark; the full and black dark of night between Nocturn and Matins when a man's sleep was heavy and his soul most vulnerable. It was then that she came. It was then that she always came.

He watched her come to him, her movements graceful and light, her hair a dark veil that moved with her. As before, he could do nothing to stop her. It was the heart of his shame.

He could not resist her. She lay upon him, tucking her chill feet against his calves as her mouth opened damp upon his exposed throat. He had strong arms, warrior's arms, fit and long, yet he could not hold her off or keep her back. She lay atop him, a light and stirring weight of femininity, and defeated his resolve.

Her mouth moved slowly up the column of his throat toward his jaw; she traced the shape of it

9

with the tip of one finger before pulling his mouth down to hers, giving him her wild and reckless heat. Dark hair spilled over her back to lay tangled on his arms and chest, cool and heavy like the night itself. They were not alone, but it did not matter. She had come for him, and he could not refuse her seduction.

All was done silently—the raising of her shift, the feel of her heat against his nakedness, the weight of her bosom pressing against him, pressing him down until his shaft rose in angry and eager rebellion. Nay, not angry, only eager. Such was the depth of his sin.

Stone walls flickering golden in the light of a single candle witnessed all. He kissed her, holding her down to him, ravaging her mouth like a wolf tearing into a hare and with as much repentance. Her legs spread over him, encasing him in soft heat, urging his seed to spill forth, to join his body to hers. Yet even now, his spirit cried out in silent torment that he had lost again. Yet again.

He was damned.

The knowledge followed him into release, his seed spurting out in unlawful spasms to lie in a wet and defeated mass upon his thigh.

The holy brother who stood in charge of all the novices in the Abbey of Saint Stephen and Saint Paul watched him in horror as the bells rang for Matins.

"Yet again, she has come to you," Father Abbot said kindly.

"Yea, Father," the novice Benedictine answered, his head lowered and his hands clenched into fists well hidden in his long sleeves.

Father Abbot looked upon the novice with concern. Almost nightly the succubus came to him, the demon sent from the Evil One to test the resolve of a man's vow of abstinence. Never had Father Abbot seen such struggles in all his years at the abbey; the resolve of the man who stood before him must be great indeed to so compel the demons of darkness to attack. And he was attacked.

Richard was a man driven.

He had appeared at their gates a little more than a year ago, just past Whitsunday, his face solemn and his manner urgent. He would give himself to God in holy service, binding himself to the Benedictine Rule for the remainder of his life, his life now strictly ordered spheres of work and prayer and sleep. He had come willingly—nay, urgently. He had pledged himself to God with the eagerness of a man being pulled from the fire, as were all who sought divine grace in a world of sin and corruption.

His fervency had not diminished once inside their walls.

He held himself to a higher and harder standard than even the Rule dictated. He battled an inner demon, one which he had brought with him into abbey life and had not done him the courtesy of remaining in the outside world. In his battle, work was his ally, sleep his enemy. He carried dressed stone for the new infirmary on his bare back. He was the oxen for their plowing, the hand that did their hoeing, the arm that scrubbed the chapel floor. He had the skill of reading, but it was a skill he undertook only when forced.

Such labor would make any man dream of sleep, yet Richard did not sleep. His succubus lay in wait for him when e'er he did sleep; Father Abbot could understand why he avoided slumber when such battles awaited him in his rest.

"The same?" he asked.

"Yea, Father," Richard admitted. Yea, she was the same. Dark of hair and pale of skin, her eyes clear windows to his own destruction; always the same, always the same result. She defeated him with her softness and her smoothness, her blatant femininity her most potent weapon. He could not drive her from him, not with prayer, not with labor, not with seclusion. No matter the obstacle he built against her, she slipped into his dreams with a smile of victory. She knew her power. She knew his weakness. In a match of strength, he was out-manned. Yet he did fight and would continue. He had no choice but to resist her.

He knew not how to do anything else.

"You work too strenuously," Father Abbot said. "She preys upon your exhaustion."

"I but buffet my body, as Saint Paul did, to master it," Richard argued.

He must have his labors. He must. She pursued him in the daylight, her vision before his eyes, unless he drove himself hard, punishing his body to control his mind; yet he could not confess such to

Father Abbot. Father Abbot could not know the depth of his failure and his sin.

"A worthy goal. Is it working?"

Richard kept his eyes on his lord's hem, his manner submissive, his heart determined. "It is helping."

Father Abbot considered his charge. Richard had come to them with a heavy heart; a year of service had done nothing to lighten it. Only sin pressed upon a man so, sin unconfessed and therefore unforgiven. Nothing could help a man but he confess it.

"You endure buffeting on every side, Brother Richard, yet is the Lord not a mighty tower? You have only to present yourself, a living sacrifice, to Him, your sins confessed, to be saved."

"I have confessed. I do confess," Richard said stiffly.

Yet not all. Clearly, not all. Richard's was a soul in torment, his agony suffered silently and alone. Among the novices he was feared, a constrained and powerful man who held himself aloof. Aloof from God? Nay, he pursued God most fervently, yet he pursued Him with a caged heart. The only one who could slip past the barriers of Richard's defenses was his succubus; an unpleasant truth and one wholly unacceptable.

"I will continue to pray for you, Richard, and what you will do is work in the scriptorium until I give you leave to return to the fields." Father Abbot could see the rebellion in Richard's posture, yet he held his tongue; none could say that Richard lacked self-control. "Let us pray that God will have His way with you, your heart and mind devoted to His will."

"Yea, Father, I pray it most earnestly," Richard answered, his head bowed.

"As do I, Richard. As do we all."

Chapter One

Spring 1155

Her dark hair flew out behind her as she rode, a heavy weight of glossy mane that the wind lifted easily in her wild ride. She would have enjoyed it, the freedom, the speed, the wildness of it; she would have enjoyed it, if not for the death that had precipitated it.

The road was muddy, thrown and broken by the horse she rode as swiftly as she could. The trees embracing the road were dark with recent rain and bright with the shrill green of new growth. The world shouted its life after a long, frozen sleep, and she could savor none of it. She had to ride. She had to find refuge in a spring world suddenly thrown back into the death of winter.

Her father was dead. She was alone and unprotected in a world that tolerated vulnerablity not at all. She searched for safety.

"Are we pursued?" she shouted forward to Edmund, her voice almost lost against the wind.

"Nay, not yet," he said over his shoulder.

She wanted to rest in his assurance, to find even a moment of safety, but she could not. Edmund was young, only a squire. He could not talk her into a place of refuge, she could only ride there, as on wings.

"Should we not ride for town, Lady? The abbey—"

"Nay, we ride for the abbey," she shouted, the wind cold in her throat, stinging her eyes to tears.

She would find safety in the abbey. The monks, though no warriors, would bar the gates and keep the world away from her. None would take her from the abbey.

Richard was at the abbey.

She ducked her head against the wind and sniffed away her guilt. Aye, guilt; she could admit it to herself. She rode hard for the abbey in a world gone swifty hostile so that she could find refuge in the place that harbored Richard.

She was not doing as her father had instructed.

Dying, his voice a whisper against the echoes of eternity, he had told her to flee. Flee the home she cherished, flee to her betrothed, to safety, to a marriage that should have taken place long years since.

Her betrothed was not at the abbey. Richard was at the abbey.

And within her own walls were knights who would eagerly pluck a maid unprotected and make her their own, claiming her lands as they laid hold of her body.

Crying, she had listened and understood the danger she now faced. An orphan with property and income was not safe in the world; she needed a protector, either father or husband. She had neither as of an hour ago. She had buried her face against her father's chest and felt his last breath shudder out of him; Father Langfrid had prayed for her father's soul as it began its ascent to heaven, urging her to flee, promising to make the burial arrangements and to handle all until she could return, married and safe. She had walked calmly from her father's chamber to the stable and ridden out of Dornei with all the serenity of death, her panic cloaked as close about her as armor. Edmund she trusted, though he was a man. Edmund accompanied her. In an unsafe world, a woman who rode alone was a fool.

She was no fool, though she did not ride to her betrothed. She rode to the man she trusted above all others, to the man whom she knew better than her prayers, to the man who had ridden away from her and not once come back.

Richard was at the abbey.

Like an answered prayer, the abbey walls rose tall and gray against the soft afternoon sky. Alone in a field, far from the town, the Abbey of Saint Stephen and Saint Paul was a refuge of stone in a green, growing world. Monks worked in the fields and walked in shuffling steps within the high walls that sheltered them from the cares of the outside world. She wanted to be sheltered in just the same fashion. The bells rang just as Edmund announced them to the porter. He had to let them in before the afternoon prayers of None; she could not wait here, in the open, so plainly seen and so easily taken.

Edmund was firm, but he was young. The porter hesitated.

"Please, Brother Porter," she said, "It is refuge I seek. Will you not grant me sanctuary?"

His dark eyes widened at the word, and he opened the gate, admitting them. Isabel rushed in ahead of Edmund and only let out her stilled breath when the bar was closed against the heavy wooden gate.

She had mentioned sanctuary; she had not mentioned Richard.

What would a monk understand of reckless and unlawful love?

"My thanks, Brother," she said softly, not allowing her eyes to search the courtyard for Richard.

"Is it sanctuary you seek, Lady?" Brother Porter asked.

"Yea, Brother . . . ?"

"Anselm I am called," he answered.

"And I am Lady Isabel. Brother Anselm, I seek sanctuary within your walls, if you will have me."

"Father Abbot alone may grant sanctuary," he said calmly, "but you are welcome until he may speak with you. It is now None. Perhaps you will be comfortable in the guest house until the good father can come to you?"

"Thank you, Brother Anselm," she answered, head bowed as he led the way to the small stone guest house. Edmund took the horses to the stable with a quick nod in her direction. She smiled his release. They were safe now. At least for the time. Let Edmund go his way.

The guest house was simple and secure, the floors dry and clean, the door snug; Isabel smiled in momentary contentment until the sound of the men at their prayers drifted to her on the clean spring air. Could she hear, in that mélange of male voices, the deep notes of Richard at his prayers?

"Your pardon, Lady Isabel, I must attend," Brother Anselm said, backing out with a shy smile and closing the door behind him. Alone, she could hear the rising voices, deep and resonant, voicing their prayers to God.

Which was what she should be doing instead of listening for the voice of a man forbidden to her.

Isabel dropped to her knees, glad for the cold, uneven stone floor, glad for the chill that encased her damp feet, glad for the distraction from the voices raised in holy anthem just within the courtyard. God must be met within the bounds of sacred prayer with a whole and undivided heart and with a soul yearning for perfection. She had neither. Yet, she prayed. Perhaps God would hear the prayer of a cold and beleaguered orphan, even as He would not heed the prayer of a disobedient and wayward woman.

For such she was, to love a man not her betrothed.

To love a man who had betrothed himself to God.

Richard.

Why could it not be Richard who had been chosen for her while she lay within her swaddling? The answer was clear as spring rain: Richard was not the eldest. Her father, and his, would not have made such a bargain. And, as much as she yearned for Richard, neither would she have. She was the sole heir to Dornei, Wiselei, and Turvestone. Her dower lands were Braccan and Hilesdun. She was a woman well propertied. Her earthly function was to marry well and produce heirs who would strengthen and increase what had already been achieved. Richard would inherit nothing. He was third born and destined to make his own way. He had made it in a monastery.

It had not been expected. He had done well in his knightly training, excelling at all he tried; he could have achieved something on his own, by his own hand and with his own sword. He had cast all down and walked into the Abbey of Saint Stephen and Saint Paul without looking back. Without coming back.

It should not matter. She was betrothed to Hubert. She was beyond ripe for marriage. But she had not ridden to Hubert. She had ridden to Richard.

She was unnatural in her desires, this she knew.

She needed to repent, this she also knew. But instead of repentance and tears, there was the knowledge that Richard was near. Richard was close. She might see him if she went in to worship. Isabel kept her knees firmly on the uneven floor. She needed repentance more than she needed Richard, none needed to tell her that, yet Richard was her hunger.

Shame swelled to wash over her unnatural desires. Shame retreated. Her desires remained.

"Saint Stephen, I am a sinner, as black of heart as Judas, betraying my lord Hubert with thoughts of another. In your mercy, give me the strength to . . ."

To go to Hubert? She did not dare pray for that for fear that it would be given. She did not want the strength to leave Richard. Stephen had endured a stoning, dying as the first martyr of Christendom; she refused to prayerfully ask for the strength of will to excise Richard from her heart. She was a poor sort of Christian.

"Give me . . . give me Richard, if it may be," she burst out, ashamed and exhilarated at once.

The monks ceased their chant in that moment, and the silence that followed was fuller for the void. In such silence, her prayer seemed to fill the room, expanding until the weight of it seemed to crush her soul.

"But only in Your will," she added quickly into the silence, her voice small and constricted. Nothing at all like the voice in which she had demanded Richard of the Most High God.

She was, in truth, a very poor sort of Christian and most in need of repentance.

A knock, definite yet delicate, and then Abbot Godric entered. She was still on her knees. He would think her pious when she was merely desperate. But perhaps he would tell Richard he had seen her on her knees in prayer and Richard would think her pious. That would please Richard, if he believed. Richard knew her very well and, most like, would not believe.

She rose to her feet quickly and bowed before the abbot.

"Thank you, Abbot Godric, for showing me the hospitality of your house."

"You are always welcome, Lady Isabel, but Brother Anselm said you came seeking sanctuary. What is amiss at Dornei?"

Isabel turned her eyes to the floor, studying the thick hem of his robe as she spoke. "All is amiss at Dornei. My father died this day. He bade me find a place of safety, for I am now a woman of great worth and much would be risked to gain what I hold."

She could feel the prick of tears and blinked them away, raising her eyes to look into the sympathetic gaze of the man before her. He was of Saxon blood, yet it did not speak against him. There was a power in him that few men possessed. She supposed it was the power of the Spirit of God, since Saxon power was a thing long past. His eyes were warmest brown and his hair chestnut lined with white, and he looked to have a care only for others, his own woes seen to by his Savior and Lord. Isabel knew she did not have the same look, since her woes were the result of a rebellious spirit and a stubborn heart.

"Poor child. But why did your father direct you here? We will surely protect you, with God's provision, but would you not have been better served to make for Hubert? He will surely be your most certain protection."

"He did not direct me here," she said with all truth, "yet your house was the closest sanctuary and I needed the comfort of that, if nothing else."

She did not mention Richard.

"Nothing else? Do not tell me that you did not seek the comfort of communal prayer for your father. You know that he will be prayed for by all here and with great heart. He shall be missed."

"Thank you," she said softly. It was a great gift; their prayers would hasten his soul to heaven.

"A message will be sent to Hubert, telling him of your need. I will write it myself and see it sent within the hour. You shall be married here, if it suits your betrothed, and then all will be settled again. I know that God will not find it amiss to have you married quickly, even on the cusp of your father's death. You must be protected from men who would steal what they cannot lawfully claim."

Godric laid a hand upon her arm but briefly, in comfort, and then turned to go. Edmund stood in the open doorway, his expression open and reposed, as was his way. There had been nothing untoward in Godric's touch; the door to the guest house had been left open to prevent just such speculation, and Edmund's calm witness showed the wisdom of the practice.

"Edmund, it is good to see you. And good to see that you have done your duty by your lady. She was well served in choosing you as her escort to our house."

"Thank you, Abbot Godric," Edmund answered. "We had safe journey."

"God be praised for that. He watches most diligently after the widows and orphans of this world. But I have news of your brother, Peter."

"He is well?" Edmund asked eagerly.

"Most assuredly. He has been knighted by Baron Thomas and has pledged his fealty. I am told he walks well in his spurs."

"He should; he practiced often enough while yet a boy," Edmund laughed. "It is good news. I would that you could tell him of my own dubbing, when a messenger passes through the abbey, but it must wait apace. I am close. He shall not outstrip me. You may pass that on if the occasion suits."

Isabel dropped her head in sudden shame. Edmund was past due for his spurs; her father should have seen it done, but he had fallen into a weakened state so quickly that much was left undone, her own wedding the surest proof of that. He had pressed for her to marry for months, yet she had always had a ready and compelling reason why they should delay. First, because she was newly home from her fostering and wanted to enjoy Dornei before becoming the bride of Warefeld, then because her father's wife, Ida, had fallen ill and needed the care only a daughter could give. Then because Ida had died and she would not leave her father alone in his grief. Finally, because her father had taken ill himself and there was none to push her from his side. And so now. She had never mentioned Richard as the cause of her continued delay, but did not God see her heart and was she not guilty of disobedience? She was not married, certain proof of her silent rebellion.

Still, Edmund must win his spurs, and only his lord could see it done. If she had gone to Hubert . . . but she had not gone to Hubert. She had run to Richard, and Richard could confer the buffet on no one. Richard had cast aside his own spurs, the symbol of his knighthood, in favor of a cowl.

"I shall," Abbot Godric answered Edmund. "Your day will come," he assured.

Yea, when Hubert came to the abbey to fetch her . . . nay, he would come to marry her. Edmund would win his spurs, and she would win a husband she did not want. Unless God answered her impossible prayer, but God did not answer prayers rooted in disobedience and willfulness, no matter how heartfelt.

"Father Abbot!" Brother Anselm said, entering the room in a flurry of black wool. "Father! A message most urgent."

"Hold, Brother Anselm," Godric soothed. "A message can wait until we are alone."

"But, Abbot Godric," Anselm said, trying for control, "the message concerns the Lady Isabel."

"Speak then, Brother," Godric said.

"Lord Robert sends word that Lord Hubert, the lady's betrothed, is dead."

He said more; she could hear the buzzing of his voice calling for Brother John, but she could not stay to hear the rest. She had prayed to be released from Hubert, and, as effortlessly as watching a petal fall to earth, Hubert had died. Such was the fruit of her careless and selfish prayer. In a gray and dim rush, Isabel fell in a swoon to lie heavily upon the cold stone floor.

Chapter Two

"You have much to learn in the art of courteous communication," Brother John said to Brother Anselm as he urged wine past the lady's lips.

Brother Anselm, good-hearted and only slightly impetuous, looked properly abashed.

Edmund looked ashamed and contrite; he clearly felt that he should have caught his lady before she fell so heavily to earth.

Brother John spoke softly to the lady as she slowly came to her senses. "You have had a shock and taken a fall. All will be well. Take a sip of wine to ease you."

She opened her eyes with effort and then made to stand immediately, her face flushed in profound embarrassment.

"Hold, Isabel," John said gently. "Be sure you are uninjured before you rise. Is your head clear?"

"My head is clear. My dignity is trammeled," she said with a rueful smile.

"You have had a shock. It is understandable. None fault you."

"I fault myself. I was taught better," she murmured.

"Rest easily," he coaxed, bringing the cup to her lips yet again, "and allow yourself to be helped. It is no great sin to lean upon others when the need is great."

"Thank you, Brother John," she said, rising as swiftly as he would allow.

John watched her, noted that her color had returned and that her eyes were clear and bright. He would not have faulted her for tears, but perhaps she did not have enough knowledge for tears, the news of death still too hot and bright. He knew her well, as well as any monk could know a woman, for he had helped ease her father's wife into eternity only six short months ago. She had stood well against that loss, tending Lady Ida in her slow march toward death with rare tenderness and skill. And now Lord Bernard gone so quickly, leaving Isabel alone. Still, Isabel would hold her place in the world, no matter what trammeling her dignity suffered.

"I am sorry, child," Godric said, his eyes soft and full of pity. "You should have heard such words in less abrupt a manner."

Anselm hung his head and tugged at his belt in silent agony.

"It would have jolted no matter the delivery," she

said, smiling her pardon at Anselm. "What happened?"

The messenger from her overlord, Lord Robert, stepped from the corner of the small room and faced her. "Lady Isabel, Lord Hubert died in Anjou fighting in a tournament but a month past. When word reached Lord Robert, he began arrangements for your betrothal contract to be transferred to the next in line of that family, to honor the bond made between your father and theirs." Geoffrey, tall and vain; she was to marry Geoffrey. The messenger continued before Geoffrey could root deeply in her thoughts. "Geoffrey fell from his horse eight days ago in a hunting accident; it was a fatal fall, my lady. Lord Robert, believing the original contract sound, wants to keep the alliance between your families. With your father's blessing, it has been arranged for you to marry the next in line of that house."

Isabel remained standing by pure will. She would not faint again, no matter the death on the messenger's lips. No matter the clamor of her guilt.

She said nothing. With one deep and trembling breath, she looked at Abbot Godric. Godric, his expression solemn and sympathetic, turned to Anselm.

"Brother Anselm, please inform Brother Richard he is needed here."

Anselm knew exactly where to find Brother Richard and he was not anxious to go. Not because he was uncomfortable in the scriptorium, which he was not, though he could not read, but because he was uncomfortable with Richard. It should not have been so. All were brothers in the abbey, each called upon by God to serve and pray until the reward of death. All were equal under the care of Father Abbot. It was only that Richard was more equal than most.

Anselm entered the scriptorium quietly, gently. One error with the quill and the manuscript would be worthless; he did not want to startle Richard at his appointed task. He did not want to startle Richard at anything, though Richard was not the sort to become startled. Only a year among them and Brother Richard was the most self-controlled man Anselm had ever encountered; for one so newly introduced to the life of the brotherhood, it was a rare thing. Still, he supposed Richard of Warefeld had come to them with that gift.

He waited until Richard lifted his quill from the vellum before speaking. "The abbot would see you now, Brother Richard. It is a matter of some urgency."

Urgent or no, Richard did not move any more quickly than he had before. He calmly set his quill aside, protected his half-completed manuscript, and turned to face Anselm. Though Anselm predated Richard at the abbey by some twenty-five years, Richard preceded him out of the room. Anselm did not take offense, though it went hard against the Benedictine Rule of precedence. Richard seemed to soar above such earthly rules without effort and certainly without malice.

"We have opened the guest house to someone seeking sanctuary today," Anselm said, hurrying to keep pace with Richard's long-limbed stride.

Richard, in keeping with the Benedictine Rule, did not engage in idle talk. Anselm felt it was not idle since the heaviest portion of the news would concern Richard himself. However, if Richard was ill disposed to speak, there was little Anselm could do without some encouragement.

"I believe you know her," Anselm prompted.

Richard moved inexorably through the golden stone of the abbey corridors, a black and silent silhouette of relentless intent.

"I believe Abbot Godric will have some disturbing news for you, Brother Richard. I would wish you prepared for what you will find when you meet with him," Anselm tried.

"My life is in the hand of God," Richard said without turning his head, his profile sharp against the dressed stone arches. "Let Him do with me what He will."

A most proper answer. Since God had obviously prepared him to marry a beautiful and wealthy woman, Anselm could only wonder at the great mercy and generosity of their Heavenly Father. But a novice monk to marry? The Lord's ways were indeed mysterious.

Richard knocked firmly upon the prior's chamber door, his face resolved and somewhat grim—his normal visage—and entered at Godric's bidding with a stride perhaps more forceful than was common for a lowly novice. Until he spied the form of Isabel.

Isabel stood like a falcon on the wrist, stiff and proud, her eyes going instantly to Richard. And Richard's eyes went instantly to her. In a glimmer, what warm recognition that had flashed in his eyes was gone, replaced by cold courtesy, and that only a veneer to shield some colder emotion. She could feel her heart shrink against his blast of grim civility, but she did not drop her gaze from his. Let him first look from her, if he could; she would not relent. She smothered her guilt; he would not have that from her, not when he was so quick to look for such from her. Let him look. Her heart and her guilt were God's province, not Richard's. Lifting her chin, she stared into his eyes, eyes so deep a blue that they appeared near black against the black of his monk's robes. She knew those eyes, that face, that form. She knew the words he spoke in his heart, the words he had never spoken to her, the words chiseled into his granite soul, words that whispered like the echo of ghosts in his dark blue eyes. Words of rejection, of disdain, of disapproval.

It had not always been so between them. Once, there had been warmth. He had not always disdained her.

Nay, he had been her closest friend.

Children still, alone within the sea of new faces and new customs at Malton, the house of their fostering, they had found each other. How to explain how they had come together? It was not that she was betrothed to the eldest brother of his house, though that was an immediate connection; nay, it had been with their first tentative exchange of words that she had found him admirable. They had been so lost at Malton, the memory of their separate homes becoming more indistinct with each Malton dawn. Yet they had found each other, the bond between them growing with the passing months.

She had been in training to be lady of a great holding, he to be a knight; how often could their paths have crossed? Yet they had found a way. They had ridden to the hunt together, he twice checking the length of her stirrup before they left the bailey. They had played the game of tables, which he had brought with him from Warefeld, and she had beaten him most roundly until he had instructed her in chess, which had taxed her skill and left him the most often winner; he had preferred chess and she tables. She had confessed that she was afraid of Hubert, his brother and her betrothed, and he had listened without censure. He had told her one summer day of the pain of grief he carried still over the loss of his mother and how he feared that he did sin with such unremitting grief over what was surely God's divine will. She had held his hand and cried with him, his pain her own.

They had shared their secrets, their plans, and their fears; he was her closest friend, and she knew that he had valued her companionship above all others. In the world of Malton, Richard had acquired few friends among the boys.

Never had she thought to lose Richard from the inmost circle of her heart. And then, one day, she had.

He had been a squire then, his first beard dark upon his chin, and she had been watching him train. She loved to watch him move. She had smiled to see him knock the sword from his fellow squire's hand and shouted her pleasure at his victory. His opponent, Nicholas, had smirked and said something murmured, looking to her. Richard had ducked his head, shaking it, and turned from her. Willingly, he had never looked at her again.

And still today.

But she would not look away. She had come too far to see him again, finding in his presence a safety he did not willfully give her. Willingly, he would give her nothing. Nay, that was not true; he would give her what he always gave her: the icy chill of reproach. And within her heart, the hot flare of guilt answered him.

he was steeped in sin. The presence of her, her very scent, roused him as nothing should save prayer. Only prayer and service could save him, and yet she was here, interfering with his salvation, interfering with his vocation and corrupting the very strands of his life.

Isabel was profoundly adept at interfering.

Richard pulled his errant thoughts back toward Godric, determined to give his abbot his full attention and starve Isabel of his regard.

So little had changed in a year.

"And so it is with deep sorrow I impart these tidings to you, Richard. Hubert and Geoffrey both, gone to their Lord in His time, if not our own."

Hubert dead. And Geoffrey also. Richard sighed and looked toward the sole wind hole in the chamber. Hubert he had hardly known, born to his father's first wife and away at his fostering before he had even been born. Geoffrey he had known better and liked less. Geoffrey, sharing Hubert's mother, was the first in this world to torment him, and Richard had swiftly learned the advantage of hiding. Proud and vain, Geoffrey would not long be missed upon this earth. Hubert, overbearing as he had been, had been Isabel's betrothed. Isabel must have brought the news to the abbey, thinking he should know the fate of his brothers.

"What was the manner of their deaths? Did they die together?" he asked Abbot Godric, ignoring Isabel completely and determined that she see it.

"Hubert died in tourney while in Anjou and Geoffrey while hunting. They did not die together but close upon each other. A sad loss for your house, Richard. Prayers will be said for them as well."

"As well?" Richard asked.

"Yea, for Lord Bernard died this day, leaving Isabel alone to fend for herself. Until a husband is found for her," Godric answered.

"My sorrow is with you, Lady," Richard murmured, looking at her hem as he bowed his head to the slightest degree.

Isabel bowed in return and said nothing.

Richard turned his eyes back to the wind hole, determined not to look at so much as her hem for the remainder of their shared enclosure. Isabel had been betrothed to Hubert from the cradle; the marriage should have taken place long ago. She was of an age to be wed. Now, because of her father's sudden death, she would be wed or risk losing all. Isabel would marry. She would not willingly give up her position in the world.

"Thank you, Father Abbot, for taking such care in telling me of my brothers. May I now be excused?"

He was already turning away when Godric called him back.

"There is more," Godric said softly.

"What more could there be?" Richard asked.

The messenger stepped forward and said solemnly, "Lord Robert, overlord of Warefeld, is most determined that the betrothal arranged between Lord Bernard and Lord Hubert be unbroken."

Richard faced the man fully and, though clothed

as a Benedictine, stood like a warrior. There could be only one meaning behind the message of Warefeld's and Dornei's mutual overlord; he was an only son, Isabel an only daughter. "The betrothal has been nullified with Hubert's death." He would not be pushed by Lord Robert's whim and not on the word of a paltry messenger.

"Lord Robert is having another written," the messenger answered, blinking rapidly against Richard's latent animosity.

The room seemed to close in on him, pressing him up against Isabel. He could hear her breath and feel her body heat, though he would not look at her. There was victory in that. He could feel her bright eyes upon him, but he would not turn to face her; he would not give even that to her.

"I have sworn myself to another," Richard said, his voice reverberating in the stone chamber.

"But not yet taken your final vows," Godric said almost reluctantly.

All eyes looked to the abbot, Richard's the most urgently. "I am sworn to another," he repeated, his voice as stubborn as his posture was humble.

"Leave us, please," Godric commanded softly.

All left, Isabel leading them, leaving Richard alone to face the lord of his chosen house. When they were alone, Richard fell to his knees and kissed the hem of Godric's robe. Against its rough warmth, he came as close as he ever had to pleading.

"My life is here. I have no wish to reenter the world."

"And what of God's will?" Godric asked softly.

"This is not God's will for me," he said, rising to his feet and burying his hands within the deep bell of his sleeves.

Godric smiled. "Is this the result of devoted prayer or your own will which speaks?"

Richard kept silent, unable to give an honest answer which would serve.

"Pray, Richard," Abbot Godric softly commanded. "Seek God's will on this. Nothing need be decided upon this hour. I will send my own messenger to Lord Robert and one to the bishop as well. Between us, we will find God's path for you."

"Yea, Father. I will pray," Richard all but grumbled.

Godric chuckled and ducked his chin into his cowl. "Pray for a submitted will, Richard; that is the measure of holiness."

Richard lifted his stormy eyes to Godric and said, "It cannot be wrong to want to give my life, every hour of my life, to God."

"Nay, it cannot be wrong," Godric agreed, "but, having given your life to God, can you then pull against the bit when He leads you along the path He has set for you? Nothing in this life is by chance, Richard."

"Yea, Father."

There was nothing more he could say. A messenger was being sent. He would set his heart to prayer. As he turned from his abbot, Richard's hands beneath the heavy wool of his sleeves clenched into fists.

Chapter Four

The messenger from Lord Robert rode into the courtyard just at the conclusion of Compline. Muddy and thirsty, he made his way directly to the Abbot of Saint Stephen's and Saint Paul's, eager to be rid of his obligation. Eager to avoid a confrontation with the novice Richard. He had heard, as had they all, lay brothers as well as tonsured, of how Richard had frothed at his lord's bidding to marry the Lady Isabel. Perhaps frothed was not exactly what he had done, but he had not submitted to a higher authority with any grace. Certainly he had shown no proper submission. And no one who had heard the tale had any trouble believing the truth of it. Richard was unlike any novice yet welcomed into the abbey; he was neither especially pious nor especially submissive, and without either attribute, he was ill suited for abbey life. Though no one would dare suggest it to him—for Richard was an especially determined man, and for some reason he had determined to become a Benedictine. God and all His saints help the man who stood between Richard and his determination.

But God's ways were higher and God would not be mocked. At least that was what the messenger concluded after being given the message from Lord Robert himself. Lord Robert was also a very determined man and had been wroth to have his arrangements questioned. But it was all Abbot Godric's headache now, once he was delivered of his message.

The abbey was quiet, the monks preparing to retire, when Godric admitted the messenger. "What response from Lord Robert?" Godric asked.

"He is firm that the marriage between Isabel of Dornei and Richard of Warefeld occur and without delay. He went to great lengths to arrange the match and obtain the bishop's endorsement of it. They are in agreement; Richard will marry Isabel."

So they had gone to great lengths. Godric smiled softly and folded his hands within his sleeves. Yea, he could well guess that a plot of prime land had been exchanged between lord and bishop to see Richard released from his vow. How compared one novice to a rich manor? Still, God would have His way, even in the exchange of land for men. There was no need to wait for his messenger to return the longer distance from the bishop. All had been arranged long before Richard had been told of his future outside abbey walls.

"Thank you. Food awaits you in the refectory," Godric said, dismissing the man.

Now all that awaited was for Richard to be told that his life's path had just taken a sharp turn. Godric let out his breath and cast his eyes heavenward; he was not looking forward to the task.

Brother Anselm did not know how it was that he managed to be in exactly the right spot to be noticed by Prior Godric and sent to fetch Richard. Again. He surely must be deficient in his prayers to be so used twice in a single day, but God did try the man who turned from Him. Anselm was more determined than usual to be better about his prayers.

Richard was in the dormitory preparing for bed, as were all the novices, when Anselm approached. Unlike all the other novices, Richard was huge in the semidarkness of the chamber, his height and breadth making him a monstrous shadow, though of much firmer form. Even a year on a monk's limited diet had done little to reduce his size, and he towered over most of the others, physically and personally.

Yet it was not Richard's size which daunted, but his manner. Even in the act of removing his shoes, he was intimidating. It should not have been so, for were they not all equal in God's sight? Yet no man in the abbey believed himself the equal of Richard; he was a man set apart from the brotherhood of the abbey even as he dwelt among them. Never had Anselm seen a man so driven to succeed, and never had he seen success weigh so lightly upon a man's shoulders; Richard excelled at all that was required of him and found joy in none of it.

Anselm could not seem to stop the hitch in his step as he approached and fixed a smile upon his face to soften what he was certain would be a blow to Richard's plan for his life. In truth, he was sorry for him. Anselm had come to the abbey as a youth of less than ten summers, and a life outside of abbey walls held no appeal for him.

"You are wanted by our abbot, Richard," he said as gently as he could.

Richard, saying nothing, bent and refastened his shoes. Still silent, he rose to lead Anselm from the chamber, the other novices watching surreptitiously and expectantly. All knew of Lord Robert's arrangements. All knew of the presence of the Lady Isabel. All knew a messenger had been sent to try and seek a release from the arrangement. None expected Richard to be granted reprieve.

"The Lady Isabel," Anselm began, seeking a path of comfort for Richard, "seems to be . . . that is, she appears a lovely and pious lady—"

"The devil can assume a pleasing shape, Brother," Richard cut in, his voice harsh and low.

Stunned, Anselm fell into silence.

Godric awaited them, his door open. Anselm delivered Richard to his destination and quickly left, his discomfort obvious. Godric was alone; the messenger had been dismissed and had left with as much haste as Anselm. It seemed none wanted to be near when Richard was informed of his new position in the world.

"I trust you have been in prayer concerning your will and the Lord's . . . and which is to prevail in your life, Richard," Godric said.

Richard said nothing. In all the chamber, only the candle flame moved, in lazy twitches that birthed twirling smoke.

"In this life, we are often called upon to submit to a course which is not of our choosing. I believe God presses us to this for a purpose, that of displaying our complete submission to His will for all the world to see. Submission is the key to a holy life."

Richard did not give any outward appearance of being submissive. Godric sighed and mentally girded himself for a battle of wills. Yet it was not his will against which Richard fought, but the Lord God's. Richard had all the appearance of a resolute foe, and foe would aptly describe him if he did not bend to God's will. No man could serve God if he would have no master; Richard was a man who was most comfortable in his own leadership, trusting none other. Not even God? Perhaps that was the wisdom of God's plan. Richard must learn to bend to a will higher, stronger, and harder than his own. He would not stand in the way or try to soften a blow of discipline from God when it was aimed upon a man, even such a man as Richard of Warefeld.

"It is agreed," Godric said, casting aside comfort and counsel, trusting Richard and the health of his soul to God Almighty. "You are to marry the damsel Isabel."

Excused by the brother in charge of novices, Richard lay on his face before the altar of Christ. Following Abbot Godric's advice, he was deeply in prayer. Like Jacob wrestling with an angel of the Lord, he wrestled with his will.

He did not want to give up the cloistered life.

He did not want to swear fealty to any but God's representative on earth, the Pope.

His course was set; he would not be turned from it by any man's whim, not even Lord Robert's.

Isabel was well dowered, he reasoned. Any man would be glad of her. Any man but him.

Her name floated in his mind like a hawk on unseen air currents, and his thoughts ran out of his control. She had changed little over the years. He had known her as a girl just short of womanhood, her skirts dirt-rimmed from play and her hair a dark tangle down her back. She had been . . . the only friend he could lay claim to. The holder of his whispered ambitions and contained loneliness. Aye, she had been a source of laughter when each day was only unremitting toil and each night aching solitude.

Malton had been noise and competition and tension, and he had understood what he was to do there: succeed. Excel. Bring honor to his name and to the name of his house. And if he did not make the friendships he had hoped for, what was lost? His duty was to become a feared and honorable knight; he did not require friends to learn his skills.

Yet Isabel had been friend to him.

Upon their growing, he with hair sprouting on his face and she with the beginning curves of womanhood, such friendship had seemed amiss. The other boys had noted it—how she sought him out and how easily she succeeded in securing his companionship; the smiles she bestowed upon him more than on any other. It was called infatuation, and to protect her name and his own, Richard had looked elsewhere. Isabel had not, and as they had grown, her pursuit of him had exceeded all propriety, all modesty, all honor.

Malton was for but one purpose for Richard: to become the most renowned knight ever to be trained by Lord Henley. He had been set well on his path when he had chosen a higher calling. But before his call to the monkhood, he had been determined to win praise as a most worthy knight.

Strangely, his most enduring memories of that time were of Isabel. She had been comely always, a fact his brother Hubert had found pleasure in. She was promised to his brother. She was not for him. He was landless, the third son, and not yet a knight. He had nothing to offer a woman, and, even knighted, it was doubtful he would ever marry. Few knights did in an age of political alliances and arranged marriages; damsels with land and property were parceled out carefully, where they would do the most good.

Which was why Lord Robert was pressing for a match between Richard's house and hers. It was a good match for Robert and King Henry. But not for him. His heart, mind, and soul were set on serving God every day of his earthly life. No man, baron or priest, and certainly no woman was going to get in the way of his call.

Richard pressed his hips and shoulders against the cold stone. The nave arched before him like a portal to paradise, the cross the road he must tread to reach it. Thoughts of Isabel had no place in this chamber. He welcomed the damp cold of the spring night, urging it to drive all thoughts of Isabel away from him. His tempest now was with God, not flesh. He must find his way to salvation, a salvation in which no woman could have a part.

He did not want to marry.

He had been commanded by bishop, baron, and abbot to marry.

And if he did not?

Then he would display the very characteristic he must not show: rebelliousness. Refuse to marry Isabel and he would be accused of a rebellious will that would not bend. Such men were not permitted to seek a life among the Benedictines.

If he did not obey, he would lose life among the Brothers.

If he did obey, he would lose life among the Brothers. And gain an unwanted wife.

He was trapped, trapped into submitting to a marriage he had no desire for. But Isabel desired him; he could feel it even within the confines of the cloister. He could see it in her eyes and hear it

Chapter Five

Just past Prime, Isabel was assisted in mounting her palfrey by Edmund. She was leaving the abbey. She had prayed the night into day, prayed for Richard to submit to the will of lord and abbot, prayed for him to take the gift from God which they had each been given. She had prayed for Richard and God had given her Richard; would Richard take the gift of Isabel?

She had seen the answer in his eyes.

Still, she had prayed for him to want her. To take her.

She had lost the battle for her pride years ago. It did not seem to matter, as long as she had not lost Richard.

But he had not come and still did not come. The hours while she had awaited the coming of Richard were many; what was one more hour upon

49

such a burden as her heart already bore?

Her pride, even so small a thing now, would not allow her to wait forever within abbey walls for Richard to make his decision. If he wanted her—but nay, he would not want her, he would only submit to having her; if he took her as wife, he would have to come to Dornei to get her. She would no longer wait while he deliberated and pleaded with God for intercession.

How could she want such a husband?

He was Richard.

Atop her palfrey, she nodded her thanks to Edmund and turned to say farewell to Brother John. In turning, she saw Richard approach. He did not come happily, she could see that though the sun was still weak and the air thick with night mist. Yet, he came. It was in his very visage, his hard and dark countenance, that she saw she was about to become a wife. Her heart trembled, crushed by her suppressed joy at his coming. Suppressed, yea—she must not allow him to see her joy, for in that he would read his defeat. But it was joy which all but choked her as Richard came to stand at the shoulder of her beast.

"By all authority, by church and king, we have been committed to marry," he said. The thin sun shone on his dark hair and against the angles of his face, making him look to her more of the lean ascetic than she remembered him. And more beautiful. For beautiful he was, with his almost black hair and dark blue eyes. A fine, straight nose he had, and a mouth that could smile and melt ice.

Though she had not seen him smile for an age. And he wàs not smiling now. "I am determined to submit to the will of those in authority over me. Will you submit?" he asked her.

Would she submit? How to contain the joy when it wanted to fly out of her to heaven itself? Submit to marry Richard? She would have walked to the shrine of Compostela in far-off Spain, on her knees, for the gift of being Richard's wife.

"Yea, I am content," she murmured, holding in her smile. "I will submit to the wisdom and guidance of those whom God Himself has placed above me in divine hierarchy."

Richard eyed her, not so far above him on her small palfrey. She appeared readily composed to accept the suddenness of baronial command. She was a woman, he surmised; such submission would come more readily to her. The whole situation was not as difficult for her as it most assuredly was for him. She had always had tender feeling for him, hardly a secret. He could see the glimmer of joy in her eyes even now, though she tried to hide it from him and the good brother at his side. Yea, it was an altogether more difficult thing for him; he was giving up a life's vocation. She was merely marrying and, thereby, fulfilling her God-given vocation.

"Come then. We shall see our duty done," he said, turning his back on her and marching across the courtyard into the chapel. Let the squire see to her dismounting; he would not look upon her any more than was necessary.

She followed, eagerly enough it seemed to him. Abbot Godric awaited them in the chapel, looking more pleased than Richard believed the occasion warranted. The ceremony, attended by the squire of Dornei, Brother John, Prior Phillip, and, of necessity, Isabel, was mercifully brief. Even so, he could feel the charge of emotion seeping from Isabel. She was happy. God forgive him, he did not want her happiness. Submission, yea. Duty, naturally. Not happiness. Never joy. He would find no joy in her. She must not find joy in him.

It was with such thoughts that he found himself married to her. Marriage: God's holy union of two souls and the bodies they indwelt. In body, life, and property they were joined. His own abbot had performed the deed, and he must indeed live with the result. How else to prove his submission?

But when in the history of Christ's holy church had any husband upon his nuptials worn the robes of a monk?

It was done now, though no exchange of rings had marked the ceremony. It only required that he transmit the kiss of peace to his newly made wife. Richard cast his eyes downward and looked into the face of the woman he had pledged himself to. She glowed. Isabel's eyes, as green-brown as moss in autumn, looked up at him, the joy she concealed within her body revealed in her eyes. Joy—not the quiet look of submission, but radiant and uplifted joy.

He stooped slightly, and she lifted her head in silent eagerness for his kiss. Brusquely, as cold and brief as a winter blast of northern air, he brushed his lips against hers. Soft, she was, and then the impression was pushed from him. He found no joy in their kiss. He made that plain to her. There was no joy for him in this union. They had joined their houses and their lands and, eventually, their bodies, but there would be no earthly pleasure for him in these things. Such pleasure he had cast beyond his reach. Such pleasure she could not tempt him to take.

"My prayers are with you," Abbot Godric said, the ceremony concluded. "My blessings as well, what little they may serve you."

"Your blessings and your prayers are most welcome, Father Abbot," Richard said. "Indeed, I covet your prayers as I reenter the world, shorn of my robes and my place."

"You have your place, Richard. God has prepared it and anointed you for it. You have only to obey."

"I have obeyed," Richard answered.

"As have I," inserted Isabel.

Richard looked askance at her. She radiated joy. What price her obedience? What value?

"And in obeying," Richard continued, "we will depart for Dornei."

And so they did, without noise or commotion. The brothers continued in their prayers and in their service to God as he rode out of the sheltering walls of the abbey into the green, wet, spring world. Father Abbot watched them go with Brother Anselm on one side and Brother John on the other. They were silent, each deep in prayer for Richard. And for Isabel, a willing bride for so reluctant a groom.

Richard did not look back. Isabel did not look back. Edmund did, and waved his farewell. It was an odd group they made, the newly wedded riding far apart from each other and the groom in monk's robes. It was a silent and solemn wedding party that made its muddy way to Dornei.

They arrived in good time, the mud-thick roads not delaying them overmuch. Birds sang with the joy of spring, and the sun rose to warm the air and clear the skies of the last traces of the damp night. Richard noted it all distantly. It was not his duty to take note of birdsong and sunlit treetops and the early blooms of spring. It was his duty to ride to Dornei. To Dornei he did ride. With his wife behind him.

The walls of Dornei rose up, a blunt vision of stone against the rising green of the surrounding countryside. Dornei was massive; double-walled and crenellated, and situated on a natural hilltop. No illegal holding, this, but a fine tower and wall built before the war for the rule of England raged between Maud and Stephen. Henry of Anjou ruled now, with the consent of both, and all had been mended. England was at peace after years of civil war. Dornei had come through that time well and intact, God be praised. Isabel's father, Bernard, had kept his holding secure in those troubled times. The land skirting the walls was divided neatly into fields just now coming into green, the earth brown and well broken by spade. It had the look of prosperity. The town clustered below the walls, a misshapen mass of brown roofs and age-blackened walls; a busy town of two roads and many merchants. The inhabitants of the town watched and whispered as their three-horse cavalcade rode past them to the gates of Dornei.

Edmund rode first to the gate and waved his welcome, then pulled his mount aside and allowed Richard to enter first. Those within Dornei's walls did not know what to make of the Benedictine monk who preceded their lady.

"Lady Isabel, are you safe and well?" the porter blurted out, his expression anxious. "Your disappearance on the heels of your father's death—"

"Lady Isabel is well, as you can see," Richard interrupted, dismounting. Edmund stayed upon his horse in flagrant violation of knightly etiquette. Richard did nothing more than mark the lapse. "She came to the Abbey of Saint Stephen and Saint Paul for succor in her distress and received such. And more beside," he added caustically.

"But, Lady, you were not here to make the arrangements for Lord Bernard—" the porter argued.

"Your name?" Richard interrupted again.

"Odwin Porter," he answered, looking uncomfortably between Isabel and the monk.

"Odwin, do you always question the acts of your lady? If so, it is a habit you will be broken of," Richard said sharply.

"If there is any breaking to be done, I shall be the one to do it, Brother Monk," a voice said.

Richard turned to face a household knight of some years, perhaps forty, with a lined and ruddy face and auburn curls streaked with silver gray. Stocky and stalwart, he faced Richard prepared for battle, even though he knew not whom he faced. Richard smiled reluctantly; worse things could be said of a man.

"I think not, unless I give you leave to do so," Richard answered stiffly.

"Lady, who is yon monk who thinks to order all within the walls of Dornei?" Gilbert asked, his hand on his dagger.

"Your new lord, Gilbert—Richard of Warefeld and now Dornei," Isabel answered, motioning for Edmund to help her dismount. Edmund came at her gesture as he had not come for Richard. Again, Richard noted it but said nothing.

His welcome into the life of Dornei was not a warm one. It was God's mercy that he did not require warmth to see his duty done.

"Your husband is a monk?" Gilbert said in thick sarcasm, his face going red to match the silvered glory of his vibrant hair.

"Yea, he is that," Richard answered for his wife. And to his wife. He wanted Isabel to know the level of his commitment to her; he had been duty-bound to marry her, and duty his service in this marriage would remain. No heartfelt bond united them. Duty required and duty met, that was all. She had to know that that was all she would get from him, no matter the depth of her wanting.

"He is Lord of Warefeld, Gilbert, and of Bledelai

and Achelei," Isabel explained, pronouncing his worth.

"Lord of Warefeld? Then brother to Hubert . . . ?"

Isabel looked down and swished her skirts, flicking off droplets of mud and water. "Aye, he is," she answered, looking up at Gilbert, ignoring Richard. It would be better said that she did not look upon him, for ignore him she could not. "The betrothal contract between Dornei and Warefeld has been fulfilled, honoring both our fathers. I must go in and see to . . . things," she said and fled across the wide expanse of the bailey. Richard remained in the bailey with Gilbert and a slouching Edmund.

"Take my horse, boy, and see him well stabled," Richard said calmly to Edmund.

Edmund, without the shield of Isabel or even Gilbert, who would not stand between any man and his rightful fight, quickly crumbled. He did not like this man who was neither monk nor lord, or perhaps was both monk and lord but was not like any man he had yet met. In that he was most correct; Richard was unlike anyone.

"Then go to your lady and see to her needs. She will have much for you to do in helping Lord Bernard on his way," Richard added, as if he expected nothing less than complete compliance. Which was true and was exactly what he received.

"Yea, Lord Richard," Edmund mumbled, grabbing for the reins.

Richard held them back, and when Edmund looked up in confusion, said, "If you have something to say, say it, boy. Do not mumble it into the dirt where only worms and pecking birds can hear you. Say it loud if you know what you're about."

"Yea, my lord," Edmund said, his eye meeting Richard's with a glint of male pride.

"Go, then," Richard said with equal pride.

Edmund went.

Gilbert did not go, but then, Richard did not wish him to.

"How many knights does Dornei hold?" Richard asked. "And how many have left since Bernard's death?"

"Twenty-five knights does Dornei hold, and but two have left and only then upon the heels of Isabel's flight," Gilbert answered gruffly.

"And you were not tempted to leave?"

"I would not leave Lady Isabel in dire need," Gilbert said stiffly.

"Or not at all, were she without need?" Richard smiled over his shoulder as he studied Dornei's defenses. All looked well enough, but then, Isabel had not been in command for any length of time. And still, what passionate loyalty she inspired. Isabel and the hold she could exert on a man had changed not at all. Dornei was as enthralled by her as Malton had been. But she could not touch him. Not again.

Gilbert did not return the smile and did not answer.

"Have a care, Brother Knight, whom you choose to hold your honor, lest you wake and find yourself a Benedictine," Richard said, his tone clipped.

Gilbert said nothing to that as Richard, his black

robes flapping, walked across the yard to the Hall.

He was expected, courtesy of Isabel. Both clerk and steward awaited him in the Hall, ready to do his bidding, or so they behaved. Richard was not fool enough to believe that all men would rejoice that a Benedictine brother had come as lord to Dornei, but he was willing to believe that they were curious about him and how well he would place as Dornei's lord. The clerk, Jerome, he instructed to wait until a later time when the accounts would be reviewed. If there was anything at which Richard excelled after a year of abbey life, it was in the reviewing of accounts and contracts. His being literate had opened many doors within the abbey; he could have made a nice place for himself in the monastic community, if not for Isabel.

Jerome dismissed, he turned to the steward. A tall man and slender, red-haired and green-eyed, he looked to be young for the position. The steward saw to all within the house; the botilers, cooks, bakers, scullions, chandlers, and grooms, all would be within his domain and authority. This man looked unripe for such responsibility.

"Your name?" Richard asked.

"Robert, my lord," he answered.

"How long have you been steward?"

"Five years come Candlemas, my lord."

"Five years?" He did not look to be above twenty.

"I have thirty summers behind me, my lord."

"It is a respectable age," Richard said. "You carry it lightly."

"Thank you, Lord Richard." He bowed. "Lady Isabel bade me escort you to Lord Bernard's chamber so that you may dress and perhaps wash the road from yourself before . . ."

Before. Richard understood what Robert could not say and what Isabel had implied. Dornei was a rich holding and deserved a rich lord to command her; in his monk's robes he did not look the part nor did he inspire confidence. She wanted him to be admired, this new husband of hers. Well, it was little enough she asked of him, and there was logic in it besides; people served better those they respected, and if Dornei's folk could not stomach a plain-clothed monk, they might swallow more easily a fur-trimmed baron.

"Come, Robert, lead on to Bernard's chamber. Let us see what manner of man we may turn out for Dornei's approval."

Blushing, Robert led the way across the hall to the stair tower on the far wall. Dornei was large— beyond large, prosperous. The hall was three stories in height, painted dark red and fluttering with colorful tapestries. The wind holes were clear of cobwebs and birds' nests, the floors of solid wood instead of packed dirt, and the rushes woven tight. It was impressive, fully a third larger than the hall at his own Warefeld.

The stair tower was narrow, as precaution demanded, but bright, the twisting stone tower lined with narrow wind holes for archers. Robert led the way up one flight to the chamber that dominated the floor—Lord Bernard's chamber. A massive bed, rich with hangings of precious damask and thick with furs, occupied the center of the room; at its foot, a sturdy bench padded with fox fur. To the left was the fire, and to the right, the trunk. Near the doorway was poised the ewer with a length of linen hanging down to almost touch the floor. All was swept and still, the space newly empty of life, ready to receive the next lord of Dornei within its walls.

Robert lifted the lid on the heavy wooden trunk and, holding his taper back to prevent spills, with a simple gesture encouraged Richard to peruse his new wardrobe. Robert, it seemed, was quiet by nature, which suited Richard well. The clothing was rich, well made, and bountiful, like all of Dornei. He had no need for such finery, but he understood the reason for having it. It bespoke wealth and security when most could only remember war. The Lord of Dornei assured all who saw him that life was good in Dornei when e'er he walked about.

'Twas a small enough service that was asked of him, to dress the part of lord of a rich holding. He buried his right hand in the trunk, feeling the soft wools and crisp linens, the colors rich and deeply dyed. These were the garments of a wealthy man, and they were now his for the taking. He was the baron of Dornei. He rubbed his left hand down the front of his black robe, a simple garment of humility and service. It was a garment he no longer had the right to wear. Because of Isabel.

Digging deep within the trunk, Richard chose the simplest he could find—a dark blue wool tunic trimmed in red cording. From the dark recesses of the massive trunk Robert snagged the matching mantle—a full circle of wine red, held at the shoulder by a golden clasp. In truth, Richard had never dressed so fine. It did not sit well with him. The sin of avarice could consume a man surrounded by such earthly riches.

Isabel's father had been a wealthy man with much property, and Isabel had been well dowered. He had known that even before the ceremony, where their separate and now combined wealth had been listed in the marriage contract. Isabel was an only child, and all had been left to her. She was an heiress of rare value, and joining their two houses had been cause for celebration for their fathers. Both men were dead now, yet he had been called upon to make good the contract made sixteen years ago. Called upon because he was the only son left living to marry a woman of such high worth.

He had never thought to marry Isabel. Even in his youth, when dreams came hard upon a man, he had never dared to dream even to marry. His was a world of men, either warriors of the flesh or warriors of the spirit; it was a world he had never thought to leave.

He had never thought to marry, yet even now her image rose before him, wrapping around his thoughts, tempting him . . . a woman with long dark hair falling against a clean white shift. Bare limbs. Seductive eyes. How well he knew her, his succubus that came to him. So bold now that she did not wait for night but attacked his resolve even during the day. Away from the brotherhood he might be, but he would not be felled by so blatant an attack from the powers of the demonic host, no matter her allure.

Dropping to his knees, to Robert's surprise, Richard began to pray. Eyes pressed shut against his personal demon, his succubus, he fought his way to sanctity through prayer. One thought followed him, one thought, like a hawk that pursued through fog and rain, knowing no barrier to its prey: Isabel had been betrothed to his brother from infancy, yet from their youth Richard had felt her desire for him glittering sharply from her hazel eyes.

So bright had been her attraction; what honor was there in a woman who made such unlawful desire so readily known?

Chapter Six

The stables were warm from the sun and fragrant with the pleasant smell of hay. The first flies of the season gathered convivially over an hour-old pile of manure, their buzzing and its odor simultaneous experiences. Louis, Nicholas, and Adam kept their voices low, the tenor of their words sounding remarkably like distant buzzing, the weight of their speech edging toward the foul stink of lost opportunity.

"I got it from Guilbert, the botiler, who was told by Robert, so there is no chance of mistake," Nicholas said. "Isabel is married."

"She flew out of here like a sparrow seeking succor," Adam said, stroking his jawline in contemplation. "Succor from us?"

Nicholas and Louis looked at Adam and then at each other in something edging along condemnation, and then the look was broken.

"I wonder if she expected to return from the abbey a matron, leaving us panting like so many hounds after her scent," Adam continued.

"It would be strange indeed for a damsel to look for a husband among monks, tonsures, and eternal chants," Louis said with a tilted smile.

"Not so strange when you consider who was sheltered within those abbey walls, chanting his prayers to the Almighty," Nicholas said. "I squired at Malton. I remember well how Isabel circled over Richard of Warefeld, her eyes only for him. As children they had been close, their heads ever together, whispering their secrets, until Richard ended it, leaving her behind in the memory of childhood. But Isabel would not be left. Where else to find Richard but at the abbey?"

"Did they have a tendre for each other?" Louis asked.

"For Richard, I could not say; he is not a man to reveal his heart in his gaze," Nicholas said, "but Isabel, Isabel with her melting gaze, was always about him. Her heart was plain to behold. Even Richard could not have missed the looks she sent him."

"Were his knight's skills lacking that he should take the cowl?" Louis asked.

"Nay, he would not have won his spurs had that been so," Nicholas said. "He was fit enough, though monk's robes and monk's habits suit him better."

They had trained together, boys being hardened

into men, and they had fought many times. And Richard always the victor. He had failed at nothing in his knight's training; he carved well, hunted well, fought well. To himself Nicholas could admit it: Richard had fought with the speed and precision that many seasoned knights never achieved in a score of years; all came so easily to him, every skill effortlessly acquired. Even Isabel he had won, and all the boys of Malton had been enamored of Isabel. Of course, although Richard had been fit enough to win his spurs honestly, he had not the brawn of Nicholas. Nicholas flexed his arm, finding pleasure in the coil of muscle.

"Henley, it has been said, had a special fondness for him," Adam said.

"True, but he was knighted fairly. He would have made a fine knight." Even there, Richard had been the blight of all the squires and newly dubbed knights for the favor he held from Henley, lord of them all.

"And now he is to make Isabel a fine husband," said Louis.

"And a lord to us," said Nicholas.

Adam said nothing.

It was into this abrupt and heavy silence that Brother John led his mule.

"Good morrow," he said pleasantly.

The men jerked and spun to face him, guilt sliding over their faces like sudden rain. The men were not known to him, not intimately; John in times past had seen them accompany Lord Bernard around the countryside, but he had not taken their measure in full. Nicholas he knew the least, but then he wondered if all who knew Nicholas knew him but a little. His hair was dark as rain-blackened bark, and his eyes the whitened blue of high summer; he was a tall man and thick with strength, with the wide brow of the Normans and the manner to match.

Louis he knew some better, for he had come to the abbey to pray when first he arrived at Dornei and its environs. Louis was the blond of wheat tassels, with eyes of darkest green; his manner matched his form, for he was tall and broad and he faced a man squarely or not at all.

Adam, smaller than the others but of a size to make a formidable knight, was blessed with eyes of clearest gray with sweeping brows of deepest auburn that were but a shade darker than his sun-brightened hair. He was a man to make a maid swoon, if another man could guess at such a thing.

"Good morrow, Brother," said Adam, smiling brightly. "May I help you with your mount?"

"Nay, but I thank you. Daisy and I are quite used to each other. I will see to her needs, if your stable will accommodate?"

"You are welcome, Brother John," said Louis. "As you see, there are stalls aplenty."

"Your pardon, Brother, but it is time for the meal. Shall we await you or can you find your way?" asked Nicholas.

"I can follow my nose to any table, thank you," said John with a wide smile. "No need to wait upon me. Go. I shall come anon."

"We will tell Isabel . . . and Richard, of your arrival. They will reserve a place of honor for you," said Nicholas.

"Were you expected, Brother?" Adam asked as they stood in the stable doorway.

All three turned to wait for his response.

"Nay, I am not expected," Brother John said as he removed Daisy's saddle.

When he turned again to the stable doorway, all there was to see was a cloud of black flies hovering over a pile of horse manure.

The sky was dotted with dark clouds as the trio of knights crossed the bailey; the wind was picking up. It was a chill wind, and they quickened their pace to outrace it. The stair to the entrance of the Hall was exposed and they hurried up it, Nicholas leading them. The smell of hot food drew them on; the sudden drop in temperature propelled them. The hall was already noisy with the clatter of plate and the hum of chatter; Isabel was at her place at the high table. She wore a gown of leaf green, as fresh as spring itself, and a bliaut of pale gold. Her hair was down, dark against the fairness of her skin and her garments, and shone with the gloss of youth and health. She was a maid to make a man's heart swell with pride and satisfaction.

Her allure did not extend to the Benedictine brotherhood.

Richard was not with her.

Nay, Richard was standing by the fire and talking to Dornei's priest, ignoring all about him—the noise, the aromas, the occasion. It was his wedding supper, and he had left his bride to sit alone. Yet, though Isabel sat in the place of power, of rank, and of might, it was Richard who emanated all the power felt in the Hall. He did not act as if he knew it; nay, he behaved for all the world like a monk seeking spiritual counsel from his priest. And perhaps that was all he was.

Nicholas smirked away that notion. No man could ignore the weight of power when it rested so upon him, just as no man could ignore the desirability of Isabel, sitting at the high table, waiting in feminine submission for the Lord of Dornei to sit beside her in his rightful place. But Richard did. Or seemed to.

A whispered word from the priest, a subtle gesture, and Richard obeyed, moving across the floor to join his wife. He did not appear an eager husband, to have to rely on a priest to guide him to his mate. Adam watched avidly and said nothing.

Smiling, Adam left his brother knights behind and made his bold way to Isabel. Being closer, he reached Isabel before her tardy husband.

"Lady Isabel," he said, kissing her hand, "I have not yet expressed my sorrow over the death of your father and my lord, Baron Bernard. How do you fare in your grief? Know it is shared to the fullest. Perhaps it will ease your burden to know that I carry an equal measure of grief in my own heart."

"Thank you, Adam," she said, smiling up at him. "Your words are as sweet as my gratitude."

She was beguiling, smiling up at him, her eyes

shining and her pale cheeks smooth as pearl. She was wasted on the Benedictine.

"You fled away early, Lady; I would have ridden with you on your journey to the abbey. There was no need to ride alone to find comfort. As to that, there was comfort enough for you within these walls," he said. *Within my arms.*

"I thank you again," she said with a slight dimming of her smile. "Yet I needed the solace, and the quiet, of abbey walls. It is a true gift to have the Benedictines within call when the need is great, is it not?"

"I cannot disagree," he murmured with a gentle smile. "We are a noisome bunch when it comes to that. And did they ease you of your grief?"

"Time alone will tell that tale, Adam. I—"

"God's mercy and loving kindness are more than sufficient for each day's burdens, Adam. Isabel is in the hands of God; what misery . . . or harm . . . within His grasp?" Richard said, intruding upon them.

He stood behind Isabel, his hands upon her shoulders, his words a barrier to flirtation as firm as any shield. He was acting very much like a husband. He spoke like a monk. Adam smiled; a man could not be both, and Richard, for all his growling protection of Isabel, was a man who clearly wanted to remain a monk.

"None at all, my lord," Adam answered calmly. "My lady." He bowed briefly and found a seat at the table. Yet, he watched them.

Richard of Warefeld had been monkish as a

squire, according to the whispers of Nicholas. He would hardly be less so after a year of monastery life. Richard might well want his newly acquired wife charmed away from him before things went as far as consummation. Looking at them now, Richard towering over Isabel, his dark hair a perfect match for hers, Adam felt a moment of doubt. Richard seemed to be standing so that Isabel was shielded from his gaze, a bulwark against male eyes and male thoughts. Perhaps Richard was less monkish than Nicholas had suggested. But in the end, it did not matter; Isabel was too sweet a prize to let fall without a tumble to catch her.

Adam smiled and then buried it in a long swallow of ale. Yea, tumbling was just the thing. And with a message sent to his uncle, who was an established ally of Lord Robert's . . . why, he could find himself the possessor of his own betrothal contract, with Isabel as his bride. If only Isabel were free and unclaimed—but he had a plan to make her so. Adam pulled deeply of his drink, hiding his thoughts in its dark depths.

Nicholas missed nothing, most especially the speculative, plotting smile on Adam's face. "Adam thinks to snare a wife from Richard's grasp," he said in an undertone to Louis. "It will not be. As monkish as he is, Richard lets nothing slip from him once he sets his eye upon it."

"Even an unwanted wife?" Louis asked, looking askance at his comrade in arms.

"You have said it," Nicholas replied. "She is his wife. He will not toss her away for another man to snatch." Nicholas stroked the hilt of his dagger, his eyes narrowed in thought. But if Richard could be convinced to return to the life he had chosen, what thought would he give to a wife and a life left behind? None, for, being married, Isabel could not remarry. Isabel without her lands interested him not at all. So, Richard must be urged to repudiate her, leaving her as unmarried as she had been yesterday. Richard had never seemed overly fond of Isabel, and Isabel had in all ways seemed more than fond of Richard. For a monkish man, doused in the church's teachings on women, the course rose clear.

"Come, let us celebrate. It is the marriage supper of our lord and lady," Nicholas said to Louis.

Louis, his own expression thoughtful, elbowed his way to a place at the table with the rest of the fighting men.

The hall was full, the tables crowded with all who lived within Dornei's walls. Elbow to elbow were the knights Louis, Adam, and Nicholas, seated below the high table. And at the high table, Aelis and Elsbeth, two young women in training to become ladies of their own halls, as well as Brother John, honored guest; Father Langfrid, Dornei's priest; and Lady Joan, who had lately served as companion to Bernard's second wife, Ida. She now served as counselor to Isabel, though Father Langfrid could see that Isabel was not of a mind to listen to any counsel which did not give her Richard. Well, that was past now, for Richard was hers; God had seen it done, no doubt in answer to the most heartfelt prayers since Abraham had prayed for a son.

But at what cost?

Father Langfrid sighed and prodded his eel with his dagger, trying not to observe Aelis's clumsy flirtations and Edmund's stiff refusal to participate in that flirtation. He tried even harder to ignore Richard's complete disregard for his bride. It did not seem the season for love, no matter what the troubadours mouthed of spring's glories. Isabel had the man of her choice, aye, and he sat in the lord's place, in the lord's clothes; Richard even had the lord's manner and mantle of power well within his grasp. But Isabel was no part of it. She was an observer, as were they all. Richard was the center, and he occupied his position of power alone.

A strong man and not given to idle talk, yet was not his wife a worthy subject of his contemplation? Isabel fair shimmered in her joy, while Richard was as dark and sharp as a midwinter night. Were two people ever more out of joint? Isabel had what she wanted in Richard, but was her marriage as she imagined it would be? Langfrid shook off his worry; God would manage all, in time. A marriage was the slow building of commonalities, the daily sharing of a life well blended.

Richard sat beside Isabel, sharing a trencher and a cup yet sharing nothing at all. 'Twas a most strange marriage feast. And all eyes watched it, course upon course, studying Richard's disdain and Isabel's devotion. Did she know? Could she feel her husband's displeasure with his state? Langfrid, knowing her, knew that she did. But in knowing her, he also knew that she would fly above such unpleasant thoughts to dwell on her success. She had wanted Richard and now she had him. Misery would have little room in her musings.

Father Langfrid scanned the room, studying the faces of those in the hall. Edmund and Gilles, both squires, served. Edmund kept his face averted from young Aelis the best he could. She was not so easily put off; Edmund knew that from experience. Still, he tried to maintain the distance he deemed both courteous and proper. What he usually achieved was a restrained disgust. Gilles was pimply and short; no one bothered to flirt with him.

Father Langfrid had never trusted Adam of Courcelle, and less so now with his open and too bright courtesy of Lady Isabel. That man looked after his own interests too well for common comfort. Louis he was unsure of; his blunt courtesy ran along the edge of incivility, yet he seemed honest enough. Not the sort of man to deal falsely with the man he was sworn to. Yet none had taken the oath of homage to Richard. Nicholas was a knight who might not swear. Nicholas had high ambitions for his earthly life, giving little thought to his eternal one. And then there were the men-at-arms and squires and household servants—all tilted on their ears to have a devoted Benedictine as their reluctant lord. But, sitting at the high table with Isabel at his side, Richard did not appear a reluctant lord, only a reluctant husband.

"A strange beginning," said Brother John at his

side. Father Langfrid had always liked Brother John; he was good with both medicinals and people and knew how to keep his own counsel.

Father Langfrid nodded gently. "Pray God it is the beginning only."

" 'Where two or more are gathered together . . .' " John quoted. "I pray it without ceasing. There is much here beyond what can be seen, but God sees all, and I am certain that He will lay all to rights. At least I pray for certainty," he added with a smile. "You know conditions here. What will Brother Richard—that is, Lord Richard—face?"

"Whether he will be Brother or lord is its own answer. Do you seek to counsel him?"

"Brother Richard seeks no man's counsel. Nor heeds it when it is thrust upon him."

"A headstrong Benedictine?"

"Nay, but a man ever certain of his path."

"A good trait in a baron, but in a monk?"

John smiled and said nothing for a pace. "Isabel appears well content in the marriage."

"She, too, has seen clearly the path of her choosing," Langfrid answered, his own smile stilled.

"She has had many stumbling blocks in her path," John said diplomatically.

"Yea, she has," Langfrid agreed. "But God and God alone knows the number of our days, does he not, Brother?"

"And the desires of our hearts," added John.

And therein lay the small seed of Isabel's misery: She believed she had caused the deaths of two men in her heartfelt prayers to be Richard's wife.

But that confidence had been whispered to Father Langfrid in the sanctity of the confessional and was not destined to be dinner conversation.

"It has been a hard season for Isabel," John said, coming too close to what had been on Langfrid's mind.

"Yea, she has been sore pressed, for every estate needs a lord. It is God's blessing that Isabel is well wed, the betrothal contract intact, overlord and king satisfied."

"All pieces in their place, each person in his station."

"Even so, Brother. God's order maintained on earth."

"Even so, Father," John echoed.

And if either man considered how many deaths it had taken for Isabel to have her heart's desire, they refrained from speaking it aloud.

Dinner proceeded apace, each dish a masterpiece to the eyes and to the tongue, richer food and more bounteous than was Richard's custom. Monks ate meat rarely, and yet he was being served venison, lamb, and rabbit, as well as eel and quail. It was more food than he ate in a month as a Benedictine. But he was no longer a Benedictine. He was Lord of Dornei, Warefeld, Bledelai, Hilesdun and all the rest. A lord of many, when all he wanted was to be a servant to One. And he had never wanted to be a husband.

Never had begun a year ago, just past Whitsunday.

Richard cast his eyes to glance at Isabel; her dark hair fell heavy and thick to her hips, unbound and glorious, a tribute to her maidenhood. He flicked his eyes forward and ate lightly of his venison; Lord of Dornei he may be, but he would not forswear his Benedictine appetites. But how long would discipline last before he slid back into gluttony?

Debauchery.

He glanced at Isabel again. She was watching him. Their eyes met. He could read her desire in the parting of her lips and the flush of her cheeks, but most especially in the clear depths of her gaze.

It was always so.

She had pursued him with her eyes as a child and then as a woman of marriageable age and now as a wife. He had beaten back her desire for him for an age, and except for one moment of sin-soaked weakness, he had resisted her. He would resist her still.

Everything about Isabel's too blatant desire for him had been wrong—wrong in God's eyes and the world's. She had been betrothed to his brother; therefore, she was his sister by marriage, her attraction for him both incestuous and adulterous. She had followed where he did not want her, her dark hair flying behind her as she watched him when he trained in the bailey. He had endured it, knowing her to be impetuous and willful and in need of training; ignoring her presence until the boys who shared his fostering at Malton had made Isabel and her hawklike devotion to him the point on which every joke, every ribaldry, was raised. Until Henley had noted it.

She had become a stone thrown against his honor and the honor of his house.

And now again. He had sought to honor God with the gift of his life, but his life had been given to Isabel. Everything in his life seemed to turn around Isabel, like the sun around the earth, the unwelcome center of all his thoughts and all his plans.

Lifting a morsel of bread to his lips, he could feel her eyes on him. Always she watched him. Without shame or modesty, she watched him. He could feel her carnal desire, see it in the flush of her cheek and the twitching of her hands. He knew all the signs of a woman's desire. He had learned at Malton.

But Malton was the past and Dornei was the present. Thinking of Malton would not help him in Dornei. Richard studied the men in the hall, dining on his food at his tables. He did not like the manner of the one called Adam. That one had been too close upon Isabel, his smile too false, his bearing too eager. Nicholas he knew too well from Malton to trust overmuch. Louis's bright look he distrusted. The steward regarded him cautiously, the bailiff suspiciously, and the men-at-arms with grim silence. Yet none of it touched Richard as much as Isabel's ill-concealed desire for him. That, he must fight, and it was the only struggle in his path which challenged his confidence, for it was a battle which he had waged often and never victoriously.

Isabel and her desire were as constant as the sun, as hot and as bright. 'Twas his battle against Isabel's carnal desires that might topple him.

But this was where God had sent him, even if only for a season, and he would master all to which he lay his hand. Brother John had come expressly to remind him of his duty as Lord of Dornei.

And of his duty to Isabel? He did not want to master or lay hand to Isabel. Not again.

With that thought foremost, he spoke to her, though he would not look at her.

"It is expected that we will consummate our marriage tonight."

Isabel dropped her knife with a clatter against the table. It left a dark stain against the cloth. Richard picked it up and handed it back to her, all the while keeping his eyes lowered, in the Benedictine fashion.

"It is inappropriate," he continued, almost without pause. "To commit such an act on the heels of Lord Bernard's death is unseemly. God would surely not smile on such behavior, and I would not begin our marriage on so precarious a step."

He chanced a brief look at her face. She was as still as a salt pillar; she did not even blink a response. Her eyes, though, gave all away.

She wanted him.

Yet she would not fight his will.

All this he could read in her eyes. Richard felt a surge of hope. Perhaps, after all, he could make it through this trial God had set before him.

"In service to God and to honor Lord Bernard,"

Chapter Seven

"He does it out of concern for you," Joan whispered. " 'Tis an act of highest chivalry."

Isabel said nothing. She washed her hands in the communal lavatory with as much vigor as if she were pounding linen. She knew Richard; a chivalric act of graciousness had not been his goal.

"He but performs his holy duty to your father. For a man on his wedding night, it is the height of self-sacrifice. You should be pleased, not insulted," Joan insisted.

Isabel held her tongue and shook her hands like a hound shaking himself after a dousing. *Holy duty?* What of his duty to her? He would like the world to think him the most devout of men, but she knew him better. She knew what he was capable of, once he removed the cowl. No matter what Joan said to appease her, she knew what Richard had done to her in the full view of all Dornei: he had insulted her. He had rejected her. He had refused the pleasures of the marriage bed and of *her*.

"One night is little enough to complain of," Aelis said, standing just beyond Joan. "You have a handsome and virile husband, at least."

Aelis, ever on the watch for Edmund, a young man on whom she could slake her thirst for romance, was betrothed to a man three times her age who was missing the most important of his teeth. She was buxom, blond, and robust; too much for her betrothed, but an even match for Edmund, only three years her senior.

Elsbeth, small and dark and fragile in appearance, spoke up from behind Isabel. "In that, Aelis is correct; one night is only that. Other nights, and days, will follow. This is but a moment."

Isabel smiled ruefully at Elsbeth. Of them all, Elsbeth understood best what she was feeling. It was humiliation; her desire for Richard was so clearly unreturned.

"A moment only," Joan said softly into her ear, giving her a quick hug. "It hurts, I will grant, but he is your husband now and nothing can change that. Remember that, my dear, and dwell on it."

If she but could, but she had known Richard for year upon year and one thing she knew above all else: Richard was an elusive prey. He was like the sun, ever in the sky and clearly seen but eternally unreachable. She had watched him, season after season, and she had yet to catch him. Once, she had thought . . . but then he had fled Malton for the abbey. She had known she had lost him then. Yet did not God work miracles? Was not Richard now her husband in fact? Aelis was right. It was but a single night.

But it was her wedding night, and instead of learning of the joys of the marriage bed, she would be praying through the long hours until dawn.

And was she so ungrateful to the God who had given her Richard? Nay, she was not. One night of prayer was not such a great sacrifice. She would pray for her father, Bernard, and his wife, Ida, and for Hubert and for Geoffrey; she would pray for them all, they who so recently departed this earth for heaven and eternal rest. She would pray. She had Richard.

Tomorrow, night would come again. Tomorrow, Richard would make her his wife in fact.

With a faint smile to show she was encouraged by their words, Isabel led the way out of the lava-tory. But she was not encouraged, she was only patient. With Richard as her heart's desire, she had learned the necessity of patience long ago. One night she had to wait, one night more, when she had thought never to have the gift of Richard in her bed and in her life. She could wait one night.

Did Richard, ever elusive, understand that he had achieved a reprieve of only one night?

The sight of Adam, smiling and handsome, in-terrupted her circling thoughts. Could not her hus-band of hours be more like Adam? More attentive, more cheerful? Nay, she had married Richard, and Richard was none of those, at least not with her.

Adam met them on the last stair, his smile wide and his posture open; in all ways he looked a man eager. She had never seen such a look on Richard. Adam, comely and winsome, meant nothing to her. In all her life, there had been only Richard.

When first she had come to Malton, she had entertained no dreams of love. Richard had been her friend, ready with encouragement when she muddled the tapestry or a grin when he bested her at chess. As they had grown, their relationship had changed, and she could well recall the exact moment when she had passed through friendship and into love. Watching him one day serving at table, the angle at which he held his head, the dark shadow of his lashes against his cheek, the pulse of blood at his throat, had ensnared her. Yet she was not taken, not completely. That had happened the next day, when she had strayed out of the hall to watch the men at their warplay. Richard had been wielding his sword, his face pulled into a frown of concentration, besting his mock foe. He was tall, taller than his opponent, and his reach greater. His fighting style had been graceful, even for a youth. At the knight's command, the battle ended. Richard pulled off his helm and ran a hand through his dark hair. A word was spoken, both squires turned to her, and Richard smiled. A hesitant smile, yet a smile.

In that moment, she was lost.

She had been lost in wanting Richard ever since. Adam's charm in no way stood against the power of the memory of that one halting smile.

"Isabel," Adam said gently.

Isabel jerked her thoughts away from memories of Richard and onto the man who stood so attentively in front of her.

"Adam," she greeted, "have you come to escort us to Vespers?"

"Indeed I have, Lady. The wind is strong within the walls of Dornei, and I fear it may try to carry you off."

Indeed, Adam was playful today. Never had she known him to be so frivolous in his speech. Perhaps he merely celebrated her wedding day. He was of a certain more cheerful than her husband.

"What will you do, then," she teased, "hold us all within your grasp? Can one man protect four women from a wind so fierce?"

"He shall have no occasion to protect me," Joan said, "for even the wind respects women of my years. Also, I wanted to wear my new wimple for Vespers, in honor of the day. Do not wait upon me. I shall not be late," she said in parting, turning to reascend the stair.

Aelis was not there to answer Adam and his offer of protection. Aelis had seen Edmund across the wide width of hall and was in pursuit of him, her hips undulating under the soft weight of her bliaut. A shaft of sunlight from the wind hole caught the gold of her hair before she disappeared.

"It seems there are but two women who need male protection," Adam said, looking askance at Elsbeth.

Look he may, but Elsbeth was not leaving.

"You have nothing hindering you from going to chapel?" he said hopefully.

"Nay, I am prepared," she said evenly.

"No need which calls you?" he pressed.

"None," Elsbeth answered without the softening courtesy of a smile. Isabel would not be left alone with Adam, of that she was determined. Adam she did not trust. He was too handsome and his charm too bright. Elsbeth did not trust him and she never had. Isabel being married did not change that.

"Then I shall escort you both to Vespers," he said with a slight stiffening of his smile.

Elsbeth answered with a stiff smile of her own. Isabel paid scant attention to either of them.

The wind was strong within the walls, swirling down in frigid blasts, carrying last autumn's leaves in its grip. It was winter's last effort to retain sovereignty over the earth, yet spring had come; winter, no matter its erratic attempts, had lost the battle. Isabel placed her hand on Adam's arm in chivalric courtesy, her thoughts wholly occupied by Richard and his stubborn will as she shivered against a sudden gust.

With Elsbeth walking behind, Adam draped an arm around Isabel.

Distantly, Isabel noted the arm wrapped around her waist. Well, it was cold and she had shivered. It was a short walk to the chapel, which was huddled against the walls and separated from the tower by only a small orchard. She had not thought to wear a cloak on such a fine spring day. His arm did warm, though she had not given him leave, by look or word, to take such a bold step with her. They were almost to the chapel. He would remove his arm shortly.

And then he slid his other hand down her arm. From elbow to wrist he traced his path down the sensitive skin of her inner arm. It was wholly inappropriate. It was too intimate, too bold, and too casual; as if he had all the right in the world to stroke her. In truth, when she looked upon his face, he acted as if he had done nothing. That, more than the stroke, offended her. Did he think that because she was now a wife that her morals had relaxed? Did he think he had the right to *pet* her?

As she was forming the words to castigate him, Richard, with Louis and Nicholas behind him, stood in the chapel portal. The hot words she had been considering fell into the hardened mud at her feet. Richard looked furious. Nay, more than furious. Explosive. Intense. Passionate. Yea, he looked fair alive with passion. Not often had she seen such a look, and it intrigued her more than his expressions of solemn dignity or cool disdain, his favored looks for her.

It was wondrous what such a look did for her mood.

She understood immediately the power of jealousy. Never before had she attempted to spark feelings of jealousy in Richard; for one, none at Malton would have believed it. And, also, she had spent all her thought and time in capturing Richard's attentions. What time had she to pretend with another? Yet now, Adam had thrown himself in her path. And with what wondrous results.

Isabel, swallowing her fury over Adam's advances, smiled up into his well-formed face, allowing him to keep his arm around her waist, his fingers upon her wrist. Certain of the intimacy of their pose and the brilliance of her smile, she looked over to Richard, her eyes guileless and bright. What would he do?

She had slavishly followed behind Richard for years, like a hawk trained to answer one call, trained to one hand. Thanks to God and Saint Stephen, she had netted the husband she had prayed for, but a disdainful and disinterested husband. Mayhap the spark of jealousy would prick his heart, releasing some matrimonial warmth. She was willing to take the chance.

She had married a monk. She wanted a man.

Richard saw in bursts, his rage flaring with each image: the male hand on her arm, the fingers lying lightly and possessively; the length of her dark hair brushing against the sleeve of Adam's tunic, wisps of black webbed against green of wool; the blatant invitation of her smile and the false innocence as she looked at him. Looked at him, her husband of hours. She displayed no maidenly blushes, no sheltered gaze, no outrage at being so intimately touched by a man not hers to claim. As shameless as Eve she was, as bent on destruction.

Just as Nicholas had implied but moments ago.

What had Isabel been about during his year in the abbey?

She was beautiful; dark and lithe and quick. Her beauty had been much commented upon at Malton. In the dark of the hall, the squires had talked of her, giggling their fascination, practicing their courtesy so as to win a smile from her; Isabel was quick to gift a smile. He had been there; he knew how much she was desired by any who saw her. And her desire had been for him, only him. Had been. Then. All had known she looked to him alone. All understood that Isabel might smile at them, but her eyes were all for him.

He had wanted her not. Did not want her now. Yet . . . yet . . . she was his wife, ordained by God, a covenant made between them until God should end it. Not Adam. Adam had not the right to Isabel.

He swallowed his rage and held it down, rendering it harmless, impotent, dead.

It was possession, not tenderness, that drove him across the dirt of the yard to stand before Adam, breaking that illicit contact. It was duty that made him say, "I shall escort my wife to Vespers."

There was no tenderness, no fondness, in his laying claim to Isabel—there was only duty fulfilled. By God's law, he had been placed in charge of her, body and soul; she would not stumble into sin with him at her side. He would not fail in this. And he would not let Isabel fail. There would be no cause for repudiation and there would be no repudiation, no matter what Nicholas hinted. He would not cast Isabel to that. He would save her. Perhaps that was the reason behind God's will in arranging this mar-

Chapter Eight

Vespers became Compline. After Compline, most made for their beds. Richard kept praying. Isabel remained at his side. Richard had insisted, and she did not know how to resist without appearing an ungrateful and unloving child, so she did not resist. Hours passed, and the full weight of night fell upon Dornei. All were abed. All was still. The night pressed against her until she collapsed against its weight and fell, fitfully, into sleep. She only knew she swayed on her knees when Richard jerked her awake.

Nocturn came, was sung, and passed.

She slept sometime between Nocturn and Matins, unaffected by his nudges.

The chapel filled at Prime, and she stirred. The air was soft with morning and birdsong, and the gentle light of dawn dimmed the candles to insignificance. She realized that her face was resting on the warm wall of his chest and that his arm was wrapped around her for support; it was comforting—and peculiar. Richard's embrace while he sang the office—an odd pairing of experiences. He was her husband and he was turning her into a nun. She had spent her wedding night in a chapel saying prayers. The only blood of the evening had been the blood of Christ. Her virgin's blood was still intact.

Upon realizing she had awakened, he put her from him. Yet she counted it as gain that he had touched her willingly.

The people of Dornei came into the chapel quietly. Of them all, only she and her husband had spent the night in prayerful vigil. And of the two of them, only her husband had stayed awake for the whole of it. The Mass that started each God-given day began, the Latin rising sweetly into the spring air. She stood at Richard's side, proud in her place as wife, though the night had not fulfilled her maidenly dreams of a wedding night. Still, if nothing else, it was obvious to all that she and her husband had spent the night together. She was a virgin, still, yet a wife, and Richard was her husband. Nothing would change that.

Truly, there was much to thank God for this day, her first day as Richard's wife.

He knelt beside her, tall and strong, a man to dream about. Worthy of every dream she had spent on him. His hair was dark, blacker than her own, and his eyes the dark blue of sapphires. His throat was fine and long, the veins that carried his life's blood thick and full. And his mouth—his mouth had fired her imagination as no other part of him had done in all her years of dreaming. She had experience of that mouth; she knew what fire could dwell there.

She twitched as she knelt at his side, her blood afire with longing and expectation. He would claim her today. He would mark her as his, as she had longed for him to do since a girl. Today the long waiting would end. God had given her Richard, and she would take the gift and gladly.

Richard looked down at her out of the corners of his eyes, his look disapproving as the Latin rolled over them, washing them in sanctity. She stilled her trembling and looked downward piously. Yet she was not pious. He could disapprove of her eagerness, but he was her husband, and a husband had duties to perform upon his wife.

Thank you, Lord, that a husband such as Richard had such duties to perform.

She hid her smile of satisfaction in a prayer.

After Prime, Richard left her quickly, no doubt because he sensed her eagerness. She did not question his departure. With Robert and Jerome upon his heels, he left to see to Dornei rents and contracts and the state of the larder. It did not matter to her how he occupied the daylight; he would be hers come nightfall.

And how would she spend her day? Why, in preparing for the evening. Tonight would serve as her wedding night, and she would be prepared for it.

And for Richard. In truth, she had been prepared for this, for Richard to touch her as a husband touches a wife, for years. She was more than prepared; she was eager. And for all Richard's monkish ways, she knew from past experience that he could be brought to eagerness as well.

Joan, Aelis, and Elsbeth followed her from the chapel. Richard was already lost to sight, but she was at rest; he was within the walls of Dornei and bound to her by holy covenant. Never again would she pine for Richard.

"Shall I fetch your embroidery, Isabel?" Elsbeth asked as they climbed the stair that hugged the lower wall of the tower.

"Nay, no embroidery today," she said sweetly, her thoughts wrapped in visions of the night. "But you may arrange for a bath; also a loaf and some ale. I will not leave my chamber today. Today I spend in preparation of my bridal night."

"A whole day to prepare for a moment?" Aelis asked with a grin.

Isabel looked at the girl, soon to be wed herself, and smiled, "A moment? Nay, it will take the whole night, if I have my way."

"It is Richard who will have his way with you, Isabel. 'Tis the man's duty," Joan said as they reached the hall.

"Let him, then. I shall not stand in the way of his duty," Isabel said in mock seriousness.

They laughed as they made their way up to the lord's chamber, unslept in last night. 'Twould not be so tonight. Nay, that giant bed would serve well soon enough.

With jokes and laughter, they selected her bliaut while awaiting the arrival of the tub. A rich azure was the choice all agreed upon, the blue setting off her dark hair, with an undergown of aureate, the golden yellow making her eyes shimmer green, or so they all agreed. For jewels, a brooch of gold set with emeralds; she lacked a bridal ring, and this lack she wanted mended at the soonest opportunity. The goldsmith in the town could fashion something for them; she would discuss it with Richard, and they would walk the distance happily, chatting as they planned the design of the ring that marked her his. She could see in her heart how it would be. It would be so, for was she not the most graced woman in God's domain, to have Richard for a husband?

The bath arrived, directed by Robert the steward. Isabel smiled her thanks and said, "Your lord has no more need of you this day, Robert, to let you attend the delivery of my bath?" Was Richard free of duty and waiting for her?

"He bade me attend as he is closeted with Jerome, Lady," Robert answered. "He reports that there is much that needs his attention concerning the collection of the rents."

Yea, the collection of the rents was important, but did her husband not wish to see her at her bath? Perhaps tomorrow, when the bridal night was past, he would overcome his monkish timidity and attend when e'er she did bathe. Yea, she could well imagine that it would be so.

Tonight would change everything.

Tonight, after the meal, they would share a bed, and all the intimacies of marriage would be theirs. There would be no excuses; she would not be put off. Her father was dead, his soul secure in heaven, his will assured. She was a wife; it had been his last command. Richard must claim her on the marriage bed or the church could annul their union. It would not happen. She would not lose him now, not after so many years and so many prayers sent into the bosom of God.

Standing before her ladies as they toweled her dry, she slipped into a memory that had sustained and entertained her for a year. A year ago on Whitsunday. The kiss.

She had followed him to the stable. It had been spring, late spring, and the air heavy with sunlight and birdsong. The odor of hay had been strong, smelling like the earth and sun combined, smelling like life. Dust had been in the air, golden and shimmering, and Richard had been a dark column of strength standing in the honeyed light of the open stable door. Seeing her, he had stepped back into the shadows, his eyes tracking her as she followed him in. No matter how dim the light, she would not lose him.

She had said nothing, too afraid to speak, too afraid he would bolt if she gave him the chance to run. He said little, none of which she could remember. It had meant nothing to her then, and she had not kept it as part of her treasured memory. She had searched him out, wanting him alone; she had succeeded, a rare occurrence.

She had walked toward him, cornering him near a stack of hay, her route sliding and circuitous, trying to ease him. Just wanting to get closer, to be closer. Just wanting to be near him.

His eyes had looked as dark as ebon, all the blue lost in the shadowed corner of the stable. His hair had fallen forward over his brow, a glossy black stream that she yearned to hold in her hand, to caress, to bathe in. She stood close enough to do it; she was close enough to touch him. And she had. Not his hair—she was not so bold as that—but . . . she had to touch him.

She laid her hand on his chest, so broad and so muscular, and felt the rise of breath and the beat of heart. His heart was pounding, she could feel it beneath her hand, and then she felt the tremor of his sharp intake of breath. He was so warm, so close. She had him, in her hand.

She did not say his name aloud, but she said it with her eyes. And he read her, knowing she was calling to him, wanting to bury herself in his touch, wanting more. His touch, his nearness, satisfying nothing. She was more hungry for him than she had ever been.

He read that in her; she could not speak it, but he read her hunger. He could read her so easily, and she was so grateful that he could. And never more than in that moment of intense and naive longing.

He groaned and swallowed the sound, grabbing her to him in the same instant. His arms came around her, hard as iron, as he kissed her mouth. It was not a gentle kiss, yet he was gentle in his fierceness. She was not afraid. Nothing he could do would make her fear.

He held her to him as if afeared she would bolt if he but let her loose. She would never willingly take a step away from Richard. He had to have known the truth of that.

His tongue found its way into her mouth, and her arms wrapped around his waist, under the arms that held her to him. When she opened happily to his kiss, when the warmth and wet of him was all she remembered ever knowing, he moved his hands down to the flare of her hips and pulled her against his arousal.

They groaned into each other's mouths in sweet distress and longing.

She had known then what she hungered for, and she had known that Richard was the only one to satisfy her.

She had ground her hips against his length, seeking succor and relief, whimpering into his open mouth, twining her fingers in the silky length of his hair. Wanting him. Trusting him.

He had pulled her from him then, with as much gentle fierceness as he had begun the kiss. She had clung, she remembered that well, her arms around his neck and her mouth seeking his, open and wet and blindly searching. Her hunger running strong. Her body aching and empty.

Richard had pushed her away then, his breathing hoarse and harsh, his eyes glittering.

The kiss was done.

All that she carried was the memory and the mark of Richard upon her soul.

He had gone to the abbey, pledging his life to God, within the week.

She had known the cause to be herself, though he had said no word to blame her. His eyes told her all she needed to know of responsibility. Yet she could not forget the kiss. She did not want to.

"You'll need no kohl to deepen the luster of your eyes," Joan said. "You need no artifice to heighten your feminine allure."

Isabel looked down at her distended nipples and flushed skin; she ducked her head and smiled, taking the ribbing in good stead.

Nay, she needed nothing but a bed and a darkened room to drive all thoughts of a celibate life from her husband's mind.

Chapter Nine

The sun was still high when she finished her toilette. The day was too long to spend it in her chamber, especially when she could go out and feast her eyes on Richard. All plans to remain sequestered vanished, and she left the room eagerly, leaving Elsbeth to tidy the space. Joan and Aelis accompanied her; Aelis making for the bailey and Joan the solar. Isabel made for Richard, wherever he had hidden himself.

Louis was ascending the stair as they were descending. They nigh bumped against each other in the close confines of the stair tower.

"Your pardon, Isabel," he said on a laugh. "I have found you with too good a will, it seems."

"You searched for me?" she asked, smiling. Could aught go amiss on such a day? "I am here, as are we all."

"Lady Joan." He nodded. "Aelis. Edmund was gearing for the quintain when last I saw him," he said with a grin.

"Excuse me, Isabel," Aelis said, squeezing by them on the stair. "It is such a lovely day. Shall I pick some straw lily for your chamber? It will add a romantic touch, I think."

"That would be most welcome, and gather some of the roots, if you would. We must resupply our medicinals," Isabel answered to Aelis's disappearing back.

"Think you she can find straw lily blooming beneath the shadow of the quintain?" Joan asked with a grin.

"She will find what she seeks there, of that I am certain," Louis answered.

"To be sought and then found," Joan mused. " 'Tis a young woman's sport. I seek my diversions in the solar, and there they happily await me. Unless you have need of me, Isabel?"

"Nay, follow your inclinations, as I will mine," Isabel answered, thinking only of Richard.

They continued down the stair, Joan making her way across the hall to the wall that divided the solar from the community of the hall. A small room, it was private and well lit and a welcome respite for the ladies when the company of men grew tiresome. Isabel could not imagine a day when she would retreat behind a wall to escape the company of Richard.

"I would have words with you, Lady," Louis said when Joan had left them.

"I am yours, then," she said, her eyes scanning the room for Richard, hardly aware of Louis's words and not at all aware of his intent.

They stood in the shadow of the wall where stair tower and hall met and merged. It was dark and quiet. Louis did not move into the full light of the hall, but kept Isabel with him in the shadows. The tables were being set for the meal, the boards laid atop the trestles and the benches positioned beneath; the hall was full and noisy. She could not yet find Richard among the throng at their labors.

"You are most gracious, Lady Isabel," he said, searching her face.

She felt his perusal and turned to face him fully; seeing his look, she smiled. "Not at all. What would you say to me?"

"I congratulate you on a match well made. You are content?"

Isabel smiled fully and said on a laugh, "I am well content."

"That is well," he said with some hesitation.

"Yea, it is well that I am content, I will agree with you," she all but laughed. "What is amiss that you look so troubled over my supreme contentment?"

"I would have you stay contented, Lady."

"As would I. We are still in perfect accord, Louis. If you seek an argument, you must choose a different topic."

"I would have you stay contented," he repeated, his green eyes intent upon her face, "but the lord of a vast estate must do more than confer with his clerk." With a subtle movement of his hand, he showed her where Richard was, off near the solar wall, conferring with Jerome.

Isabel felt the laughter seep out of her like a slow wound. Richard looked very scholarly, his hands on the parchment of contracts and agreements. A lord must fight to hold and keep all under his care safe and secure. How long had it been since Richard had used his sword arm for other than crossing himself?

With Louis at her side, stalwart and solid with muscle, she considered the specter of Richard as she had not yet done, forcing herself to see more than the dream of him. Forcing herself to see the man to whom she had pledged her life and her lands and her people.

He was more slender than he had been at Malton.

Here he was, closeted within the shelter of Dornei's walls on a day fair and mild. Why was he not practicing arms or hunting for meat? Why stay indoors? So as not to miss the next office of monkish prayers? Such a lord as this would lose all that her forebears and his had fought to gain and hold.

Richard was the husband she had prayed for, aye, but not this monkish man. A man of war was needed to lead Dornei and Warefeld to prosperity, not a man of prayers.

None of these traitorous and newly born thoughts did she share with Louis, but the seed was planted in her mind and heart.

"He has much to learn of Dornei's accounts," she said in mild defense.

"Aye, and that can be done when the moon is up or the weather foul," he answered.

"He would not wait for the chance of rain to learn his duty."

"And others may not wait for their chance," he said in warning.

She could not ignore it. Word of a Benedictine lord would spread on the wind, bespeaking Dornei's vulnerability. Even now, Warefeld sat untended, her lord recently dead and the one born to replace Hubert and Geoffrey sitting in a warm hall reading the accounts. No, it could not be borne. Their lineage demanded more.

"Prayers and accounts have their purpose," she said mildly, "as do arms. You have a thought which would guide me?"

"I have a plan," he said bluntly. "Release me."

"Release you? This is your plan?"

To release Louis to run wild in the land, broadcasting Dornei's weakness, was not a plan she was prepared to follow. How well could Louis be trusted?

"I will not betray," he said, looking as trustworthy as always.

Yet, how well could she trust him? He was a knight, and of a fact, all knights swallowed deeply of ambition.

"You have not yet paid homage to my husband as Lord of Dornei," she said.

"I will do so on my return. I will swear him fealty without pause," he promised.

He was asking her to trust him in a world where misplaced trust could kill.

"You will vow, here to me, that what you are about will aid Richard?"

"Not only Richard, but Isabel," he said, his entire demeanor bespeaking earnestness.

"You will vow?" she repeated, searching his face for falseness and deceit.

"I will vow. This is for Dornei's gain."

She paused on the precipice of decision. He was Louis; she knew him. Yet how well could any man be known when such a prize as Dornei stood in his path? But his eyes were so earnest and so intent. Could she distrust the urgency of his gaze?

"Then go," she said, her decision made. "God guide you in your endeavor."

Louis smiled and kissed her hand in response. She smiled in return, praying to God that she had done well to trust her heart.

From across the long hall, over the noise of tables and benches being dragged into place, through the gloom of stone, Richard marked the kiss and the answering smile. And liked it not.

The girl Isabel had become a woman in the year he had become a monk, but how far a woman? As far as Nicholas suggested? Isabel had the fire of desire buried but lightly beneath her skin, this he knew too well, but would she have betrayed all honor and chastity by giving her body to a man not lawfully hers? Nicholas would have him believe it of her. However, he was not disposed to believe Nicholas in anything.

The kiss Louis had bestowed upon Isabel could have been merely a kiss gently passed between a knight and his lady, a kiss of chivalry and of friendship.

The kiss he had bestowed upon Isabel had been neither gentle nor chivalrous, but full of fire and instantly consuming, as tinder to flame. Unexpected it had been, but long fought against. He had lost that fight, for an instant, for the instant in time it took for a man to want a woman and begin the road to claiming her. He had lost the battle within himself and had taken Isabel with him into carnal defeat. She had come with him happily enough and with no apparent regret.

She did not look regretful now, with Louis still touching her hand, fondling her with a near caress.

Jerome, standing next to him, he had forgotten completely in his study of his wife.

Adam rushed to her side then, an obvious witness to the kiss, and forced Louis to release her hand. Adam, with his soft smile and bright ways, coaxed a laugh from her, a laugh she seemed more than eager to give. Louis remained at her side as well, his smile subdued and his manner contained: a suitor outmaneuvered.

And her husband watched all from his side of the hall.

Richard looked around him in that moment, struck by the weight of uncomfortable quiet. All in that hall watched Isabel. All in that hall watched him watch Isabel. Including Isabel. Of course Isabel; jealousy was a woman's snare. He knew that well enough.

Father Langfrid broke into his tumultous thoughts, his interruption a blessing. "When will you accept the oath of fealty?"

The oath of fealty, the oath which would bind the people of Dornei to him and he to them as their lord. A binding ceremony which would set him in his place as lord, as binding a ceremony as marriage. Or even more so, since there was no chance of repudiation with the oath of homage.

Richard did not take his eyes from Isabel, could not, though he knew it fed her to have him watch her so.

Nicholas moved toward Isabel, and Richard's eyes took it in, noting the smile of speculation and the look of pregnant question in Nicholas's eyes as he watched Richard watch Isabel. Yea, he needed to bind these men to him if he was to keep Isabel from sin, though God knew better than he how little that helped when two souls were bent on destruction.

"Today," he answered Father Langfrid, his eyes still on Isabel and her circle of men. "Now. Before the meal."

Chapter Ten

Once word had gone out, it had gone quickly. Kneeling before him, hands clasped and heads bowed, they had sworn to be his men. But he had noted that Nicholas had hesitated to bend his knee. He had also noted Adam's half-hidden smile as he bowed his head. The men-at-arms had submitted quickly enough, but that tale told little. Betrayal came easily to most men, even those who held honor high. Still, it was done.

Except Louis. Louis had left upon some errand for Isabel, so said Isabel. Where, how long, and concerning what were all questions she could not or would not answer. Searching her face, so small and delicate in its dark beauty, he had seen the lie in her crystal eyes. And said nothing. What point in demanding the truth of a liar?

But Isabel had not been a liar at Malton; bold,

yes—too bold for a maiden pledged to another, but not a liar. What other changes had taken place in the last year? What else would she feel the need to lie about? In order to find out, he would need to talk to her.

Once he had passed into manhood, talking to Isabel was a task he had avoided. She invariably offended his dignity, making sport of him, laughing at the wrong time. And she always found a reason to argue with him. With maturity, he had understood that her constant pricking had been the evidence of her frustrated desire for him.

And his avoidance of her, because he had returned it.

Comely and bright, she had been watched by all the squires. Isabel had returned the interest with smiles and flirtations while keeping the heart of her interest in him. He had felt the heat, and none had been blind to the glow of attraction that had shone from her onto him. For himself, he thought he had done well and kept his unlawful fascination with her well hidden. But Isabel had known; by that kiss, so urgent and wild, he had shown himself the sinner he was. All long ago now.

How many men had she kissed since then?

How many lies would it take for her to hide beneath pretended innocence?

Nay, he did not want to talk to Isabel. He did not want to drive her into a lie. He did not want to look the fool.

Only to himself would he admit that it was a poor beginning to his lordship of Dornei and Isabel.

After the homage ceremony, Isabel had suggested they go hawking, to celebrate the day. He had wanted to stay within, having much more to discuss with his clerk and his bailiff, but the fighting men had been instantly enthralled by the suggestion, and he had little wish to thwart a celebration commemorating his lordship of Dornei, no matter how little he himself wished to celebrate such an event. He had his duty to perform. It was all that mattered to him.

He found suitable clothing for himself, determined not to feel irritation that Isabel had not arranged for a boy to see to his needs, and was mounted and ready with the rest of them. Isabel was mounted and ready as well. Isabel, it was clear, had decided to hunt with them.

The day was fair, the sun full and strong in the sky. The strong wind of yestereve had passed away in the night and left behind a sky as blue as deep water and as cloudless. The world was growing green in the warmth of a gentle spring, and he could not but help being gladdened by the bounty of God's grace in providing such beauty to the eyes.

If only Isabel and Adam would not ride so close together.

She was a woman who did all she desired, no matter where her desires led her. He knew that better than any man in this company, or he hoped he did. How far had she strayed since leaving Malton? Her father, Lord Bernard, had not been a stern man; he had let his only child run wild, letting her fancies direct her in the most unwise fashion.

She rode ahead, showing him her back and her long fall of hair and the trim curve of buttock poised atop her mount. She should be wearing a cloak, shielding herself from male eyes, no matter that the weather was mild. She was not mild, and she did not inspire mildness.

Adam, at her side, did not look mild.

Richard reined in his annoyance. They were in a large company of armed men; nothing would befall. Not here, not now. He should ride up to the head of the party, being lord of them all, yet he did not want to ride to Isabel. She would see his coming to her as a victory; she made victories out of wet kindling, making something of nothing. Yet, he would not willingly give her even the fantasy. He would stay to the back, well away from her.

He cast his eyes downward, upon the earth, striving for peaceful and contemplative thoughts. Yet his eyes again and again rose to watch Isabel share her laughter with Adam.

When next he looked up, she had disengaged herself from Adam's side and was making her way along the edge of the party back to him. Was it not so? Did not Isabel always seek him out? He kept his eyes forward and did not greet her when she came alongside him. She did so neatly, her mount well mannered and well managed; she had always been a capable horsewoman, he would give her that silent compliment.

" 'Tis a wondrous day for hawking, is it not?" she said with a smile. Isabel smiled too often, he thought, and at too many. Always she had a smile for any man who spoke two words to her.

" 'Tis a fair day," he answered.

"I am so happy that you agreed to this adventure, Richard. I fear to bubble up with joy because of it," she said, her eyes glistening with emotion.

She was joyous because he was hawking? 'Twas ridiculous. He said nothing and did not stop the frown of irritation that crossed his features.

She noted his frown, and her smile faded. He did not feel the least bit guilty.

"You do not share my joy," she said. "Are you so unhappy to be out of doors, or is it your married state which drives you into dismay?"

He could hear the trace of wounded pride in her voice and felt a small surge of grim satisfaction; not all men would tumble into the dirt at the radiance of Isabel's smile. She must know by now that he never would.

"I have been forced to give up my heart's desire, Isabel, as you well know. How joyous did you expect to find me?"

"Can you find no joy in me?" she asked.

"I find my joy in duty, as you would do well to learn." He looked at her askance. Her bosom was high and full against her bliaut, her profile white and delicate against the background of trees coming into full green; he knew the look of her and could not stop looking. "It is obvious that you have lost none of your appeal to men. Under dire consequence to your soul, you would do well to remember that you are now a married woman."

Her ire was up. She was ever up and down, her emotions pulling at her like the wind, without direction or control. He did not care that her anger had been pricked; in fact, it pleased him. She had lost her joy in him. It was enough to satisfy.

"Perhaps after tonight I will not have trouble remembering," she said, holding his eyes with hers.

"If you cannot remember now, you will not remember later," he answered, looking down at her.

"We shall know for certain on the morrow," she said, striving to keep her voice pleasant.

"You assume much about tonight," he said, prodding her again. She would find no rest in conversation with him, particularly on this topic.

"I assume that we will share the marriage bed. 'Tis past time."

He snorted lightly, the sound coming through his nose with all the arrogance he intended. "You are overeager." He said it as an insult. She received it as such.

"Perhaps you are merely undermanned," she snapped back, her eyes as hot as sparks. "Will you pray through another night?"

"You mock me for praying for the souls of your father and his wife? For my brothers and your betrothed?"

"Nay, naturally not—"

"I begin to think there is little 'natural' about you," he cut in sharply, his voice on the rise.

"I would have said that you have long thought me too 'natural'!" she shouted.

"We will scarce find game with such a row as

113

this," Nicholas interrupted, pulling up beside them. His smile was as wide and as treacherous as a river in flood. "Even the boar run in fear."

"You forget yourself, Knight, to speak to your lord and lady thus," Richard said heavily, swinging his anger round to an equally just target. Nicholas and his arrogance he would ill tolerate.

" 'Twas said in jest, Richard," Nicholas said, bringing up old taunts with such words. It was uneasy ground between them, old and bitter ground, and Richard was ill disposed to give way.

"And not well done," he said. "Mayhap you should return to sit behind Dornei's walls, since hawking is not to your mood today."

Nicholas seemed on the verge of opening his mouth to argue, but, looking again at Richard's face, he snapped his mount around, called for his squire, and rode back to Dornei. Even when they were fellow squires, Nicholas had learned the folly of argument when Richard's temper was prodded. Richard rode on silently. Isabel rode silently at his side, thinking hard and holding her tongue against further insults. 'Twas not the way to lure Richard into her bed.

Richard was obviously going to try to find a way to avoid the marriage bed, and he seemed determined to be miserable in his husbanding of her. Could the hawk catch the sun? Such it had always been between them, but she had the advantage now; they were husband and wife. He would not slip the snare that easily.

Did he think to insult her by declaring her overeager for the marriage bed? Was she not supposed to want her husband to possess her? Had she not been imagining it for year upon year? How did he manage to make it sound sinful for her to want her own husband? How did he manage to make guilt rise in her like an upward draft of hot air? That was the worst of it; she felt guilty. Richard always made her feel guilty. He clearly did it by design. No man could be so successful by accident.

But, among the stone of words he had thrown, had she not heard the glimmering pebble of jealousy? Jealousy was her ally, for at least it showed he had a heart to bruise in regard to her. At least she could make him feel *something*. If jealousy, could love be far behind? But how deep could love grow if he avoided the marriage bed?

He must not avoid it. Richard would claim her tonight. It would be so, for she would make it so.

They returned to Dornei having caught nothing, the hawk unblooded.

Chapter Eleven

With Richard well married and the oath of homage declared, Brother John departed while the day was still fresh. However, Isabel did not miss the sympathetic look Brother John pressed upon her or the grim longing in Richard's eyes as John rode out of Dornei's gates and back to the abbey. No more longing for life away from her; that would change tonight. The only one he would look after longingly would be her, once he had tasted the delights of the marriage bed.

He acted ill disposed to taste.

Perhaps it *was* an act, an act given for her benefit. Richard had never been effusive in his treatment of her. Isabel sighed within herself and confessed the truth: he had treated her with little more than courtesy, and that tinged with disdain, for years.

Yet the kiss told another tale, a tale more to her liking.

He must feel some warmth toward her to have behaved so. Richard was ever and always proper in his deportment, serious in his outlook, and reverent to his duty.

Isabel looked across the hall to where Richard stood in conference with Jerome, again. The answer lay in her hand. Her husband was a man who stood by vows of duty with full honor. Well and good. Was it not his duty to bed his wife? Yea, it was. Isabel smiled, her heart tumbling within her ribs. He would do his duty by her. He would. And she would see him put aside all such unmanly behavior as squinting over accounts in the full light of a mild day.

Edmund was at her side, his duties since Lord Bernard's passing slack, mumbling again of Aelis. Isabel listened with half an ear, her mind on finding Father Langfrid.

"Can you not find more for her to busy herself with? She trails me like a hound after a hare, and I have no liking as the hare," Edmund complained.

"What offends you, Edmund? She finds you beguiling. Other men would not take offense at that," Isabel answered.

"I have done nothing to beguile her," he snapped. "And a man likes to find his own pursuits."

A man he called himself, and she could not fault him. At seventeen summers he was surely a man by any measure, yet he was such a boy when stood next to Richard. Had ever Richard been so young? In years, aye; in deportment, never.

"She will marry soon," she said in comfort and dismissal.

Ducking his head, Edmund veered off toward the smith. He had seen a flash of blue across the bailey; blue was Aelis's favored color.

Isabel slipped into the chapel, but all was still. Father Langfrid was not within. On her way out, she spied Elsbeth with a basket of loaves and cheese.

"Where are you to, Elsbeth? Have you seen Father Langfrid?"

"He is where I am bound," Elsbeth answered. "Giles the carpenter is a father today; I am bringing this small offering to ease the mother. Father Langfrid is there, offering his blessings and good cheer."

A fresh and potent flare of guilt shot upward like a bolt from Isabel's contrite heart. Elsbeth performed what was *her* function as Lady of Dornei. She had been too occupied with trying to arrange for Richard to tumble into her bed to mind her other duties.

"Wait upon me, Elsbeth. I will fetch a skin of wine for the household. This is a day of great joy."

Elsbeth waited while Isabel ran across the yard to the kitchen, shooed Edmund off to the tiltyard, and hurried to lead the way to the carpenter's abode. All it took was the slightest effort and a little time; in truth, it was not so great a task to see to the needs of her people.

By the time they arrived and greeted Giles, she had forgiven herself.

Father Langfrid, all smiles, was just ducking his head through the portal as they arrived.

"A fine lad with his father's bright look," Langfrid said to them all, Giles included. Giles smiled his thanks. "A blessing upon Dornei this day in the easy birth of so strong a son."

" 'Twas not as easy as all that, Father," the carpenter's wife, Sifurtha, said from her bed in the corner.

"The next will be easier still, God willing," Langfrid said in good will.

"God willing," she echoed.

Giles, thinking of the bloody sheets that had been carried out by the midwife, said, "One for a start is enough."

With all the talk of childbirth, Isabel's problem came fresh upon her mind, driving all thoughts before it.

"Father, may we speak?"

"Certainly, Isabel."

He looked at the wine she carried. Isabel passed it to Elsbeth without a word, and Elsbeth carried all the gifts from the Lord and Lady of Dornei into the carpenter's abode. Her duty fulfilled, Isabel walked with the Father back up to the hall.

She could think of no words to say what needed to be said. How to tell her priest that she was eager for the consummation of her vows but her husband was not? She confessed all to him, it was true, but
· this was so strange a tale, and put Richard in so

119

poor a light, that she did not know how to address such a topic.

Fortunately, Langfrid did.

"It was kind of Richard to spend the night in prayer for those in your combined families whom you have so recently lost. Most husbands of an hour would not be so generous."

Generous? That was a word for it, but it was not her word. Though Langfrid was right: Richard had lost both Hubert and Geoffrey in the same instant, with the same breath. And she had lost her betrothed; surely the world and the saints expected her to mourn for Hubert. Yet all her thoughts were of Richard. Perhaps she was as unnatural as Richard claimed.

But she was a wife, her duty here and now. And Richard's duty, too. They were lord and lady; they must consummate and produce an heir. All else was secondary.

"Yea, he is generous in his prayers," she said, the truth of it unpleasant to her ears. "Yet while we prayed, we did not . . . fulfill our union."

"Yea?" he asked expectantly.

They were almost to the hall, the scurry of people upon them. She did not want to discuss this in the open, for all ears to hear and eyes to watch.

"May we go into the chapel? My words would come more easily there."

"And more softly," he said, understanding her.

The dark of the chapel, lit by two precious pieces of glass, was soothing to her. They had been married by a priest, their vows taken in God's full sight and by His divine direction. Surely, He would want the marriage on right footing. 'Twas all she wanted as well, and if the sight of Richard's blue eyes and wide shoulders pleased her, was there sin in that? Nay, for she but desired the man given to her by God. 'Twas right and proper for her to desire her husband and lord.

"You know I am well disposed to this marriage," she began.

"Oh, yea, that I understand well," he said with a soft light in his eye. Did he laugh?

"But my concern is that . . . is that," she stammered, her eyes darting around the sacred hall, lighting everywhere but on Father Langfrid. "Is that . . . is the marriage legal without the . . ."

"Consummation?"

"Yea," she breathed with a smile, relieved.

Langfrid shrugged and went to straighten a tilted candle. "The church does not require it in unusual circumstances."

"There are no unusual circumstances here," Isabel insisted, following him. "My husband and I are living under the same roof, and we are both of an age."

"That is true," he agreed. And said nothing more.

For a learned man, he was a trifle obtuse. But then, he had long lived a celibate life. Isabel, too close to the heart of her troubles not to strike, blurted out, "Then would you communicate that to Richard? As soon as possible and certainly before nightfall?"

She would have done it herself but she knew it

would only irritate Richard, giving him more to charge her with in the sin of being "natural." Besides, such counsel would weigh more heavily coming from a priest.

"I will do what I can," Langfrid said, his cheeks rising rosy pink. He *was* laughing.

"You may laugh, Father," she said with a rueful grin, "but I know Richard. He requires this push toward the matrimonial bed."

"As you say, Isabel. He is your husband."

Isabel smiled fully and said, "Yea, he is."

She left then, back to the hall, where she had set herself the task of rousting Richard into the tiltyard and away from his parchments and prayers.

Langfrid, watching her go, thought that Isabel was one bride who would not faint for fear on the bridal bed. Of Richard, he was not so certain.

The passage from the outer bailey to the inner was small and narrow and dark; it was there that Adam waylaid her. Of a truth, she had seen more of Adam since a wife than she had ever seen him as a maid. And when had he ever been so forward?

"Isabel," he said, laying a hand upon her arm, halting her. "I have been searching for you since the hawking. You looked so unhappy, I thought to cheer you."

"I was not unhappy," she said, looking down at his hand, willing him to remove it. And she had not been unhappy; she had been angry.

"Nay?" he said, running his hand along her arm

in a blatant caress. "Yet you did not have the look of a happy bride."

"You are mistaken," she said, removing his hand. "I am very happy to be a bride."

He smiled. Had Adam always smiled so often and for so little cause? She could hear the sounds of smith and laundress, the high voices of children, the low murmur of men; yet she remained alone with Adam in the shadows. A faint bell of alarm rang softly in her mind, but she did not know how to respond to its call. She had never felt such uneasiness in the company of a man.

He stroked a hand against her hair, and she jerked her head away. Truly, he was too bold, yet had she not encouraged him just hours ago, in her efforts to birth jealousy in Richard's heart? Of what possible use were his inappropriate attentions upon her if Richard was not there to witness it?

"I would make you happier," he said, pressing her against the stone walls, his body a sudden and unexpected weapon which he held against her.

"Adam!"

"I but give you what you want, Isabel. Do not protest," he said, pressing a kiss upon her mouth.

She slid her face away, more in irritation than panic. Did he not understand that such behavior did nothing to her purpose? He said that he gave her what she wanted, but she did not want any of him without Richard there to behold; and she had never expected nor wanted such a display as this! Perhaps she had misled him in that?

It galled her to think on Richard's words regarding her behavior while out hawking. He could have been right; perhaps she was too bold. Adam's current posturing certainly indicated it. Yet how to dissuade him without maiming his pride?

"I must protest," she said, her voice a muffle against his chest, her hands pressing against him to no avail. "You must stop this, Adam."

"I cannot find the will to stop. Your beauty, as dark and rich as a summer night, beckons me. I am powerlesss, caught within your grasp. Deal gently with me, fair Isabel."

It was she who was caught. One of his hands clasped hers while his mouth forced kisses upon her; they were wet and cold and excited within her only revulsion. It was when his other hand groped at her skirts that she abandoned all thoughts of salving his pride.

"Adam! Stop this!" she snarled, thrashing and pulling her hands from his. He only tightened his grip, smothered her with his mouth, and laid a heavy hand upon her breast. "You are a fool!" she managed to say against his mouth.

"For you," he returned, forcing his breath down her throat.

Her breast ached with his rough handling, and she could scarce draw breath with his weight pressing her back against the stone. His kiss was suffocating her.

And then it stopped.

Richard had come into the barbican, his size filling up the opening, closing off the light. Never had she seen him look more forbidding; never had she welcomed his presence more.

Adam released her and stepped back, his face the color of chalk.

"Whatever she may be, she is mine," Richard said, his voice tight and low.

Whatever she may be? 'Twas an insult and nothing less.

"Leave Dornei now," Richard said, looking only at Adam, "and you keep your life."

He looked very calm, little more agitated than when deep in prayer, yet his breath was heavy and loud.

Adam hesitated, his color returning. He had heard the insult to Isabel and was considering. Richard was so recently a monk, a man forbidden to take up arms . . .

"Go, Adam," she said. "There is no place for you at Dornei. Go to Braccan."

She sent him to her dower lands because she felt some guilt in encouraging his flirtation. She had never intended that he should so misread her. At her words, Richard's face took on the grimness of God at His judgment seat. She realized in that moment that she should have kept silent, not coming to Adam's aid against his wrath, not when he was so clearly jealous.

He was jealous. It sent a thrill through her that erased all memory of Adam's mauling treatment. Mayhap Richard, seeing her in the arms of another man, would realize that he loved her and that their marriage was a gift from God. Surely a man so protective of his wife would want to claim her fully on the marriage bed.

When Adam waited yet another breath to decide his course, Isabel watched in amazement as Richard pulled his sword free, his movement fluid and swift. No monk would own such an act. In that moment, Adam was gone, back toward the outer bailey and the open road.

"He has not his mount," she said, unable to curb her tongue and still fighting her guilt. Adam was a knight, and a knight was nothing unhorsed.

"He has not my wife either," Richard said, resheathing his sword, the gleam of metal lost in the shadows. "I will send his squire with his equipment. Would you care to join the escort?"

"Naturally not!" she huffed, thrusting out her chest like a gamecock.

"Naturally?"

"Yea, naturally," she rejoined, refusing to back away from his taunt. "You do not think I welcomed his hands upon me?"

"Lady, you would be wise not to ask me what I think," he answered, his voice a near growl.

He could growl, but she had seen the glimmer of desire and possession in his eyes and he had drawn steel in defense of her. Mayhap she knew his thoughts better than he.

They were still alone, the darkness and the stone an embrace, all sound muted and muffled. She could not resist him. She could not resist the moment.

Drawing near him, she stood with her breasts on

a level with his hand upon the sword hilt. He was a tall man, seeming more so in the close confines of the corridor, his shoulders blocking out the light that struggled to enter. She could feel his heat, the very pulse of his blood and the beating of his heart.

She was close enough to almost, almost touch.

"You are my husband. I would know all your thoughts," she said softly. Seductively.

She could see the shadow of his black beard, a dark impression on his cheek and throat. She could see the thin golden flecks in his dark blue eyes. She could see his chest rise and fall as his breathing quickened. She could see the pulse of desire flutter in the hollow of his throat.

He was so close, and it was so dim in the confines of the barbican.

His mouth was so close. If only he would bend to her, taking her mouth as Adam had done. His assault she would welcome. His touch she craved. Surely he would follow his natural impulse.

As he had before.

As he had in that blazing kiss that shone in her memory like a star.

"Stand away from me," he breathed, his voice harsh and guttural.

Before she could react, he was gone, back toward the inner bailey. Leagues from the marriage bed.

Chapter Twelve

They may have been alone in the forced closeness of the barbican, but what had passed there was not long a secret. Mayhap the young squire Gilles, who had been set to the task of cleaning out the latrines for breaking his knight's favorite harness, had not yet heard, and that only because he smelled so foul. But everyone else knew, fortress and town alike. And knew not enough to keep silent.

Joan accosted her first, catching her as she crossed rapidly in front of the chapel, eager to avoid Father Langfrid.

"Are you well, dear?" she said, laying hold of Isabel's hands and clasping them within her own, her cheeks bright with misery and concern. "What was Adam about that he thought to avail himself of you in such a way? Surely the man had no cause to think you would return his regard, and with you so firmly wed to the man of your heart."

Something in the way Joan spoke made Isabel feel guilty to her knees.

"They say he lifted your skirts . . . did he truly attempt so much, and in the open passageway of the barbican?" Joan asked, her concern warring with her curiosity.

"I only remember that his attentions were most inappropriate and unwelcome."

"Of course they were," Joan soothed. "And he is most fortunate that Richard is such a forgiving man. I cannot think of a husband who would react with such gentle admonition to such a blatant attack."

Unless Richard felt that she had provoked it? *Whatever else she may be.* He had certainly reacted as if Adam were only partially to blame. And was he wrong? She had flirted with Adam openly, but only to attract Richard. Yet how could Adam know that? Guilt, like nausea, rose, gagging her.

"He has ever been a thoughtful man, slow to anger," Isabel said, quoting God's ideal of manhood. But was it hers? She would not think on it; Adam was gone, and by Richard's word. All was well.

Joan left her with a hug and a pat on the cheek, off to visit the carpenter's wife and new babe with a small bag of herbs to ease the discomfort of nursing. Isabel had brought wine; her duty there was done.

Elsbeth found her next, upon the outside stair to the hall. The sun was breaking through high clouds and warmed the stone, casting all beneath them in soft and gentle light. The wind was high, pushing the clouds across the heavens toward the distant sea; just as Elsbeth was pushing Isabel up the stair and into the sheltered portal of the hall entrance.

"I always knew Adam had it in him," she all but spat. Such vehemence from Elsbeth was hardly normal. Yet, it had not been a normal day. "He was lacking in chivalry—profoundly lacking."

"It does seem so," Isabel said, unsure of her own measure of guilt.

"And is so," Elsbeth said, giving her a quick, hard hug. "Dornei is well rid of him. Lord Richard did right and protected you well."

"Yea, he did," Isabel said, warming to the memory. Richard's fury had been hot upon seeing Adam's hands upon her. Surely such heat would accompany him to the marriage bed.

Aelis, finding her in the solar, led her thoughts in another and less pleasant direction.

"Of course, all are tittering about Richard's rage in finding Adam laying hands upon his wife," Aelis said.

"All?" Isabel said, fighting the flush of embarrassment.

"All," Aelis said bluntly. "Between the inner and outer bailey it is all that is whispered. That, and wondering why you did not shout for help. Surely someone could have come to your aid before Richard found you."

She had been silent, it was true, but it was because she was too shocked to speak. Did any think her willing to accept Adam's touch? Did they take her silence for consent?

Did Richard?

"She did not cry out, 'tis a fact all know," Nicholas said to Richard as they walked through the outer bailey.

"All?" Richard asked, not looking at Nicholas, forcing Nicholas to match his stride.

"Of course all. She could have been heard in either bailey if only she would cry her need."

"Not all cry when in need," Richard commented.

"A woman?" Nicholas snorted. "When does a woman not cry her need to heaven and beyond?"

"Isabel is not like all women," Richard said, knowing it for the truth.

"Nay, she is not," Nicholas agreed coldly. "A man not pledged to her backed her to a wall and laid hands to her, and she uttered not a word of protest. She is most assuredly—"

"Unique," Richard finished, looking at Nicholas out of the corner of his eye. "I have known Isabel long. When she is gripped by fear, it is as a hand to her throat. If you would tattle within the walls of Dornei, speak of that. Better yet, do not speak at all if you have so little control of your own tongue."

"I am only trying to help you understand—"

"There is nothing to understand," Richard said coldly. "I am husband to Isabel."

"But is she wife to you?"

"According to the church, she is." At Nicholas's

look, he added, "Do you question that there was a ceremony?"

"Nay, but perhaps . . . the legality of it."

"We were joined in the abbey with the archbishop's blessing. We are legally wed."

And would stay so, no matter what Nicholas plotted. It did not matter what Adam had done with Isabel or what Isabel had done with anyone else; and it did not signify that his blood tossed like hot poison in his veins when he saw again in his memory the sight of Isabel's exposed legs and struggling arms. He did not want her anywhere near him, with her seductive eyes and her velvet skin, yet he would allow no one else to have her.

He would not repudiate her.

He would not cast her away, not in that fashion. Isabel was his wife, by God's will, and she would stay his wife. Since Nicholas could not keep the rein on his bothersome and slanderous tongue, it would be Nicholas who would go.

"And I would have you travel to Lord Robert and tell him so," Richard said, ending the conversation. "I would have the marriage confirmed in his mind, so that he may know that all is well in Dornei." And it would be Nicholas's own foul tongue which would declare the permanence of his bond to Isabel.

Richard could not help but smile at the look on Nicholas's face.

And then he noted how strange it felt to smile. There had been little call to smile within the abbey and little more at Malton. But this was Dornei; perhaps he could find some small joy in Dornei. Being lord had its advantages, Nicholas's face at being so ordered one of them.

" 'Tis naught to smile on, Isabel," Father Langfrid scolded. "The talk runs to the degree of your purity."

He had found her in the solar, where she had been pretending not to hide, and marched her back to the chapel for a private conversation under Christ's holy cross. Unfortunately for Langfrid, he had come upon her too late; she had already made peace with Adam's odd display of courtly love and the level of her own guilt. She had none. She had never in any way encouraged Adam to touch her; she had reviewed it all, and she had never encouraged that.

And if the talk ran to the "degree of her purity," that would soon be laid aside as well, for Richard would know the level of her purity once he made her his true wife.

As to all the rest, the only man she'd ever kissed had been Richard. He should know her heart well enough to know that. Father Langfrid knew her for a virgin still, though Adam had come uncomfortably close to robbing her of that virtue. The blessing was that now Langfrid was as anxious as she for Richard to seal their marriage with a conjugal night.

In all, Adam had performed her a good service in prompting Father Langfrid to so firmly unite with her in purpose: Richard must consummate the marriage.

"The talk will end when Richard does take me to the marriage bed," she said. "Communicate this to my husband, please. He has husbandly rights. And if that fails to move him, remind him of his husbandly duty. Richard is ever and always about his 'duty.' "

"I will speak with him," Langfrid replied, "but I hardly think it will come to that."

Chapter Thirteen

"You must understand that you are expected by the church to give your wife children; on your present course, she has grounds for annulment," Langfrid said, growing hoarse with the effort to convince Richard to undertake sexual relations with his wife.

Richard rose from his knees, where he had been in most earnest prayer. God gave enlightenment to all who asked for light and understanding, and so Richard understood well who was behind this spiritual call to conjugal duty.

"Isabel will not have her marriage to me annulled," he said.

"Then you will perform your husbandly duty?"

Richard could almost find amusement in the idea. Most men would not find coupling with Isabel a duty. Most men would not have to be threatened with annulment to lay Isabel down on the marriage bed.

Images of dark hair, a bleached linen shift, and the feel of a woman's arms wrapped around his neck mingled with the sight of Isabel's legs draped in fabric and the obscene memory of Adam's hand tugging at that fabric.

He should have killed him.

Richard bowed his dark head and quickly confessed the murderous thought before it took firm hold in his mind and heart; such thoughts were unworthy of one who had committed his life to Christ's holy service. He struggled to regain his calm sense of earthly detachment.

This was what Isabel always wrought in him, this turmoil, strong emotion, wild thoughts of violence and passion. Needs. Needs that shamed him.

Life had been more peaceful in the exclusive company of men, celibate and prayerful men. There was nothing of peace in the presence of Isabel.

He believed in the perfection of God's providence.

He believed that God's ways were above his ways.

He believed that he was called to be perfect as Christ was perfect.

And because he believed all this, he willed himself to believe that God had ordained his mating with Isabel. He had dutifully married her. The mating was what he had yet to accomplish. The mating was what he most passionately did not want to do.

He would not repudiate Isabel, no matter what she had done, who had touched her, or how often.

Richard suppressed the turmoil that rose to blind him at the thought of male hands touching Isabel. He would allow no annulment. Being Lord of Dornei was where God had placed him, and here he would remain until God and God alone moved him.

And God could move him, back to his heart's desire, when he had performed his service here.

Yet what was needed in this earthly moment was for him to consummate the marriage; he had to mate with Isabel.

Of a faithful servant, God asked much.

"Yea, I make Isabel my wife tonight," he said, facing Langfrid, his blue eyes dark with resolve. "You may tell Isabel that I will follow the course of duty."

Langfrid blushed to his eyes in embarrassment, and Richard could not fault him. He knew Isabel, and the lengths to which she pushed a man, even if that man be a priest.

After Father Langfrid had delivered his blushing message that Richard would do his duty by her on the marriage bed, Isabel spent the hour before the meal searching for stains on her gown and snarls in her hair. She had to look perfect. If all went as she hoped, Richard would watch her walk across the floor to the high table, be speechless with admiration of her beauty, captivated by her conversation during the meal, and helplessly in love with her by the final course. He would rush her upstairs on a current of love and worship her with his body, as he had promised to do in their wedding vows.

She could hardly wait.

Joan knocked and gained admittance just in time to help with the final arrangement of her hair.

"He prefers it down, I am convinced, so merely wind this ribbon throughout and let it cascade among the curls," Isabel instructed. She was blessed with softly curling hair, of which she was truly grateful. Richard had seemed, from his earliest days, fascinated by her hair.

"Since neither your mother nor Ida are here to help you . . . prepare . . . for your bridal night, I feel I should . . . say something," Joan said, fussing nervously with Isabel's hair until it was more tangle than cascade.

"Yea, I would hear anything you would impart to me," Isabel answered eagerly. What had she to fear on the bridal bed, since Richard would be her partner?

"Oh," said Joan, nonplussed at Isabel's open eagerness. It hardly matched her own memory of her bridal night so long ago. "Well"—she cleared her throat—"he will . . . that is . . . men are different from us . . . fashioned by God to be . . ."

"Yea, I know that men are different," Isabel helped, turning to face Joan and take her hair out of the elder woman's hands, where it was becoming more tangled with each struggling word Joan spoke.

"Ah, good, you understand," Joan said in relief.

"Wait! How is that difference manifest on the marriage bed?"

"Well," Joan said, turning an unbecoming shade of red, "they are . . . bigger."

"Bigger than what?" Isabel asked.

Joan coughed and pulled at her wimple. "Richard could explain it better, I think. He will guide you. Trust him, and all will be well." She turned and was gone, speaking the last words to the still air of the stair tower.

It was advice Isabel could happily follow; trust Richard she always had. He was a man who inspired confidence and trust, even as a squire. In that pack of boys reaching toward manhood, Richard had stood apart as a natural leader. Henley had seen it and taken special care to spend more time with Richard, to train and teach him the ways of knight and lord. All had seen that Richard was exemplary, none more than she.

Smoothing her gown over her hips, she took a deep breath and walked out of her chamber. She had nothing to fear; she had known Richard for most of her life. She felt she had wanted him for the whole of her life. And now she had him. He would know what to do, and she would trust him.

With the memory of their single kiss blazing her in eyes, Isabel fled gaily down the stair tower to meet her beloved husband for dinner.

She entered the hall with the confidence of

Queen Eleanor herself, her eyes glowing and her step both measured and seductive. Her gown glimmered in the patchy light of the great hall, the candles setting the golden hue aglow with the radiance of the sun, and the azure of her bliaut the deep blue of a summer sky; she looked lit from within, as on fire as the sun that burned in the heavens. And Richard, knowing the reason why, could not help but be amused by her.

"I see the good Father delivered my message," he said when she reached her chair.

Isabel looked over at Richard as she sat, carefully arranging her skirts to fall most prettily. Was he making a joke? Richard never joked. She knew him well and knew this of him: He was stalwart, loyal, honorable, handsome, and duty-bound. He did not engage in frivolity. Did he?

"What message was that?" she asked, testing the waters of ill-tested humor.

She held his eyes, expecting him to look away from her in embarrassment, which he would do if he understood what she was asking him to say.

But no matter the provocation, Richard never looked embarrassed; a year at the abbey had not changed that about him.

"That I will see to my duty upon the marriage bed. With you. Tonight," he said calmly.

Calmly he said it, when her heart beat faster just to hear him say the words. He showed all the emotion of a clerk looking over the account books—which, in any regard, was all he seemed to want to do.

Isabel picked up her knife and speared a chicken pasty, cutting into it viciously and eating it voraciously. She would not look at him, sitting so elegantly beside her, his black hair gleaming in the light and his eyes dark and unfathomable. Yea, she noted the length of his fingers as he broke his bread, and she could not ignore the fine black hairs that climbed the back of his hands to his wrists, nor the web of veins that crisscrossed his hands and the perfect shape of his well-trimmed nails. Those hands would touch her soon. They would caress her as they had on that long-ago kiss, when he had gripped her to him as if she were the sum of his world and all that he cared to possess.

He had been on fire then. Now he was cold, calmly telling her that he would do his duty by her on the marriage bed. He showed more passion when reviewing the accounts with Jerome.

He was nothing like a real lord, who spent his time hunting, hawking, and fighting. Nothing. Richard may have worn her father's clothes, but he was still a monk at heart.

Sitting at her side, he could feel that her mood had changed. Gone was the queen at her adoring court; in her place sat an angry girl.

It was so typical of Isabel and of his converse with her. Never could he fathom the maze of her thoughts, except to know that all her thoughts led to him. Her fascination with him was as constant as the earth. Should she not then be happy that she found herself his wife and that he would take final possession of her tonight on the marriage bed?

The thought made his blood thicken and pulse heavily, and he shifted his weight in his chair, praying for control. Always it was the same—he prayed for control over his rebellious body, fighting the images and urges that had long plagued him. Always he was successful. Yet he fought the same battle again and again, never gaining firm ground, never able to leave the battlefield of physical lust.

He looked at Isabel sitting at his side. She was not the enemy in his battles against his own urges; she merely made it more difficult for him to win. Perhaps because she was so very determined that he lose. The thought made him smile. He watched her eating furiously, the food in her mouth barely swallowed before more was shoved in to takes its place. She chewed as if her food were an enemy to be devoured.

He found he could understand it. And he smiled more fully; Isabel had always amused him, though she confounded him just as often with her impulsive ways.

"I did not see you in the yard today," she blurted out between mouthfuls. "I suppose all that reading tired you."

He looked at her over his wine, sipping slowly, enjoying the disparity in their eating styles and wanting her to be aware of the difference. She thought him tired? Where would this lead? He would not have long to wonder since Isabel was not adept at hiding her thoughts; although he could not help but wonder if she had ever tried.

"Reading never tires me," he answered easily, studying her. "I am accustomed to it."

Isabel grumbled under her breath and shoved a piece of bread into her mouth, answering over her food, "There is no doubt as to that."

"Would you like instruction in reading?" he answered pleasantly, sure that the enjoyment he was getting in prodding her was a sin. Still, he didn't have the heart to repent. "It would help you in your management of Dornei in the event of my absence."

Lords of vast estates often traveled, leaving wives behind to manage all. Lords of vast estates, even small holdings, fought and were gone in their warlike pursuits, satisfying overlord and king. She could hardly picture Richard doing that, unless he carried a scroll rather than a sword.

"I can read, thank you," she answered sharply. "I pursue other pleasures for my entertainment. Do you not do *anything* else?"

Richard looked into the dark liquid of his wine and cursed the image that rose in his mind. Yea, he did more than read; he battled the succubus who visited him nightly, but he was not going to admit that to Isabel. She would probably think it a fine joke.

"Yea, I do more than read. I pray," he answered, prodding her, swallowing his smile.

"I had noted that," she said.

"That is good," he answered, knowing it would prick her. "I would be a worthy example of Christian service to my wife."

For answer, she drank half her wine in a series of loud gulps and picked at a second chicken pasty. Her knife became a weapon and her food the enemy. Isabel was blatantly irritated.

He could not fathom the cause. Yes, he teased her now, but he had agreed to bed her, had he not? He was the one being forced to bend his will; her will was being satisfied on every level. He should be the one in turmoil, not she. He was married, as God willed, and he was obedient, succeeding at this latest task to test his commitment to the Holy Father.

And he would not think of the passion of Isabel's kiss or the feel of her beneath his hands, though the memory scourged him.

His agreement to consummate the marriage was spiritual service, not lustful action. He would take no pleasure in it. He must not.

While he battled his determination to do his marital duty against his rising passion for his wife, he listened distantly to Isabel talking about hawking and sparring and the waning of his knightly skills. He had not remembered her as being shrewish; then again, he had avoided her company at every opportunity.

"Fret not," he said, cutting her off. "I know well what is expected of the Lord of Dornei. In fact, I must journey to Warefeld and the other estates which we jointly hold so that all may swear to me. Once matters at Dornei are in hand, I will leave for Warefeld."

Isabel was certain that she was one of the "matters" to which he referred.

Had he always been so cold-blooded? Could a man who spoke of their joining in such terms inspire confidence that he would do well at his "task"? He was clearly, nay, proudly, only interested in reading; she was not at all certain he could perform in the marriage bed. The memory of their kiss was less vivid the more time she spent in his company. This "monk" was hardly capable of inspiring ardor—until she looked at him from under the fringe of her lashes and noted him boldly studying her.

He was beautiful. His skin was without blemish, his eyes the color of sapphires, his hair dark as a lake in midwinter; and he was looking at her as if he actually wanted to make her his wife. His body to hers. His mouth to hers. His hands . . . touching her, without restraint, without censure, without . . . sin.

The thought struck her hard, and she knew the thought was his, coming to her from his eyes. Coming to her from his heart? She wanted to believe it so.

Her heart fluttered wildly, a bird trapped in a cage, her pulse jumping to fly free of her body. She returned his stare. Caught. So willingly caught.

Mayhap more would happen tonight than communal prayers.

Gilles pouring more wine into their cups broke the moment, but she had a new memory to add to the memory of their kiss. And, God willing, memory upon memory would be added tonight.

Dinner was concluded. A light rain was falling, the sky darkening outside the wind holes so that extra candles were lit. The dark was coming early, and she could only praise God for His impeccable timing and bounteous grace. The inhabitants within the curtain wall broke into groups of quiet activity. Elsbeth drew Aelis into helping her repair a tapestry that Isabel's mother had fashioned in her day as Lady of Dornei. Aelis came reluctantly, and only because Edmund had quit the hall before the final course, leaving the duty to Gilles. Isabel knew she should help with the tapestry, but she did not want to give up her place near Richard. No matter how monkish he had become, she could not imagine him sitting to mend cloth, needle in hand. What to do to keep him close and occupied before he found something else to read or another prayer to chant?

"My lord, would you care to play a game of chess?"

By his look, he was preparing to refuse her. But today was not going to be a day of refusals.

"Have you lost your skill at chess as well?" she prodded.

"As well?" he answered, turning to face her.

"As well as losing your skill at hawking and swordplay and—"

"I have not lost my skill, merely my desire."

"A result of your abbey confinement," she rejoined. "They are greatly skilled at subjugating a man's natural desires."

146

"You may praise God and Abbot Godric for that, Isabel, else I would give in to my desires now. You would not be happy at the result."

He looked very stern, very severe. She did not care; it was his look. She knew it well.

"I think I would," she said with a fetching smile. "I have always been happiest when you followed your natural desires."

His eyes glowed dark, the blue lost, becoming black as night sky. He was remembering their kiss. Nothing could have given her more pleasure.

"I think you would not, little Isabel," he growled, "for this desire is more violent than any you have yet seen from me."

"I am ready for any desire you choose to bestow upon me. More than ready. Eager," she breathed, staring into his eyes, challenging him. Unafraid. He was Richard, after all.

He shivered then, a tremble that traveled from his head to his feet and swallowed whatever retort he had been ready to make.

"Set up the board," he said instead.

Smiling, victorious, she did.

"Who shall have first move?" she asked.

"You, naturally," he said with a small grin. "You always make the first move."

"Only when I am compelled by my—"

"Opponent?" he cut in.

"Partner," she said instead. "My partner's inability to do so."

She moved a pawn forward.

"You mistake lack of desire for inability," he said, moving his own pawn.

She stared into his eyes and said, "You will never convince me of a lack of desire, not when it comes to . . . play," she finished with a wicked grin.

Richard shook his head and laughed lightly. "You never would be convinced of something you did not want to know."

"Is that unusual?" she returned. "Besides, I think I know more of this game than you would credit."

Richard's look turned dark, and he studied the board, refusing her eyes. "I pray that is not so, Isabel."

"Play with me and you shall judge," she said, moving her knight. She played aggressively, as they had both known.

Sitting under the weight of the tapestry, Aelis giggled and Elsbeth blushed. Joan, returning from the garderobe, asked, "What is funny? Have I missed something?"

Richard moved his queen, Isabel her bishop.

Elsbeth tucked her head and kept her eyes lowered. Aelis only giggled the louder. But neither girl was compelled to answer; Richard answered Joan's question.

"Isabel admonishes me to play upon her body, bringing us both to desire and its result."

Isabel felt the heat rush into her face. Gilbert and Robert, sitting behind them, coughed and left the room. Gilles ran out, laughing. Elsbeth buried her face within the tapestry. Joan could only stare, her mouth agape.

"Richard!" Isabel protested, her voice a squeak.

"I am glad that you are still capable of healthy shame," he said, moving his queen again.

"You have the ability to make me flush with shame most regularly," she snapped, her eyes bright and hot. She moved her knight absently, her emotions charged and her tongue ready for his next assault.

Richard moved once more and she was in checkmate, the game over.

"For a woman most eager to play, you do not play very well," he said, rising to leave her.

"I but need practice," she shouted to his retreating back.

Richard turned slowly, his eyes smoky and dark, and smiled grimly.

"And you shall have it. After Compline."

149

Chapter Fourteen

He walked away from her swiftly, desperate to leave behind the blatant temptation of her. She did not suspect, God willing, the effect she had on his resolve. She was so bold, yet he could admit that she would be as tempting were she a shy damsel, hardly able to meet his eyes. Yet, her manner added to her allure. Could anything subdue her? He had not seen it yet if there were. She was bold, fearless, impulsive to the edge of recklessness, and an innocent, for all her pretense at courtly sophistication. He knew her a virgin still. Her very blushes confirmed it. And, he could admit quietly in his own heart, he did not believe that Isabel would have freely given her body to any but him.

He saw again the image of Adam lifting her skirts and her mute and desperate struggle.

He should have killed him.

Would he have been able?

According to Isabel and her shrewish harangue, he would not, his knightly skills having been lost in his Benedictine year. Was she right? As a monk, he had no need to fight, except against the unseen forces and principalities of the spirit world, but now he had reentered the world of men and would need to fight flesh and bone as well as the unseen demoniac foe.

Life had been simpler in the abbey.

Richard traversed the inner bailey, ignoring the light rain, which was warm and gentle and most welcome to his troubled thoughts. Gilbert approached him, carrying two swords. Richard smiled, remembering that Gilbert had been seated nearby during the meal and would have heard Isabel's harangue concerning his knightly prowess. Taking the proffered sword, he went with Gilbert to the practice yard. One thought followed him: Was he doing this for himself or for Isabel?

Did it matter, in any regard?

"How long has it been?" Gilbert asked, his sword arm at rest.

Suddenly he swung, his sword alive and glistening with rain against the silver sky. Without thought, Richard blocked the blow that would have bloodied him.

"Not that long," he answered, his smile wide.

He had forgotten the pure, animal joy of battle.

They parried and blocked, each man testing the other, refraining from the harshest of blows, learning the skill of his opponent. Richard remembered everything; all the skills so long left behind rushed to the fore, his movements swift and effortless, his reactions instinctive, even after so long a slumber. He was covered in sweat when Gilbert tipped up his sword, signaling a truce.

"Eat more meat and you will not tire as easily," Gilbert said as he studied Richard.

It was another reminder that he was no longer a monk. If he was going to sustain himself in his life as Lord of Dornei, a fighting man, he would need heartier fare than a monk's portion.

Richard nodded his acceptance of Gilbert's counsel; it was only the truth he spoke, and wise words would always be welcome to Richard's ear.

"Your casting out of Adam was timely," Gilbert said, checking his mufflers, not making eye contact. "Had she been mine, I would have killed him where he stood."

Had Richard not thought the same, and had he not struggled against the urge to kill the man who laid hands on his wife? Was this yet another Benedictine legacy which he would leave behind him? Mayhap he should have killed him.

"Louis and Nicholas are gone as well, I note," Gilbert said.

"Louis was not of my doing, though his time may come," Richard said, wiping his brow with the back of his sleeve. The rain had stopped, leaving only mist that swirled into the air like vines climbing bark.

"Any man's time may come," Gilbert said carefully.

"Aye, for I will not stand idle should any man attempt Isabel," Richard said in warning.

He did not know Gilbert, and a man would be a fool who did not desire Isabel.

"That she made it out of Dornei without a husband could not have been easily done," Richard said, studying Gilbert's face. He was not so old a man that his blood could not still burn.

"It was a close thing," Gilbert admitted, "but few expected her to act so quickly. She can act, that one, when action is called for. She does not suffer from indecision."

"Nay, not that," Richard smiled in agreement. "You urged her to go?"

Gilbert nodded and studied the sky. The clouds were rushing east in an unbroken mass. It would be clear by morning. "Aye, but I never expected her to run to the abbey."

"And marry a monk?" Richard asked, dark eyebrows raised in wry humor.

"Do monks carry swords?" Gilbert returned.

Richard smiled and hefted his sword in answer, their battle resumed.

Aelis stood to the side, leaning against the stable wall, and watched them battle. It would be better said that she watched Richard. He was a very handsome man, even for an almost monk. He was tall, muscular, and strangely graceful, his movements supple and fluid, unlike some knights who hacked with little strategy and much vigor. Aelis crossed her arms under her ample breasts and sighed her pleasure in watching such a man at his battle play.

"Why stand you in the rain?" Elsbeth asked, coming quietly to her side.

"It has stopped raining, and why do you ask why I stand here? Can you not see Richard honing his battle skills? Is he not a man to stop and watch?"

"He has been forced to give up his heart's desire, the path of holy service. I would not enjoy watching him wield a sword."

"You are ridiculous, Elsbeth," she scoffed. "Any man can pray all day, but a true and valiant warrior—"

"The world is peopled with warriors," Elsbeth argued, "and could do with more prayer."

"By such a man as that?" Aelis pointed. "Should such a man, with those eyes and that form, be hidden beneath the cowl?"

"God sees the heart," Elsbeth maintained, her posture rigid and her tone inflexible. "What matters a man's external parts?"

"I am not God. They matter to me," Aelis laughed.

"He is wed to Isabel," Elsbeth said censoriously.

"Almost wed," pronounced Aelis with a gleam in her blue eyes. " 'Tis no true marriage without the bedding. Even the church finds it so, so do not bother to argue with me, Elsbeth."

"What matters this to you, Aelis?"

"It matters little to me," she answered, shrugging. "But 'tis interesting, is it not?"

* * *

From the opposite side of the bailey, Edmund watched Richard at his swordplay. And watched Aelis watch Richard at his swordplay. He also noted how well and truly Aelis ignored him.

Shifting his eyes from Aelis, Edmund could not help but be impressed with Richard's skill with a sword. The man knew his moves; all he lacked was the strength to fight on. Time and red meat would cure that ill. It was a relief to see that Dornei was not in the hands of an incapable monk more concerned with chants than battle cries.

But did Aelis have to look so impressed?

Not looking into his motives, Edmund walked more directly into Aelis's line of sight. She did not spare him a glance. Stupid and inconsistent girl. When had Aelis not flown to him like an arrow?

He would not go to her. He had never pursued Aelis and he would not start now. He did not even like her, or so he had oft told himself and all who would stop to listen. Nay, he would not go to her, but he could fetch shields and maces, offering a diversion from the sword for the two battlers.

They thanked him offhandedly, Richard covered in a fine film of sweat, Gilbert breathing hard. Richard was smiling. Edmund had not yet seen the Lord of Dornei smile; it was a warm thing, more so since he did it so seldom, and transformed his face from forbidding to winsome. Was that why Aelis hovered?

"Do you need a rest?" Gilbert asked, huffing lightly.

Richard smiled and tossed Edmund his sword.

"I have worked myself harder in a night's prayer vigil, but if you—"

"I need no respite," Gilbert said quickly, "yet if the boy would care to try his hand—"

"I would!" Edmund offered, all smiles. He was honored. And now Aelis would, of necessity, be forced to watch him.

They worked with the maces, each man finding his rhythm. Richard was even better with the mace than with the sword, and Edmund was quickly outmatched. With Aelis as witness. In his eagerness to salve his pride and appear fierce, he attacked precipitously and lost his footing. He fell hard to his knee and hung his head in public shame.

"Do not let her scorn touch you, boy," Richard whispered, keeping his martial distance. "She but plays with your heart."

Was his rejection, then, obvious to all? It was shame piled upon shame, with all of Dornei to witness.

"She is striving not to see you," Richard said more urgently. "Can you not see it is a game she plays to win your regard?"

"How do you know?" Edmund asked, in awe of Richard's gentle counsel.

"I know the games of women, boy," Richard answered, glancing toward the stair tower, where Isabel stood, watching him.

Isabel watched Richard battle, as she had done time after time during her years at Malton, and was just as enraptured. He was handsome, graceful, strong—everything a baron should be. And now he was hers. She had been so foolish to fret that his prowess had waned. The Richard she knew excelled at every endeavor; she supposed he had been a successful Benedictine. But that did not signify. He was a monk no longer. Tonight would prove that.

Watching him move, his hair dark and gleaming, the muscles of his back and arms bunching, she scanned the cloudy sky for a hint as to when night would finally fall on this endless day. Aelis seemed to find Richard equally fascinating, which made an odd sort of sense, but was she not enamored of Edmund?

Yet when Edmund and Richard stopped their mock battle and Edmund carried the maces to the armory, Aelis's eyes followed Richard. Isabel found her unexpected behavior mildly alarming. Fascination for a comely squire was one thing—had she not felt the same herself for Richard?—but to contemplate with such blatant interest a married man was most unbecoming. Entirely inappropriate. Extremely disturbing. And so like Aelis.

Isabel looked heavenward again; it was hours yet to Compline. Hours before she would make certain that Richard was most definitely married.

In the interim, Aelis needed guidance on proper deportment. As Lady of Dornei, it was her duty to train the girl. She had been sadly negligent in that duty; Lady Bertrada had trained her better.

Isabel allowed herself one more look at Richard, who was standing and talking in easy rapport with

Gilbert, before she turned to walk toward Aelis. Aelis needed a firm hand, and she was just the woman to do it. It was her duty, after all.

Isabel looked once more at Richard, at the mist lying on his hair like jewels, at the breadth of his shoulders and the length of his legs, without giving herself permission. And she never realized she had breached her own vow of restraint.

Aelis ignored Isabel's approach, her eyes and all her attention on Richard. It was most irritating.

"He is a brilliant fighter, is he not?" Aelis said.

Isabel had always thought so, but she did not enjoy hearing the words on another woman's tongue.

"I believe he is quite capable," Isabel answered.

Aelis merely sighed.

"And such beauty on a man; he is most fine, your Richard," Aelis said, not taking her gaze from him.

"Yea, he is mine," Isabel said sharply and then tamped down her anger. Aelis was a girl in need of instruction; she was no threat to Isabel. Richard was hers.

"Oh, I know he is," Aelis said easily, "but do you note how hot Edmund's looks are? Has he ever looked more interested than he does now?"

It was true. Edmund was fairly piercing Aelis with his gaze; he looked miserable. Aelis, on the other hand, looked delighted. Isabel understood then that this was a game that Aelis played upon Edmund's heart, and she felt herself relax. And yet, was it not overbold of Aelis to flirt so with the Lord of Dornei?

"Yea, he looks quite engaged," Isabel agreed. "But it is more the behavior of a lady to make her interest less blatant. Such bold behavior is—"

"Is what has caused you such renown," Aelis finished.

"I beg your pardon?"

"Your interest in Richard while you were betrothed to another is known by all," Aelis said without the slightest breath of condemnation. Why, then, did Isabel feel such shame? "I was only a child when you were both at Malton," Aelis continued, "yet it is a tale well told and often. Isabel loved Richard and was betrothed to his brother. Yea, everyone knows what passed during your years at Malton."

Shame washed over Isabel. Had she truly been so bold that all knew and all tittered over her love for Richard? Had Hubert, his brother, heard the tales as well? And how would Richard have responded to such a charge? What could he have said that would not have damned them both? Worse, had Richard felt the shame of her regard for all these years? The shame she was just now feeling?

It was a very uncomfortable thought and she longed to rip it from her.

Unfortunately, she did not know how.

Chapter Fifteen

Richard appeared at the light meal that marked the end of the day with damp hair and a jaw scraped raw by the blade. Isabel could not help but wonder if he bathed for Compline or for her. She did not truly want an answer, which was strange behavior for her. She could only blame her conversation with Aelis as the cause.

She had spent the better part of the afternoon, the part not spent in watching Richard at his swordplay, trailing after Father Langfrid, too nervous to speak and too guilty to leave. Guilt, which had touched her but lightly before she found the means to cast it off, would not leave her now. Had she truly pursued Richard as Aelis hunted Edmund? She knew Edmund liked it not; he spoke his annoyance at every opportunity. And he spoke of the gross impropriety of Aelis's behavior. He was not flattered, and he was not disposed to return her regard.

Had it been so for Richard?

She had believed, with no small thrill, that Richard had flown to abbey life because of intemperate love for her, love he could not realize because she was promised to his brother—a raw love that had revealed itself in that one searing kiss. A kiss of urgent need and mating and passion. An erotic kiss. A forbidden kiss.

She could not have him, yet she had wanted him to burn for her; to take his wanting of her, his need, into the whole of his life, even if that life lay within the abbey. To burn for her in his prayers and in his sleeping and in his very dreams.

As she had and did for him.

Now she had him, past all hope in her most fervent prayers, but had she lost his regard in her pursuit of him? Did she have a husband who did not like her?

It did not mean anything; their lands, monies, peoples were joined. *They* were joined by church and king. Liking, even love, certainly love, did not matter in this bond of families.

Yet it did matter. It mattered because it was Richard. He had always held her heart, though she had never believed he would hold her hand in marriage. What did he think of her? Did he shun the marriage bed because he shunned *her*? It might be that he did not want to be a monk, he only did not want her. Edmund did not want Aelis.

To Father Langfrid she had not been able to confess her fears, but she could talk to Richard, searching his mind on the matter. She had to know what Richard thought of her, and, for the first time, she wanted to know what he had thought during the long years of her pursuit. If he felt anything of what Edmund felt for Aelis, she would attempt an apology. She had not meant to cause discomfort, and certainly not shame. What would she say? *I ask your pardon, Richard, that I wanted you too much?* She snorted in self-derision and earned a puzzled look from Richard.

"Did your wine go down amiss?" he asked.

"Nay, I . . . nay," she said, looking down into her lap, watching her fingers twist upon themselves.

A simple "nay" from Isabel? Richard was intrigued; when had Isabel been known for the brevity of her speech? Or the twitching of her fingers? By all appearances, she seemed nervous, yet he could not credit it. Isabel was never nervous, never hesitant.

But how often had it been her bridal night?

Nay, she had been eager enough last eventide, thinking her deflowering hard upon her. Isabel was ever bold, eager, and impulsive. He found it something of a miracle that she had lived to pass out of childhood and into womanhood, given her nature.

Still, a virgin would have fears . . .

She was a virgin, no matter her impulsive nature, and he was right to ignore Nicholas's hints to the contrary. He was certain of her purity. Mayhap she was only behaving normally, fearful of the coupling to come, ignorance fueling her fear, dampening her natural desires.

Yea, natural. She had desired him from the start, and he could not but believe she desired him even now, though her skin had gone milk pale and her lips were red from self-inflicted bites. It was odd, the way God turned things around; Isabel was reluctant when he was suddenly so resolute. He would fulfill the vows he had taken; he would bed her, ripping her maidenhead and making her his wife. He was as determined to do his duty as Lord of Dornei as he was determined not to enjoy it.

There could be no sin if he did not enjoy it.

He was safe if he did not burn with lust.

Richard studied her, her eyes bright, as green as the emerald brooch she wore, her manner distracted, her movements abrupt. He had known her long, for most of his life; he would not have her fear what was to come. He had been forced to it, but he did not want her to suffer the terror of the unknown.

"I will not hurt you," he said, searching her eyes.

She jerked her wine goblet, spilling a stream of red onto the cloth that covered the table. She grabbed for the bread and broke off a mouthful, the air filled with the smell of yeast and wheat. He took hold of her hand before she could hide her emotion in food, swallowing with the bread all she wanted to say.

"It will hurt," he said, stroking her palm with his thumb when her eyes went wide. It was like looking into cathedral glass; her eyes were so clear, her thoughts so revealed. "Though I will do all I can to keep from hurting you any more than is necessary to see my duty done."

"Your duty," she repeated, looking into his eyes, the hurt blatant even in the dim and golden candlelight.

"Aye, my duty. We have a duty upon the marriage bed, Isabel; it was you who reminded me of it. Would you have me say less, do less, now?"

"Nay, naturally not," she said, turning back to her small feast of bread and cheese, chewing the bread with as much gusto as if it were venison.

"It is natural, what we undertake," he said, still holding her hand, his thumb making circles on the inside of her wrist. "God created, God ordained; the joining of two bodies into one, a sacred union, a bond both spiritual and physical."

Her eyes had gone wide, pools of mossy green fringed by lashes so dark and long they reminded him of butterfly wings beating against the summer air. His body hummed his awareness of her, of every nuance of color in her hair and skin and eyes, of the sweet and spicy scent of her, of the fine texture of her skin, and the way her hair fell down in glistening waves. She was as light as a lark and as active, her voice sweet and her movements quick and agile.

She had always been so. Even in her awkward age, she had not been awkward.

It would have been easier for him had she been less beautiful.

But she had never made it easy for him.

God and all the saints, and all of Malton, too, knew how difficult she had made life for him. Yet, strangely, he did not think that Isabel knew. She did not look about her, as most in the world did, seeking approval or agreement; nay, Isabel fixed her eye and flew straight to her target, all else lost, inconsequential. And all his life, for as long as he could remember, she had fixed her eye upon him. Yet now, now she could not meet his gaze.

He would never understand her.

Now, when he had acknowledged that he had the right—nay, the duty—to lay his hands upon her, he could not stop touching her skin. His hand traveled up her arm to the bend of elbow, and there he caressed her. Through the fabric he could feel her heat. Her very slenderness, her fragility, enticed him. She was so small, so delicate, so feminine.

She was, in all ways, all that he was not.

In an hour, her body would accept him. In an hour, she would take him inside her, sharing her heat. In an hour, he would feel her surround him, blessedly trapped within her. In an hour, he would lie upon her, encompassing her as he took her. In an hour—

"It is time for Compline," Father Langfrid said into the haze around him.

Richard stood woodenly and helped Isabel to stand. "Praise God for each and every miracle," he said hoarsely, his hands tightened into fists, refusing to touch her. "I was close to taking you before Compline."

165

He left the hall, looking to all a man in firm control. Isabel followed behind, her face a mask of shock. She had almost ranked above his prayers? God was a god of miracles in truth.

Compline passed in a choral blur, and Isabel escaped as soon as it was over, leaving Richard in holy conversation with Father Langfrid.

Her hour was upon her.

She had never thought to be afraid, not with Richard, and she was not; at least, not that much.

She was in the lavatory, rubbing a cloth over her face and . . . private parts. She suddenly and urgently wished for another bath, yet there was no time. Compline was over. Richard would come. The sun had not yet set, but Richard would come. He had his duty to perform, did he not? And would it be only that? Would it be only duty between them?

He had offered nothing else.

She had believed—nay, she had dreamed—that if only he were her husband and lord then all would be well. She would have everything she wanted. But she had wanted a willing husband. Richard was not willing. Richard was determined. There was little room for passion in determination.

Perhaps there had never been any passion in Richard at all; perhaps she had only inspired embarrassment. But their kiss had not been tinged with embarrassment; she could console herself with that. It was small consolation; the kiss was long ago and the marriage bed faced her. It seemed a big bed, cold and hard when shared with a man chained to it by biblical duty. What sort of kisses would such a bed inspire?

Nervous, with no outlet except the one which loomed before her forbiddingly, Isabel scrubbed at her feet, washing away the ash and dirt of the bailey. Joan came upon her then, and Isabel tucked her feet under her gown, unaccountably embarrassed. Joan, bless her, said nothing about her grooming habits.

"Your night is upon you," Joan said, her chin high and her courage bolstered by five cups of wine. "Trust yourself in Richard's hands; he will know what to do. There is naught to fear."

"The pain?" Isabel managed to ask.

Joan kept her chin high, looking at a spot somewhere above and to Isabel's right. "There is some . . . discomfort at first, but, because it is Richard, you will heed it little. This is a night all women must face. Face it well," she said.

It did not sound pleasant if she must be admonished to "face it well."

Joan made her departure as abruptly as her entrance, turning at the portal to say, "He will not be looking at your feet."

She supposed that was a blessing, as they were still somewhat dirty.

She would have liked for Joan to stay, a feminine companion to ease her into the marriage bed, to be a link between wife and husband before the link was fully forged in physical union. She would have liked not to have to wait in the lord's chamber for

Richard all alone. But it was not to be.

Richard had come.

Isabel looked ready to fly about the room in agitated nervousness. He supposed it was natural for a bride facing her loss of maidenhead, but it seemed unnatural for her. Where was his bold girl? He did not know how to deal with this Isabel. Isabel was fire and spark, not damp dismay. He did not know what to do, so he did what he had come to do; he pulled off his tunic.

Why did she not disrobe? She knew what they were there to do.

Thinking about her at supper, sitting next to her, breathing her scent, he had been hard and ready. He had throbbed with need all through Compline, disgusting himself. He had changed not at all. He was unfit for the brotherhood of holy men and had been cast out of it; God had seen his heart and the succubus who plagued him. A year of prayer and fasting, and he had not changed. He was stiff now, just thinking of performing his husbandly duty, hardly caring that Isabel looked like a mouse who had spotted a circling hawk.

Yet what did she have to be nervous about?

Was she not, as she always did, getting what she wanted? His life had been turned inside out, while she had a husband she had wanted since her hair grew past her shoulders. He was being forced by duty to take her, fouling his purity, so hard-won after such diligent effort. Yea, he had failed; his thoughts had betrayed him, though his body had remained pure.

He lied. Did not Jesus say that if a man lusted in his heart, he had committed lust in fact?

He had lusted. He could not outrun his desires, and so he had done what was left to him; he had killed them. Desire was a memory he killed nightly, hacking and hewing with prayer what he could not touch with sword. Aye, he was a mighty warrior who battled daily, yet his enemy sprang up again and again, refusing to die.

Perhaps he did not have the will to truly kill his passion.

And facing Isabel now, her body his to take, what path was left him? Only one: to take no pleasure in their coupling. Mating without desire was the way; it would be duty fulfilled and desire thwarted. It was the only way he could succeed at this task. It was the only way he would not drown in lust. And lust built with every moment he was with her, breathing her scent, watching her hair tumble down around her, fighting the urge to fondle her softness, delighting in her delicacy. He had to take her soon. Now, before the fire within him burned him to ash and he was left with only his failure.

She looked at him now with eyes both sad and afraid; he did not want her to fear him, yet the strength of his passion frightened himself. He had been hard for hours, and each moment of delay only stoked his ardor. He needed to find release. The release of duty. Never the release of desire.

169

She came near him, her hands clasped in front of her, looking penitent and shy. She could not fear him, not now, now when had to take her and mark her as his. The sky was amassed with gathered clouds, gray and pink in the setting sun, flying to the east to escape the constraints of land and earth. The wind blew through the wind hole, setting her hair loose, raising it from her shoulders to blow about her with all the gentle movement of a mother's hand. He should not touch her. He would lose all control if he touched her.

He had been commanded by God to touch her.

He stood before her, naked to the waist. She still wore her undergown and bliaut, the azure dark and mysterious in the dim light, the silk threads throwing sparks of light.

He wanted her.

It was his shame.

"Forgive me," she said, and he was startled to hear her speak. He was lost in his battle, and her voice was sweetly urgent, calling to him through the blaze of desire. "I never meant to cause you shame." Her voice broke.

Yet he was the one broken.

She came near him, even though she had just confessed that she knew the source of his shame. He would not share it; it was not a battle for any eyes except God's.

She came near him, her scent wafting to him, her hair reaching out to him, blown by the wind at her back. He saw himself then, lifting her skirts, plunging into her where she stood, her legs useless, her arms clinging to his back, her black hair covering them both.

He saw it.

He felt it.

If she did not step away from him . . .

"Stand away from me!" he growled in command.

He had said much the same to her before and for the same cause. He burned for her.

He had said much the same to her before and she knew the cause. He hated her.

How could her dreams have ended here? How could her prayers have played her so false? She had only wanted to love him and to have her love returned. Instead, she had taught him to hate her by her shaming of him at Malton. He could not even accept her apology.

She tried again, trying to find the words to express her sorrow; she had not understood the delicacy of a young man's honor. She had seen nothing of honor. She had seen only him.

She tried to find the words, but the words froze within her at the look in his eyes. Almost, almost she was frightened.

He was desperate. He was desperate that he not enjoy their mating. He had to bed her, to get it behind him, duty performed, service rendered. It was what he did best. He did not run from his duty.

And Isabel? She knew nothing of duty. She knew only desire and fulfillment. She had him; it was all she had ever wanted. He had to lose his dream so that she would have hers. Anger flared within him, but it did not diminish the heat of his desire.

"Make yourself ready," he said, his voice a rumble, stripped of all emotion save urgency.

Was this the night she had dreamed of? Was this what it was to be Richard's wife? This cold, stern man making his desires known through blunt orders? This was not as she had envisioned Richard inviting her to the marriage bed. This was the man she had shared her heart with, the man who understood her better than any other, the man whom she had loved hopelessly for years. Could he not understand the sweetness of this moment, the sweetness of having her as wife? Looking at him now, his face hard and set, she knew. He could not.

She slowly slipped out of her bliaut and undergown, the pale linen of her shift following. His eyes followed the shift to the floor. And then he surveyed his bride, his desire masked by grim purpose.

Her luminous eyes were like twin moons, wide and bright and shining.

Her legs were shapely and slender, her hips rounded, her belly soft. Her breasts were full and plump for so small a woman, and he could not but stare at the gentle pink of her nipples. She was all ivory and pink and black, only her eyes disturbing the harmony with their earthy green hue. She was like his succubus, his nightly tormentor. She was his wife.

Looking, seeing what God had created to test him, made the battle more difficult. He blew out the taper near the door, leaving them in the mild darkness of early evening.

Duty required, service rendered. It would be nothing more, though he could feel desire wrap itself around him, robbing him of air so that his breathing was labored and loud in the still chamber. He could not want her, not Isabel. He could not lay hands to her or he would burn as he stood. He could not. He could not.

Yet God had left him no other path.

He pushed her backward, his hands light on her shoulders, ignoring the softness of her skin and the dark hue of his hand as he laid it upon her. She fell upon the bed, supine but not relaxed.

He throbbed with need and closed his eyes against the images assaulting him. So many ways to take her, so many ways to touch her, so many places his mouth begged to travel, but all that was required was his duty. He must do no more than his duty by her, ripping her maidenhead, drawing blood, claiming her, by God's command.

"Kiss me, Richard," she said, her voice atremble. "Please, kiss me like before."

Kiss her? He did not even want to be in the same room with her. She wanted the blind passion and raging need of their first and only kiss; she wanted to fall into desire's inferno. Never again.

Her mouth was soft and pink, even in the fading light of a rain-soaked day. He could not stop looking at her mouth.

"I do not want to kiss you," he said.

He stood on the edge of the bed, looking down

at her, willing his eyes to close against the sight of her. His eyes refused to obey his will. He laid his hands upon her thighs, pulling them apart, ignoring the fact that she fought to keep her legs together, ignoring her hands upon his wrists, ignoring the violent desperation with which he touched her.

He leaned down, against his will, and kissed her throat. Her blood surged and she turned her head, exposing her throat to his mouth, submissive. Afraid.

Her fear did not stop him. Nothing could stop him from fulfilling his divine duty.

He trailed the fingers of his right hand up the inside of her thigh; she was soft and warm and trembling. He touched her dark curls and felt of her; she was dry, unready.

"I do not want to touch you," he whispered in her ear.

He slid his hand up her, skimming over hip and belly to cup her breast. It was heavy in his hand, the nipple rising instantly. He did not want to hurt her. He did not want to take her unready.

It mattered not. He was not going to stop. Such was the depth of his sin, his carnality. He was past redemption to take her as she was, frightened and reluctant. Even beyond redemption's reach, he touched her.

"I do not want to feel your breasts, their softness, their weight."

He caressed her, his hand learning the feel of her, though he fought against the knowledge. Her nipple found his fingertips and compelled him, against his will, to fondle her. He rubbed against her, fighting the picture of what he was doing to her in his mind. He was failing. There was too much passion in this, though he knew she felt none of it.

She felt only wounded. Isabel held herself still, uncertain and afraid. Each terse declaration was a blow that killed as surely as a lance. These were not words of love and desire. This was not as she imagined.

He did not want her.

He did not love her.

The dream she had of him, of them, shattered, and only she seemed to realize it. Could he not hear it breaking?

"Then do not," she cried, backing away from him and from his hands. She was glad of the darkness of both cloud and night; it hid her nakedness. Her absolute nakedness. He felt nothing for her; it was displayed in every touch and every word.

"Do not?" he asked, glad of the darkness so that she could not see the depth of his sin. His hunger for her, despite his battle against it, was burning him to ash. "I must. I must do my duty as your husband. You know the truth of that, Isabel."

He lied, to himself and to her; he touched her because he had not the will to stop. He would take her because he was an animal who could not turn from sin and desire, though the woman was Isabel. And now Isabel would see him for what he was. Even the knowledge of that could not stop him. He had to have her, to feel himself in her, to wrap himself around her; he was cast so far and wide from God's grace that damnation would have been a softer penance than the one which raged within his soul. To use Isabel in such a way and to blame her for his lust . . . even he had not known how far a man could fall into depravity.

She heard his words as a reproach because she had been the one to use duty to force him upon the marriage bed. But she had not expected this. He acted as if he hated her.

She had to ask his pardon. Perhaps all would be well if he understood her repentance and granted her pardon.

"Forgive me, Richard," she said over her fear. "I did not understand until I saw Aelis what it was I did to you."

She crept backward over the bed, holding his wrist, trying to catch his other hand and pull it from her breast. She could not have him touch her this way. Yet he seemed everywhere; she could not escape him, not on so small a spot of earth as the lord's bed.

"I shamed you, I know. Forgive me. I only wanted so much to be yours. I did not mean to pray for Hubert's death; it was only that I wanted you to be Lord of Warefeld in his place. I did not think what it would mean . . . that he would die."

He released her breast, and she thought the worst was over. For a moment she thought so. His hands gripped her thighs and pulled them apart. She felt the cold air of the chamber, pushed by the night wind, in her most private parts.

"Forgive me. Because of my prayer you were taken from abbey life, a life you chose because of me. Because of what I did. Because of what we did. Because of our kiss," she cried.

She had come to the end of the bed. He pulled her back, her legs hanging down from her bent knees. She could not stop the tears from falling and she could not stop fighting him. This night was no part of her dream. But she had prayed irresponsibly, selfishly; this was her penance. He held her there, his hands hard upon her, as she cried out her guilt.

"Hold, Isabel, that we may accomplish the task God has set for us," he said, his voice colder than the night wind. She asked for forgiveness when he was poised above her to take her in violence and lust? She knew not the quality of the man to whom she was mated. But, nay, perhaps now she did.

He slid down his braes; she could hear the cloth against his skin, but she could not see. Her eyes were swollen with tears. "Please," she sobbed.

" 'Tis a task I did not seek for myself on a path I did not choose to tread," he said, his body a black shape in the shadowed room. He loomed over her. Never had she found his size so formidable, so frightening.

"I do not want to bury myself in you," he grunted. He wanted the words to be the truth. He did not want to be the sort of man to take a woman like this. Yet he could not stop. He was lost, lost in sin, in lust, in carnal desire. And Isabel was caged with him, trapped within his sin as he longed to be trapped within her tight heat.

All he had known of himself was proven true, the truth hammered out upon Isabel's unwilling body.

Holding her hips within his grasp, he plunged into her. She knew she was called to submit, but she could not stop scrambling across the bed on her back, trying to be free of him. It was pain, only pain, within and without. It was her penance, and she could hardly stand against it.

"I do not want to want you," he whispered as his seed was released within her heat. Isabel could not hear him over her tears. Once more, he was glad of the darkness.

Chapter Sixteen

"Forgive me. Forgive me. Forgive me," she repeated through her tears, her chest heaving with her sorrow.

He slipped out of her, still standing by the edge of the bed. She had drawn her knees up to her chest and curled like a child in the middle of the bed, crying out her pain and her guilt. All he wanted in that moment was to wrap her in his arms and rock comfort into her, giving her his warmth and his strength. He had known the same desperation, the same hunger for forgiveness.

Poor Isabel; her sins were as splinters to his logs.

"Do not ask forgiveness of me," he said, his voice far above her.

So, he could not even forgive her. He would never forgive her. Mayhap if he understood, if he would only give her the chance to explain her heart, then he might find the grace to forgive her.

"I could not help wanting you," she said over her tears, the words choppy and wet, like a sea in a storm. "I never meant to shame you. It was only that . . . it was only that I wanted to be near you."

She made herself uncurl her body, made herself speak slowly, made herself look at him. He was not looking at her; his face was to the unlit taper, as if he would light it with a look. He was most likely angry enough that he could see the deed done.

"Did you not want the same? Did you feel no fondness for me?" she asked, hating the tremor in her voice. "Our kiss . . . that single kiss . . . in the stable that day . . . I know you must remember it. It marked us both, did it not? You were for the abbey soon after, and . . . I knew . . . or thought it was because of our kiss. And because you could not have me as I could not have you. Because of Hubert."

She was crying again. She could not seem to stop, and she knew that Richard was not overfond of womanish tears. She had to stop the tears. She had to convince him to forgive her.

"I prayed to be released from my betrothal, but I said nothing, neither to your father nor mine, and not a word to Hubert. I did not shame you in that, Richard. I only spoke to God, telling Him the desires of my heart, imploring Him to grant me the man of my heart. It was not wrong, was it, though all are now dead? I did not think that they would die. I never meant . . ."

She looked at his back, so broad and implacable; he would never forgive her. Her marriage was broken before it had begun.

"You did feel something for me, did you not? And could you not still find something in me to love?" she said. She sounded pitiable, she knew, yet she could not stop herself. She was fighting for Richard, and he was worth any price.

"Richard?" she asked, her voice hoarse with crying. "Forgive me," she whispered, burying her face in the bed cover. "Forgive me."

It was all there for him to see, her fears and her burdens laid out for him; her heartfelt contrition was obvious. Her hair fell about her, masking her shape in the faint light of the rising moon. The moon rose above the clouds, defeating them, shining forth over the earth as if the day had never known rain. And once, long ago, it had been so; the earth had not known rain until God, sickened at heart over the world's sins, had caused it to rain for forty days. He had washed the world clean. Would that Richard could wash this marriage clean.

But he could not.

What he could do was share Isabel's burden of guilt and blame; he could not allow her to bear the weight of so much false guilt. Let her see the man she had pledged her life to, not this youth she had admired from afar. She had wanted the image of him. Let her see him as he was.

"You have done nothing which requires forgiveness," he said to her bent form. "I bear you no enmity. Face me, Isabel, and read my face. You will see that it is so."

She lifted her head, the moonlight shining off her tear-streaked face, her eyes black with hurt and darkness. Isabel . . . her emotions ran so wild and hot.

"My decision to join the Benedictine brothers had naught to do with you," he said from his side of the room. He would not stand near her, not when he could smell his seed on her and see her breasts gleaming white through the dark snakes of her hair. He knew himself better than to stand near.

"What, then?" she asked, her voice a croak. He could see that she did not believe him; her memory and her dreaming had told her another tale, which placed her at the center. But it was a dream that wounded, and he would not stand idle while Isabel suffered hurt. The fault was not hers, but his. She must see that.

"What did you see when first you saw Malton?" he asked gently.

Isabel studied him, her tears slowing, before she shrugged listlessly and answered, "A fine hall of darkish stone dominating a strong river."

"I saw my destiny," he said. "I saw the place where I would make my name."

"All young boys would see it so," she said.

Richard looked into her eyes and said, "But I was going to *make* it so. 'Twas no idle dreaming for me; Malton was where I must and would prove myself."

"And you did."

Richard looked beyond her, out to the moon, well above the clouds now, shining white and strong, the only light in the night sky. She did not understand. She had placed him too high.

"It was difficult at first for me there. At Malton. I do not mingle easily. I cared only about my task, that of becoming a great knight. I had no time for games or the jokes one boy plays upon another." He would not tell her of the ribaldry that followed him when her devotion to him became obvious; whatever chance he had hoped for to bond with another squire had been snuffed out with her adoration. Yet he did not fault her; it was her nature, and her intent had been innocent of evil. "Henley marked my devotion to advancing my skills and drew me in, close to his side. You remember?"

"I remember he thought well of you and that he spoke of you fondly."

"Like a father."

"Yea, like a father," she agreed.

"Bertrada, his lady wife, she also . . . drew me in."

"They were both pleased with you. I do remember it," she said. She did remember it as she was so often in Bertrada's bad graces for not attending to her duties. But she had not wanted to sew; she had wanted to follow Richard.

"She was a worthy lady, did you not think? So generous and gracious. So beautiful," he said, his voice trailing off. He looked down at his hands, clenched into fists before him. "I worked hard, thinking to please her."

"And Henley."

"Aye," he said jerkily, "and Henley."

"And you did," she said, her tears dried upon her cheeks so that all that remained was the glimmer where they had been. "You did well at Malton. You won your spurs."

"I won my spurs," he said woodenly. "I did not achieve my goal. Or at least, I did not make the name for myself I had imagined when first I beheld Malton as a youth."

Isabel was at a loss. Richard was making no sense. She did not even know the words to ask. But Richard did.

"Did you not note, you who were ever at my heels, how often Bertrada came near? She understood my determination. She understood what was in my heart—words a youth can hardly think to form. With her I felt . . ." His voice trailed off. "I felt . . ." he said softly. Valued? Understood? He did not know the word for what she had made him feel, not then and not now.

Whatever the word, sin had been the result.

"I committed a cardinal sin. That is why I joined the Benedictines," he said finally, his tone clipped and cold.

A cardinal sin? Isabel ticked them off in her mind, thinking Richard was surely exaggerating. Pride. Envy. Sloth. Intemperance. Avarice. Ire. Lust.

Nay, he would not have clouded his soul with any cardinal sin . . . though perhaps he edged close to the sin of pride.

His words echoed in her mind. He had felt . . .

something . . . in Bertrada's company. A tickle of warning ran along her ribs and settled in her middle. When did Richard ever speak of "feeling"? Richard was duty and purpose; he did not prate on about "feeling." He had never confessed to "feeling" anything for her, and she was his wife. The woman he had kissed with a raging passion when she had been promised to another.

She had been promised to another. His very brother.

The tickle turned hard and heavy within her, like the weight of a hand pressing down.

How different the memory of their kiss looked when turned upon itself.

How much honor lay in a man who would display his ardor for a woman who could never be his?

All the words came together in her mind then, in just the correct ordering.

Lust.

Bertrada.

Benedictine.

Isabel flinched against the horror of it, shaking her head, willing away the truth. It could not be so. Yet Richard said it was so, in his awkward way.

He had lusted after Bertrada, his lord's wife, the untouchable woman in the center of Malton's orbit. She was mother to them, lady to the same lord Richard had sworn to uphold. It was akin to incest; had Richard not gone to Malton at the age of ten? It was certainly adultery with the one woman among them who could not, must not, be touched.

Bertrada had taught her, trained her to be a noble lady and blameless wife. And Bertrada had copulated with Richard.

"It is why you left Malton so abruptly?" she managed to ask, determined that he say it, confess it to her openly.

"Yea," he only said.

And she knew it for the truth. Richard had run to the Benedictine brotherhood to expiate his sin with a lifetime of prayer and service. It had not been because of their single kiss; she had been so naive, so foolish to place such import on a single, chaste kiss. She was a fool. Had they shared a love, a passion, that could not be fulfilled? Nay, he had respected no such boundary with Bertrada. There had been no boundary with Bertrada. He could not resist Bertrada.

It came to her then, sitting upon her marriage bed in the dark, that she had been flattered beyond measure to think that Richard had given up his spurs because of thwarted love for her. There was sin in such pride, and she was reaping her penance now.

But that was not the worst of tonight's confession. The room was dark and Richard a darker shadow within it, the moon long since beyond their sight, yet she could see all as bright as day. Richard could not hide from this truth, no matter the depth of the darkness, and neither could she.

"But hiding in the monastery, cloistered among the brothers, did not work, did it, Richard?" she asked, her voice hard and unrelenting. "You love her still."

Chapter Seventeen

He spent the night in prayer, in the chapel. It was almost as if he had never left the monastery. Except that instead of wrestling with his succubus, he had wrestled—and bedded—his wife. Isabel. Her tears clung to him still, no matter that the dawn was sliding up the sky. It was time for Matins, and for the first time in a year, he was not eager for another hour of prayer.

He truly was a married man.

And he had spent the night on a cold floor when a bed and wife were within reach.

She had charged him with loving Bertrada. Still, after all he had confessed, she did not understand the man she had wed. She attributed love as the cause of what had gone between him and Bertrada. Isabel—such an innocent, to think that love must precede fornication. Love Bertrada he did

187

not; not even at his most innocent had he believed he loved her. Desired her? Yea, it had come to that, and he had acted on his desire, as he had acted on his desire with Isabel when he had unleashed his passion on her in their solitary kiss. His was a sin most deep. He battled lust daily, knowing himself to be insufficient to the battle, losing daily. Hourly.

Isabel was angry. Her pride had been wrenched from her by his confession, to lie as bloody and torn on their marriage bed as her maidenhead; this he had done to her, with his words and with his hands. A night of prayer had not absolved him of his sin with his wife of a day. She had wanted to believe that their kiss had driven him into the holy brotherhood; such thoughts would well please a young woman in love with an unattainable man. Now she had been told he had not been running from her, and such knowledge would dig deep into pride.

And he had hurt her. Their coupling had not gone well. The performance of his duty had been a disaster. She had not been ready for him. Ready? With her tears fresh on her cheeks and her hands pulling at his, scrambling to be free of him and of the marriage bed? Nay, she had not been ready. But he had. He could not have waited longer. His need, his hunger, had been hard upon him, and his duty had compelled him to proceed, even against her unreadiness. God knew he was such a man as to take a woman unready. And now, Isabel knew as well.

Tonight would be better. Tonight he would not fail. Isabel deserved better, even from such a man as he knew himself to be.

Richard stood, his knees stiff from a night of kneeling, and turned to leave the chapel.

Tonight would be better. She was no longer a virgin. Her fears were behind her. He would not fail her tonight.

He would not fail.

With that thought, Richard walked out of the chapel with a smile on his face. Those who saw him wondered at the change a night of marriage had wrought in their new lord and smiled in return.

Isabel was not among their number.

Isabel awaited the dawn alone in her chamber, sitting upon the great bed of the Lord of Dornei with her arms clasped around her knees and her face turned to the wind hole. Thus she had spent the night. She rocked herself gently, humming beneath her breath, searching for comfort and finding none.

What comfort with Richard as husband?

Tears sprang fresh and fell from her eyes; she did naught to stop them. To what purpose, when they only fell again? Never had she imagined that marriage to Richard would bring anything but joy and yet now she knew that she would never feel joy again. Joy had flown by her, to stay out of reach until she was caught up in the clouds with Christ. Would that she could fly now, fly away from here, out over the fields and forests until Dornei was just a dark speck on the sodden horizon. God, let her fly away. Away from all her misery. The Lord seemed of a mind to answer her prayers; perhaps He would answer this impossible request for deliverance.

Yet, if her fortune ran true, she would be caught, hooded, and kept chained to her master's hand. As she was now chained to Richard throughout this life. Such joy at the thought yesterday; such sorrow today.

And all because Richard loved another.

Isabel turned from the window and all thoughts of escape and pressed down the pain that rose like the sun to sweep through her, burning away all hope of happiness.

He loved Bertrada.

The words would not cease repeating themselves in her mind to echo in her heart.

He loved Bertrada.

It was sin at its most blatant. He could not love Bertrada, not in that way, not with touch most intimate and kiss most profane. Courtly love, yes; such was allowed, even encouraged, but never this. Never adultery. Incest.

How had it come to this? Where was the boy who had caught her cheating at chess and laughed at her deception? To marry Richard had been to marry the only person who had caught hold of her heart, understanding her thoughts and moods as no other. He was the man she had wanted even when he had cast her off, for she had believed— nay, she had known—that he loved her. There had been no hope for them, and so he had turned from her though he had loved her. And she, not strong enough to turn away from the sight and presence of Richard, had loved him.

The Richard she had loved could never have committed so foul a sin. The Richard she loved was honor and duty and purpose most resolute. The Richard she loved. . . .

Isabel sighed and slid off the bed to stare out of the wind hole. The Richard she loved did not exist. She had created him, created him out of fair looks and lean visage, out of dreams and sighs and girlish memories. He did not exist, this man she had loved so long from so great a distance. She could not love a man who would so foul his vows of honor and duty, who would kiss a young girl with such passion while bedding another.

Yea, there lay the heart of her misery. He had lied to her. All had been lies. The bond she had believed they shared beyond any two people in the world—a lie. His laughter—a lie. His purity—a lie. His devotion to duty and perfection and accomplishment—a lie. The very character of the man she had set her heart on—a lie that tore her heart from her to be cast out of the wind hole, to fall and fall and shatter. All had been a lie. His kiss had been a lie and she had believed him. Nay, more than believed, she had set her world around him, he the sun to her every day. It had all been deception and deceit. He had lied to her with every breath and every step and every reluctant glance. She had seen and watched and studied only him, the world shrunk to him and his deeds. What dark deeds he had committed while she watched and saw only what she wished to see.

He loved Bertrada.

The feeling of being trapped weighed heavily, crushing her more completely with each painful realization. She had been betrayed. She had been a fool.

He had never loved her. He had never wanted her. Yea, he had kissed her, probably out of pity at her foolish and naive infatuation with him. She saw that now, now that she cared to see the truth of all his years of avoidance of her, of his carefully downcast eyes, his mumbled responses, his running retreat whenever she had tracked him down. But then, she had not cared to see. She had seen only Richard. Richard had seen only Bertrada.

Even with his confession, it was impossible to think of them together, though she could not drive the shadowy images from the deepest corners of her thoughts. It was impossible to believe that the man she had held in such high honor, who carried himself with such pride, had stolen the virtue of Henley by soiling his wife. Small wonder he had fled to the abbey. No matter how deep his fall into sin, Richard was a man of honor—this she knew though all the evidence spoke otherwise. She could not have been so far wrong in her knowledge of him, could she? Was he not a man who valued honor and duty above all?

How hard and fast she clung to the lie of her memory when the deceiver Richard was stood before her. He had sinned with Bertrada. By his own lips, he had confessed it.

And such a sin. Having been given by his father into Henley's household, Richard had become part of that house, his honor bound to Malton and to Henley. His sin had stripped honor from them both. He had defiled his lord's marriage bed.

He had defiled hers.

This Richard she knew not. This Richard was not the husband she wanted. How well would God hear that prayer?

The sun had topped the trees, lighting the day. The trees, washed clean yesterday, shimmered green in the morning sun, their color darker, truer, than just yesterday. So much could change in a day.

She turned from the wind hole and walked across the stone floor, ignoring the cold seeping into her feet; such small discomfort as cold feet she could easily ignore. Opening her trunk, she lifted out the first bliaut that came to her hand; it was old, a gown of her mother's that had been reworked for her years ago. The soft red of the finely worked wool brought a smile to her lips; such lovely memories she had of seeing her mother in this gown. She had been a child, easily tucked under her mother's arms to bury her face in a warm bosom, her problems small and her mother's love a great bastion against all pain and all disappointment.

It was the perfect gown to wear on such a day as this, for now she was no longer a child. She had

left the naive child she had been on the soiled
sheets of her marriage bed. The child Isabel had
died with the same blow that had killed her love—
nay, it had been mere infatuation—for Richard.
That Isabel, foolish and hopeful, was dead. It was
a woman who faced the day, a woman who would
not live in the lie of dreams.

A woman who did not love Richard.

Chapter Eighteen

He had heard her tears. Any who had an ear to hear would have heard her heart-wrenching sobs and pleas of the night before. His had been such an ear.

He had not dared intrude upon them, their conjugal duty a private thing that required no human intervention, but he had prayed that God would be merciful and Richard gentle in his dealings with Isabel.

He was not certain how God had answered his prayers.

When Isabel exited her chamber, he would be waiting, to offer comfort if needed.

Isabel came out then, and from the look of her, she did seem in need of . . . something.

"Good morrow, Father," she said calmly.

"Good morrow, Isabel," Father Langfrid answered somewhat tenuously.

Isabel did not stop to chatter with him about her conjugal night. Isabel did not throw herself into his arms and sob out her confusion. Isabel did not grin and proclaim her victory to God and the world in claiming Richard as husband, true and proper. Any of these responses he would have expected, perhaps each in its course; yet Isabel did none of these. Isabel preceded him down the stairs, her head erect and her step stately; her mouth closed. Langfrid did not know how to speak to this Isabel.

"When you did not attend Prime, I—" he began.

"Nay," she interrupted, her dark hair flowing out behind her, lifted by wisps of wind as she descended the stair. "I was most fatigued. But do not fear, I said my morning prayers in my chamber. Let Richard have his treasured spot in the chapel."

Sharp words for a wife on the morning after her deflowering.

"I could not help but hear your tears, Isabel," he said gently, laying a hand upon her arm to slow and stop her descent. They were upon the hall, and he would not have this conversation in public. "I am here. You have only to speak out your distress to me—"

Isabel turned to face him, and he pulled away from her in surprise. Never had he seen such a look on a woman's face. But then, he had never been married.

"I am not in distress," she stated, her tone as flat and cold as her eyes. "If you would offer counsel and comfort, seek out Richard. He is the one in need, not I."

"But, Isabel—"

"Excuse me, Father, but I must be about my tasks. Meaningful work awaits me this day," she said and continued her descent, her step rapid and hard upon the stone stair.

Meaningful work? Such words, such intent, from Isabel rang sharply in his ears. Isabel's intent had always and only been Richard. What had happened in that bed last night? Isabel had directed him to Richard, so to Richard he would go; perhaps the comfort he longed to supply would be welcome there.

It was not to be.

Richard was in the hall, though not in his preferred corner talking accounts with Jerome. Nay, Richard was on his way out to the bailey, his visage as dark and forbidding as his hair in the welcome sun of a spring day.

"Good morrow, Father," Richard offered, his words hardly more than the barest greeting.

"Good morrow, Lord Richard," Langfrid said. "You were up early. The first in chapel for Prime, as usual."

"I spent the night in prayer, Father, as is my custom," Richard said, looking out into the bailey, clearly eager to be away.

"So?" Langfrid said. "Yet were you not . . . I thought I heard . . . did you not fulfill your marital duty?"

Richard turned to face him. Langfrid thought

how odd it was that Richard's look matched Isabel's almost exactly; and he still could not read what he saw in their eyes.

"Did I not proclaim that I would?"

"Yea, but—"

"And I have done so. Isabel is a virgin no longer."

"Yet you went back to the chapel?" Langfrid may not have been married, but he knew this was not usual male behavior for a man recently wed.

"Yea," Richard answered curtly.

"But—"

"Excuse me, Father," Richard interrupted, "but I have much to do. Edmund!" he called across the bailey. "Find Gilbert and bring swords for a bout."

Richard strode across the bailey in the rough clothes of a man about to undertake a physical battering, his black hair gleaming and his carriage erect. Langfrid stood, open-mouthed, and watched, his thoughts whirling. Isabel in a hurry to set about her tasks as lady. Richard in a hurry to train in arms.

What *had* happened in their marriage bed?

The morning was still young and Richard was covered in sweat. He was sadly out of wind and stamina, but time and training would cure that lack. His battle skills would be honed, and he would once again attain the heights of prowess he had left behind at Malton. He would. He would achieve what he set his hand and his heart to; what he had mastered once, he would master again.

Why was Isabel not watching his progress?

His eyes scanned the perimeter of the tiltyard, searching for her without direct intent. She had always watched him train. It had always been so, since he was a youth of more joint than sinew. Always she had stood to watch him, her translucent eyes claiming him even if her voice did not. To hack and hew without Isabel to mark his progress . . . his eyes flicked away from Gilbert, scanning for Isabel.

"You look for a distant foe when you have one much nearer," Gilbert chided, laying a blow that Richard just managed to block with his shield.

He had to concentrate. He could not be looking for a flash of black hair and curve of hip when he faced a sword drawn and pointed. He could not and he would not. Isabel would come. Isabel always came.

"Riders come!" came a shout from the sentry atop the walls.

With the words, Richard imagined Adam, Louis, and Nicholas riding upon him to claim his holding. But nay, they would not be so careless with their lives. Even Nicholas would not be so bold as to return with Adam. Louis? What would Louis do? He did not know Louis well, though Isabel . . . nay. He cast that suspicion away from him. None knew Isabel as well as he. Last night had borne the truth of that.

All eyes turned to the sentry, waiting for his next words.

" 'Tis Louis, with two knights and a squire unknown to me," he called down.

Louis. The name settled in his gut like a weight of stone. Louis had returned to Dornei with two knights unknown. Returned to Dornei or returned to Isabel? Of a certainty, Louis's loyalty did not rest with him. What errand required him to bring two strange knights within Dornei's walls?

Isabel flew across the bailey like a bird set to soaring flight, so eager was she to greet Louis and his escort. The insult could be felt even by a man who had so recently been a monk; she would fly to Louis and not to him?

"Open the gates, Odo," she called gaily, her eagerness plain for all to see.

The gatekeeper, Odo, looked down from his perch to Richard, waiting for his consent to Isabel's overeager demand that Louis be admitted. Richard could see the flash of irritation spark behind her eyes and could not summon the piety to be ashamed at the perverse pleasure her irritation gave him. She had wanted him as husband, did she not, and he would be a poor sort of husband if he allowed a man of questionable motives to ride gaily into his domain.

With a nod, he gave his consent, and the outer gate was opened. The inner gate of the barbican was not. In a moment, the men were trapped within the outer gate, which closed behind them, and the inner gate.

Louis and his comrades made admirable targets.

Isabel was furious. Richard, growing more pleased by the moment, cheerfully ignored her.

Richard climbed the stair to the top of the barbican and looked down into the small, stone-walled space that confined his "guests." Their horses were pressed together, yet remained calm. That told him much about their ability as knights, for it would take a well trained knight to keep his animal calm under such circumstances. See him they could not, for he was protected by stone, yet he could study them from the slit that would allow boiling water to be dropped upon them if they proved untrustworthy. Looking at Louis, he allowed his wishes to take him where they would.

"A fine barbican," one of the knights remarked.

"If the Lord of Dornei wants us to compliment him on the skill of his stonemason and the firmness of his mortar, I can observe as much in his hall," the other said.

The unknown knights were tall and full across the chest. The squire who accompanied them was of similar breadth, but with the spareness of youth.

"I thought we were needed," the squire said to Louis.

"Needed for what?" Richard said into the midst of them.

"Lord Richard," Louis said, relieved and embarrassed at once. "I have returned—"

"I can see that," Richard said. "Returned from where and with whom?"

"He does not recognize you," one of the knights said to his mysterious companion.

The second knight remained silent but flicked back his cloak, which fell in precise scarlet folds.

"From Greneforde, my lord," Louis said, his face

reddening. "This is William le Brouillard, Lord of Greneforde. At his side is Rowland the Dark. Ulrich is the squire who rides at William's back."

"I have heard much of William le Brouillard and Rowland the Dark. Little of Greneforde," Richard said. "Why have you come to Dornei?"

"To give you aid, Lord Richard," William said, toying with his mufflers. "We are here to assist you."

Richard glared at Louis, though he knew that Louis, coughing uncomfortably even now, could not see him.

"This was your errand? To find knight nurse-maids to help the monk hold his tower?"

"He does not seem to need help," Rowland remarked lightly to William.

"But, my lord, William is more than knight, he is Lord Greneforde. You have some need in knowing your neighbors?" It was said as a question when clearly it was not. Louis was a poor liar. Richard pressed down the anger and humiliation he felt that a knight in his household would think he needed help in holding what God had ordained for him to hold. He was not so frail a man as that.

"Open the gate," he commanded tersely. "And have water heated for a bath."

At Richard's words, Rowland said to William, "He does know you."

William merely grunted his reply.

Once free of the barrier of the barbican, the men took each other's measure. It was not done subtly, though none took offense.

Richard was dressed in warrior's garb of leather

gambeson and was sweat-slick, his sword held easily in his grasp. He felt more than a match for any man who faced him, and it showed in his bearing.

William he could have identified by his beauty and his deportment. It was a known fact that William le Brouillard had a face that would rival a woman's and the fighting skill to match a demonic wraith. He stood tall, his hair black and curled, his eyes the silver gray of steel, his manner pleasant and sure. He was a man who was certain of his worth, and equally certain that his worth was acknowledged by all, though, as all was done with a certain wry humor, it was impossible to take offense at such pride.

Rowland was a dark man, his eyes as black as his hair, his skin burnished brown by long years in the sun. He was tall, broad, and a warrior to the bone in manner and by reputation. Even among the Brothers, Rowland and William's battle tales had been repeated with a certain unholy relish. Yet for all that battle history, he appeared a mild man, his gaze soft and dark and cloaked. Yea, cloaked was a word which suited Rowland well. Dark were the depths of him, unlike the shining brightness of his comrade brother, William. Well matched they were, and if the tales were correct, as true to each other as cradle-mates. From all Richard knew of them, such men would not seek to deal treacherously with any man, especially one not known to them.

But what of Louis? What did he know of Louis, who had brought these men into his domain? Richard looked at Louis then, enjoying the sheepish look in his eyes.

"What, then?" Richard asked, laying the burden of talk upon Louis.

"My lord?" Louis asked.

"Explain yourself."

"My lord," he said falteringly, "I know Adam and Nicholas. I heard their talk, and thought you needed—"

"Help?"

"Support," he insisted. "From trusted men."

Richard said nothing, but thought that Adam and Nicholas would not have spoken openly of their plans and thoughts if they had not believed Louis one of them in spirit. He would deal with that later, in private.

"All is in hand," Richard informed them all. "Adam and Nicholas are both gone. I am true Lord of Dornei."

Richard did not miss the blush that spotted Louis's cheeks. To be true lord meant that he had bedded Isabel. And why should Louis blush at that, unless Louis held a tendre for his wife? Isabel attracted admirers as easily as a dog fleas.

William nodded toward Isabel, who stood as if rooted at the base of Dornei Tower.

"Your lady wife?"

"Yea," Richard answered, his tone as firm as his intent.

"You have been blessed," William said with a smile.

Blessed? The word jolted Richard. He had never

considered himself blessed at having been compelled to take Isabel to wife. Obedient, yea, but not blessed. He had been doing his duty, proving his submission, living out his service to God. He had not been blessed.

Had he?

"Come," he said, throwing off all thoughts of blessing. "Take your rest. You are welcome to Dornei."

At that, Isabel came forward to greet their guests, as was proper in her role as Lady of Dornei. Yet did she have to greet Louis with such warmth? And did he not detect the flutter of eyelashes when she was introduced to William of Greneforde? Nay, he was seeing what was not there to see; she was merely being gracious and welcoming. Yet he did not imagine that she ignored him. That was a truth he could not help but see, and she seemed ill disposed to hide it. When had Isabel ever ignored him?

Now.

Today.

'Twas intolerable.

"Isabel," he said, forcing her attention to him. She looked upon him like a dog in need of bathing, her expression sour and forced. "Make a chamber ready for our guests and see about the bath. We must not disappoint."

He could see the effort it took her to bite back a retort to his command and felt a flush of pleasure that he had managed to prick her. Let her fly at him in rage or sulk, he did not care which, but he would have a response from her. Ignore him she would not.

"Ulrich," William directed, "go with Lady Isabel and take these supplies with you."

"Yea, Lord William," Ulrich said in a rushing breath, trotting off after Isabel, who was striding briskly toward the tower.

"Your soaps?" Richard asked drily, motioning toward the pack Ulrich carried.

"Only a few," William answered with a smile. "It would take an ox to carry them all."

Richard nodded, smiling at the humor of the man. The tales had been true concerning William le Brouillard.

"You have been but recently married?" William asked as they walked toward the tower.

"Yea, two days now," Richard answered.

"Ahh," William smiled at Rowland in response, his eyes shining like new coin in silent mirth.

Richard said nothing. William had achieved the last word, and all three knew it.

Chapter Nineteen

Isabel charged up the stair tower like a leaf blown by a hostile wind, so furious at being ordered about by Richard that she felt as if she were flying apart. She could hear Ulrich, squire to Lord William, panting somewhere behind her, straining to keep up; she should slow, but she could not. She could not because Richard's command was still ringing in her ears, as if she did not know how to be hospitable, as if she were a child to bid, as if she were a wife.

She reached the chamber, on the top floor, and noted that a new coverlet would be needed. She had not been up to this room in months and only now saw that dust was white upon the floor and the bedding was musty. From the look, it appeared that one of Dornei's cats had made the bed her own, for it was covered in white hair and muddy footprints. It was an embarrassment.

Ulrich, breathless and a trifle red in the cheek, came hard upon her into the chamber.

"Many thanks, Lady, for your hospitality."

"You are most welcome, Squire, but let me have the room cleaned. I had not known of its condition—"

"Oh, Lady Isabel," he said, his breath coming back, " 'twill do most well for my lord William. All that he requires to be content is his daily bath. I will shake the cover. He will expect no less of me, though it be fresh from the laundress."

"Oh, you are kind." She smiled. He was a disarming lad, very broad of shoulder and handsome in his youthful way. "But I will see to a new coverlet and a good dusting before any guest of Dornei is admitted here. What you do at Lord William's command after that is between the two of you."

"Very well, Lady." He smiled. "And may I say, you run a fair race up your stair. I doubt my lady Cathryn will believe I have been outrun."

'Twas Isabel who turned red then and ducked her head with a contrite smile. "You think me a most improper wife, I daresay, yet I have only been married for two days and have not much practice at being the Lady of Dornei. You must not spread word of my indiscretion to your lady, Squire, or I will be undone."

"Lady, I would do nothing to harm you," he said with a grin, taking her measure.

Isabel returned the look, liking the lad before

her. He had a way about him, a charm that flowed like river water, bright and sweet and clear. Would that Richard were more like him. This lad was not one to throw his lordly weight about a hall. Would that Richard found the grace to curb his high-handedness. 'Twas intolerable.

"Squire, you hold my reputation in your hands." She grinned back.

Aelis burst into the chamber.

"Lady," she breathed, thrusting out her bosom and looking as earnest as she might, "may I be of help to you in preparing the chamber?"

Ulrich's eyes took on a speculative look, which Isabel could hardly miss and which Aelis had hoped for.

"Yea, run and fetch a fresh cover from the linen chest," Isabel said. "This room needs airing and dusting."

Aelis was looking at Ulrich, her pretty blue eyes taking in his form and face and finding all very pleasing. Ulrich did not blush but returned her look, measure for measure. Isabel felt distinctly unnecessary.

"Aelis?" she said.

"Oh. Aye, I will," she said, still looking at Ulrich.

"Would you like help in finding the linen?" Ulrich asked, his eyes merry.

"From you?" Aelis asked. "How could you help me when I know this place and you do not?"

"I know how to find what you seek," he said.

"Do you?" She smiled, holding his gaze. "I have heard those words before and been disappointed."

"Oh, have you?" He smiled too, rising to her challenge. "I do not disappoint, Aelis. My training does not allow it."

"You speak of your knight's training?"

"Did I say so?" he said, his voice husky.

Aelis smiled and looked at the floor, her chest heaving with the sensual exchange.

Isabel remembered it. She remembered it all. The seeking, the finding, the taunts and the innuendos; she had pursued Richard in just such a way and her blood had raced to find him. She had teased him without mercy or measure and she had loved every minute of it. Had Richard? He had not behaved as Ulrich did now. She had loved to hunt out his whereabouts, loved finding him and flirting with him, loved being with him, but perhaps she had not loved *him*. Perhaps it had only been the pursuit of him that had fired her. Watching Aelis flirt with Ulrich, she could not but think it, for did not Aelis flirt with as much joy when Edmund was her target?

Edmund came into the room then, which was becoming a trifle crowded with bodies.

Aelis ignored him. Ulrich faced him openly, his expression guiltless, which naturally he was. Edmund looked as black of visage as the Lord of Dornei.

"Lady Isabel," he said, looking at Aelis and Ulrich, "Lord Richard asks if the bath is ready."

"You can see that it is not," Isabel said, more fatigued than she could say at being so ignored in her own hall. "Tell your lord that I will manage all and that he does not need to tutor me on how to be a wife. In fact, you may tell him that I had all the tutoring I shall ever need from Lady Bertrada."

She would have felt a bit ashamed at so losing her temper in front of a guest, but no one was paying her the least heed.

"Off with you, all of you, until the room is as I like it," she said, shooing them out of her sight. Edmund left angrily, his eyes stormy. Aelis left smiling. Ulrich left cheerfully, his temper unaffected. If not for Edmund being in the midst of them, she was not uncertain that Ulrich and Aelis would have left together.

Isabel was disgusted with them all.

Aelis should content herself with the husband arranged for her. It was what Isabel should have done herself, but in her blindness, she had demanded Richard, and Richard loved another. The very woman who had taught her what it meant to be a woman held Richard's heart.

Tearing the dirty cover from the bed, Isabel could only rage in her heart that God had answered her prayer.

"God has answered your heartfelt prayer. Where is your joy?" Father Langfrid asked.

She had finished preparing the chamber, setting the servants to clean and scrub, scolding them for not doing their duty in keeping it clean, finding fresh linen only to realize that the laundry was backing up. She had been on her way to the laundress to find out exactly how remiss in her duties she had been, when Langfrid had found her. She had no answer to his question. Her joy? It was gone, vanished on the marriage bed as surely as her virginity. Yet she would not tell him what had transpired there, proclaiming Richard's sin to the sky. Richard's confessor knew all and was the only person who needed to know. Richard certainly had not needed to tell her, and she could not decide if it was an act of cruelty or vulnerability on his part in telling her the depth of his sin. There was no need for Father Langfrid to know unless he heard it from Richard himself.

But Father Langfrid was determined to mend the breach between them, and to do that, he must know the cause.

"Was it that the conjugal night did not meet your expectations?" he asked.

"Yea," she answered, trying to mask her sarcasm, "it did not."

Langfrid seemed to relax, at ease to have a cause for the breach in her joy. "This is the normal way, I am told. You will accustom yourself to it in time and will even learn to find pleasure in it."

Impossible. She was never going to allow Richard such intimacy with her again. All she could hear was her own voice begging him for forgiveness, pleading with him, the tears choking her. Let him bed Lady Bertrada again instead.

Nay, she did not mean that; it was her anger and her hurt, for she would not wish Richard to sin to such a degree again, no matter how deeply he had hurt her. But it was a truth that he did not want her. He had never wanted her. And she would never allow herself to want him again.

She said none of this to Father Langfrid, naturally, yet he seemed to read something of her rebellion on her face.

"You will, Isabel, and you must. 'Tis the way of marriage. He is your lord. You must submit with a good will."

"I did submit," she said, charging ahead, hoping to outpace him.

"With a good will," he said, "for your own sake."

For her own sake she would avoid the marriage bed and Richard with it.

"Excuse me, Father, but I must speak with Elfrida about the laundry."

Her meeting with Elfrida went well as she was in a fine mood for delivering a good scolding, which Elfrida heartily deserved for so neglecting her duties. Langfrid waited for her to return. He was determined to continue this conversation—almost as determined as Isabel was not to have it. Leading the way into the chapel, Isabel resigned herself to listening to Langfrid discuss her conjugal relations.

It was most unpleasant.

"You do understand that only men find pleasure in their coupling the first time they attempt it."

With the way God was treating her lately, she found she was not surprised.

"Women blessed with a husband, particularly a husband such as yours, come to yearn for their husband's touch; it is merely a matter of learning . . ."

A husband such as hers? A husband who did not want her and yearned for another? Nay, Richard would never touch her again.

"Do you not yearn for a child?" he asked into her silent and sullen face. "Without pleasure, there is no child."

"No child?" she asked, speaking out for the first time in his diatribe.

"Nay," he said, clearly exasperated. "For unless you achieve your pleasure, no child can come."

A child. Yea, she wanted a child. Richard she could never have. But Richard could give her a child. One child was all he would have to provide. He could give her nothing else, but he could give her that.

"How do I get my pleasure from it?" she asked intently.

Langfrid blushed. "I cannot answer as to that."

"I refuse to ask Richard!" she snapped, knowing that was exactly what Langfrid would suggest.

"Richard will know," he urged. "You must trust yourself in his care. He is your husband. He will know what must be done, how the thing is to be achieved."

It was advice she could hardly follow, but she kept the retort to herself, swallowing the words as she strode from the chapel. But she did not need to speak; she was Isabel, and all was written upon her face for all the world to see.

214

Chapter Twenty

"You did not pledge to me," Richard said.

"I will. I only thought to serve you," Louis answered.

They were alone in the hall, the light strong and bright against the stone, the cooing of nesting birds in the high wind holes soft and peaceful to the ear. It was well, since there was little that Louis said which sat soft upon Richard's ear.

"By bringing armed knights not sworn to me into my fief?"

"They are not treacherous. Not like Adam and Nicholas."

"So, you know they are gone from here and you seek to distance yourself from their plotting?"

"My only plot was to give you aid in becoming a strong lord for Dornei."

"And for Isabel?" Richard pounced, sensing the weakness in the man before him.

Louis dropped his eyes for but a moment and then lifted them with resolve. "Isabel is your lady. There is no other claim."

"Nor shall there be," Richard declared. "God has given Isabel to me. No man shall take her from me; only God has the right."

"You speak not as a monk," Louis said, a smile trying to light behind his eyes.

"I am not a monk," Richard stated. "God has seen to that." *And Isabel.*

Isabel had robbed him of his will to serve God and God alone. He had taken pleasure in her last night: sin magnified. And given her none in return: sin multiplied. She hid from him now, because of his confession, when she had always and in all times hunted him. The day felt . . . empty . . . without her.

"And in your efforts not to be a monk, I but sought to aid you," Louis said. "It was only for this that I asked William and Rowland to come to Dornei."

It was less than flattering that Louis thought his skill at arms so lacking. Yet the truth was, he had been practicing and could use a fiercer foe than Gilbert, who was the best Dornei had to offer. Perhaps some friendly swordplay would not be amiss. Who better to test his skill against than William le Brouillard and his shadow companion, Rowland? For their battle prowess they were known well, yet also for their valor. For that alone he would allow himself to trust them. But Louis? He did not trust Louis. Louis yearned for Isabel. What man did not?

"She has no yearning for the marriage bed," Rowland said.

William grunted and sank lower into his bath. It sounded painfully familiar.

"A marriage of two nights. Give him time," William said.

The chamber in which they were guests was clean and well presented. The sheets were white from the sun and smelled of lavender; the cover was wool dyed blue and stitched with red thread. A bouquet of spring flowers lay upon the ledge by the wind hole, the soft wind carrying the scent of flowers into the room. William was well pleased. Even his bathwater had arrived hot and ample.

Ulrich scrubbed William's back with his favorite scented soap. Rowland stood leaning against the far wall, his arms crossed over his chest, relating what he had learned of conditions at Dornei. Louis, friend to Ulrich, had requested most urgently that they come to Dornei's aid. Richard, Lord of Dornei, was not as Louis had painted him, for no soft monk had held them trapped within the barbican. Yet Richard was a man unused to battle, and such a man would not meet Dornei's needs easily. How often was a monk called upon to bear arms?

"Give him time," William repeated. Time cured most ills, he had discovered.

"I would give him eternity, but the lady . . ." Rowland shrugged.

"There is more to marriage than the marriage bed," William said.

Ulrich snorted in dissent and disbelief, while Rowland laughed soundlessly at the squire's youthful display.

"But we can do nothing as to that," William continued, giving Ulrich a dark look which Ulrich smiled away. "He is a man trained to knighthood, a man who chose the cowl and was forced to give that up but recently. Not an easy step, from the cloister to the battlefield."

"So," Rowland said, reading William's intent, "we help him learn again to hold his ground in battle. And leave it to him to learn to hold his lady wife."

His face both serious and regretful, William answered, "I can only do so much, Rowland."

Ulrich's laughter rebounded off the walls, frightening the lark that had been searching for a place among the scattered flowers to build her nest.

Hard upon the midday meal, the men adjourned to the bailey to commence their battle play. The day stayed fair, the sun bright, drying the mud of recent rain and urging the flowers to come forth and spread their light perfume upon the air. At the moment, within the bailey the only smell was of sweat and manure.

"I had heard," Richard said to Rowland, circling with his blade sharp and ready, "that you two fought ever at each other's backs, single combat being . . ."

"Being?" Rowland prompted.

"A skill you little used," Richard taunted, baiting the knight who stood to fight him. He was glad for the chance to test his long-neglected skills and enjoyed prodding for the temper of the man before him. But Rowland appeared a man of no temper. He spoke little, smiled only with William, and fought . . . he fought with the feral joy of a lion.

Richard found pleasure in the company of such a man as Rowland the Dark.

The ring of swords meeting, deflecting, seeking more than air, filled the bailey. The dull thud of wood absorbing metallic blows accompanied the scudding of sudden clouds across the sky. The sun fought for dominance of the spring sky and was slowly, silently defeated by wave upon wave of clouds until all was gray and still. Still except for the ringing of swords and the beat of weapons against shields. It began to rain, a light rain which all within the bailey ignored. It fell lightly, just more than mist, and almost as soft upon the skin. The circle of watchers within the bailey increased with each strike, each circle, each pass of blade against moving quarry. But Isabel was not among them. Isabel did not watch.

With a blow that caught him unprepared, Rowland cracked Richard's shield in half, the smell of fractured wood rising into the wet air. Rowland stood poised to strike.

"Such loss of concentration leads only to the grave," Rowland said softly, his sword the dull gray of pewter in the dim light. "If you want her to watch you train, ask her."

He was so obvious, then? Even to a stranger? Yet Rowland had been so blunt in his observation and so unemotional in his advice that Richard could not take offense.

"Ask her?" he said.

Did he truly want Isabel to watch him at his swordplay? The answer surprised him; yea, he did.

"Ask her," Rowland repeated. "She likely does not know it would please you."

That was likely true, since her attention in the past had always displeased him, but it disturbed him far more to have her missing. But whether she would do anything now to please him was something he did not want to consider too closely. He did not understand a world in which Isabel was angry with him and kept her distance. He did not know what to expect or what to do.

Rowland stood back while Richard rose from his knees. Once Richard was standing and with a new shield from Edmund, Rowland retreated to the sidelines. William le Brouillard took Rowland's place. If Rowland was the Dark, his thoughts and plans hidden, William was the Fog, for although he was seen, he was impossible to hold and, like the fog, was silent in his battle skills. They would be well matched in battle.

Richard was determined to be a good match for either of them.

"You have a mighty arm . . . for a praying man," William jested.

Richard smiled, accepting the compliment. "The devil is a mighty adversary; my arm has grown strong in my battles against him."

With smiles of men born with the love of fighting in their blood, the ring of steel once again dominated all sound within the bailey.

Chapter Twenty-one

Elsbeth stood on tiptoe to see out the wind hole into the bailey. She was fortunate in that the men were staying in a small area to do their fighting; her view was unobstructed, even by the rain which felt like a cooling mist.

"His concentration was broken and he was felled by the dark one. Now he fights Lord William," Elsbeth said, not taking her eyes from the battle in front of her. When last she had looked away, Isabel had scolded her most roundly.

"They rest while he has none," Isabel muttered. "It matters not to me," she said loudly, for Elsbeth's edification as well as her own.

And it did not. It was what a woman could expect when she chose a husband from among the abbey brethren. Now, if there were to be a battle of chants, she would wager that her husband would win most resoundingly.

If he could not fight and fight well, he would lose all. And what would that matter if she had no child to gift with the lands and manors and towers won through the years?

She needed a child. Dornei needed an heir.

The clang of weapons was sharp, even within the chamber, and she forced her mind away from Richard's mock battle and onto her real one. She had to get with child. She had to get pleasure from the marriage bed to get with child, according to Father Langfrid.

He could be wrong. He was not married. He had no child.

She would not proceed without further information; she would not ask pleasure from Richard if she could possibly avoid it. She would not let Richard touch her if she could possibly avoid it.

"Elsbeth," she said slowly.

"Hmm?" Elsbeth answered, keeping her eyes to the action in the bailey.

"Have you ever heard that a wife must receive pleasure in the marriage bed to get with child?"

Elsbeth turned to face her, her eyes wide, her mouth silent.

"Have you?" Isabel prompted. Elsbeth's mother had given birth ten times; she must have told her daughter *something* before sending her off to her fostering.

"Yea, my mother told me that was so."

"Did she?" Isabel asked in disappointment and rising despair. Why had no one ever told her these details? The answer was that her mother had died while she was very young, too young to be told the truths of the marriage bed. Ida had been her father's wife during the years of her fostering. And Joan? Joan could not speak about the acts of marriage without a goblet of wine in her grasp.

"Yea," Elsbeth answered. "It was why she was three years barren before my eldest brother took root in her womb. After him, she bore a child nigh on every year."

Three years! She did not want to try nightly for three years. She did not even want to live with Richard for three years. Let him go back among the monks where he could pray and dream of Bertrada.

The sound of blows could be heard, stronger now, and then the sound of a body hitting the damp earth.

Isabel was on her feet and partway to the wind hole before she made herself turn aside. She was finished with making a fool of herself over Richard. Elsbeth was facing the wind hole, her expression startled. Isabel inched forward, completely against her will, and asked, "Is Richard . . . well?"

Elsbeth turned, her face still and white. "It is not Richard, but Edmund and Ulrich, and it is not a battle but a brawl, Isabel. They look to kill each other."

Isabel tossed aside her vow of disinterest and hurried to the wind hole.

* * *

They battled, churning the soft earth into mud, their footing becoming precarious. They did not note it. They battled on, as only two young men with more heart than brains will do.

It did not last long.

William blocked a swordblow that would have bloodied Edmund and sent Ulrich's blade flying through the air to land in the mud. "Hold, boy," he commanded his squire.

Ulrich, trained to heed that one voice, obeyed, his body panting and quivering with the effort. But he did obey.

Richard tossed Edmund to the ground with a swipe of his hand and held his own sword to the lad's throat. Edmund swallowed hard and studied his lord. Richard's expression was severe, his black brows pulled low over his dark blue eyes, his breathing heavy with suppressed anger. Edmund had raised arms against a guest of Dornei; death could be the payment for such ill-advised action. To his credit, Edmund awaited his lord and said naught in his own defense. Content that Edmund would hold in place on the ground, Richard scanned the crowd that watched them. When he saw Aelis, looking both shocked and excited, he spoke. To her.

"Shall he die, girl? Shall we give the troubadours fodder for a stirring tale of two squires who came to blows over you? He should die for attacking a guest without provocation," Richard said, his voice carrying easily over the rain and the horror of what he was suggesting.

The vast bailey was still. None spoke. Richard looked down again at Edmund. He was white, the color of summer clouds, his eyes huge and bright and the only color in his face.

"His attack was not unprovoked, Lord Richard," Ulrich said, his voice a quaver on the air, as thin as a shaft aimed high and far, yet he spoke in Edmund's defense. "I bear Edmund no malice."

It was valiantly done. William had a worthy squire and had trained him well. Would that he could say the same of Edmund.

"What say you, Aelis?" Richard prodded, still awaiting her response. "Was this unchivalrous attack unprovoked? Do not you yearn to see just a little blood spilt on your behalf this day?"

Lady Joan elbowed Aelis hard in the ribs, urging her to speak. Shaken and trembling, she did. "Draw no blood, my lord, I beseech you. Edmund bears no fault." Her voice broke on saying his name, and her shoulders shook with emotion.

Richard had the answer he sought.

Richard looked down at Edmund and whispered hoarsely, "You have trusted your heart to a woman and she has stolen your honor. Remember this hour well, boy."

Richard sheathed his sword and turned away from Edmund, leaving him in the mud. He would not insult the boy by playing nursemaid to him. Ulrich rushed over and offered Edmund his hand. Edmund, without hesitation, took it and was lifted to his feet. Heads down and shoulders together, the two squires left the circle of spectators, their voices low and confidential. Gilbert's booming voice scattered the rest of Dornei's folk until only William, Rowland, and Richard remained.

"They will be fast friends now," William said. "You dealt well with them."

Richard grunted away the compliment and asked the question that plagued him.

"And do you think young Aelis has learned not to play with men's lives? That was also my intent."

"You may have made her fit only for the convent," William laughed lightly.

"Not that one." Richard smiled slowly in return. "She is betrothed, and to a man past his prime."

"Ah," said William, "and so she tries her skill on squires."

"You call what she does skill?"

"William is from the Continent, where such skills, in man or woman, are highly prized," Rowland said in wry humor.

"Had I left those pups to try their skill, she could have tried her skill at needlework," Richard said, turning to walk toward the armory. His guests walked beside him.

"Nay, you dealt aright," William said. "Either the boys understood not her game or she did not. All are taught now."

"Pray God 'tis learned," Richard said, speaking from his heart.

Rowland and William, as was their way, shared a glance rich with meaning, yet said nothing.

*   *   *

Elsbeth found Aelis hiding behind the kitchen. She had been crying, which was all to the good as far as Elsbeth was concerned, but was past it now. She was hunched over, hiding her face against her knees with her hair as curtain to hide her shame. Still, Elsbeth would have her say.

"What did you do to drive them to a fit of arms? Could you not be well content to have them both vying for your regard? Did you have to spur them to combat?"

"I have just been pinched and scolded by Dame Joan," Aelis sniffed. "I do not need to hear more of it from you."

"Do you not?" Elsbeth hissed softly. "Hear yourself; you are sulky, not contrite."

"I was contrite with Joan," Aelis insisted crossly.

"A contrite heart does not turn sulky. What did you do?"

"I do not know," Aelis said, beginning to cry again, which cheered Elsbeth. "I only know it went too far."

"So you have learned something."

"I only wanted what Isabel has—the man she chose for herself instead of the man chosen for her. She pursued Lord Richard and now she has him."

"You believe your course of action hers?" Elsbeth said, seeming to tower over Aelis in a dark and slender rage. "Ask her if she encouraged Richard to blows with another. Ask her if all her dreaming got her the husband she wanted. Ask her."

"I shall."

Elsbeth left then, after giving Aelis a fresh square of linen for her nose. She knew what Isabel would say. She knew how miserable Isabel was.

Chapter Twenty-two

The moment Aelis opened her mouth and confused guilt poured out of her, Isabel understood that Richard's display in the yard had been for Aelis's benefit. And that it had worked. Her duty now was to finish what Richard had begun, so that such a display as had just occurred in the bailey would never be repeated.

"You think your attempts to avoid your marriage to Lord Ivo will be endorsed by me?" she asked sternly. "You thought amiss. Think you that you can arrange a contract for yourself with Edmund? Or is it Ulrich who now charms you? Have you forgotten that my marriage to Lord Richard was arranged by Lord Robert and the bishop himself? Think you I had any say as to whom or when I would marry?" When Aelis only stood shaking, her tears rolling down her pink cheeks, Isabel continued, "Nay, you thought not at all if you could think I would be happy that Richard's two brothers died. You are profoundly in error, Aelis. I did as I was bid, as so shall you. And with good grace, if you are wise."

She had not been wise, and look where it had landed her.

Aelis left with fresh tears upon her cheeks, and Isabel did naught to stem their flow. God willing, Aelis had learned. God willing, this would be the end of Aelis's constant flirtations.

Did Richard see Aelis in Isabel? Had she been as wayward? She hoped not, for she did not want Richard to think such of her, no matter how little she cared for him now.

And with such a man she had to provide heirs.

It would be a miracle of most amazing proportions, since she could not imagine allowing him alone in the same room with her.

But it was folly to torture herself with such thoughts when the day was still so fresh. Her duties awaited her. She did not have time, not anymore, to dream of Richard. She had her duty to sustain her, her duty as Lady of Dornei, which did include producing heirs. *Three years*? Could she abide Richard in her bed for three years? Nay, she could not and would not. Every word out of his mouth proclaimed his revulsion for her; every action and every look shouted his dismay at anticipating a lifetime with her. She would not take him into her bed, not for year upon year; he would have to do his duty by her more efficiently than that. Richard was a model of efficient and diligent duty; he would manage it more quickly than Elsbeth's doddering father. And then, the moment her menses ceased, he could take himself off, back to the chapel and to his beloved chants. Back to the chapel, to dream of Bertrada.

Yea, he would do his duty by her and she would do hers. She knew how to perform her duty as well as he.

And now her duty entailed arranging for baths for her guests. She was just moving to the stair, searching out the steward, when Joan rushed breathlessly into the hall. Isabel half expected her to turn and run off, as she had been doing all day. Clearly, Joan did not want to discuss the marriage night. They were well matched in that.

"Isabel!" she gasped, pushing back her wimple. "Dornei has guests."

"Yea, I am aware of that. Lord William of Greneforde and—"

"Nay, Isabel," she said, her voice thin and taut. " 'Tis Lord Henley who has come to Dornei."

He could not refuse them entrance. Henley had been the father of his fostering; he could not turn him away. His face a mask of stone, Richard watched Henley and his retinue ride into Dornei.

He was not prepared to greet guests. He and William had been at battle, he learning rare skills in combat that William had learned in fierce battle with the Saracens. He was sweaty, dirt streaking his leather gambeson. His muscles quivering with exertion, he faced the last man on earth he wished to face.

All within the bailey could feel his tension. William lowered his sword and drew near his side. Rowland stood just to his back, his presence a dark weight which comforted. Gilbert grunted and fondled his hilt, his distrust obvious. Yet Henley had done nothing. It was Richard who was deserving of their suspicion. He knew it. Isabel knew it.

He looked toward the hall for her then, yearning suddenly to see her and yet not wanting to see her at all. Let her be spared this. God in heaven, let her not bear witness to his shame.

"Who is he?" William asked softly.

"Lord Henley of Malton. I was fostered there," Richard answered.

"A hard fostering? You are not pleased to see him," William stated. It was no question.

Richard did not answer, for what answer could he give? With a prayer of submission on his lips, he shook off his sense of doom and walked over to Henley, prepared to greet him. If he were any man at all, he would tell Henley all that had passed between himself and Bertrada. If he were a man, he would face the death that was due him without protest, as Christ had done, though Christ had been innocent and he was not.

But there was Isabel. He did not want to leave Isabel alone, without a protector.

He did not want to leave Isabel.

Then all thought left him. Henley had not come alone, nay, and the men who rode at his back lifted off their helms. One face stood out, the sun glinting off hair the warm color of polished oak, gray eyes shining with joyful malice. Adam was within Dornei again, having come with Henley. Adam, whom he had cast out, had returned.

Before he could speak, Henley preceded him. It was his way; he was a man full of the pride of life and overflowing with bluster. No simple and courteous greeting would stop him from declaring what he knew and what he wanted.

"Stay you, Richard," he commanded, his voice as thick as his torso. "Adam is pledged to me. He is as freeborn as you and may pay homage where he will. You have no authority over him now, not when you cast him out."

William and Rowland came forward to stand side by side with Richard, their hands ready upon their sword hilts. Never before had anyone stood with him; always he had stood alone. It was good to stand with trusted men, and men who, without explanation or apology, trusted you.

"The man committed offenses against my wife," Richard said evenly. "He is not welcome in Dornei."

Henley smiled. His smile was big and harsh; he had lost a tooth in the year of Richard's monkhood. "You did, perhaps, take the point too sharp, a trait I remember well in you, Richard. Adam has sworn to me; he is my man now."

It was a speech designed to shame Richard, as if he were a boy crying from a simple fall and needed urging to become more the man. It was a technique which Henley had perfected and which Richard remembered well. But his year in the abbey had taught him something of self-discipline and the danger of wild blame and false guilt. He was not as easy to shame into compliance as he had once been.

Henley continued, "Can you not forgive? Or do you seek to pluck the splinter out of his eye when the log is in your own?"

It had come. A year of running and praying, and still, it had come to stand before him in the bright light of day. There was no hiding from such a moment, though he fought the urge even now.

Richard felt the wind suck at his soul with the words. Damning words accompanied by eyes bright and hard with knowing.

Henley knew.

Henley knew all.

What had passed between himself and Bertrada stood naked and white within the bailey, there for all to see. Shame and guilt rose afresh within him, as if his year of repentance and prayer had been a night's dream. Even Adam sat his horse, smiling down at him as if he, too, knew of his sin and shame.

All would withdraw from him now; the sudden friendship of the two good and godly men at his side, men who had walked the Way of the Cross, would be ripped apart, like a weed from tilled soil. As it should. They should not bind themselves to him, he who had fallen so far and so deeply.

Into it all, flew Isabel. Wild, impulsive Isabel,

who should stay as far away from this turmoil of
male pride and fleshly sin as she could; yet she did
not. She flew straight to him, as straight as the hawk
which plummets to snag the sparrow. And her anger was writ large for all to see in her clear and
shining eyes.

And she cared not who knew it. Henley was
gloating; she could see it and remembered instantly all the many times she had seen that same
look when he had dealt with man or maid younger
or less powerful than himself. He was a proud and
pompous man, and she was glad her contact with
him had been little, though the shadow he cast was
long and all within Malton had felt its chill to
greater or lesser degree. Richard had felt it most
sharply, for, while Henley had kept Richard close
to his side out of favor, therein lay the problem.
None were at peace who dwelt long in Henley's
shadow. To bring Adam with him, to thwart Richard's will in who would or would not enter Dornei's
gates, spoke all that needed to be said of the man.

And Adam—how he gloated upon his horse. All
his good looks vanished with such a countenance,
his pride and malice so clear to see.

She rushed to them, her eyes taking it all in—
the silent support of William and Rowland and Gilbert, the mute rage and desperation of Richard.
Oh, aye, desperation, for she knew well what Richard was suffering at seeing Henley again, now that
she knew of Bertrada. Her husband suffered under
an affliction which most men avoided for a lifetime: holy integrity. He faced the man he had be-

trayed, and she could almost feel the knives of guilt ripping at her as they surely ripped at him.

He looked at her then, his blue eyes as dark as deep water, and her anger fired higher, higher than the clouds, higher than the sun itself, for she could read his eyes, and his eyes told her that he expected her to join in the attack that had commenced against him within his own bailey. He expected her to stand with Henley, against him. Stupid man! Was ever a man born who understood a woman less? Did he not know that she would always stand with him, even when she did not want to be anywhere near him? He did not know her at all.

"Welcome, Lord Henley," she said, her words welcoming if her voice was not. "Welcome to Dornei. Dismount. Take your rest. I will have food prepared for you."

Henley eyed her as he eyed all who stood below him, with speculation and mild contempt. "Thank you, Isabel. You are now Lady of Dornei, I see, in deed and in truth."

"Of course I am," she bit back. She would not play his sharp and pointed games of speaking words which were shaded unto darkness and deceit. "You knew that well, I think."

"I knew it." He smiled, his missing tooth a black hole that his lips could not cover. She found malicious pleasure in that, and did not care that he would read it in her eyes. "I did not know how well you would do as lady of a great holding; you always seemed a bit dreamy to me, though Bertrada assured me well and often that you would come into your time. She read you right, it seems."

She could feel Richard's tension pounding outward from him as one can feel the buffeting of the wind, and she knew well its cause . . . and cursed Henley for it. So much came back to her of Malton then, so many memories of dinners with Henley. She had thought her memories had been the stuff of childhood, of a girl far from home in a household unfamiliar to her, but she had remembered aright. She did not like Henley. And she did not care if he knew it.

"We all come into our time, my lord, and pass out of it as well." She smiled maliciously, enjoying it. "With Bertrada as my instructor in the household arts, how could I do less than succeed? Or do you think her incapable?"

Henley grunted and dismounted. "Your wife has a sharp tongue, Richard. She wants discipline. Can you not tame her?"

Richard quivered and clenched his hands into fists, the muscle in his jaw working with the rhythmic force of a pulse. "I am well content with God's provision for me. Naught is amiss in Dornei."

"Each man has his own standard," Henley grumbled spitefully.

"And mine is met in Isabel," Richard said, his silent and controlled rage a living thing which threatened to consume him.

"And Dornei will see to your needs, Lord Henley, while you are here," Isabel interjected.

She did not heed Richard's words of being well

content with her; she knew that it was merely a part of the verbal sparring with Henley. They had bested him, between the two of them. 'Twas a fine moment. No longer were they children, under his command and control. Now they were lord and lady, and they did not need to tolerate his oafish insults. Let Richard understand that and leave off his anger. Did he not see how it fed Henley?

"Edmund," she directed, "show Lord Henley the way to the hall. Robert, see that a light meal of chicken pasties and cheese is spread for our un-expected guests. Aelis, run and see that water is heated for bathing. I am certain that at least one bath will be required today," she said, smiling at William.

He smiled in return, and in his eyes she could read admiration. It warmed her.

Henley walked off, Adam and the rest of his men trailing behind him, as was their place in life. Adam—he should have gone to her dower lands and stayed there, as she had bade him.

Upon their leaving, Richard eased his shoulders and said, "Make certain there is enough water for two baths, Isabel. Rarely has my need been so great. Does Dornei possess a tub great enough to wash the whole of me?"

"It does," William interjected. "I have it."

For the second time in a single day, Richard smiled.

Chapter Twenty-three

Dornei had more than one tub. Richard was soaking in it, Edmund attending him, when Isabel entered the chamber. He had sent for her, knowing he would be naked and covered in naught but water when she came to him. He did not understand his own motives. He did not want to look too deeply into his heart to find them.

He soaked, wanting to wash away the odor of Henley's presence in Dornei. And Adam's. Their arrival had opened wounds barely closed from last night's confession on the marriage bed. He knew only that Isabel was angry with him. She did not seek him out. She thought him in love with Bertrada. Yet she had stood with him as he faced Henley in the bailey. He had not expected such from her, yet, knowing her as he did, he should have expected nothing less. Always she had stood by

240

him and for him, when he had done nothing but endeavor to ignore her for most of their long years together at Malton. Even now, when she had every right to spurn him, she had come when he had beckoned. And now she stood within their chamber, her eyes flashing her anger and her rejection.

Would that he could ignore her anger.

"Edmund!" she said, targeting him for her outburst, ignoring Richard. For the moment. "What was in your mind that you would attack a guest of this house and without provocation? For no matter what Ulrich said to offend you in the bailey, I know he would not have prompted anything but a smile from the stoniest heart."

"Lady," Edmund said, his eyes beseeching, his hands clasped, "I did not think—"

"That has been well documented," she cut in, "by all within Dornei."

"Hold, Isabel," Richard said, pinning her with his dark eyes. "Leave off. The boy has answered for his deeds. All has been dealt with. Say no more to him. A boys' fight, nothing more."

Nothing more? When swords had been drawn and blood sought and eyes alight with battle lust? For such she had seen, even from her perch within this very room. But she was to say no more about it, when it concerned Edmund, whom she trusted as a brother, because the Lord of Dornei and Warefeld had commanded her silence? Richard's high-handedness was intolerable. But she would say no more, not now, when it would impair Richard's credibility with those he must command; in front of Edmund, she would say nothing. To Edmund, she would say nothing more about the fight; she could acknowledge that Richard had dealt well with the matter, if only in her heart. From her lips, he would hear nothing. Would that she never had to speak to him again.

Would that he would not lie about so languidly in his tub.

She had seen little on their conjugal night; the night had been dark and her eyes had been tight with tears. Now she could see all clearly.

He looked nothing like a monk.

His arms were chiseled with muscle, his thick veins prominent, even in repose. The column of his throat was long and supple, the shading of his shaven beard a dark outline of pure masculinity that traced its way down to a lightly furred chest. His chest was broad and muscular, his stomach banded by lines of muscle that pushed at the water when he shifted his weight to sit straighter in his tub. Yea, he was lean, but not in the way of a monk. He was warrior lean and hard, battle-ready, and eager to fight. This was the Richard she remembered. This was the man she had sought as her own.

Before she had known of Bertrada.

Before she had understood the lie of his kiss.

She looked into his eyes, forcing herself to look away from his stern masculinity. He stared back at her, his eyes so dark and rich a blue that she wished to tumble into their depths. Until she killed the thought. She would not be the fool for Richard again. She would leave girlish dreams and fancies behind, in her girlhood, where they would stay. She was a woman now, and a woman knew her duty.

"Leave us, Edmund," she said, and in the same moment, Richard commanded, "Be gone, boy."

Edmund left, so obvious in his eagerness to be quit of the tensions in the chamber so clearly respectful of Richard as to be deeply irritating to Isabel. When had Richard become so firmly Lord of Dornei that even Edmund had abandoned his attachment to her to fasten it on the monk who stood head over them all?

But Richard was no monk. Had she not noted it? He was less the monk each day and more the warrior he had trained to be. Why, then, was she so miserable?

Bertrada.

How easily the answer rose within her.

With the closing of the chamber door, Isabel's eyes focused again on Richard. She could not stop looking at him, it seemed. And cursed herself for her folly.

He leaned back against the wooden tub, the planes of his face sharp and clear in the afternoon light, his eyes like sapphires against the ivory of his complexion. Such beauty in a man was . . . compelling. Sinfully so. Had those hands, which now were so lazily draped over the rim of the tub, held her thighs apart with such gentle force? Had that mouth kissed her throat, seeking her pulse with its moist heat? Had he truly thrust his member, so large and firm beneath the thin veil of water, into her, making her his? Was she his?

Isabel swallowed heavily and closed her eyes against the sight of him. She had lived in a dream world for most of her remembering, constructed out of memories and plans and tiny bits of contact with Richard. She did not want to live there any longer. It was a child's game. She was a child no longer.

Was she his?

Nay, he was Bertrada's.

She had a husband who did not want her.

She had a husband who did all out of a sense of duty.

Richard's sense of duty had shaped his life, even when a young squire. Such could not be said of her. She lived on impulse, she could see that now, but Richard had the right of it. A man's days on earth were allotted, and each man must do as God directed; she would do her duty as Lady of Dornei and she would ignore the ache in her heart at dreams both realized and lost.

Duty was a splendid shield against pain.

"Isabel, we must speak. There is much I would say," Richard said.

She forced herself to look upon her husband. Yea, he was a man to make a woman dream, but dreaming was not part of her duty.

"Speak, then. I will not hinder you," she said, her expression calm. Her eyes, her incredible, translucent eyes, were shuttered.

He could not read what was in her, and always,

always, he had been able to read her eyes.

He did not know this Isabel.

How could Isabel be so calm, so composed, when he was naked and in the same room with her? 'Twas not possible. Should she not be agitated and distracted in even the smallest degree, as was he?

He had taken her, made her his own, on the bed behind her. He had cupped her breast, her ivory breast, in his hand just hours ago. He had kissed her throat, feeling the heat and life of her pulse beneath his lips. He had laid his hands upon her thighs, preparing her to accept him into her body.

But she had not been prepared.

Therein lay his answer. Or part of it. He had assaulted her body, shattered her dreams of girlhood love, and revealed to her a sin which shamed him every hour of his life. A heavy burden he had laid upon her. That she did not publicly revile him showed the mercy and generosity of her character. That she had shuttered her heart against him he understood. But he could not allow it to stand. He wanted access to Isabel's mind and heart. He needed it. His brief conversation with Rowland had opened a door he had not known existed; he wanted Isabel in his life. He wanted her regard, her attention, her everything.

He wanted her.

He did not know how to get her.

He and Isabel had shared a bond of intimacy from their first meeting. In all of Malton, she alone had been able to make him laugh. She alone had sought out his company. She alone had listened to the whispers of his heart. He did not know what he had done to win her regard, and so he did not know what to do to regain it. In all his experience, he had only to breathe to have Isabel.

For once, it was not enough.

He did not know where to begin. He was not a man of courtly words and compliments. He did not know how to flatter. He knew how to fight and he knew how to pray. Such were not skills which won a lady. He did not imagine they were suited to win a wife.

But he would try.

"I would thank you," he began. It was always good to begin by giving thanks. Even prayers began in such a way. "I would thank you for so efficiently hosting our guests. For so many unexpected guests, you have provided well. I did not know you so capable."

The Isabel he had known from childhood would have flared at the implied insult. The Isabel who faced him now did not. He would welcome, happily, any response from her, even anger.

"I did nothing beyond my duty as Lady of Dornei. I seek no praise for it," she answered stiffly.

At that, he had exhausted his efforts at flattery. He did not know how to interact with this strange new Isabel. The atmosphere within Dornei was strained enough with the arrival of Henley and his veiled accusations; he did not want Isabel suddenly to be less than he knew her to be. Where was his impulsive, infatuated girl? Mayhap, if he pressed her into closer proximity, she would tumble into the Isabel of yesterday.

"Since we have dismissed Edmund, would you . . . ?" and he held the square of linen out for her to take.

"Would I . . . ?" she said softly, her eyes round and still.

"Wash my back?" he said as innocently as he knew how.

To her credit, she only paused for a moment before grabbing the linen from him and attacking it with a sliver of soap. She did not need to know that Edmund had already washed him thoroughly. Surely, with her hands upon him, she would feel *some* response to him? It would be so, he consoled himself as he leaned forward in the tub. Isabel had little experience at resisting him; surely she would fail before long.

She did not.

She scrubbed the length and breadth of his back, and his buttocks besides, with all the dispatch of a serf. Very efficient. Not at all intimate.

He was badly shaken by the experience. More so because her hands upon him, neither slowed by passion nor frantic in seeking passion's release, caused desire to pulse within him. He quaked, and he did so alone.

Was she truly so cold to him? Had all her feeling for him died?

True, she had experienced no pleasure in their coupling, but few virgins did. The darker possibility was that she could not forgive his sin with Bertrada.

She had been shocked by his confession, as was right, but he had, he realized now, expected her devotion to him to remain unchanged, no matter what sins he had committed. Such was the surety he placed on her feelings for him. He had been wrong, and he could add the sin of pride to his growing list of divine offenses.

But, no matter what wounds he had inflicted upon himself, he had hurt Isabel beyond bearing in allowing her to believe that he had joined the brotherhood to escape Bertrada and his illicit love for her. Worse, that he loved Bertrada still. Such knowledge would weigh heavily on a woman, and he could not allow her to bear such an ill-conceived burden. He would have to speak of Bertrada, as much as he hated doing so.

Isabel was leaning over him, her hair curling with the moist heat of the bath, her face intent on her duty and devoid of any emotions he could read. He must speak. He must tell her all and of how wrong she was to assign love to his involvement with Bertrada.

But he could not speak, not when she was so close, not when she was touching him. Her hands were so small and white, the skin of her cheek so smooth, her lips so red; she was a beauty, desired by all who knew her. Her smile was ready and quick, her laughter light and musical. When had she last laughed? Surely not since becoming a bride. All she had wanted was him, and all he had done was wound her. He was not a man for any woman to want, yet all he wanted now was for her to want him.

He was hard for her, and he closed his eyes against the desire hot and heavy within him. He would not act on his desire when she did not want him. He would not force her. He would never force her again.

He would only try to force her to desire him.

Yet he did not know how.

He had to speak; he had to free her of the lie of his loving Bertrada. He would look the worse for it, but it did not signify. Isabel must be free of this. And his desire would be denied until she wanted him again.

"I want to tell you about Bertrada," he began. She jerked upright and dropped the linen into the water. "It is not as you—"

"I am not your confessor, Richard. This is between you and God," Isabel said, her eyes fierce. "But if you wish to speak about something, I am eager to talk about the performance of our marital duty on the marriage bed."

Richard could only stare at her in stunned amazement. Did she truly want the intimacy of their bonding again? Mayhap he had misread her—

"I have been told that in order for a child to be conceived," Isabel continued, wiping her hands dry and laying the linen precisely over the bench when she was finished, "I must experience pleasure on the marriage bed." She turned to face him, her arms crossed over her chest and her chin lifted.

Claudia Dain

"I am not certain exactly what is meant by that, but I am certain that it did not happen last night."

Richard gripped the edges of the tub in grim silence.

"I understand that your chosen path lies with the Benedictines. I will not stand in any man's way when he chooses to follow God. Once I am delivered of a healthy child, you are free to return to the abbey, where I am most certain you are eager to be. My duty is to see that the line is ensured, and that is what I intend to do."

She was gone, her dignity intact to the last, before he could manage breath to stop her.

He was not entirely certain what he could have said to stop her. In the cooling waters of his bath, he had shrunk to the size of his thumb.

Chapter Twenty-four

As soon as he was dressed, the wool of his tunic clinging to his wet back, Richard sought out Father Langfrid. The good Father was in the town, visiting the goldsmith, whose wife had died of a winter fever. The man, Edward, had three small children and was prayerfully considering a new wife. Father Langfrid was disposed to gently guide him toward the widow of the armorer's assistant, or so it seemed to Richard as he came upon them.

"She is a kind soul who had her husband's high regard," Langfrid said.

"But she is older than I by some years," Edward said.

"And do you think your children will mark the difference?" Langfrid replied. "As to that, you cannot tell me she is not a comely woman. She bears her years lightly."

"I will not deny it," Edward said.

"Especially to his priest," Richard said with a wry smile.

"My lord," Edward bowed in greeting. "If you have need of any work, I am here. My workmanship is skilled and my shop profitable."

"And you are not modest," Richard said.

"I am only truthful," Edward responded.

"And skilled," Richard teased.

"And skilled," Edward smiled.

"I do have need of you," Richard said on impulse. "But now I have come seeking my priest. If you will come with me, Father? I will return and will return Father Langfrid to you, if you are eager to be convinced of a bride."

Father Langfrid and Richard moved off, walking the single street of the town merchants. There was no privacy, but Richard did not want to wait, the question was so hot on his tongue. Taking the Father by the arm, Richard edged toward the pond that bordered the brewer's hut.

"What is it, my lord?" Father Langfrid asked, a trifle winded by their pace.

"It is Isabel. Something has happened to Isabel. She has changed," Richard said in a low voice, though even he could hear his urgency and commanded himself to serenity. The Brothers in the abbey would smile to hear him so distraught, he who had always displayed such self-control. Women were a man's most arduous test in this life.

"The only thing that has happened to Isabel is that she has married," Langfrid said.

A hard answer. The only conclusion Richard could draw was that he himself was the one who was responsible for the change. It was an unpleasant conclusion. He wanted another.

"Yea, she is married, as am I," Richard said. "Yet she has come to me," he said reluctantly, "with . . . a plan . . . the idea that . . . she . . . we . . . have not met the requirements for conception."

"Ah," Langfrid said with a smile, "so she did come to you. I am well pleased. I instructed her to go to you with her questions, knowing you would have the answers."

Richard could only stare at him blankly.

"Is it not well that Isabel is so resolved to do her duty?" Langfrid said with a toothsome smile.

Richard found the idea of being Isabel's duty less than pleasant, but Langfrid, having never been a husband, would not understand. Richard said nothing in response to his question.

When the sound of their footsteps had faded toward the inner bailey, William and Rowland, who had experience of wives, did understand. And they enjoyed a fine and quiet laugh over their tankards of ale within the brewer's cottage.

"I wish him well. It is not an easy task to train a wife to enjoy the pleasures of the marriage bed when she is determined not to," William said as they left the hut.

"He faces not the same challenge," Rowland said. "Though Lady Isabel carries wounds which only a man can inflict."

"You know something," William stated.

Rowland shrugged. "Only what any man can see. She loves him. According to the gossip, she always has."

"And how would loving a man now her husband wound her?"

"Have you forgotten that she snatched him from the abbey?"

"Aye, I had forgotten. But he seems determined now to be Lord Dornei. In all ways."

"Now," Rowland smiled sadly. "The bedding was last night."

"But they have been married two days . . ."

"As I said, the bedding was last night."

William winced. "That would hurt a woman's heart. And her pride. How did he spend his wedding night? Do not tell me 'in prayer,' for I shall not believe you. She is a fair damsel and would set any man's blood afire."

Rowland remained silent as they climbed the hill back to the tower. The gate was open, the bailey quiet.

William looked askance at Rowland. "He spent the night in prayer?"

"Aye," Rowland answered.

"He is either a fool or the most self-disciplined man I know."

Rowland smiled and said, "I believe he is both."

"And what of Henley?" William asked as they crossed the bailey. "What have you learned of him?"

Rowland's face grew solemn and he dropped his

dark-eyed gaze to his toes. "Henley plays a game with Richard—a foul and unholy game."

William frowned. "Richard is not fond of games."

"It is a game, a courtly game," Ulrich insisted as he polished William's shield. " 'Tis no shame in it."

" 'Twas no game," Edmund said stiffly.

"Not as you played it, no," Ulrich said.

When Edmund looked up from his own polishing of Richard's helm, his eyes dark with anger, Ulrich laughed and punched him in the arm.

"All men and women play this game, 'tis no sin," Ulrich said. "You must not make it more than what it is."

" 'Twas she who made it something," Edmund grumbled.

"You are betrothed?" Ulrich asked. "As is she?"

"Aye."

"Then what more can it be?" Ulrich grinned. "You are promised. What words and looks are shared within Dornei's walls remain here. No one is harmed."

"If all know 'tis a game," Edmund said slowly in comprehension.

"Aye," Ulrich said cheerfully. " 'Tis a fine way to spend an afternoon, I can assure you."

He winked.

"And how does your lord look upon your activities?"

"Why, my Lord William," Ulrich said with heavy pride, "was master of this game before he wed, and now he plays the same with his wife. They are most happy."

"He plays at love with his wife?" Edmund said, forgetting his polishing completely for the moment. "I cannot see the purpose in that. I am certain Lord Richard would frown on such frivolity."

"Well," Ulrich shrugged, continuing his polishing, "your lord was recently a Benedictine. My Lord William is French."

"Ah," Edmund said. It answered all.

" 'Twas a game to me, that is all," Aelis said.

"No game has such consequences," Elsbeth said.

The two stood together in a corner of the hall, arranging flowers in a terra-cotta urn. The sun shone through the wind hole, bringing with it a fresh breeze full of the smells of damp and fertile earth, rain, and early blossoms. 'Twas a happy smell after the long cold of winter which smelled only of wood smoke and sweat and melting snow. The two girls made a striking pair, if any cared to look, one so fair and one so dark, one full and lush, the other slim and fragile. Yet Elsbeth was not fragile. There was a hard core to her that few bothered to see. Aelis knew that, of the two of them, she was the more easily bruised, no matter that she was the bold one. She was bruised now, still hurting and confused after the afternoon's unexpected battle. That she had been the cause still shocked her.

"Nay, but—"

"But?" Elsbeth said in disapproval.

"But it was so nice when it was just a game,"

Aelis said wistfully. "Edmund is young and his looks are so fine. And he rides with such style. And who else is there for me here? Gilles?" she snorted.

"There is your own betrothed," Elsbeth scolded. "Think you Lord Ivo would be cheered knowing you cavort with Edmund while he waits for your maturing before making you his bride?"

"I am not cavorting."

"You will call it what you will," Elsbeth said, snapping a blossom off in her irritation, "but it is not seemly. Nor is it wise. Where is your contrition?"

"I am contrite," Aelis said. "But I am also bored. How wrong can it be to trade looks with Edmund?"

"You saw how wrong it was this afternoon. Would you have him killed to ease your boredom?"

"Nay," she said. But she said it with less conviction than she had an hour before.

"What of your duty?"

"I will do my duty. I will marry Lord Ivo when the time is upon me," Aelis said stoutly, and then with a tentative smile she remarked, "But it is not upon me yet."

Isabel walked the rooms of Dornei, checking for dust, rodents, mildew, and fresh linen; never again would she assume that all was well and well attended within her domain. The servants needed constant watching, even with Robert in his post as steward. The man could only be in so many places, and his primary concerns lay with the food and its presentation. The general condition of Dornei fell to her; she was Lady of Dornei and it was both her right and her duty.

Fairly certain that no more questions regarding the details of the marriage bed would be forced upon her, Joan walked at her side, suddenly eager for conversation.

"You are busy today, Isabel," she said. "Marriage seems to have changed you."

"I would say that I am fully prepared to meet my duty as Lady of Dornei," Isabel said, bending to check under the bed in Lord William's room. There was no dust, but there was a gauntlet. His, it was to be assumed, and therefore Ulrich's responsibility.

Joan laughed easily as Isabel left the chamber, closing the door behind her. "There is a duty that I remember most fondly from my own married state."

"What duty is that?" Isabel asked, walking toward the stair tower where a small pile of dirt had been pushed into a corner. Unacceptable.

"Very amusing, my dear," Joan chuckled. "Richard is very handsome, as you well know, and your lifelong attraction is no secret, as well as being no mystery. What a waste it was when he joined the Benedictines. I tell you, many a woman sighed in anguish over that decision. 'Twas a loss to us all, such a man clothed in abbey cloth, hidden away from appreciative eyes. I do not have to belabor the point with you, Isabel. You have a fine man as husband. I am certain you must thank God every hour that you are compelled to perform your marital duty with such a man."

Isabel was scarlet by the conclusion of such a confidence. She had preferred Joan when she had been awkwardly silent; this level of confession was impossible to tolerate. Why did people suddenly seem to think they needed to bare their souls to her?

"I do not," she said. "I do not find any joy in that duty."

"Spoken like a bride," Joan said, giving her a quick hug. "I had forgotten. With Richard's diligence, that will change, my dear. And soon, I think."

Isabel did not think it would, not soon, not ever. She could hear again Richard's strong and determined voice repeating, *I do not want to touch you. I do not want to kiss you.* Nay, she was not eager to endure that ordeal again.

Not when she still wanted his touch and ached for the passion of that long-ago kiss, desires which rose despite her resolve not to be caught in the lie of Richard again. How to keep her heart and her pride intact when he preyed upon the desire for him that lived still in her memory?

Oh, aye, bathing him had been the worst torture he could have devised. He likely did it apurpose. He knew how he looked. He knew she had yearned for him for a lifetime. He knew that he could command her to touch him, to run her hands over his skin, to feel the tight and taut strength of him, and that she must. But she could not command him to touch her in tenderness. She could not command his heart to want her. She could not make him love her.

Three years.

She could not. She could not endure three years of his nightly possession and his daily presence when he gave her no part of himself. Worse, he gave his heart and his desire and his dreaming to another.

Endure it she could not, yet she wanted a child. Only Richard could give her one.

Rushing down the stair tower, leaving Joan behind her, Isabel tried to ignore the low slanting of the sun's rays. Endure it again? She must. Dusk was fast upon her.

She would not endure it waiting, waiting for the sun to creep down the sky, waiting for the birds to fly to their nests, for the dogs to curl upon the hearth, the men to sit and game before the crackling fire. She would not wait. She had her duty to occupy her.

What duty awaited her now?

Richard always seemed busy about some task. Surely there were tasks which depended upon the Lady of Dornei; the hall was clean, the laundry fresh, the tapestries beaten. Yet the menu awaited. Isabel sighed happily, her duty discovered. The menu for tomorrow must be planned today, the spices sorted and chosen, the meat prepared, the dough set to rise. Yea, much called to her from the kitchen; she had her duty before her.

With a sprightly step, she made her way down

the stair into the dark recesses of the undercroft. The spices were stored here under lock and key, and the Lady of Dornei held the key. She jangled them in her fist, enjoying the heavy ringing; they were the sign of her authority over her domain. She alone would unlock the chest that stored such flavorful treasure. She would carry up what was needed for tomorrow's meal. Let Richard read his accounts; she was in charge of the larder. No longer would she unrepentantly pass the duty on to Joan, who had taken it when Lady Ida died; it was her duty and she would perform it.

In the still and quiet undercroft, lined with trunks of fabric and spice, she gazed about her. She had played here as a child, an act of daring, for it was a forbidden place to any who did not have the authority to trespass here. A dark place, which swallowed the feeble light of the torch she carried as it swallowed sound. All was subdued, the sounds without coming as if from a far distance, muffled by dirt and stone.

Isabel shook off her mood and placed the torch in a ring set into the stone. She had the authority to be here. She was Lady of Dornei.

For so many guests, both welcome and unwelcome, a fine table must be prepared. Capon with eggs would suit, and it required saffron, sea salt, pepper, cinnamon, ginger, and cloves. And for the creamed fish, saffron and ginger as well. Chicken pasties were a favorite of hers, and she added more ginger and black pepper to her mental list. It was the season for spring greens, and she liked them best without seasoning.

She did not know why she had put off this duty. It was most pleasurable. Isabel loved a hearty meal as well as the next, and planning what savories she would put in her mouth tomorrow was a thrill. Having made her choices, she proceeded to collect them. 'Twas not a great task; the spices were delicately packaged in small sacks, her mother's invention to prevent spoilage from damaging the lot, and one which had become Dornei tradition. She was turning to take her torch when she gasped and took an involuntary step backward.

She was not alone.

Adam awaited her, a smile on his lips. He stood with his arms crossed over his chest, blocking the stair, trapping her.

Trapping her? It was a foolish thought birthed by her childhood fear of the undercroft. There was nothing to fear from Adam. In truth, *he* should fear *her*; had he not disobeyed her instruction to go to Braccan? She could feel her irritation rise just looking at him, him so confident and handsome and nonchalant. Richard never had the bad taste to look so . . . so condescending.

"Why are you angry, Isabel?" Adam asked, uncrossing his arms and coming toward her. "Because I am here or because I left?"

Such arrogance; Richard might be proud, but he was never arrogant.

"Richard cast you out of Dornei. You should not be within Dornei walls now," she said, clutching her bags to her breast and lifting her chin decisively.

"But what do you want, Isabel? You are the Lady of Dornei."

No matter how great the chasm between herself and Richard, she would not suffer Adam's clumsy attempts to wedge the gap wider. Moving to retrieve the torch, she answered, "I want what my husband wants. He has said you are not welcome in Dornei. Heed him. You are not."

Adam only smiled, his smile as wide as his obvious disbelief, and blocked her approach to the torch. Very well, she would leave it and send Robert down for it later. She had not forgotten Adam's amorous attack nor the insult such liberties implied; she did not want to remain in the most isolated part of the tower with him for a moment longer. When she darted toward the stair, he stalked her, stopping her, trapping her.

Aye, she was trapped. She could call it what it was. Had she ever thought Adam charming? She could not remember. Was she afraid? Nay, but her anger grew with each affront to her person and her dignity. This was not a game she cared to play.

"Come, Isabel." He smiled, the torch lighting his hair to amber red, his pale eyes like pearls in the flickering light. "Come and let me show you what you truly want."

Before she could respond, he grabbed for her and she dropped a bag or two of spice upon the widely spaced stones of the undercroft. His arms encircled her as if in play; but it was not play. There was nothing charming about being touched against her will.

"Leave me!" she commanded, her anger high and bright, impossible to miss even in the flickering shadows. "You know not your place, and you clearly know not mine."

He pressed her against him, his hands hard upon her back, his breath in her face. The smell of him was repellent. Another bag tumbled over her arms and to the ground.

"I know more than my place," he said, his voice soft and urgent, his hands roving. "I know how you must ache for a true man to teach you the meaning of passion. All here know that your one night with Brother Richard was memorable for all the wrong reasons."

"Release me," she hissed, struggling against him, dropping all the bags willingly so that she could push against him.

"A man more monk than man would not know how to bring a woman to her pleasure. I am no monk, Isabel. I can make you scream for release."

"I am screaming now," she whispered.

But she was not. She could not. Fear had her trapped, and she could not see a way to freedom. He had her, his arms and hands everywhere, his mouth upon her, wet and open, touching her where she did not want to be touched. Doing things she did not want done. And none to help her.

None knew where she was.

None would hear if she screamed.

Yet she could not scream, she could only fight in silence, losing with every moment that passed, with every unlawful touch upon her body.

And the thought that held her captive above all his hands could accomplish: Did he think her willing? Had she somehow invited this attack?

His mouth covered hers, his tongue hard against her teeth and his hands hard upon her breasts.

Nay, 'twas too much. No man could think a woman would invite this.

The keys were still in her hand and she swung them against his face, thinking of nothing but driving him from her. The red of contact rose quickly on his fair skin and he lost his smile. He did not release her.

Grabbing the keys and throwing them across the room, he snagged both her hands and held them above her head. He had lost his smile, she could see. He did not think she wanted this; 'twas he who wanted it. And he would stop at nothing to get what he had set his hand to.

This was no game.

With a snarl, she kicked him hard and felt the joyful thud of bone against her foot.

In the next instant, her breath was gone as he knocked her down to fall on her back, the stones driving the air from her lungs.

He was all she could see, his form blocking even the struggling light of the torch. She could not breathe. She could not move.

He moved.

His head was jerked back by some unseen force,

his throat exposed and white in the dim light. She saw the dagger slice its way across, leaving first a dark red line and then a gap as wide as the sky, opening, spilling blood, pumping blood, out, out, a flood of red to cover her.

And then she saw Richard.

Dark he was in the darkened room, dark and glorious, his face stern and set and unrepentant, his dagger red and wet. He reached for her, but she could not reach back, though she wanted to. All she could see was blood, blood covering the stones, covering the bags of spices, running across the floor in trails which grew ever wider, like a stream in flood.

"Isabel!" he said, his voice an echo from afar. "Are you harmed?"

The blood slowed, the pumping stilled from the wedge in Adam's neck. And yet the blood looked to fill the room.

"Isabel," Richard said, taking her in his arms, cradling her, pressing her head against the warm and solid mass of his chest. "Speak! Did he hurt you?"

Hurt? She was not hurt. She was covered in blood, the spices ruined, her keys lost.

All was broken.

"Nay," she said, her voice a tremble which came from the center of her to shake her soul.

She could not hear the weight of unshed tears in her words. Richard could.

He carried her in his arms, her weight light as down, her trembling the heaviest thing about her. He carried her to their chamber, a place familiar to her, a place of safety. She was safe now. She must know she was safe.

William and Rowland met him there, their swords unsheathed, their faces determined.

"Watch her," Richard commanded. "I have more yet to do."

"With a will," William answered.

Richard was already turning away. He had laid Isabel upon their bed and covered her with a thick marten fur. She trembled still, curled in a ball so tight she could scarce draw breath. But he must leave her for now, for danger still awaited in Dornei.

Rowland followed him, a silent wraith of vengeance. They shared a look of dark intent and then rushed down to the undercroft. It was full of the silence of death. Without hesitation, Richard hacked the head from Adam's white and lifeless body. Lifting the head by the shimmering auburn hair, he mounted the stair swiftly.

A crowd was gathering, clustered in the bailey, pressed into the tower stair, shuffling into the hall. They massed to see the gruesome sight and were more haunted by the memory of Richard's grim visage.

Here was no monk.

Richard paid them no heed. He strode with his prize into the hall. Henley was playing chess with one of Malton's knights, and both watched Richard approach, their faces expressionless. No thoughts of Bertrada intruded, no pain at facing his sin, no fear at receiving well-deserved judgment at Hen-

ley's hands—all washed away in a tide of blood by
his need to protect Isabel. All Richard could see
when he faced Henley was Isabel and her mute
struggle not to be defiled.

Richard tossed the head to roll and land at Henley's feet.

Henley jumped out of the way.

"You brought this dog into my domain, against
my express will," Richard said, his voice heavy and
strong. "He laid hands upon my wife. Death was
his payment. So it will be for any man who harms
Isabel. Take what is left of him and leave. Now."

Rowland stood at his back, in all ways backing
him. Yet it was not necessary. Henley had no desire
to fight, and if he had, Richard was more than a
match for him. This all knew who stood within the
hall. Richard was an adversary who had faced his
demons daily; such a warrior had little fear left in
him, and, in truth, his strength had grown mighty
in his battles against the unseen forces of darkness.

Henley looked at the head with its bloody and
ragged stump and then at Richard's face. Without
a word, he left the hall, his knights following him.

"I will escort him to the gate," Rowland said.
"Your lady needs you."

Richard nodded his thanks, breathing deeply,
forcing himself to calm. He would have killed Henley gladly, given the need. Gladly and without a
prayer for forgiveness. How far he had come from
the Benedictine brotherhood. The knowledge
brought him no pain, no loss. He was no monk.

But that was past; Isabel needed him now. Rowland had the right of it.

Once again, he mounted the stair, seeking out his wife. When had he ever approached his prayers with such eagerness and urgency? William stood with his back to the open door of their chamber; beyond, Richard could see Isabel staring out the wind hole, her fingers white on the stone ledge.

"She did not want to be alone," William said softly in explanation of the open door.

Richard did no more than nod, dismissing William of Greneforde; his thoughts were all for his wife.

"Isabel," he said, her name as sweet on his tongue as the Eucharist.

She turned to him at once, and the tears which she had held in such rigid check burst forth. Silently they fell, as she was always silent in her distress. This he knew of her; he knew so much of her.

She was covered in blood, as was he. It smeared her hair and stained her gown and covered her hands and face. It mattered not.

She rushed into his outstretched arms, burying her face against his chest, her sobs echoing within his heart.

Isabel.

He lifted her against him, rejoicing in the feel of her against his length, reveling in the comfort of just feeling her breathe, the ecstasy of the solid pounding of her heart against his chest. She was alive. Alive, whole, and unharmed.

The rushing joy he felt covered him as naturally

as a cloud covers the sun; it was familiar, this joy in her. Familiar and natural. He had cast her from him, this woman who knew every corner of his heart. He had been a fool. He had listened to the taunts of Nicholas and the others, shamed that a girl betrothed to his house was his only friend, shamed and convinced that by his affection, his need for her, he committed an act unpure. And so he had shunned her, leaving her bewildered and hungry for his presence and leaving himself alone. In all of Malton—nay, in all of his life—there had been only Isabel.

And that thought, that unexpected knowledge, made the breath catch in his chest.

Chapter Twenty-five

It was with no great surprise that Richard watched the bath being delivered to the lord's chamber. William still stood at their door and directed the tub inside.

"I told you that you were not needed," Richard said to him as the tub was carried in.

"You told me nothing. You nodded your head at me, in greeting, I surmised," William answered. "I arranged for a bath, to soothe and cleanse."

"Your answer to all occasions, it seems," Richard said a trifle stiffly.

"In this, it will serve you well," William said seriously, drawing Richard close. "Your lady needs to wash this event from her body and from her mind. Let her be clean again. 'Twill heal her, washing away her guilt."

Richard studied William, looking deep into his

silver-gray eyes; he shielded much pain behind light words and banter. And perhaps there was wisdom in that.

"She is guilty of nothing," Richard said.

William smiled. "Well said, Lord Richard of Dornei, and true. But a woman's mind runs not straight, but winds like a hare on the run from a hawk. Such confusion must be eased out of her, gently and tenderly."

"With bathwater?" Richard said on a smile.

William shrugged elegantly. "To be clean is never a hindrance."

"Nay, it is not," Richard agreed. "And for Isabel I have only tenderness. Your words on this were not needed, but appreciated."

William smiled and clasped him on the arm, hard, before turning away. "And the bath?"

"Appreciated."

"And needed, for my nose never betrays." He sniffed comically, walking off.

Joan passed Richard, brushing by him in her hurry to comfort Isabel, who sat upon the center of their bed, shaking, silent. The tub was steaming, the special packet of Flanders soap given to them by Lord William added to the water, and Joan, talking nonsense to fill the air with her own style of comfort, undressed Isabel.

Rowland came up the stair, his cloak flowing out behind him with the regal silence of flight. Richard closed the door upon the sight of his Isabel and turned to face Rowland.

"Henley is gone. His men with him," Rowland

said. "Gone without a whimper or a backward glance."

"You expected more?"

"For a man who struggled so to gain entrance, he did not struggle so upon leaving."

"You understand not the man," Richard said. "Henley charges forcefully upon the field when certain of victory. With the possibility of failure, he is just as quick to leave it."

Richard could see the question, the logic, as it played out in the shadows of Rowland's black eyes, but he possessed too much chivalry to voice his thoughts. But the logic was clear: Why had Henley been so certain of victory in entering Dornei? Because he had been certain of Richard.

Henley had always and ever been certain of Richard.

Through the heavy door, Richard heard a smothered sob, and he turned at once to join his wife, leaving all thought of Rowland and Henley behind him.

Isabel was staring at the blood-soaked bliaut Joan had just removed from her, her eyes wide with fear and dismay.

" 'Tis naught, Isabel," Joan said, holding the cloth in her hands for Isabel to see.

In two steps, Richard snatched the gown from Joan's hands and threw it out of the wind hole.

" 'Tis gone, Isabel," he said.

Isabel looked at him, her eyes wide.

She was stripped of her clothing, her skin cloud-pale, her wrists bruised where Adam had mauled her, her face still streaked with blood; yet she was whole.

"Come, Isabel, come and wash. Do you not wish to be clean?" he asked.

She stared out of the wind hole and said on a whisper, "I wish to fly away."

"Without me?" he asked, and then cursed himself for such vulnerability displayed for Joan to see. But Joan had left them. The door was closed firmly. They were alone.

He wanted her. Even now, when she was bruised and bloodied and lost in terror, he wanted her. More than wanted, needed. And she wanted to leave him.

"You flew away," she said, her hair wet and sticky, molded to her skull. She looked like a new-hatched chick, fragile and damp. "You flew away and left me."

"I am here, Isabel," he said, wrapping his arms around her, lifting her into the bath.

"Now," she accused softly.

"Always," he promised.

The word caressed her, and she wanted to nest in its comfort. Would that it were so, but she knew that it was not. She was no fool. Richard was worried; he would say anything to give her rest. He would not stay. He could not be a Benedictine Brother in Dornei.

She allowed him to bathe her, his hands gentle and slow, the soap sweet and soothing. The heat of the bath penetrated her bones, forcing out the chill of Adam's touch and the cold terror of his attack.

Had she caused it?

The thought would not leave her.

Perhaps she was just like Aelis. Perhaps she drove men to violence. Perhaps she was responsible for his death.

Richard was thorough in his washing. Her arms and hands he touched, finger by finger, joint by joint. Her legs and feet he massaged with soapy water, the linen soft and slick. Her hair he washed, his hands tender as he rubbed her scalp, forcing the blood to relinquish its hold on her. All done as lovingly as a father to a child or a monk to a penitent. 'Twas no husband who washed her so.

He wanted her so badly that he fair shook with passion. Nay, 'twas more than passion, it was a tide of need, longing, and gratitude which washed over him as surely as water washed Isabel clean of all memory of Adam's foul attack. Isabel was whole and safe; 'twas all that mattered to him. He thanked God that he had sought and found her when he had. And he prayed to God that he would not harm his wife by showing his desire for her when she plainly did not want him, not as a man. She needed his strength and his protection; his desire for her was a burden she had shaken off last night on their marriage bed.

Lifting her from the tub like a child, he dried her with a length of linen. She stood still, unresisting, unresponsive. Docile, as Isabel surely never was.

Once dried, she hopped upon the bed and cov-

ered herself with furs. Yet still she trembled. It tore
a hole in his heart to see his wild, bright Isabel so
chained by fear.

He stripped off his own bloody garments and
tossed them out the wind hole to land where they
would. Isabel followed the action with her eyes,
and then kept her eyes upon him as he sank into
the water she had so recently vacated. 'Twas cooling, and he hurried about his task. He would be
washed of all sign of his killing before he touched
her again. A symbol only; he felt no remorse for
killing Adam. And he felt no guilt for his lack of
remorse. Protecting Isabel was his only goal, and
he had succeeded, by bare moments. He had almost failed her.

Never again.

"We will have no clothing left if you keep throwing it out the wind hole," she said with a hesitant
smile.

"Is not Dornei prosperous?" He smiled back.

"Yea, but only because we wear our clothing
more than once." Her gaze dropped to her lap, and
she said tonelessly, "That gown was once my
mother's."

"I am sorry, Isabel," he said softly, his eyes
searching hers. "My mother had many gowns
which would please you. When we ride to Warefeld, they are yours."

She nodded her reply.

She could read the desire in his eyes, and her
trembling increased. He had looked just so when

he had kissed her that long-ago time. Perhaps that kiss, that one kiss, had not been a lie.

No matter. She did not want to want him, not as she had; it hurt too deeply when Richard changed his mind and changed his life.

She did not trust him. She did not dare. With her life, yea, and with the keeping of Dornei, possibly. But with her heart? Nay, she would not trust him with her heart.

He had looked at her once before as he was looking at her now, his blue eyes deep as dusk and as shining as the stars. His brows slashed low and dark, his lips full and tight against his teeth—it was the look of a man trapped in the chains of desire. Once before, she had seen such a look on Richard's face and she had believed what she would never believe again: that Richard loved her. Men could battle desire and lose without once touching love; Richard and Adam together had taught her that.

Richard rose from the water hard and ready, his body revealing the depth of his desire. His dark eyes were as hot with passion as she was certain hers were cold with caution. He walked to the bed without even drying himself, the water running from his hard body, rivulets that ran together to catch in the hair on his chest and belly and thighs. His eyes dominated the room, his cheekbones sharp on his face, and his mouth relaxed; he was coming for her, to her, wet and hard, dark and lean, no matter that she trembled on the bed.

He could not know that she trembled for him.

277

The sun was just setting, a gentle sunset of pink and yellow, the low-slung clouds purple-gray and hovering over the treetops. Even in so faint a light, she could read the ardor in his eyes. Always desire and never love. Guilt would follow hard on passion's heels, and then he would reject her. She had only to remember that single kiss to know what would happen between them tomorrow.

"Isabel," he said, leaning over her, his skin shining and moist, the scent of soap sweet and fresh. His hair was slicked back from his face, black and gleaming, the ends dripping onto his shoulders . . . and onto her. "I want you," he breathed, as if speaking it would make it so.

She could not speak. It was as if he had stolen all the air from the room and left her none. His body was so hot, she could feel waves of heat rolling off him, drying him more quickly than any cloth. She resisted the urge to touch him, to feel the coolness of water being burned away by his heat. He would burn her.

She could not look into his eyes. She would lose all if she stared into his heart. She looked instead at a slender thread of water making its hurried way down his furred chest, over his heartbeat, into the hair of his groin, where it was lost, consumed.

Never again.

She could not do this. Not for three years. Not for a night.

"I need you," he said, his voice hoarse with emotion.

Desire only. Not love. He needed her? Nay, he

needed a woman. Tomorrow he would run from her, as he had before.

Yet what did she need? A child. She needed a child. For tomorrow and tomorrow and tomorrow, she needed a child. Richard was the means. If she could only remember that, if she could do her duty in that, to give Dornei a child to feed its legacy, she would be free of this agony. She would be free of him.

"Take me," she said, closing her eyes against the sight of him.

She would submit to him; it was her marital duty, but she was not commanded to open her heart to the pain he would leave in passion's wake.

It would not be difficult; he would be quick and furtive, guilt goading him to hurry. She had tasted of his skill last night; she knew what to expect. Men and their maulings were so similar, so predictable.

With his first touch, she knew.

It was nothing like last night.

His hands stroked her face, fingertips exploring the shape and scope of her features. He traced a finger down her nose, around her lips, and to her throat; so gently, so tenderly did he touch her that she shuddered her response. He pulled her to the edge of the bed, just like last night.

Nothing like last night.

She could see the thudding of his heart beneath muscle, the water of his bath gone like morning mist. She closed her eyes and pressed them tight; she would starve her awakening desire by refusing sight of him.

His hands spanned her skull and he kissed her temple, his breath warm and sweet. Nothing like Adam's breath, nothing like Adam's smell. Richard smelled good to her, so good that she yearned to bury her face in his chest and breathe deeply of him. She did not. Her duty did not require it. This bedding was all of duty; she would make it so.

"You are well, Isabel?" he asked, and she could feel his scrutiny of her face through her closed eyes. "This mating will not . . . hurt you?"

He was asking her about Adam, this she understood. But Adam was a dim and fading memory, pushed away by Richard's hands and Richard's look and Richard's scent. All that was left of Adam was the guilt she felt. Richard was so much more than Adam.

Yet she would not admit it to him.

"Nay," she said, forcing herself to look at him, forcing herself to keep her eyes cold and her manner dignified. "You may proceed. I am ready."

Richard's eyes were so dark, so full of pain and passion, that she looked away quickly before she was undone.

"Nay," he breathed, "you are far from ready. Yet I will take you there."

Fear and anticipation rose within her in equal parts; she did not want to to be taken, not in the way he meant the words. Why could he not simply part her legs and be done with it? What more did duty require?

But Richard was beyond duty.

She was so still, his Isabel, so still and quiet. She

held herself in, like a hooded falcon on a tether, stiff and still and careful. The eagerness and hope she had displayed as a virgin on her marriage bed was gone, replaced by this cold woman who only wanted him to hurry. He had done this to her; he had transformed her.

He would heal her.

He wanted the Isabel she had been, before he had crushed her spirit.

She sat on a pelt of marten fur, her drying hair falling around her slender nudity. Never had she looked more fragile or more desirable. Never had she been so unreadable. Yet even in that, she spoke volumes; Isabel had barred the gate against him. Always she had been as open as the sky at midday, sparkling, sunny, warm. Now she was night—dark, cold, and mysterious.

Yea, he did not know how to read this Isabel, yet the night held its own pleasures, the night hosted the stars, familiar and bright. He would learn Isabel in all her moods, be they light or dark, and he would find his way. He would not lose her.

Not again.

Not any more than he already had.

She would not even look at him.

Very well, then he would reach her by touch and touch alone. God willing, he would succeed.

He ran a hand over the length of her hair, so dark and smooth, still damp from her bathing. He lifted the mass of her heavy hair from the base of her neck and fanned it out, letting it fall to her back, cloaking her nakedness. For a moment only, before he repeated the gesture, lifting, falling, lifting, falling; her body sheathed, then exposed, and again, to his eyes. It was an erotic dance he played upon her hair, teasing his eyes with the sight of her.

"Your hair is wet," he said.

"As is yours," she answered, her eyes firmly closed against him.

"Nay, mine is almost dried. Touch and see," he said.

"Nay!" she snapped, clasping her hands together in her lap.

She would not touch him.

Yet he would touch her.

He pulled her hair forward, over her upthrust breasts, covering her. The ends pooled in her lap, curling, drying. He allowed his hands, his willful hands, to have their way, running down the length of her hair, feeling the fragility of her chest, the soft mounds of her breasts, the slenderness of her ribs . . . the hammering of her heart.

"Your hair," he said, playing with a curl that rested on her hip, absorbing the velvet texture of her skin; "your hair has called to me for season upon season, night unto day, year after year."

Her breath caught and she trembled. And kept her eyes closed against him.

"I would pray most diligently, most fervently, that you would bind your hair. Hide it beneath a wimple, tie it off in a plait, anything to keep it from my eyes. Yet you would not. How did you know that your hair was my undoing, Isabel? How did you know me so well?"

"I did not know," she said softly.

Richard smiled and followed the long trail of a curl with his fingertip. "You knew."

"Nay, I—"

"You knew how I wanted you, how every moment of my life at Malton and beyond was filled with the fight of refusing you. Refusing every look, every sidelong glance, every smile, every touch. Yea, you knew how I wanted you. You know me too well not to have known."

He curled his hands around her breasts, and she gasped, her nipples hard and hot beneath the cool weight of her hair.

"Your hair is almost dried," he said, fondling her.

Isabel dropped her chin to her chest and moaned softly.

This was nothing like the last time.

Richard was making no claim of performing against his will a duty he had no desire to perform. This was too close to her dreams, too much of what she had imagined coupling with Richard to be like. Even his words were designed to ignite a flame in her. Did she not long to hear that Richard had desired her for as long as she had wanted him? She could not stand long against this assault. She could barely stand against Richard and his allure when he was aloof; how well when he was as passionate and determined as only Richard of Warefeld could be?

She had to keep her heart safe, even as she allowed him into her body. If only he would hurry and be done. This seductive adventure would be her undoing, in spite of her refusal to behold him in his natural glory.

He was a man. No monk looked as he did, spoke as he did, touched as . . .

Richard's mouth was at her throat, his hand once more upon her breast, and the dual sensations tumbled her heart into her hips, where it continued to beat most urgently. She squirmed against the weight of desire as it settled between her legs; she felt hot and full.

And empty.

His mouth moved up her throat, to her jaw and then her cheek. So gentle, so delicate were his kisses, like sun on skin after a long, cloudy day; so welcome. She sighed her satisfaction and could feel his smile as his hands spanned her waist, his thumbs resting beneath her breasts.

This would not do.

Would she never stop tumbling into Richard's arms if he did but smile at her?

But he was more than smiling now.

His mouth kissed the corner of hers, and she trembled before the tingle that surged through her body. When had Richard learned to be so tender? So gentle? The kiss they had shared in the stable had been nothing like this.

She jerked upright, pulling her mouth from his. Naturally, it had been nothing like; he had learned such tender arts from Bertrada, the instructor of all.

"I do not want to kiss you," she said, opening her eyes to impale him with her rejection.

Richard jerked upright at the words and stared

into her crystal eyes. He understood. Sharp were his own words thrown back at him in such a moment. Sharp must have been her pain, an untutored virgin, upon hearing them on her marriage bed.

Yet he would not stop. He would not take her unready again. But he would take her.

His hands stroked her breasts, their eyes locked in silent battle while his fingers played upon her rosy nipples.

"I do not want," she breathed almost on a gasp, "to feel your hands on me."

God above, he knew what she was about, and yet the words were like knives into his soul. Not feel his hands on her? He would touch her until Christ called him home.

He pushed her back onto the bed, and she fell wordlessly and without protest, except that her eyes, her amber-green eyes, held his. She hated him. She wanted him.

How well he knew the strength of such opposing desires. He knew she was trying to hold back the harness of reigning desire. He knew. He had tried to keep himself from wanting her with the same words and the same intent. Only he knew how completely he had failed. And knowing all that, her words drew blood still.

He lay upon her, casting caution and gentleness aside, wanting her beyond consideration and chivalry. Wanting her . . . and demanding that she want him.

She was soft and small and curved, her hair a

black wing flung out beneath her white body. He kissed her, pressing his hips against hers, making her feel his arousal and what she had done to him by simply being Isabel.

She surged back against him, hip to hip, groin to groin, yet she covered his hands in her hair with her own . . . and pulled his hands from her. Even as her hips sought union with his. He ended the kiss as violently as he had begun it, her mouth a red wound upon her ivory skin.

Gasping, her breasts heaving, she said, "I do not want to feel your weight."

"Nay?" he asked, his eyes glittering in desire and anger commingled. "Have you forgotten that in order to conceive you must be brought to your pleasure?"

He was braced above her, his arms long cords of strength as he awaited her answer. His hips still pressed against hers, and she ignored the urge to grind into his weight. He was Richard as he had been in the stable, wild and hot and demanding. And again, she was not afraid, not of him. Only of herself and her weakness with him.

Once she conceived, he would return to the abbey and the Benedictine brotherhood. Leaving her. But leaving her with child. She wanted a child.

"I know my duty to both our houses," she said, looking at his throat, the dark shadow of his beard on a column of both strength and vulnerability. The intensity of his gaze would burn her through, leaving her exposed; she could not look into his eyes. She was exposed, as vulnerable as his unprotected throat, but she did not want him to see. Desire and dreams she had set aside in favor of dignity and duty; he must leave her that. "Do what you will," she said.

The sun was disappearing behind the trees, a rosy mass of heat quickly covered by the black silhouette of forest. In the last warm light of the day, she could see his look of solemn determination before he began his most earnest seduction.

She had given him permission to seduce her. He took it.

His assault, for it was nothing less, was as violent as it was thorough. She had dreamed, hour upon hour, of his kiss in that sun-flecked stable; he met her dream a thousandfold.

His kiss was hard against her mouth, yet he did not bruise her. His tongue toyed with her lips before demanding entrance; she could scarce take breath to hold him off. Hot and full, swift and hard, his tongue ravaged her mouth, his lips insistent that she hold nothing back, that she withdraw not a hairsbreadth from him. She could do naught to stop him.

It was God's good mercy that she was not called upon to try.

His hands rested upon her breasts, where he palmed her nipples to tingling sensation. She arched into his hands, helpless to stop her response to him, shamed that he could so effortlessly wring a reaction from her. Where was the dignity she sought to hold in defiant defense of his freedom with her body?

Gone, flown away with his first touch, his first kiss, his first look.

She must not succumb to him so easily; he would leave her with nothing, nothing save a child and her duty rendered.

His mouth left hers and suckled his way down her throat to her breast. With his hand and his mouth he fondled her, sending rivers of sparks shooting along her limbs and to the seat of her womb. She bucked against him, wanting more, ashamed at her wanting, fed by her desire, and torn by the conflict.

She had felt none of this in their stable kiss. But he had. She knew then why he had pushed her off, why he had avoided her, why he had not dared to look into her eyes. If this was desire, it inspired fear as well as yearning. Such passion was controlled only by its own hunger, heeding no other sanction, obeying no voice but its own.

Yet Richard had forced his passion to obey God's will and his own.

In a flash of divine understanding she saw Richard as he was: a man of rare strength and discipline. A man who had bedded his lord's wife and taken the cowl to redeem himself. 'Twas a contradiction. She did not understand how he could be both.

But she was not allowed to think, not now, not when Richard was sliding his hand down her torso, feeling his way from breast to waist to hip to thigh. Still nipping at her breast, his mouth hot and wet upon her aching nipple, he caressed the back of her knee, urging her to relax her leg, to bend, to open. And she did.

Passion was calling to her. She did not have her husband's strength of will to turn from its voice.

She shook. Her legs and arms trembled, plucking at the sheets beneath her hips, arching into his touch, where e'er he touched her, be it mouth or hand. Wanting his touch, wanting whatever he could give her, even for so short a time as the minutes between dusk and dark upon their marriage bed.

Yet, in all her submission to his touch, she trembled to keep her heart intact. For him, it was passion commingled in a snarl with duty. And so it would be for her. She would not let her heart fly into such a tangled hedge as the one which protected him. She would not, for he would leave.

His hand cupped her, tangling in her curls, feeling for the opening to her womb while his mouth kissed her hard upon the neck, bruising her. She craved his bruising, reveling in the pleasure-pain of his passion, turning into his every touch, welcoming his desire as she guarded her heart.

She was wet for him, her mound pulsing with pressure aching to be released. Her nipples ached, arching for his hand. She was open, ready, more than ready . . . and he withdrew. First his hand from her heat and then his mouth from her throat, and then he lifted his glorious weight from her and looked deep into her eyes.

She panted up at him, her eyes unfocused, her lips red and chapped.

Why had he stopped? Was this not the moment when duty was to be performed? How was she to plump with child if he did not continue?

He stroked her body, calming her, a slow massage that kept the fire smoldering within her but did not allow it to spark into fulfillment. He kissed her brow gently, his breath soft and sweet, and kneaded her shoulders. He lifted her and pulled her hair from beneath her, straightening out the tangles with his fingers, all gentleness, all chivalry. He touched her throat at her pulse point while she stared up at him, her eyes slowly focusing.

"I have marked you," he said, tracing the bruise with his fingertip. "I have not the will to repent."

Always he spoke of repentance. Always he would search for absolution, an absolution she could not grant.

Taking a deep breath, feeling the slowing of her heart, she watched him. He was dark and lean, lethal to her senses, his hard beauty a draught tinged with poison, for he would destroy her if she allowed it. He stroked her hair, skimming his fingers over her hairline, caressing her brow. With a fingertip he traced her brow line and the delicate and sensitive line of her nose. With his thumb he outlined her lips, and she breathed in sharply, leaning into his hand with a will untethered.

It was the only signal he required to begin again.

His hand behind her neck, he lifted her to meet his mouth, his kiss a summons, urgent and fast. She met him willingly, her mouth opening, inviting him to enter, to find her, to take her. To know her. And he came, plunging in, his tongue a sword, quick and light, determined and deadly. His assault was bold and sure, his manner the same. His hands upon her were confident, touching her at will, holding her as it pleased him.

He held her pressed against him, his arms hard around her back, her hair hanging down to the sheets below. She cautiously wrapped her arms around his neck, allowing herself to touch him willingly. Nay, not allowing . . . not strong enough to fight back the desire to feel his skin beneath her hands, to feel his heat and his strength, to touch him freely, if only for this night.

Three years. Would three years of nights such as this be enough to last a lifetime?

She returned his kiss fully, rubbing the softness of her breasts against the hard shield of his chest. He was so broad, so hard, so tall. He enveloped her, and she sighed happily at the loss of self she felt in his arms.

He tugged on her hair, and her throat was exposed to his mouth. He trailed kisses, hard and hungry kisses, down her neck, soft and pulsing with need, to her breast and bit an aching nipple. She gasped, her voice sounding raw and heavy to her own ears, and held his head to her breast, silently demanding more. She could not see him, her hair held tight in his fist, her face to the ceiling far above her, but she could feel his hands on her body and his mouth on her skin and it was enough. More than enough.

He nipped his way across her breast, his evening

beard scraping along her sensitive skin, and feasted on her other nipple, sucking hard and biting without warning. She wound her fingers through his hair, holding on, holding him, holding back so very little. He kissed hard, sucking the plump skin of her breast near her arm, bruising her. She wanted it; she wanted his mark. She wanted anything he could give her.

She squirmed against him, and he released his hold on her hair. She attacked him with her mouth, her kiss a hard bite on his throat, and he groaned his response. He tasted good, like salt and man; the feel of his blood pulsing beneath her lips was intoxicating. She wanted more. She wanted to be a part of him.

He rose to his knees and pulled her with him. She was shaking, her hands clumsy and her vision blurred. But she had the strength and will to hold him to her, to run her hands across the incredible width of his shoulders and down his back. He did the same, his hands skimming, possessive, titillating. He followed the curve of her spine to the swell of her bottom and held her fast, his hands warm and rough, his every breath proclaiming her as his to do with what he would.

She had yearned to be possessed by Richard for all her life, and she could not but welcome his touch now. No matter where it led. As long as it left her heart intact.

He was hard and he pressed her against him, showing her the strength and length of his passion. She was soft and hot and she welcomed him, straining against him, opening her legs to allow him entry while he caressed her from behind. Urging him to lie down with her. Urging him to take her.

What he did was take his hands from her and push her down to sit upon the bed. She was wet with wanting, aching and tight, her body pulsing like a wound.

He tormented her.

It was willful—no man could be so successful by chance. No man was so ignorant. Nay, it was done apurpose.

He pressed her back by her shoulders to lie upon her back. She did, her eyes a beacon of confusion she struggled to hide, her breathing labored and loud. Richard got off the bed and stood next to it, staring down at her, his eyes a smoldering fire of blackest blue.

She would not speak, she would not ask why he waited, why he tormented her. She would not reveal her pain and her weakness to him. She would not be a fool for him.

Richard kissed her softly on the mouth, and she was disgusted by the moaning sound she made at that light contact. She schooled her features to sterner dignity and closed her eyes against him. She was so highly aroused that the smallest touch was like pain, yet she yearned for more.

She was a fool.

Richard touched her knee, a gentle touch, yet the fire skittered there and she commanded herself not to open her legs to him, though that was her desire. She wanted to wrap herself around him, skin to skin, heat to heat, until they were indistinguishable. Indivisible.

But it was not to be.

With firmer touch, he stroked her thighs, a hand to each, rubbing, caressing, massaging, but there was nothing in his touch that relaxed her. With each stroke he rose higher to the source of her heat and her ache. He played upon her. She would not reach for him, though her hands longed to pull him down to her, to make him kiss her, to make him fondle her, to make him take her. She would not. She wound her hands into the bedding, her fists holding on to her resolve and her dignity. Her part was to do her duty, nothing more.

His part was to bring her pleasure; he did not. He brought only pain.

He spread her legs, slowly, casually, his hands warm and sure, his breathing loud.

She would not look. If she saw the fire in his eyes she would melt away. She clutched the bedding, submitted to her duty.

He spread her wide. She could feel how wet she was, how swollen; it was a relief to spread herself. Yet he had done the spreading, not she. She would not enter into this bedding eagerly, only in dutiful submission. 'Twas the only way to save herself.

"I could bathe in the scent of you," Richard said on a rasp. " 'Tis richer than perfume."

She could feel the blush starting at her breasts, rising to her face. She kept her eyes closed.

He massaged each thigh, his thumbs coming

shadow-close to the seat of her ache. She pounded her anticipation and frustration, her blood alive and wild, her skin vibrating, her breath shallow. She wanted him. Needed his touch. Now.

She skittered toward his hands on a whimper. He flicked at her arousal once, twice, and stopped. She near cried aloud her anguish. His hands went to her breasts, plucking hard, and she bucked against his hands, her hips twitching, grinding against air.

Now.

"Richard," she begged.

"Look at me, Isabel," he said.

She obeyed instantly, without thought. She could not see; he was a dark shape against stone and moonlight, and then her eyes cleared. He was looking down at her, his face grim and still, his eyes alight with unearthly sparks.

"When does duty end and desire begin, Isabel? Only then shall you find release," he said, his voice as hard and unyielding as the stone that surrounded them.

He wanted, nay, demanded that she surrender all to him. He would leave her stripped, without her dignity, without her adherence to duty and duty alone. He would have her beg, to have her admit that he was her desire. Nay, she would not.

Never again.

Yet she ached . . .

"I do not want—"

"Tell me not what you do not want," he growled.

"Speak only of what you want, and I will deliver it unto you."

When she was silent, he bent to take her in a rough kiss, and she surged to meet it. Savagely they attacked each other, their hands hard and demanding, their mouths wide and wet. They asked for no quarter and they were given none. In their desire they were perfectly matched. His arms were wrapped around her, holding her hard to him, bending her back and stealing her air. She had no need of any air she could not steal from Richard's lungs. She clawed his back, twining her fingers in his silky hair, holding him to her, demanding the release he withheld.

He would not yield.

He would not touch her and give her what she needed.

"Give me a child," she said against his mouth.

"Not good enough," he almost snarled, nipping her ear. "Tell me what you seek in this bed, by my hand."

When she would not speak, he unleashed the power of his hands.

He closed her legs, the pressure on her fullness exquisite pain, and traced the path he would like to follow, if only for her stubborn will. With a finger he deliberately and delicately toyed with her arousal, touching lightly now, missing altogether, pressing hard for but a moment and then gone, like the lark at dusk. She quivered, her body screaming for release, so close at times and then so far, his hand an ally and an enemy who changed allegiance moment by moment, stroke by stroke.

He kissed her, his kiss full of promise and passion. A coaxing kiss. A kiss to lure. A kiss to believe in.

She relaxed into his kiss, his breath her own, his scent covering her, while she strained against his tormenting hand.

She was close to tears.

"Only name it," he said, pulling back from their kiss, "and it shall be yours."

The world had shrunk to the marriage bed, to what they gave and what was stolen. He had stolen her resolve and the snarled threads of her dignity, but there was one thing which Richard could give.

"Pleasure. Give me my pleasure," she commanded.

With a growl of satisfaction, Richard obeyed.

He spread her legs wide and cupped her fully, his hand wet with her need. With his fingers, he strummed her. Relentlessly he plucked and teased her arousal, while his hand snaked up her trembling body to squeeze her nipple in urgent command.

Isabel's body obeyed.

Her convulsions started deep within, and Richard plunged into her to meet them. He felt her pulsing around him, squeezing him, enveloping him in rigid spasms, releasing her seed to meet his. With his hand in her hair and his mouth on her throat, he joined her in her release as they had been joined in their torment. Duty was forgotten as desire was fulfilled.

She had achieved her pleasure; he had given it to her.

He smiled in satisfaction and kissed her temple, stroking back her hair.

He lay within her, one with her, and sighed his contentment.

For Isabel, there was only defeat.

He had delivered her unto her pleasure, the force of it stunning her. He had given himself over to his passion, unleashing his desire upon her. She knew what was to come.

He would reject her, withdrawing from her in body and mind.

It was all duty for him. He had to get a child upon her in order to be free to return to his chosen life. And it was all duty for her. But she prayed that she would soon be carrying; she did not think that she could endure night after night of Richard's determined attentions with her heart intact.

She pretended it was intact now.

The mother-of-pearl clouds were building again, turning the night sky gray and masking the shining moon. Richard lay next to Isabel, his breathing deep and steady, his arm tossed over her waist, his face buried in her unbound hair.

"Do you think it possible that I am with child?" she asked.

Richard lifted his head and looked at her delicate profile outlined by the radiance of the moon. How many wounds had he inflicted upon her? Too many to count. But he would heal her.

If he only knew how.

"We have done all possible to see that it is so," he said, tracing a fingertip down the fragility of her profile. "At least I have." He smiled in jest.

But Isabel did not understand his purpose. He could feel her tension and her withdrawal. She would not forgive. She wanted nothing of him save his seed.

"It is more than possible," he repeated, "yet too soon to know. We must be diligent."

She remained quiet, her silence a cloak lying heavily upon them both. What held her tongue? Had she suffered so greatly at his hands this night? He had brought her to her pleasure, had he not?

And the method he had used to force her to demand satisfaction from him shamed him now. He could have seen to her needs without driving her into frenzy, yet he had demanded that she want him, as she once had, before she had known of Bertrada.

Bertrada, ever in the midst of them, even upon their marriage bed.

As was his pride ever among them. Could he not, even now, let go the sin of pride?

Richard rolled over on his back and crossed his arms under his head. Isabel had been mauled at Adam's hands, and he had bedded her as soon as she was wiped clean of the man's death blood. He was a poor sort of man to treat his wife so, yet he had not found the will to stop.

And therein lay the worst of his cardinal sins. His body ruled him. He was little better than a beast of the field or wood—worse, since he possessed a soul. Such had been his sin with Bertrada, and now he brought his foul nature into his marriage.

Yet he had wanted to possess Isabel, to drive clean the memory of Adam's touch and impress his own scent upon her. That he had done, and now he had a wife at his side who was frightened into silence.

"Does the performance of your marital duty distress you, Isabel?" he asked the ceiling.

She was silent long. The sounds of the hall came to them as they lay upon their solemn bed—the snap of fire, the first deep snore of the evening, the slosh of water being carried in a bucket, soft male voices in melodic conversation, a woman's gentle laugh. And still Isabel was silent.

"Nay," she said at last. She was lying on her side, turned from him, her hands pressed between her knees. "Does it you?" she asked softly.

"Nay," he answered at once. "I find the duties of the marital bed to be less than onerous."

He heard her sigh and heard the tremble within it. "I but jest, Isabel, and badly. There was little call for humor in the abbey, and my frolicsome parts are as ill used as my warlike ones."

"You are a fine warrior," she said immediately.

"You defend me gallantly, at least in part," he said.

He could feel her smile in the dark and smiled in return.

"As you defended me," she said into the night, thanking him.

" 'Twas my right," he said dismissively, "and my duty."

"Your duty," she repeated, her tone flat.

"My pleasure as well, if I must confess it," he said. "Pray for me, Isabel, for I feel no remorse for sending him to purgatory without a prayer to follow him."

She turned onto her back and lifted her knees, her feet braced against the bed and her arms crossed over her.

"And should you not pray for me, if you can, for being the cause of his death?"

He turned sharply to look at her. "How are you the cause when it was he who mauled you like a wolf tears into a hare? You the cause? Nay, 'twas my blade which sent him out of this life and into the next; 'tis I who need prayer over the matter of Adam."

Isabel turned her head to look at him, her arms still covering her. "And I do not? Did I not . . . entice him? Was it not I who—"

"Does the hare entice the wolf?" he interrupted, lifting himself onto his elbows to look down into her troubled eyes. "Nay, do not think to rob me of needed prayer, Isabel. I am in dire need. The time will come when I must pray most diligently for you. But now is not your time."

He released her from her guilt with the words; in full knowledge, he released her. He did not hold her accountable for Adam's assault, he did not blame her for her flirtatious ways, which was in his right to do. And with his words, so carefully and comically spoken, she was released.

She looked up at him, her smile slow and brilliant. "Now is not my time?"

"Nay," he said with a returning smile, "now is not. You have done nothing. Nothing, Isabel."

"And you will tell me when I am in need of most urgent prayer?"

Richard kissed the curled end of her hair and smiled. "Let us both remember that you have asked me to tell you when you have erred. 'Tis a fine way to begin a marriage."

"So say you," she snipped with a grin as wide and white as the moon.

"Naturally, and am I not a monk, knowledgeable in all things spiritual?"

"You are no monk," she said gently.

"Nay," he agreed, "but I am a husband, and as husband I bid you sleep, Isabel."

"Will you stay?" she asked.

Would he stay by her side all through the darkness or would he, as any Benedictine would, rise to pray in the chapel throughout the night? He was a husband, not a Brother; he would stay. He would stay by her side for all his life.

"Naturally, I will stay," he said, kissing her lips gently.

She was asleep, her breathing soft and deep, her limbs heavy and still, before he had finished his first Paternoster. She jerked awake, her fear leaping up and filling the room, her open-mouthed cry silent.

"Sleep, Isabel," he commanded, forcing her fears to run from him. "None shall touch you while I live."

She was asleep almost before she had known she had been awake, her fear a memory of the night, misty and fantastical. He laid his hand upon her back, rejoicing in the simple rise and fall of her breathing. She was alive and safe; naught else mattered, save that she was his.

She was his. The words struck a chord in his heart that rang distant and discordant. *None shall touch you while I live.*

Why did he yet live?

He was a man who had taken the wife of the lord of his fostering. Henley, knowing that, should have killed him. Henley had the right, just as Richard had taken the life of Adam for his presumption in laying hands on Isabel. It was a husband's right, and none disputed it.

A husband now, he looked upon his trysts with Bertrada with different eyes. Where had Henley been during the first signs of illicit attraction? During the times when Bertrada had been so assuredly alone?

He knew the answer now, looking back on that time, and for the first time saw more than his own guilt. Henley had been there, seeing all, saying nothing. Allowing matters to proceed apace, leaving his wife in Richard's path for Richard to take and hold, even for an hour. Henley had seen all and done . . . nothing.

Why?

He could not grasp the thought. If any man touched Isabel, he would follow Adam to the grave. Isabel was his and would stay his. Only his. What sort of man would allow otherwise? A coward, certainly. There was the matter of Henley's abrupt departure, with no inquiries made as to the death of his newly sworn man, and with no apologies.

Not the acts of an honorable man.

And a dishonorable man was capable of anything.

Chapter Twenty-six

Isabel awoke to birdsong and the howl of a kicked cat. While her eyes were yet closed, she heard Edmund and Ulrich laughing in the hall and Elsbeth's soft and muffled response. With her first languorous stretch, from fingertips to toes, she heard Joan say something sharply to Aelis. She did not hear Aelis's reply.

'Twere all the sounds of daybreak at Dornei and she was deeply content, from her skin to her bones. Content and slightly sore. Richard had used her hard last night; he was a hard man, she had always known it. How hard she could not have guessed.

Smiling, she stretched again, and noted that she was alone in her bed.

Alone, when he had promised to stay with her. He had promised not to leave, even for the space of the night, and it was a promise he could not keep. No matter that he had absolved her of guilt in Adam's death, no matter that he had driven her to her pleasure. No matter that he had spoken to her like a wife, a treasured and precious woman to be protected and defended for all her days. His days with her would be brief.

How could she have forgotten?

Last night had been duty. Today would bring more of the same. Day upon day of duty until she bore a child and Richard hurried back to the abbey. Perhaps he would not even wait until the child was born, but would feel he had done his part when life plumped her belly; after all, it was *her* duty to bring forth a healthy child.

Again she awoke alone in her bed. Richard was gone, busy with his prayers, no doubt. Duty following duty. She should be at her prayers as well.

She straightened the coverlet over her prone body and turned her eyes toward the wind hole. She did not rise. It was a gray day, heavy with cloud; the sun was completely overcome. A brisk wind snaked its way into the wind hole, bringing the smell of rain and raw earth. She pulled the cover up over her nose.

Last night. She did not want to think about last night.

All she wanted to think about was last night.

The terrible intimacy of what they had done together, the biting and kissing, the scents and tastes, appalled her. Intrigued her. Embarrassed her. Aroused her.

Richard had been ferocious in driving her to her pleasure.

Isabel shivered and buried her smile beneath the marten fur that lay upon her bed.

She had known he possessed such passion; their stable kiss had revealed it. Yet she had not known where such passion led.

It would be difficult for her to give that up when Richard rejoined the Benedictines. Would it be as difficult for him? Nay, he had made his meaning clear when he had first taken her; he had not wanted any part of the passion of the marriage bed. He had made all as clear as a sunshine with his toiling repetition of *I do not want.*

Yet she had done the same, said the same with her mouth while her heart felt differently, and duty had had no part in it. Perhaps it had been the same for him.

Perhaps? She had lived her life out hoping and dreaming that perhaps Richard would love her and want her and need her. She was grown. It was time to put dreams aside when duty was so clearly before her.

Isabel forced herself out of bed to stand on the cold floor, the lack of sun and her nudity chiding her to hurry. She was a step from the basin next to the wall when the door to the chamber opened wide. Richard stood upon the threshold, and grinned hugely.

Before he could say a word, she was back in bed, the coverlet protectively embracing her shoulders and covering her completely.

"Good morrow, Isabel," he said. "I came to see how well you fare, yet I can see you fare quite well."

"I am well," she said stiffly. He had thought her ill, to stay so long abed. It was long past the dawn. "I will pray at Terce."

"You need not keep the hours of a Benedictine," he said.

Yet where had he been? Not with her.

"You do," she said, her eyes as cool as the morning.

"Out of long habit only. You need not acquire my habits."

Naturally not, since he would be returning to the abbey and she would not.

"And you seem incapable of acquiring new ones. But then, you have not the need."

Richard closed the door behind him. In his hands he carried a mug of ale and a fistful of bread; he came as servant, to break her fast. She was a churlish bride to be so sour.

"Untrue," he said evenly. "I have discovered many habits I did not anticipate a fortnight ago."

"And many sorrows," she said, taking the ale with an apologetic expression.

"Nay, sorrows I have always had. To you I bring tribulations."

"This does not taste like tribulations," she said, sniffing at her ale, trying for lightness when her heart was so heavy. 'Twas not his fault he had been trapped into a marriage not to his liking. He would leave her, aye, when his duty to her was done. Did any woman fare better? Now he was hers, if only for a season. In truth, what did being churlish win her but an uneasy stomach and a sore head?

"You have a kind tongue," he said, sitting on the edge of the bed. His hair fell forward over his brow, a dark and shining leaf against pale water, his eyes the blue of dreams.

"You are the first to remark upon it. Some say my tongue is sharp, even bitter."

"None who have tasted of it would say so," he said seductively.

"Now you are kind," she said over the top of her mug.

Would it be so difficult to spend a season or two with this man? She had yearned for just such intimacy, such bonding, all her life; why cast all away because the pattern of the dream was not to her liking? The weave was hers, let God fashion the pattern; she would be content with it. Mayhap He would give her three years. Three years with Richard was no tribulation.

"I am not kind," he said. "You know this best of any. I am proud."

"You are," she agreed pleasantly.

"Clumsy."

"Only with words," she soothed, patting his hand compassionately, her smile as sharp as talons.

"Some would say I am too solemn," he said, toying with her fingers.

"I have always preferred the word 'grim.' " She smiled cordially.

"I have heard the word 'handsome'—"

"But never in your hearing," she finished.

"Stalwart?"

"Determined."

"Pleasant?" He frowned, his black brows low and compressed.

"Polite," she said instead.

"Romantic?" He slipped a band of gold set with emeralds onto her finger. Her wedding band.

It was beautiful.

It was perfect.

It was not as she imagined it.

It was better.

"Hopelessly," she said, leaning forward to kiss him, dropping the protective and unnecessary barrier of her blankets.

He wrapped his arms around her and she was instantly warm. The wool of his tunic rubbed against her skin, irritating and arousing her at once. He was fully clothed, his hair combed, his teeth cleansed, his boots on; she was naked and arrayed in nothing but her hair.

Perfect.

He nipped her ear.

"I have marked you. You are dotted with bruises," he said.

She twined her arms around his neck and arched against him. He lifted her onto his lap, her legs straddling his hips.

"I should be about my prayers and the duties of the day," she said against his neck. She felt his pulse jump beneath her lips and smiled.

"Nay, it is my duty to worship you with my body.

This will I do," he said, running his hands over her breasts, palming her erect nipples.

"You are ever about your duty, I have observed," she said, kissing her way to his mouth.

"And?" he said, lifting her hips with his hands and controlling her rhythm against his straining length.

"And," she gasped, "never have I been . . ."

"Aye?" he asked, holding her derriere in his hands while his mouth trailed across her breasts.

". . . been . . . so impressed with your . . ."

He spread wide her cheeks, and she came down hard and wet upon the wool of his tunic, his manhood a rod that pulsed with eagerness. His mouth snagged her nipple, suckling hard. Sensation shot through her like sunlight through clouds, hot and bright, a welcome burning.

". . . diligence!" she finished.

He bucked beneath her, holding her down to rub against him, his hands hard upon her hips, his mouth merciless at her breast. She strained against the fabric, wanting his possession, desperate to have him enter her.

He dallied.

His hands left her hips and gripped her head, holding her for a scorching kiss while her body sought futile union with his.

"You admit to being impressed," he said against her mouth, his lips sliding over the flushed and tender skin of her throat, hovering at the swell of her breast. His hands spanned her back, holding her away from him by the width of a finger. She

311

wanted his touch, to feel the heat of him, the solid
strength of him, the hard and pulsing length of him.

He refused.

"By your devotion to duty? Aye," she moaned,
searching for his mouth.

"Ah, duty." He smiled. "Hard words upon Isabel's lips."

"You think to insult me," she smiled lazily, "but
is it not my duty to find pleasure in the marriage
bed? This I do. Or try to do," she added.

She groped at the fabric which encased him,
searching for the opening that would release him
to her, pulling and tugging, her hands frantic.
Whining her distress that he would not spring free.

Richard bucked hard against her, crushing her
against the promise of him, flicking her nipple with
his tongue.

"You lack restraint, Isabel. This I have noted often."

"And you, Richard, have all the gaiety of a
shroud."

"A shroud?" he said. "You followed long after a
shroud. What was it that you found so compelling?"

His hands played upon her breasts, and when
she came close to finding her way past the wool
that protected him from her hands, he snatched
them off, holding her two in his one. Her hands he
held behind her back, a gentle cuff she could not
break, her breasts thrown forward toward his
mouth, her legs wide and open upon him.

Struggle she did not.

"Compelling," she breathed as his mouth teased her nipple, his free hand likewise flicking the other into hot sensation. "Why, 'twas your body, if you must know."

His hand snaked down, skimming lightly over ribs and belly to hover near her curls. Her aching need grew by the moment, and she twitched her hips uncontrollably toward his hand. In a single movement, he plunged a finger into her, sliding deeply and easily, while he bit hard upon her distended nipple. She groaned and threw her head back, straining toward his hands.

"And that," he murmured, his eyes sparkling like summer stars, "was the reason you watched me in the yard, season upon season? To watch my body?"

He had removed his hand. She could feel herself drip upon him, her body's call for release from this exquisite torment. He looked at her, his mouth a half smile of predatory domination, his hold on her secure.

"Summer I preferred," she said, her voice a rasp of shattered passion, "for then you would take off your gambeson."

"Summer is upon us," he whispered.

He was asking her to watch him train, in Richard's subtle way. He wanted her to watch him. He wanted her eyes upon him, wanting him, desiring him.

"I am eager for it," she said, her eyes alight with impatience.

"Ah, Isabel, ever eager," he said softly.

Her hands still held behind her, he released his

shaft with a quick movement of his fingers. He sprang forth with all the vigor of life. She quickly lifted herself above him while he held his shaft ready for her. She slid down, impaling herself on his sword, groaning at the contact, the fullness of possession. She kissed him hard upon the mouth, breathing his scent, sharing his air, and then she rode him. Hard. Fast. The size of him glorious. Reveling in her body's effort to accommodate him. Reveling in him.

Her hands were freed and around his neck, urging him to take her breasts. He complied, his hands quick and light upon her nipples, his mouth at her throat.

Her pleasure came long and swift, hard and effortless, slicing through her to carry her off, out of herself, into the air of heaven to tumble in a twirling spiral into the sun. Powerful. Frightening, if not for Richard's arms around her, Richard's mouth on her skin, Richard's scent in her nostrils. Because it was Richard, she was not afraid to soar beyond all the boundaries she had known.

Even now, his seed might be planting itself within her.

Isabel relaxed against Richard, his hands easy on her back, stroking her, soothing her, easing her back to earth. She lifted herself off of him, the scent of their mingling strong. He kissed her gently and with shared smiles they fell back upon the bed to lie softly in each other's arms.

She most assuredly had achieved her pleasure.

She grinned and sighed, turning into his arms,

wrapping herself around him with arms and legs.

"You have found the joy of duty, I think," he said, his voice a rumble in his chest, stroking her hair.

Duty; aye, there was joy in duty. Her duty was to bear a child, and it could have begun now, today.

Today, she thought, frowning. Each time he spilled his seed within her, she was one day closer to losing him. She could not stop it, or stop him. Richard was most adept at bringing her to her pleasure, and she was most thankful for his skill.

Is this what Bertrada had felt in his arms?

The thought took hold and would not leave her. She did not want thoughts of Bertrada here, to defile her marriage bed. But Bertrada was between them, always.

Did Richard think of the woman he loved while he lay with his wife?

Richard, attuned to Isabel as he was to no other, felt the change in her.

"Have I used you too hard, Isabel?" he asked, one hand still on her hair, the other light on her arm flung over his chest. "My passion—nay," he snapped, sitting up, dislodging her, "let me name it aright, my lust comes upon me strong and hard. I do not control it as I should. As I must."

Isabel sat up with him, her eyes troubled and searching. Her hair tumbled down her back, black against white, bounty against delicacy; she was a woman of rare delicacy. He should not have taken her as he did. Yet had he not wanted her to know the man she had bound herself to for life? He had told her of Bertrada; let him now tell her of his darker sin, of which Bertrada was only the evidence. Did he even need to speak? Did not Isabel, of all women, know the heart of his shame?

Even now he shrank from speaking it, wanting to hide it from the eyes of men, and from Isabel most of all. He did not want to lose her. Confessing this, he surely would. But the time for hiding, if ever there was such a time in the life of an honorable man, was done. He would keep silent no longer. He would hide from Isabel never again.

"You must know," he said, staring into her eyes, wanting to see the exact moment when she would turn from him in revulsion.

"Know what? Your meaning is hidden from me," she said, brushing her hair back behind her shoulders. Did she not know how the sight of her aroused him, even now, when his seed had so recently been cast?

She had known him long, yet she knew him not at all.

"Then hear me, Isabel, and know me," he said, rising from the bed, away from her and temptation. "I am awash in sin."

"As are we all," she said quickly.

"None such as I," he said. "You know of Bertrada." He watched her stiffen and lift her chin, awaiting the assault to her pride.

Never had he felt such pride in her.

She sat naked on his bed, prepared to listen to him speak of another woman. Her strength astounded him, and he took pride in her. She was a wife to make any man proud—and he had not wanted her. Nay, that was not the truth; he had wanted her unto depravity. Such was the blackness of the stain of sin upon him.

"This is not of Bertrada," he said, turning from her to gaze at the sky. 'Twas a thick day of cloud, the trees shrouded in mist, the birds flown, taking their song with them. A dark and heavy day for confession. "This is of me. I lust, Isabel."

"You feel you have made a profound statement, this I can see, Richard," she said, pulling the marten skin over her. "Do I offend if I point out that we all, all God's creation, lust?"

"Not as I," he said softly, turning again to face her. "I lust always. Always it defeats me. Can you not see the truth of that in Bertrada? Would I have taken my lord's wife if I were not beset with this sin and consumed by it?"

Isabel was struck by many thoughts at once and she hurried to put them in order. Firstly and most importantly, Richard clearly did not feel any special bond to Bertrada. He attributed his coupling with her to his battle against lust, not his devotion to Bertrada. The thought sent relief to settle like a soft mist in her heart. He did not love Bertrada. Yea, this was foremost.

Secondly, Richard battled lust . . . and lost. Or so he said. For herself, she could not see it.

"Lust defeats you," she repeated, scooting off the bed to stand near him. "Daily?"

"Hourly," he said.

"For this to be so, you must have copulated with every woman in Malton. How was I missed?"

Stiffly Richard turned from her and set his face to the wind hole. "This is not an occasion for jesting, Isabel. I bear my soul and its tribulations to you."

"I do not jest," she said, standing at his back. He was tall and broad and . . . wounded. Who had inflicted these wounds upon him? Richard was sensitive to duty and honor, but this . . . this was overwrought. " 'Tis only that I do not understand how you can battle lust and lose without a bedding to mark the occasion. How is it done?"

She was jesting, just a bit, for she could not bear to see him so forlorn. Surely he suffered more from the sin of pride for thinking that he and he alone of all men and women upon God's earth suffered so extravagantly from the sin of lust.

"No woman is safe from my desires," he said. "Have you not proof enough in your own memory? Surely I do in mine."

"Do you speak of now, today? Surely it is not lust to couple with your wife."

"What of our kiss?"

"Do you speak of our solitary kiss in the stable that warm day in Malton? I remember it well and am gratified that, with your list of lustful moments, you can manage to remember it, too."

"To jest of such sin is not seemly," he said, his face dour.

"As I said earlier, the word 'grim' applies well to you." She smiled.

He did not love Bertrada.

"And what of our kiss?" she asked, turning him to face her. "A single kiss—"

"A kiss of passion," he said.

"Yea, of passion," she agreed with a wide grin, "but not of fornication. And 'twas you who pushed me off. I may well have continued, so caught was I in . . . lust? Nay, it could not have been lust. 'Tis you and you alone who suffer so greatly."

"There is Bertrada," he said, and she struggled not to feel the pang his naming of her brought.

"Aye, there is Bertrada. And who else at Malton must I face? Who else partook of you?"

"Why, none," he said.

"But have you not said that no woman is safe from your desires? Bertrada was not the lone woman at Malton. I, as I have said, was most assuredly excluded from the reaches of your sin. And then there is Dornei; who have you ravaged here? Aelis is most comely and has found her own joy in watching you train in the bailey. Must I banish Aelis to protect her from you?"

"Nay!" he snapped. "What is there in Aelis to lust after? She is hardly more than a child."

"What to lust after? Why, she has breasts and lips, soft and ready for any man."

He studied her, his expression hard, yet his eyes were soft with questions.

"You do not think I battle lust."

"No less than any man. Certainly no more."

She laid a hand upon his arm and looked up with her translucent hazel eyes, giving him her acceptance, her humor, and her love. Yea, she had loved him long, his Isabel, through every tribulation and every sorrow, and still she smiled. And loved him. Her love had followed him all his life, and, so accostumed to its glow, he had been blind to it. But no longer. William le Brouillard had the right of it; Richard had been blessed with Isabel as wife.

He bent and kissed her, a gentle kiss. His first kiss of love. But perhaps he was wrong in that. Perhaps he had always kissed her in love and was just now seeing the truth of it.

The truth. Aye, the truth. The world shifted just a bit, allowing him to see what he had not. Henley, Bertrada, Malton; all seen suddenly with eyes cleared of low-slung cloud and magnified by the gift of distance. And Isabel the crystal that brought all into focus.

He knew then what he had to do to kill the worm of guilt which had eaten at him throughout the long year of his Benedictine penance.

He straightened and turned, his face as grim as Isabel described it.

"I am for Malton," he announced, making for the door.

Snatching up her linen shift, Isabel said, "As am I."

Chapter Twenty-seven

She was upon her palfrey while Richard was still arranging the party. She was not going to be left behind, no matter how stern his look. Oh, aye, he had confessed to having no love for Bertrada, but she was no such fool as to let her husband go to Malton while she sat quietly in Dornei. He and Bertrada had a bond, though it be sinful, and Richard would not face the woman of his sinful bond without his wife at his side. In all her worrying, she had never contemplated Richard running anywhere but back to the abbey. In the abbey, the door would be barred against her, and he would be lost to her forever. And to Bertrada. Yet that day was in the future; today he rode to Malton. And she beside him.

"We ride with you," Rowland said, his tone implacable.

"I need no nursemaids," Richard said.

"Good, for we are none," William said, "but we shall ride with you. You cannot stop us, Richard; we may ride where we will. Your lady wife rides with you," he said, his tone for once serious. "Do you not wish her fully protected?"

It was the only argument that held, and the three men recognized it.

"Ride, then," Richard said, turning from them, "but think not that I give you charge over me. I have my own purpose for traveling to Malton and will not spend time in argument on any point."

"Agreed," Rowland said, hand to sword hilt.

"But Lady Isabel," Richard said, drawing close so that his voice would not carry. "Stand by her, whatever happens. Protect her, if God wills."

"Rest on that," William said. "She will be well protected. You can rely."

Richard gripped William's arm in accord and then Rowland's. "I do." He smiled. " 'Tis an honor I bestow upon you; none else have I trusted. Ever."

"You have chosen well," Rowland said. "Your trust will not be betrayed."

"You have chosen poorly," Elsbeth said, her eyes downcast, her hood up, shielding her face. It was a poor shield; her profile was glorious.

"*I* have not chosen, Lady, but my heart," Ulrich said, his eyes merry and compelling.

"What of Aelis?" Elsbeth asked with a slight frown. "Did you not prefer her even yesterday?

Your heart must change purpose with every heart-beat."

"Every heartbeat sings only of you, Lady," he said, a hand to his chest, his sigh dramatic. "Only and always, this I swear."

"Swear not to me," she snapped, clutching her cloak about her, hiding within its folds. "And speak not of only and always. I did not know you a week past. You will leave here at any hour."

"And leave my heart behind, with you, at your feet," he said.

" 'Tis a sight I would cherish to see," she said with a wry smile, which she ducked to hide in her cloak.

"Ah, you are cruel." Ulrich grinned, taking her hand, which she quickly snatched from his. "But 'tis the emblem of love. I am heartened by it. Be cruel to me, Elsbeth, for by this I know you care more than is wise."

"I am wise," she said, "and I do not care. I do not trust you, Ulrich."

He grinned playfully and answered, "Be wise, Elsbeth; do not trust me. Love me. Your love I will not betray."

He reached for her hand again, his eyes relentlessly charming. It was with greater reluctance that she pulled her hand free. Ulrich noted the reluctance and smiled.

"You betray your betrothed by speaking thus to me," Aelis said over her shoulder. Her blonde hair was a bright beacon in the gloom of the day; she

323

knew this, and so her hood was down.

Edmund frowned for a moment, looked over his shoulder at Ulrich and his amorous attack on Elsbeth, and shrugged off his indecision. 'Twas a game, after all. He was prodigiously good at games.

"I betray no one but my own heart," he said, trying the words on his tongue, finding them pleasant. "You have chased me, Aelis. I am found. Turn and face your treasure."

She turned, her face livid. "You are no woman's treasure! Think you that any maiden would find you as precious as you obviously find yourself?"

"I do not find myself precious," he stumbled, "I only wish that you would."

"Wish all day, pray all night," she said, her blond hair tumbling around her face, "and you will find yourself still alone with your prayers and your wishes."

"But did you want me, Aelis?" he said, his confusion plain. "I thought . . . I thought I pleased you."

"Yesterday. All yesterday. Today I know my duty is to my betrothed."

"And tomorrow?" he said, edging near her, his leg brushing against the wool of her skirts.

"What of tomorrow?" she asked, letting him tangle himself in her clothing.

"Tomorrow will find us in Dornei, with spring bursting forth her sights and smells for us to savor. Far away from our betrotheds. Close upon each other." He was doing better; these words seemed to sit well with her.

"Aye, 'tis so," she said softly, his breath upon her

cheek, his hand hovering over her back.

"Should we not then take what is offered by time and convenience?"

"Convenience?" she snarled, turning away from him. "Was I fashioned for your convenience? Nay, speak not, for I dare not find myself poisoned by your oafish reply."

Aelis stalked off, leaving Edmund with a perplexed look. Over her shoulder she said sharply, "You were more attractive when you spoke little. Pray resume the practice."

"He wants practice," William said to Rowland as they stood by their mounts.

"He shall find it hard battle to practice again with Aelis," Rowland said.

"I'd wager on him," William said. "Aelis is too eager and the field too empty. She'll engage Edmund for lack of any other."

"What of Ulrich? And Gilles?"

"Ulrich does not foster in Dornei, and Gilles has not come into his time."

Rowland smiled and shook his head. "You rate Ulrich too low; he needs not days when hours will do. And Gilles? His time is nigh upon him."

"So say you, but what says Aelis?"

"A wager?" Rowland said.

"Ten marks that Edmund gains ground with Aelis."

"When?"

"By sunset tomorrow," William said.

"Done."

"You think Edmund will not succeed?"

"Nay, 'tis that I think Ulrich or e'en Gilles will strike and hit the mark before Edmund finds his tongue for wooing," Rowland said, brushing back his black hair with a careless hand. "You will not instruct him?"

"Is that part of the wager?" William laughed.

"Does it need be?" Rowland asked with raised brows.

William, for answer, only laughed the harder.

"I attend because you will need me," Elsbeth said to Isabel, glad for the excuse to be away from Ulrich and his wit.

"I will not," Isabel said. "A ride to Malton does not require—"

"Please, Isabel," Elsbeth said quietly. "All know of conditions between Dornei and Malton. I would lend support, even by my prayers."

Isabel looked down at Elsbeth, standing so quietly and so determinedly next to her palfrey; she was a maiden of intense and tranquil strength. Such a companion would be most welcome in any circumstance.

"What do you know, or think you know?" Isabel asked softly.

Elsbeth ducked her head and hid her face from view. "Adam riding into Dornei with Lord Henley at his head told all. Malton is at odds with Dornei."

"Yea," Isabel said, her eyes misty with her thoughts, "that is so. And for right cause."

"Aye, Lady, for right cause," Elsbeth said, thinking of Adam without his head. "Yet did not the Lord of Hosts command us to love our neighbors as ourselves and pray for those who persecute us? I offer my prayers to such an end, Isabel."

Isabel looked down at her, her eyes sad and the smile of acquiescence she tendered even sadder. "Then come, and welcome, Elsbeth, and be our prayer warrior, for this adventure needs much prayer to sustain it."

"I will," she answered, her eyes alight with divine purpose, "and gladly."

"You appear less than glad that I have come," Isabel said to Richard as they rode through the wet morning.

"You read me well," he said, keeping his eyes on the track before them, keeping his eyes off her. "You did not need to come."

"Yea. I did," she said stiffly.

Leave Richard to face Malton without her? Never. Malton had been the home of their youth, Henley and Bertrada acting as father and mother to them both, though in Richard's case Bertrada had been more than mother. What had driven him into her arms?

Isabel gazed at Richard, his profile strong and sharp in the heavy light of a cloud-thick day; he was not a man to jump from one woman's bed to another, though he had been convinced he was just such a man. And who had done that service on his soul? Malton held the answer, she was certain, because Malton was the source.

327

"It is a raw day to be riding," Richard said, tightening his grip on the reins.

"I am not so frail," she answered, lifting her chin defiantly.

"Nay," he said, turning to her, his eyes dark and shining, "you are not."

She was not. With all that had passed between them, he knew she was a woman of rare strength and determination. Had he not tried to best her for years, and did he not now find himself wed to her? Aye, she was strong, but what awaited in Malton would require more than strength of purpose. Would she not turn from him when he had accomplished his mission?

Would he blame her?

Nay, he would not.

Such a trial was asked of few, and were it not for his weakness of spirit, she would be spared now. But he had only recently come into his strength. Isabel had only recently become his wife. Isabel could not be spared, but mayhap she could still be spared the sight.

"Do you need to go?" Isabel asked, voicing his own thought. "Was there nothing that could have been said or done to make this journey to Malton unnecessary?"

He could hear her concern, even her fear, and knew it was for him. But he was beyond fear. He only wished to spare her what was to come.

"Nothing," he answered. Malton awaited. There could be no turning, not for him. "I do not need an escort," he said.

Isabel snorted delicately. "I am not your escort. I am your wife."

"I do not need—"

"If you say you do not need your wife on this journey I shall bite your lip when next you do kiss me."

"You assume much." He smiled in spite of himself. "You are certain I will kiss you?"

"Naturally." She smiled smugly. "Am I not married to the most lustful and depraved sinner in all of King Henry's domain? Kissed? I am certain to be ravaged before the sun has set."

Richard grinned and shook his head. Only Isabel would dare jest concerning his most besetting sin. Into his life she brought the miracle of laughter.

"You do not seem alarmed," he said, his smile broad.

"Do I not?" she asked innocently. "It must be because I have seen his worst. It is nothing to me."

"Nothing to you?" he said, his eyebrows raised precipitously. "I perceive I have been challenged."

In response she only looked at him, her look cool and assessing, her smile superior.

Yea, he had been challenged.

There was nothing that fired his blood hotter than a challenge.

Isabel, naturally, knew this.

"It will go better next time," Ulrich said to Edmund, their mounts riding close.

"Next time?" Edmund said with a sigh. "She will

knife me ere I get close enough to speak with her again."

Ulrich chuckled. "Then shout your compliments. She will turn to hear them."

"I seem not to have the skill for courtship."

"With the need for feminine company, the skill arises. You will find your way to her heart. She wants you to find your way. With both of you in such earnest effort, you will succeed."

"She wants it? I think not," Edmund said.

"Think you Elsbeth wants my attentions?" Ulrich asked, looking ahead to where Elsbeth rode at Isabel's flank.

"Nay, Elsbeth wants no man's attentions," Edmund said easily. "Elsbeth wants only prayer and the solitude to enjoy her sojourns with God."

"You are wrong," Ulrich said, his blue eyes serious for once. "Elsbeth needs my soft words and light heart more than any woman of my acquaintance, even more than Marie, who needed me most desperately."

"You are wrong," Edmund said. "Elsbeth needs no one."

"Elsbeth needs me," Ulrich said and then shook off his solemnity. "Because I am laughter and ease when her heart knows only worry and disappointment. And I am more than disposed to provide cheer, as well as a few kisses, to train her in the art."

"Aye, you think of her welfare," Edmund chuckled.

"Aye," Ulrich said with a smile, "and if you would

only think on Aelis's, then your courting would run smooth. Think not on what to say, only of what she would hear; give her what she wants and you will win only smiles from her. 'Tis a simple thing to please a woman."

"He seems to have found the way to please her," Rowland said, watching Isabel and Richard as they rode at the head of their company.

"I did not doubt him," William said, ordering the folds of his cloak with a flick of his hand. "He is a most determined man."

"Determined to ride to Malton," Rowland said softly. "What drives him, I wonder."

"Not vengeance," William said.

"Mayhap pride," Rowland said thoughtfully.

"He killed the man who assaulted his wife and his pride."

"But not the man who forced his way into Dornei."

William looked at Rowland askance. "That was strange, was it not? How that Richard did allow it? He did not want Adam within, for just cause, and yet lifted not a hand to stop his entry."

"Henley fostered him."

"A fostering that forged more loyalty than to a wife? Nay, he is not a man to tumble to that," William said, frowning. "There is something amiss there, something unholy which binds Henley and Richard to each other."

"A tie Henley uses when it pleases him," Rowland said, his eyes on the dirt being crushed beneath his mount's hooves.

"Agreed," William said. "The question is, does Richard ride to Malton to break the tie or knot it stronger?"

Isabel felt the coming of Malton in the turn of the road and the shape of the wood banding the fields. She had lived here, riding to her fostering as a child of eight, frightened, excited, alone. It had been spring then, too, though later in the season, the jonquils high and bright, the wind warm. Bertrada had greeted her, arms outstretched in welcome, her pale gown fluttering at her ankles, a woman younger than Isabel was now. Isabel had been entranced at once.

Had Richard?

Isabel cast a glance at her husband. He appeared unmoved by land, the shape of Malton surrounding them slowly. Richard almost always appeared unmoved, except when she made him laugh. Or made him angry. He was neither now and would likely not be moved to any emotion when his will was so focused on reaching Malton.

On reaching Bertrada?

Such thoughts, traitorous and sharp, were unkind.

But were they true?

Richard had claimed no love for Bertrada, a claim he well believed.

Richard had claimed to battle with the cardinal sin of lust, the source of his tumble into sin with

Bertrada, a claim Isabel could not believe.

He believed he lusted indiscriminately and that Bertrada had run afoul of him. How could it be true when Isabel had thrown her body in the way of his hands for an age and he had never tumbled with her?

Richard was a man of more honor than he thought. Could such a man fornicate with his lord's wife without some stronger emotion driving him? Was there not, indeed, something more than lust which had wrapped around him as surely as Bertrada's arms?

Did he not, in some way, love Bertrada?

Did she want to know?

Her thoughts kept tumbling upon themselves, like battling birds tumbling through the air, all flutter and beak and desperation. There was no answer which would give her ease, no answer to pursue which would free her, yet still she strained, a hawk straining against the jesses of history and circumstance.

Malton rose in the distance, a great tower in a large plain. Tall and gray and crenellated it rose, casting a deep shadow on the town which huddled at its stony feet. A strong tower with many men to arm her.

Isabel felt the hairs on her arms rise up in alarm and dread anticipation; would they be admitted? Henley had little reason to allow them entrance. And if not, would they be killed in minutes?

Richard kept riding, his dark eyes on his goal, when every prayer on her lips was for him to halt and return to the safety of Dornei. For him, there was no safety at Malton and 'twas all she wanted for him, beyond honor and pride. Beyond duty.

Be safe, her heart pulsed. *Live*.

The horses kept moving forward, against every prayer, in direct contradiction to every beat of her heart.

Richard would not call on William and Rowland to fight on his behalf, not when Henley's cause was so divinely just. Only Richard was guilty of wrong and only Richard would be held accountable, if Richard had his way.

Only Richard would die.

But not alone. She would not leave him.

"Let me go to the gate alone," she said. "I will seek peaceful admittance. Surely he will grant us entry. We come with no ill intent." Yet even as she spoke, she wondered. Why had Richard come to Malton?

Even as she spoke, he could read the uncertainty in her eyes.

"He has the right to kill me. You know that for a truth, Isabel," he said.

She had no answer. Isabel, whose answers were ever quick, was silent.

William and Rowland rode up and joined them, their faces wiped of any emotion.

"Need we muster a battle plan or will we be admitted?" William asked.

"There will be no battle plan, for you will not battle on my account. Whatever fighting there may be, it will not be your fight," Richard said, his tone clipped, the subject closed.

"I am certain there are enough men for all of us," Rowland grumbled.

William smiled and said to his comrade, "You have met a man who guards his battles as jealously as you guard yours, Rowland. You will mark how irritating it is."

Rowland only grunted.

"There will be no battle," Richard said.

"They will open for us?" William asked.

For answer, Richard said, "They will open for me."

The air swept down the plain, cold and wintry of a sudden, the sky filling with dark clouds and skimming birds suddenly eager for their nests. The wind creaked through the trees, tossing them hard upon themselves, branch rubbing against branch, new leaves just unfurled showing sharp green against the darkening sky. It was cold, as if spring had been a dream of warmth on an endless winter's night.

Ignoring the chill, Richard dismounted. Dismounted and disrobed. His battle gear he laid aside, stripping off his helm, his cloak, his surcoat, his hauberk. Edmund, stunned motionless at first, hurried forward to help his lord. None spoke. The only sound was the whine of wind and the chink of metal as it landed on the damp earth.

He stopped at his breechclout. He stood before them, more naked than clothed, the wind hard in his hair, blowing its blackness to whip against the gray sky. He was defenseless. How could a defenseless man appear as lethal as an unsheathed blade?

He would be admitted. Because he was without defense, even the defense of pride and bearing.

"You are not going," Isabel said, her voice shaking.

"I am," he said, his voice strong, determined, impossible. "And I am going alone."

Isabel ignored him, or tried to. Without aid, she dismounted, her skirts catching in the stirrups, her toes catching in her skirts.

"Nay," she said. "I am going with you. I can disrobe as well as you," she snapped, pulling at her cloak and throwing it from her. The wind caught its weight and sent it flying, a dark green woolen bird clumsily finding its wings.

"Touch one lace and I will beat you," he said. He was so calm, so resolute; she had never so wanted to kill him.

"With what?" she said, her eyes filling with tears, shaming her. "You have nothing with which to fight. You have *nothing!*"

Richard watched her, her hands at her laces, her eyes full of womanish tears. The shame and terror she fought within her heart was magnified a thousand times by the wash of tears over her crystal eyes. Because of him. All because of him.

He had nothing? She was wrong. He had her, this gift he had not wanted and had run from all his life. This divine gift named Isabel.

By this act, he could lose her; in all ways, he could lose her. He held her out to God with an open palm, and held his own life out as well. Let God do what God would do; he knew what was required of him. He would run and hide no longer.

Richard had finally found the strength that was to be found in a will submitted to God.

Sword would not be needed. It would not be that sort of fight, a fight of arms. No armor could save him, be it chain mail or monk's robes. Henley could kill him, he had the right; but Richard had to go. He had fled Malton, leaving Bertrada; he had to return.

"I have all I need for what I must do," he said, his hand covering hers, stopping her tugging at her clothing.

"To die? Is that your plan? You cannot walk so willingly toward death. You cannot leave me. I am not conceived of a child. You have not done your duty to me. You cannot leave. Not yet."

She was crying, the tears falling in rich drops to stain her bosom, her voice tight with lost composure.

They stood alone apart from the others, the clouds near black and covering the sky, the smell of rain heavy and full upon them. They stood alone on that large plain, the tower of Malton a darker stain on the sky. They stood alone, and he would push her from him to stand with William and Rowland and Edmund and Elsbeth and all who were clean, as he was not.

"I must walk this path, Isabel," he said softly, "no matter what awaits."

"Why?" she cried, her eyes red and swollen, her

cheeks white with fear. "Does she mean so much? Can you not forget?"

She hung her head then, her sobs coming from her heart, through her lungs, robbing her of air. Because of him.

"Nay, I cannot forget," he whispered. "Can you? Does she not stand between us always? Ever in your thoughts, even now?" Her face was milk white as she lifted eyes red with tears to his, her pain plain for him to read. In her greatest distress and distrust, she had the strength to show him her heart. Such was the strength of Isabel, the strength of a love that would not fail nor falter, though she lost herself in the giving. Bertrada never dreamed of such strength. "There is more of you in this than Bertrada."

"I do not drive you to this!" she said, angrily lifting her chin.

"Nay, you do not," he said, running his hand lightly over her hair. It was swept wild and high by the wind. "It is God Himself who urges me forward. This is my duty to God," he said gently. "Would you have me turn from it?"

Of all the things he could ask of her, to this she could give only one answer. She wanted to hate him for it, for all of it. For his sin with Bertrada and his determination to destroy himself and his arrogance in asking her to sanction his own destruction. More, the destruction of her dream. Yet had she not stopped living in her dreams? This was the choice before her, and she knew her duty as Richard's wife; she knew the duty Richard required of her and, through the pain of her own loss, found the grace to do it.

How had she come to love him so completely? Such selfless love she had not imagined when she had dreamed of loving Richard. This was love without gain. Love that was all of giving and loss and emptiness. Sacrificial love. It was the love of God in sending His son to certain death. As she now sent Richard.

How was it that such an unromantic love could fill her heart to breaking?

Her tears a remnant, she laid her hand upon his naked chest, feeling his heart pound and his blood pulse, feeling the heat of him, feeling the strength of his will, the force of his life.

"Nay," she said, her voice as strong as she could manage. "Do not turn. Only let me walk it with you."

He laid his hand over her own, a bond of hand to heart to hand. Their eyes met in full understanding, for when had it ever been that Richard could not read Isabel, and when had Isabel not known the heart of Richard?

"You cannot, Isabel," he said, his voice a caress, "though I would find joy inexpressible in your company."

It was the finest compliment he had ever paid her. And he had saved it to mark his death.

He turned from her and from them all, his hand slipping from hers with all the graceful departure of the sun melting away on the horizon. They watched him walk, his nakedness a wound upon a loving eye, in the chill wind that was blowing dry the cold spring earth. They watched him walk the track to Malton, half expecting an arrow to fly down and pierce him, but the sky remained clear of all but cloud.

It was when they watched the gates swing wide and Richard walk into the shadows of Malton that Rowland spoke.

"He is as a penitent on holy pilgrimage."

It was then that she clearly understood what had driven Richard into Malton.

With a muffled cry, she mounted and kicked her palfrey toward that still open gate. Richard would not be alone in his duty to God, not when it was her duty to stand by him.

Chapter Twenty-eight

They followed her, naturally. It was their duty and so she did not begrudge them, but neither would she be talked away from her purpose. Her hair was lifted from her back to fly out behind her, the ends tangling upon themselves with as much nervous purpose as wringing hands. Her cloak was gone, the wind having taken it on a brief flight until casting it to earth, a length of green wool to mix with the brown mud of early spring. Her bliaut did little to warm her, yet she had not a thought for the chill wind that pressed against her frame. All thought was for Richard.

And then she was through Malton's gates, the memories closing on her with the iron force of manacles. It was all as she remembered it, though perhaps a bit more forbidding, or perhaps that was because of her purpose. She had to save Richard.

It had started.

Henley stood in the deep mud at the center of Malton's bailey, his posture bold and his manner sure. He stood within his own domain, where all within were sworn to him, and within this domain stood Richard, nearly naked, clearly penitent. Alone. Until now.

Isabel dropped from the back of her horse like a stone and rushed to stand at Richard's side. More slowly, her approach cautious and careful, Bertrada moved across the yard to join them, her favorite woman holding her elbow against a fall. All signs of age, yet Bertrada was not old—nay, she was as beautiful as Isabel remembered her.

Her hair was long and thick and blackest black; she wore it loose, always, a simple band at her brow holding all in place. Her skin was as pale as spring petals and as fine. She wore white, always, knowing that the color flattered her as no other, the fall of her dark hair all the darker and richer for the white that surrounded her slenderness. Her eyes were as black and shining as her hair; huge and expressive and thickly lashed. She was a woman to make a woman envy instantly; she was a woman to make a man sin. Aye, she was, and even as a child, Isabel had sensed that Bertrada knew her own skill and did not find fault with it.

Isabel had wanted to be Bertrada without having truly liked her; such was the power of her magnetism.

The walls of Malton were lined with bowmen and household knights, the yard quickly filling with squires and knights newly dubbed, cooks and blacksmiths, falconers and stablehands. Richard may have wished to walk into Malton alone, but he was not alone now.

He felt her at his side, this she knew, yet he did not turn from Henley. No matter; she was with him. He would not face Henley alone.

Henley's look was smug, his tight and unpleasant smile telling that, though he did not understand the purpose of Richard's visit, by his visit he signaled his defeat. Such a scene—both Henley's crass superiority and Richard's restrained submission—caused a flood of memories to wash over her, memories she had left behind at Malton which, at Malton once again, rose fresh and unspoiled by time. Only the memories of Richard had she kept for herself, stoking and nurturing them as tenderly as a babe. Other memories now rose so violently that she fought the urge to retch.

They had been much alone, the two of them. Both young and fair, both far from home, for had not Bertrada been a wife newly made, and had not Richard been alone within the throng of Malton? Yea, a leader he had been, she had seen that aright, yet a boy alone; no bond had formed for him, such as the one she now witnessed in Rowland and William. All men needed such a bond, yet Richard had had none. Henley he had shadowed, and Henley had much relished the role of sun in Richard's life, both burning and warming Richard as his mood dictated. From Bertrada, from fair Bertrada, there had been only soft smiles and gentle words. Isabel had felt the proof of that herself; Bertrada was a soft and gentle woman, and it had caused Isabel many brushes against sharp guilt that she was not more like her.

She remembered how Bertrada had smiled and how Henley had watched and how Richard had stumbled. It had been no secret; now that she was a woman bedded, she could read the signs of desire and fulfillment. Henley had known.

Before she could speak, Richard growled, "I did not want you here. I did not want you to see this."

"The whole world may watch, but not I?" she flared. "Always you push me away, and you have yet to learn that I will not be pushed." Her anger was high and her eyes full of stinging tears.

Richard turned to her, his chest and shoulders a shield to hide her from the curious eyes of Malton. He would shield her when he stood naked and repentant in front of Henley? The tears overflowed, and she wiped her cheeks with her hands.

"I do not push you away, Isabel," he said. "I push you away from me. To protect you. I do not . . . I have never trusted myself with you," he finished, his eyes the blue of a moonless night, dark and soft and full of hidden pain.

Oh, aye, it made sense to her, now that she understood what he believed of himself. Rejecting her? Nay, he had been protecting her from the sin which he felt gnawing at him day and night; he thought himself as wild as any beast and had sought to protect her from being devoured. Could any man be so wrong about his own nature?

"How strange that is," she said with a smile more tears than mirth, "because, naturally, I trust you. With all. Without fear."

"You have ever lacked caution, Isabel," he said smiling.

His answering smile was brief and then faltered completely as he turned again to face Henley. William, Rowland, the squires, and Elsbeth stood near the gate, unwilling witnesses to whatever Richard had planned. They did not know, but Isabel did. She knew because she knew Richard and the depth of his honor and commitment to God. Did any know Richard better than she? But she did not want him to do this, no matter that he called it his duty to God. Let him fulfill his spiritual duty in the abbey, away from her, locked behind abbey walls . . . yea, even that.

Her tears coursed down, a torrent that flooded her face. To be so discomposed in front of Henley and Bertrada was a worse humiliation than she had ever thought to bear, yet she could not stop. And she would not leave.

She would hand Richard over to Father Abbot herself if only he would not take this next irreversible step.

"You have gained entrance. What is your purpose here, Richard?" Henley asked in sarcastic courtesy.

"Go to the abbey," Isabel hissed, tugging on Richard's hand, ignoring Henley and all of Malton. "Give yourself to God in spiritual service. I will not hinder you."

Richard looked down at her, his hand strong and warm in hers, his countenance solemn. Never had he looked more determined or more broken in spirit.

"I ran to hide within the embrace of the abbey once before. I will not again," he said softly, his eyes for her alone.

"You must," she begged, tugging at him, trying to pull him from this path that must surely destroy him.

He took both of her hands in his and smiled, a smile so sad and so true that her heart stopped within her. Her tears stopped. Even the wind stopped. All was as still as a world in prayer to hear what Isabel had prayed her whole life to hear from Richard's lips.

"To do so I must leave you, Isabel. I will not give you up. Never again."

Joy and suffering twined as one and pierced her soul. He would not give her up. He would destroy himself in trying to keep her.

She did not want his destruction. She wanted him safe, even if it meant losing him. In that moment of selfless love, Isabel left the remains of her childhood behind forever. She carried a woman's love within her heart, a love sown years ago and which had taken many seasons to ripen, and she understood fully the weight of pain such love required.

No matter what happened to her, Richard must be well.

"Did you ride to Malton so that I could be privy

to your mattress whisperings?" Henley scoffed. "If I left you to it, you would no doubt tumble her in the mud at my feet."

Richard turned to face Henley, his face set and resolute. "Nay, I am not a man for that, though I believed so for a time." Richard paused and let the implied accusation stand. Henley remained silent, though his eyes revealed his surprise at being contradicted on a point so carefully nurtured.

Richard was not the boy he had been. Henley had convinced him well, with lectures and taunts, of his lustful nature and lustful thoughts—thoughts common to all boys coming into manhood. Richard could see that now in Edmund and Ulrich; 'twas nothing more than a season which a man passed through on his way to maturity. But Richard had not had the counsel and company of other squires; Richard had only had Henley, and Henley had convinced him that his very nature was flawed.

Yet, still, he had sinned with Bertrada.

"Nay, Henley," Richard continued, "I have come to publicly confess and to seek your forgiveness. And if not that, your retribution."

The wind stayed silent and still, as if listening for Henley's response. Isabel commanded her tears to dry, for she would face Henley and Bertrada and all of Malton with as much dignity as her husband. He deserved no less and required so much more; yet she could not give him what he most needed: a clean heart and a spotless soul. Only God could give him that, and only God would think of using

Henley as a tool for Richard's redemption.

Henley was as white as winter wind. "Nay, you dare not," he whispered, eyeing all those who thronged within Malton's walls to hear Dornei gossip.

Bertrada's pale complexion was bled of all color, her beauty a mask drained of all save horror. She made to leave. Richard called her back.

"Stay, Bertrada, and hear my confession. Let all within Malton's walls, where first I did fall into sin, hear."

"You will ruin me," she whispered, her hand extended in her plea.

Richard smiled, looking for all the world like a monk offering comfort to a lost sinner. "Bertrada, we are already ruined. This will make us clean."

"Slander my wife and I will slay you," said Henley hoarsely, sounding more like himself.

"You will slay me for telling the truth, yet you let me live after joining my body to your wife's?" Richard intoned. "What man chooses such a path?"

"He knew," Isabel hissed, her eyes on Henley, her heart on Richard. "He always knew."

Richard turned to look at Bertrada, leaning against her woman, her curves turned upon themselves as if she wished to sink into the mud that stained her hem.

He remembered, daily, how Bertrada had sought his company, how she had touched him innocently, how she had made him smile and eased his loneliness. How the innocence and comfort had been a shield to hide her longings. Aye, he had learned of women and their ways while at Malton. Only Isabel did not play at women's games. Only Isabel was bold with both her intent and her words. Isabel hid nothing—not her desire, not her heart.

His look for Bertrada was all of pity. Pity and naught else. For Henley he had only cold disdain.

Henley had known? Of course he had known. What man turned aside when his wife sought the company of another?

"You used your wife, used her as the stick to drive me. And the gain?" He smiled grimly. "A man under a weight of guilt such as mine would hardly say nay to the lord he had sinned against. But such is not the path to redemption laid out by my Lord. Public confession is required; public confession shall be given."

The population of Malton stamped and jostled in their curiosity and impatience. The Lord and Lady of Dornei presenting themselves to the Lord and Lady of Malton was a spectacle irresistible to any. Children sat on shoulders, women elbowed their way to the front, and the curtain walk was three deep in armed men; all waited, all were hushed to hear more than the mumbled emotion of the quartet in the center of them.

Richard, his body lean and hard, knelt in the mud at the feet of the Lord and Lady of Malton. His face was calm and composed, like a man at prayer. What he did was as holy as prayer, this Isabel understood. Richard sought release from his burden of sin and guilt, and though it would likely ruin him, she would not hinder him in his holy duty. Nay, she would stand with him.

Erect and proud she stood, her hair a flag of victory, her chin high and her eyes clear. She stood at his side, his mate in all things, even this most public of humiliations. Humiliation was a small word when held against the presence and the power of Richard.

Richard's voice was loud and strong, carrying to all parts of Malton, compelling each ear to hear his confession of sin.

"I have defiled the marriage bed of Henley and Bertrada," he boomed. "I have committed the cardinal sin of lust. I have betrayed my lord. I ask forgiveness."

He knelt, mud-covered and head up, seeking Henley's decision, his soul at rest.

All was quiet. The wind started again, sweeping across the sky, pushing dark clouds before it until they cascaded across the late afternoon sky. It threatened rain. The sky was heavy with water, ready to burst open and wash them all. An errant breeze, cold and clean, shot into the bailey, blowing Richard's dark hair. Isabel could see his flesh rise in bumps at the contact, but he did not move. He waited, trusting in God, though it was Henley who stood with a sword at his side and archers at his command. Richard had laid his life in God's hands; he would not snatch it out for fear of Henley. Not again.

The crowd was titillated; she could feel it and hear it in the excited whispers all around her. Henley's silence grew until the weight of it pressed against her, crushing her lungs and flattening the beat of her heart. Richard could wait silently and at rest for Henley's decision; Isabel could not.

"Can you not forgive the man who stumbled," she hissed between her teeth, "when you are the man who set the trap?" Henley's eyes widened, and Bertrada gasped. So, Bertrada had not known. But Henley had known. "How much forgiveness will you need to seek from Richard, if God is capable of softening your hardened heart? You used your wife as harlot, Henley. How much forgiveness for that?"

"Enough," he spat. "You were ever a bothersome chit."

"Speak well of Isabel or speak not at all. Do what you will to me, but she will not be harmed by even a wayward glance from you," Richard said coldly.

How was it that a man, kneeling and naked, could carry such a weight of lethal threat behind his words?

"Please, let it be done," Bertrada implored her husband, her eyes black holes of pain and humiliation.

"Very well," Henley grunted out, the veins in his forehead throbbing. "It is done. You are forgiven."

Richard leaned forward and clasped Henley's hand, kissing it. "Thank you," he said.

Isabel took her first full breath of the afternoon. It was over. But it was only beginning. Isabel had not perceived how far Richard's duty would take him.

"Bertrada," Richard said, standing, his near naked body holding all eyes, "seek your lord's forgiveness, as is right. Confess and be healed."

Bertrada looked little disposed to ask forgiveness of the man who had smiled and looked the other way while she sported with another man, but Richard was determined that she walk the path of cleansing he had just trod. It was the only way. It was all that could save her. Otherwise, Henley, his pride publicly shorn, would kill her, and none would fault him. Bertrada must confess and obtain forgiveness. Bertrada must be saved or he would be responsible for her death.

"Enough," Henley growled, his heavy face red with anger and impatience. "You have what you sought of me, and it is more than you deserve."

"Forgiveness is always more than we deserve, yet who has not sinned? Who among us has no need of it? Come, Bertrada. You know 'twas not well done, what you continued. Lay down your weight of guilt and be free," Richard said, his eyes kind, compelling her to act.

She had little enough defense to stand against him. She had pursued Richard, innocent though they both had been of where such flirtations ended, to meet the lack in her own marriage bed. She had not conceived, and Henley was not a man to keep a wife not fruitful. She had to bear a child, and if not by Henley, then by someone else, someone who would never speak of his betrayal. Richard, strict in duty, beautiful in body, alone in spirit, had seemed perfect. Their hurried couplings still shone in her memory like starlight, dark and bright. Exposed now to daylight, her decision seemed tawdry. There had been no honor in their gropings, only desperation.

She dropped to her knees, her face hidden in her hands. " 'Tis true. I have been sick at heart for what I allowed to happen. Forgive me, Henley, please forgive me. I would only honor you, with my life, or with my death if you cannot forgive. I await," she said, raising her dark eyes to his. "My heart is at rest."

It was a moving sight, her beauty and her piety blending seamlessly with her womanly submission. It was a balm to the eye, and those who watched sighed in satisfaction and nodded mute approval.

Henley looked like a man trapped. He had known—aye, he had manipulated to have the two of them spend much time together, knowing where it had to lead. Bertrada was a beauty, but he was not a man to be stirred by a woman's beauty, and after breaching her on their marriage night, he had not found his way to her bed again. She had hungered for a man until her eyes had settled on Richard, for it was Richard whom he had placed under her eye. Again and again, he had set them together, speaking words of praise concerning the boy to Bertrada, teaching Richard that he was a man soaked in sinful lusts and ill equipped to quench them. He had done his work well. If all had gone as he wished, Bertrada would have conceived a child and Richard would have drowned in guilt, ready to grant Henley any service to expiate his crime. But Richard had run, Bertrada had not conceived, and he now faced the public exposure of his secret acts.

Bertrada waited, her piety and submission obvious to all. To kill her now would leave him none the richer in pride or regard.

"Up, Bertrada. You are forgiven," he ordered roughly.

Instead of obeying him, she sobbed into her hands, kneeling before him. He offered his hand to help her to her feet, eager to end this display. Bertrada rose, leaning into him, her sobs shaking her. And still Richard stayed, waiting.

"Begone," Henley barked, motioning with his hand toward the gate. "There is nothing more for you here."

"Is there not?" Richard said calmly. "Only you can know, Henley, if there is any sin you must confess to me or to your wife. If your soul is without stain, then I will go."

Richard stood unmoving, waiting, his expression expectant. Henley looked a man in torment.

"It was not I who fouled my vows," Henley said in an undertone.

"Nay?" Richard responded. "To love, honor, and protect, lifting your wife as holy and blameless to the Lord of Hosts?"

"Words spoken at the marriage ceremony," Henley said. "Am I expected to remember and keep every vow I have ever sworn?"

"Yea," Richard said, "you are."

"Did you plan all this when you stripped and walked through my gates?"

"I only wanted forgiveness. For all who have sinned."

"You are more monk than man," Henley grumbled.

"It does not take a monk to see sin before his eyes, or in his heart."

"Must we all kneel in the mud today?" Henley snarled, his anger obvious.

Richard stepped close to him, the visual force of his nakedness a blow against Henley's guilt, and said in a hoarse whisper, "I know what you did."

Henley looked up abruptly, and Richard's eyes pierced through the layers of deceit with which Henley had covered himself.

"You set us together. Again and again, time upon time. A woman of beauty who hungered for a man's touch and a youth just coming into the full force of his manhood; you taught me well that my lusts could not be contained, that I was ruled by passion and sin and could never hope to quench their fire. I believed every word you spoke," Richard growled softly, his eyes smoldering. "You needed a child, an heir, Henley, and I was the vessel which was to provide one for you. And knowing how I had sinned against you, knowing the guilt which would ride me all my life, you hoped I would grant you any service to expiate my crime. But Bertrada did not conceive," Richard hissed sharply. "And I will not hide this sin any longer.

Will you stand before God and declare that you do not need forgiveness?"

Henley was trapped. There was naught he could do. If he did not ask for forgiveness, would Richard then speak aloud his guilt? Such a path he would not risk. Richard could see all his dark thoughts in the frantic shifting of his eyes; Henley, his motives and his methods, were as clear to him as rainwater. Even now, he plotted. Bertrada could be plumped with child another way.

Henley dropped to his knees at Bertrada's feet, his movements stiff and quick.

"Do not kneel to me, my lord, 'tis not—"

"Hush, woman," he barked. "Can I do less than others have done?"

All waited, shocked that Henley had been driven to this. Yet did not eternity weigh more heavily on a man than this temporal life? Not a one of them would have chosen differently.

"Forgive me, Lady, for taking such a course. 'Twas ill done," he said.

For answer, Bertrada knelt with him, throwing her arms around his neck.

'Twas done.

Richard smiled and silently thanked God for His mercy. And then thanked Him for holding Isabel's tongue during this display. He had felt her urgency and her fear, her anger and her distrust, yet her lips had remained sealed. 'Twas nigh on a miracle. Turning, he walked with Isabel toward the open gate, and Dornei.

She understood more than what had been said

in their public confession and mutual forgiveness. Richard knew that Henley had done more than turn his head away from the adultery of his wife; he had actively pursued the alliance, forcing his squire and his wife to spend much time together. Also, he had convinced Richard to owning the cardinal sin of lust; a young man of such serious and godly bent would have taken such instruction to heart. Such had Henley not confessed. And she also understood what Henley had hoped to gain. An heir, no doubt, for Bertrada had never borne one. But she would say none of it. It was left behind, with Henley and with all memory of Malton, to be forgotten. Let God deal with Henley in His own way and time. Richard had done his part.

"What has he done? I comprehend it not," Edmund said to those who waited with him near the gate.

" 'Therefore, confess your sins to one another, and pray for one another, so that you may be healed.' " William quoted. " 'The effective prayer of a righteous man can accomplish much . . . My brethren, if any among you strays from the truth, and one turns him back, let him know that he who turns a sinner from the error of his way will save his soul from death, and will cover a multitude of sins.' The Book of James, chapter five."

"You know as much holy writ as a monk," Edmund said, looking wide-eyed at William.

"Yea," he said woodenly. "I do."

He did not seem pleased with his skill, Richard noted. Richard and Isabel were at the gate, and now he would see where his confession had taken him.

William and Rowland faced him squarely, their expressions solemn. He could not read them and prayed anew that God would not desert him in this first of many steps back into the world of honorable men.

"You have heard the depth of my sin," he said, facing them.

"Because we have heard your confession," William said, his silver eyes glinting like polished steel.

"I have sinned much," Richard said, prompting them.

"As have I," Rowland said.

"As have we all," William added.

"You have walked the Way of the Cross," Richard said, his voice revealing his awe and, perhaps, a touch of envy.

"Aye, and mayhap for the same cause for which you joined the abbey brethren," William said. "Great service to expiate great sins?"

Richard smiled lightly. "It does not work."

"Nay, it does not," William answered. "But few have the heart to do what is required."

"To walk in the Way, even to far Ashkalon, is an easier journey than the one which brought you here," Rowland said, his dark eyes soft and expressive. "Few men would have the strength to do what you have done here today."

"I had to obey my Lord," Richard said, the words simple, the meaning profound.

"Aye, and that is your strength," William said. "A

man of such strength is a welcome comrade. Even if you do hoard your battles," William said with a pained smile.

"A single flaw," Rowland answered with a grin. "None can say you hoard your clothes."

"Did none bring my clothes?" Richard asked, his expression comical.

"We brought ourselves only," Rowland answered, "certain you hurried to your death."

"I was dead," he said with a grin, his face alight; "dead in sin; now I am alive. And cold."

"You expected less?" William said. "I wager you will not start a new fashion being thus clothed."

"Unclothed," Rowland corrected.

They passed through Malton's gates, leaving all darkness there within her dark tower. None stopped them, and they left with as many in their party as they entered. 'Twas God's grace and nothing less.

The wind was hard outside the walls and the sky the forced gray of an early and stormy dusk. 'Twould be a cold ride home. Home. He was leaving Malton, not running, and he was going home. To Dornei.

"Edmund, fetch my—"

But Edmund was mounted and gone before he could finish, off to fetch Richard's clothes where he had left them on the road, off with the reins of Richard's mount firmly in his fist. All mounted with smiles, he behind Isabel on her palfrey. Isabel, of them all, was strangely silent. Certainly God's miracle over her tongue could now come to an end?

She sat before him without protest. Also without joy. He wanted her to speak, to let her words tumble out, to berate him, tease him, question him. Not this silence. Not from Isabel, who hid nothing from him. He did not know what to say to her when she was so silent. And he was afraid to ask her what was in her heart. Richard smiled ruefully; he had faced Henley and Bertrada and all of Malton. He had faced his sin, seeing it for what it was and what it was not. He had shouted his transgressions to heaven itself and had felt none of the fear he felt now with his wife in his arms. A word from her and all the joy he had just won would vanish.

But he must speak. He could not lose Isabel, even to silence.

"I need your forgiveness, Isabel, if you can find the grace to grant it."

With a soft sigh, she took breath and answered him. "For what should I forgive you?"

"For Bertrada?" he said. How easily he said the name now; all the power of that name was gone.

"Better you should ask if I can forgive Bertrada, for taking what I wanted most in all the world," she said, her voice a tremor of heavy emotion.

"She took nothing which I did not freely give," Richard said softly, holding her against him to ease the pain of his words.

"Oh, aye, you can say it," Isabel said brokenly.

"I did it, Isabel; you know the truth of that."

"Yea, your body she took, the intimacy of you and the heart of you and the dream of you. Nay, I will not cry for the dream of Richard; that is gone," she said, throwing her face to the sky, blinking back the tears.

"I am here, Isabel," he whispered, his voice a soothing caress against her hair. "I am yours."

"Because of God's ordaining."

"I can find no fault with the path of God's choosing for me," he said smiling.

"Did God plan for you to tumble with Bertrada?"

"Nay!"

"Nay, you *chose* Bertrada!"

Yea, if she believed that, it would grieve her spirit. Would he not have ripped open his chest to hurl his heart upon the ground if he did believe that Isabel had chosen Adam?

"I did not choose Bertrada," he said.

Isabel inched forward and turned her face to scour him with a look. "I understand well the part Henley played in the game he had devised, but do not deny that you found her beautiful and that—"

"I deny nothing," Richard said sharply, "most especially my own responsibility. Henley played his part and Bertrada hers; yet no one forced me to her bed. I found my own way. I knew what I did. No fog blinded me."

Isabel was silent, each heartbeat painful in a chest crushed by sorrow. No fog had blinded him. It was not true. He was not the animal he imagined; he could not have coupled with Bertrada unless he loved her. He loved her. He had chosen her.

Richard had not chosen Isabel. God had forced her on him, a direct result of her prayer. It was the truth, she knew it for a fact. Had she not prayed for

Richard and had Richard not been given to her in the next instant?

"What is it, Isabel?" he asked, his voice soft again. They rode at the back of their company, their words heard by no one.

"I believe you," she answered, her voice unsteady and thin. "I believe you. You would not have lain with Bertrada unless you had strong feelings for her, feelings stronger than lust. Feelings of love. None could have manipulated you into her arms without your heart being engaged. You love her."

"I do not love Bertrada," he said roughly, pulling her against him, his arm hard around her narrow waist.

"Perhaps not now—"

"I never loved Bertrada!"

"You must have," she said simply, her knowledge of him her surest guide.

"Isabel, you rate me too high," he growled. "Usually, I find it hard to criticize such a tendency, but now—"

"I know you, Richard," she argued. " 'Twas not blind lust which drove you into her arms."

"Nay, 'twas lust for you!" he barked, jerking the reins in his anger.

Lust for her?

Lust for *her?*

Impossible. Richard had never lusted after her; even when he had been convinced of being a lustful beast, when all his lustful thoughts had found their fruition, he had never touched her. He had only touched Bertrada. And 'twas not uncontrollable lust which drove Richard to act; this they now both knew.

So, with this knowledge planted firmly in her heart, she answered him.

"You did not lust for me," she said dismissively.

Richard barked his answer, a cry of laughter covered with frustration.

"You beg for words and then discount their meaning! I tell you what I *know*. Do I not know my own thoughts? My own heart?"

"I have often wondered," she said.

"Wonder no longer. I tell you, though it shames me, though how it could after all this day has brought, I do not know. This is my day for shaming and confession, so hear, Isabel, what I have hidden from you all these years."

She waited. It would be horrible; she could hear the horror of it in his voice. It was his day for confession, public and personal; she would not stop him, though she cringed to hear what he would reveal.

"That day in the stable," he began, his voice tight with emotion. "You remember it?"

Remember it? She had lived upon it. Would he now admit to the lie that kiss had been?

"Do you?" he barked.

"Yea, I do remember it," she said.

He was hard against her back, his arm a band that trapped her against him. His very blood seemed to pulse and vibrate, so hot was his tension.

"That day, that moment," he said hoarsely, "signaled my defeat."

She slumped against him and hung her head. 'Twas just as she had known it. He had not wanted her; his kiss had been—

"Do not lose yourself in dreaming of what you think I am saying, Isabel," he commanded. "Listen to my words and hear their truth. I am baring all to you. Appreciate the gift of my debasement."

"I hear you very well," she said stiffly. "Kissing me was a moment of defeat for you."

"Aye, it was," he agreed, "for could I hold honor high when I lusted after my brother's betrothed? I, who watched you and the black gleaming flag of your hair every moment I was not honing my skills? Did I not know that you watched me? Do you know what it does to a man, to know he is desired by the most desirable of women? Did I not hear every laugh you gave to the others? Did I not burn for you every hour of my waking and in every dream of my slumber? I burned, Isabel, and I ran, to keep from burning you with the fire of my unlawful desire."

He had burned for her. 'Twas a dream impossible. But where did Bertrada fit into dreams of Isabel?

"And what of Bertrada? I can hear the question, though you do not speak it," he said. "Bertrada was no more lawful for me than you, yet she was no virgin and she was not to become my sister. Bertrada was . . . there . . . willing . . . and as alone in her desires as I."

"Alone? What of Henley?"

"Henley," he smiled. "Henley does not worship her body as a husband should; his tastes are not . . . natural."

"Oh," she said, her eyes wide and her mouth slack with shock. "Poor Bertrada."

"Aye, poor Bertrada," he echoed. "She is to be pitied, and pity, more than desire, was what drove me to her bed."

"But there was desire," she said.

Richard laughed without a trace of humor and lifted his head to the twilight sky. "Isabel, you drive a man hard. Yea, there was desire. For you."

"I do not understand how that can be so."

"Then you do not understand your own allure. When I kissed you, no gentle kiss for an inexperienced maid, I . . . had not intended it."

" 'Twas I who kissed you. I who followed you. I who first touched you," she said. "You are the one who ended it." She had pursued him. He had shown no signs of wanting her. Not ever.

"If I had not ended it then, you would have found yourself on the stable floor with your bliaut ripped from your body."

The violence of his words shook her. She did not doubt the truth of what he said, of his believing it, but he was wrong. Richard would have never—

"Do not doubt me, Isabel," he said, his hand sliding up her torso to caress her bosom. His naked chest pulsed heat even in the chill of the day. Where was Edmund with his surcoat? Where was their party? William and Rowland were far ahead and Elsbeth was sequestered with Ulrich, her hood shielding her face. Richard pulled Isabel hard against him, his arousal a blunt blade riding the small of her back. "Do not doubt the strength of my desire for you, nor my battles against it. I fought for control daily, hourly. I told you I battled lust. I lied. I battled you."

Sweet words to heal years of rejection; how she longed to believe him. But she would not let his words turn her; there was still Bertrada. There was still the truth that he had not wanted to marry her. How much could he have wanted her, if he wanted her at all, if he had not wanted her as wife?

"I battled you and lost," he continued. "And lost again. And so it was that I came upon Bertrada, with images of you surrounding me, taunting me. Bertrada endured her own hauntings in her place at Malton, and so we met our needs in each other. I knew it was wrong; I make no excuse, but all my thoughts then were wrong. What was one more upon another? Was to want my lord's wife so much more a sin than wanting my brother's bride?"

"You did not want to marry me," she said, trying to ignore the pain in his voice and the pain in her own.

"I did not want to leave the sanctuary of men," he said. "What control would I have with you when I had none sequestered from you? You were with me in the abbey, Isabel, in every hour, every office, every prayer. I burned from within, and not with the holy fire of righteousness. I burned for you."

She bent her head and let her tears fall into her hands.

It answered. It answered all. Henley's lies, Bertrada's need, Richard's desires, and her own pursuit of the one man she had wanted; all tumbled together to produce a man in search of redemption and a woman in search of a monk.

"Will you go back?" she asked softly, holding his arm against her, feeling the silkiness of his hair and the raw muscle which was the man. "When I am with child, will you go back to the abbey?"

It was her last question, her last fear. He had chosen life among the Benedictines, and though his reasons were gone, he had found peace and purpose in that life. His duty to both their houses fulfilled, even his desire for her fulfilled, would he return to the life that had suited him so well?

"I cannot go back to burrow in the abbey," he said, laying his cheek to rest upon her head.

"Why?" she whispered into the misting rain. The sun was near set, the sky dark with cloud.

"Because," he said, and she could feel him kiss her hair, "it is as I said. I cannot leave you."

The sound of hoofbeats was their only warning. "Your clothes, my lord," Edmund said, his intrusion rude and jarring.

Richard slipped off Isabel's palfrey and quickly donned his clothes, rapidly done with Edmund's help. His own mount waited, as did the rest of their party, and he was mounted and riding at Isabel's side before the first heavy drops of rain fell.

He could not leave her. Yea, 'twas what he had

said, but were these the total weight of words of love she would hold against her heart for all her earthly life? 'Twas not enough. 'Twas not near enough.

"Tell me again," she said, "before Edmund interrupted. You said you could not leave me . . . ?" she prompted.

William and Rowland, hearing her, laughed as men will do, the sound full of pride and hidden meaning, and rode ahead. She wished them well and gone. Elsbeth blushed and pulled her hood around her, against the rain and searching eyes. Ulrich rode at her side, urging her horse to match his canter. They were free to go; Richard would never declare his heart with so many ears and eyes to take witness. Edmund rode behind—a length behind after Isabel's sharp look to push him back. Did a squire need to ride at her tail to be useful?

All for naught.

"That is what I said," Richard shrugged, smiling. "What more must be added?"

He kicked his mount into a canter to match Ulrich's, and she did the same to match his. The sky was gloomy and the rain hard as it hit; they would not make Dornei before Vespers. The setting was unromantic and the mood uninspired. And Richard did nothing to help.

"Perhaps to tell me why you cannot leave me?" she coaxed.

"You are my wife. I will not leave you. 'Twould be unnatural and neglectful of my—"

"Richard," she snapped, "if you say 'duty' I will—"

"—most natural desires," he finished huskily.

She looked over at him, for when had she ever been able to resist the sight of him? She knew him well. She had loved him for years. She was to be married to him for a lifetime, a most cherished answered prayer. The teasing smile he wore now was bright enough to part the low clouds that enshrouded the earth and pressed upon them.

Richard might not be adept at courtly banter, but did it matter when she could read his heart?

"Will you or will you not admit that you love me?" she asked.

"I would rather show you," he said, grinning.

Isabel smiled in return and then kicked her horse into a run, leaping into the lead in their unannounced race for Dornei. "Then show me, my lord," she said as she left him behind, "and I will then give you the words to tell me."

Richard caught up with her in moments, his mount easily overmatching hers. "I will leave you too spent for words, Lady," he said, his eyes gleaming with dire promise.

"Think you that is possible?" she panted. Dornei was just through the next stand of wood, a dark and tangled mass of branches in the pelting rain.

"I see it as my duty," he said, his words a delicious threat.

"And when does duty become desire?" she asked, echoing him, slowing her mount.

"With you, Isabel," he said without hesitation and without restraint. "With you."

Chapter Twenty-nine

He rode out of the wood slowly, his chain mail glinting with rain. His sword was out, shining even in the dim light of a stormy spring dusk. His identity was no mystery; they had known each other long, had grown to maturity together at Malton, had supped together at Dornei. And he had been sent to Warefeld and been told to remain. Yet here he was, in the wood surrounding Dornei.

Nicholas, his sword raised for battle, his shield ready, rested upon the back of his warhorse and waited.

Richard drew his sword instantly, knowing there would be no parley. This battle between them had been coming for an age. Nicholas and his malicious tongue had seen to it that Richard had cast Isabel from him with both hands. He had been a fool. Worse, what he had done to Isabel because of this man's caustic words shamed him. There had been no place for Richard among the other boys at Malton, no rapport; he had stood alone, always alone, as Nicholas had stood in the center of the boys, shunning him.

Richard smiled his eagerness. They each stood alone now.

Edmund held his shield, and Richard held out his hand for it. The boy kicked his horse forward, his face white and his eyes firm with purpose. The arrow came from the wood, piercing Edmund through the hip. The boy fell from his horse without a cry, the shield rolling from his outstretched hand.

'Twas Isabel who cried.

"Nay! What is this? Did you not swear homage—"

"Attend the boy, Isabel," Richard commanded, his eyes not leaving Nicholas. "Is there an arrow for me?" he asked Nicholas.

"Only my sword," Nicholas said.

"What of me?" Isabel said, her voice high and angry as she knelt beside Edmund and pressed the length of her bliaut to his wound. The blood soaked the fabric through in seconds.

"For you he plans a wedding," Richard answered, speaking Nicholas's intent.

Nicholas smiled grimly. "She is too rich a prize to let slip."

He attacked then, kicking his mount to run at Richard. Richard waited, letting him close the distance over the sodden earth, and Isabel could not smother the whisper of doubt which wondered if Richard was afraid to meet a fellow knight in combat. Did he pray, even now, for divine deliverance?

The sound of running horses, heavy with the weight of armored men, came from out of the wood. "Saint Stephen," she mumbled, "let it be aid."

Her prayer was answered.

William and Rowland rode out of the wood, their own swords unsheathed and ready for blood. With a sigh, she thanked God for His mercy in delivering Richard, for who could defeat both William le Brouillard and Rowland the Dark in battle? Quickly she turned her full attention to Edmund.

Of all the skills which Bertrada had taught her, the mending of flesh and the setting of bone were matters at which she excelled.

Her eyes kind, she urged confidence and comfort. "Can you feel your toes, Edmund?"

"Aye," he whispered.

"Can you move them?

"I dare not try, Lady," he breathed.

Isabel smiled down at him. "Then do not try. I must remove the arrow. It must be pushed, the fletching cut . . ."

She needed to work quickly, before his pain increased. And it would. She had learned that the pain of injury only grew as time passed and that any aid was best given soon.

She had no knife.

A knife appeared out of the rain.

Looking up, she saw Rowland towering above her. "You know what you are about?"

"Yea, but Richard—"

"Richard has no need of aid. You do," he said with a soft smile.

Richard had no need of aid? 'Twas not so. Richard had merely waited while Nicholas rode him down.

Isabel looked up, away from the blood that pumped out of Edmund. Only for a moment, only hoping to see that Richard was safe. Surely William fought Nicholas. What could Richard have done without a shield to protect him?

He had done much.

Nicholas's shield was shattered and his mount lame. He and Richard were standing facing each other in the cold and driving rain, their swords wet and shining and lethal. William of Greneforde held the reins of Richard's horse, an easy and nonchalant spectator to the battle being played out before him.

"Nay, he cannot—" she whispered, not able to take her eyes from Richard.

"He can," Rowland said calmly. "And has."

"How?"

"The boy needs attention, Isabel," Rowland reminded. "How may I aid you?"

"Cut the fletching off. A clean cut with no splinters, mind . . . and you may tell me how Richard unhorsed Nicholas," she said tartly. 'Twas not possible. Could prayer unhorse a warrior?

"Aye," he smiled, bending to the boy and gripping the shaft firmly. "Hold, boy; it will be quick," he comforted. He sliced through the shaft, his knife sharp and working cleanly through the wood.

Looking to Isabel, he asked the question with his eyes, his hand on the blunt end of the shaft. With a nod, she answered him. Without pausing to take breath or to prepare Edmund, Rowland lifted Edmund upward and shoved the shaft through to the grass behind. A fresh burst of blood poured through, and Rowland looked for something to stanch the flow.

"Let it bleed out," Isabel said, kneeling beside Edmund, who was white and silent, his hands clenched on Rowland's arms. "Whatever wood remains within will be washed out."

"He will lose much blood."

"Only for a moment. We need something to bind him, something without the stain of mud and field," she said, looking down at her own muddy bliaut and Rowland's splattered surcoat. "I have only my shift," she said and began to strip off her clothes.

Let Richard beat her, if he lived.

She watched Richard, her fingers hurrying with her laces, the rain making all stiff and unyielding and cold. The ring of blades striking, loud and strangely melodic, beat against the pounding rain in uneven rhythm. The two men circled each other, Richard the aggressor, his point up, dancing almost gaily in search of kindred steel. Ever graceful, he advanced over the uneven and sodden ground, his hair a black and shining cap, his eyes dark and alive as his hand sought death. For the fight was to the death. It could be nothing less.

Nicholas had ever been a strong fighter, his arm

sure and tireless in all his mock battles. But this battle had nothing in it of knights in training or tumbling squires; never before had he faced a man intent on his death. Never before had he faced his death in another man's eyes.

He had not expected a monk to be so fierce.

He had forgotten that Richard of Warefeld was no monk.

"Hurry, Isabel," Rowland murmured. "Richard suffers not. Edmund needs you now."

He kept his eyes on the boy while she stripped to the skin, keeping her linen shift off the ground as she pulled it from her soaking body. She shivered when the full swell of wet wind hit her body; her cloak was gone, a sodden bird lying in the road before Malton, and her bliaut would take too long to don. She could not wait; nay, 'twas Edmund who could not wait.

Naked, she knelt at his side, Rowland lifting him, the grass beneath him black with spilt blood. Ripping the shift in two, she pushed the fabric into his dual wounds, one in front and one behind, seeking to touch her fingers within the wound, connecting the fabric, blocking the wound and stopping the flow of his life out upon the grass. 'Twas the best she could do until a cauterizing iron could be heated and applied.

Edmund's eyes rolled and he was still, his breathing shallow and his pulse thin. He had lost much blood. But that was over now. The linen was holding.

Laying the boy back to earth, Rowland removed

his cloak and pressed it round her shoulders. 'Twas wet, but it covered her. She hardly noticed; kneeling at Edmund's side, her eyes were all for Richard.

Nicholas was a big man, thick with muscle and with arrogance. He fought a man who had succeeded at every endeavor to which he had applied his skill, yet a man he had bested in his proud heart for year upon year. Richard had always been the best with sword and mace and lance; his skill had flowed from him, making every effort seem one of effortless ease while all around him struggled clumsily to master what he had mastered at a touch. Nicholas had hated him within a week of his arrival at Malton. How not to hate such a man? When Richard had flown like a startled thrush to the abbey, he had rejoiced. When Richard had appeared with Isabel at his side as his wife, he had marked how much a monk Richard had become. Such a man could not fight; the skill and inclination had been prayed out of him. Such a man as Richard now was, he could defeat.

How such a man could stand against him now was beyond his reason. Looking down, he saw that he bled from a single slice across his thigh. 'Twas of no matter; no man would die of such pricks as Richard dealt.

William and Rowland saw what Nicholas did not. They too had fought the man, and understood his style. Richard was no hacker. He did not hack and hew his way to victory, but struck lightly, as effortlessly as lightning and as quick and sharp. And, understanding the rage of a man who defended his wife, they knew he toyed with Nicholas, to prolong his suffering and his penance for so heinous a desire. No man would have Isabel save Richard.

Isabel saw only that Richard was unharmed. 'Twas all she needed to see to ease her heart.

With a smile, Richard lunged and sliced Nicholas again on the thigh where his hauberk ended; Nicholas's wealth was not such that he could afford mail that went below his hips. Isabel's wealth should have taken care of his lack.

But had Richard missed? Looking down quickly, Nicholas could see but a single cut. And yet, was it not deeper than before? Had it not been a mere scratch, and was it not now the depth of a finger's width?

Looking up, Richard smiled. Nicholas thought that most odd; it was well known that Richard did not often smile.

Never had Richard had such cause.

Another lunge and Richard's sword swung down. Nicholas tried to block the sword with his own, but his sword encountered only air. His leg pained him, the blood running hard and fast. So much blood from a single, shallow wound?

But 'twas not shallow, not anymore. The red and gaping cut now gleamed with the white of bone.

God above, 'twas not to be borne. If he did not strike soon and win, he could lose the leg.

And still he could not lay his sword to Richard; the man moved as light, as sun, seen but not able to be grasped. Nicholas could not lay his hand or his sword to Richard. Without doing so, he could never lay his hand to Isabel. He had arranged it all; his uncle was high within the bishop's household, and, with Isabel widowed, his name would appear on the marriage contract. His uncle had him assured that it would be so, that such arrangements could be made, that Isabel and Dornei could be his. His part had only been to make Isabel a widow, and he had gladly taken up his task. To kill a monk would be no effort. Yet he bled and Richard, the monk, did not. He could not comprehend it.

Richard's grin was as wide as the wound on Nicholas's leg; he was enjoying the slow death of his enemy. He could see that Nicholas was befuddled and still thought to win. Such arrogance was killing him.

Richard moved in close, his sword a gleam of death that was reflected in his eyes. "Did you think you would take her from me? She is a gift you shall never touch, not even with your sight," he growled. With a twist of his arm, his sword a shining extension of his intent, Richard pierced Nicholas's left eye. His eye was gone in a burst of blood and pulp.

Isabel gasped and turned her head from the sight, fighting the sudden upthrust of nausea that roiled within her. "Richard, nay!" she cried, her voice a moan of horror.

Her voice, coming to him, piercing through his animal rage, checked his hand. He heard the pain in her cry and knew in that instant that if he did not stop his torment of Nicholas, 'twould be Isabel he tortured and not the man who stood bleeding in front of him. His revenge against Nicholas stood as nothing against his need to protect Isabel.

Without hesitation, he slammed his sword into Nicholas's other eye, piercing the brain. Nicholas, his reason gone, stood for a moment, just an instant, and in that instant Richard said, "Isabel is mine." With that, Nicholas, who had cast his eyes upon a prize he could not touch, fell to the ground with the heavy thud of man and mail and blood.

Turning, Richard looked at her, kneeling in the mud by a boy gone white and silent with pain and blood loss. Her eyes were as dark as the earth, her hair the color of sodden bark, her skin the flawless white of cloud; she watched him and he saw her fear. She was as still as Edmund and as silent, her eyes glistening with the same overriding terror as when he had delivered her from Adam's touch. The violence of battle assaulted her; she could not bear the sight of death. Warm skin and soothing words would ease her.

" 'Tis done, Isabel," he said, hurrying to her. "All is well."

She watched him come, her eyes wide. He enveloped her in his arms, slipping his hands beneath her cloak . . . and felt her nudity. Pulling back from her, his hands holding firmly the edges of the cloak, he frowned and said, "It appears I must beat you, after all." Soothing words they were not, but why was she wet and naked?

Isabel snuggled within his arms and said with a trembling smile, "Did I not say I could disrobe as well as you?" She pressed her face against his chest, her nose cold and wet. He held her to him, giving her his warmth and the proof of his life.

"The boy?" he asked, looking down at his squire.

"Shot through," she said, pulling away from him, remembering her duty as Lady of Dornei. "We must get Edmund home and dry and warm. He wants better care than a cold, wet field and the remains of my shift."

That answered as to her nudity and he could not fault her; her duty had been clear, but he thanked God for Rowland's cloak.

She need not have spoken; Rowland had lifted Edmund into his arms and was carrying him to William, who sat upon his horse. Gently he laid the boy in William's arms and, as one, they rode softly for Dornei. No time was spent in straightening the sopping mess of her bliaut; Edmund could not wait for a woman to do her toilette in the rain. Her gown was draped over Rowland's mount, as wet and muddy as her long-abandoned cloak surely was.

"The archer?" Richard asked as they rode.

"Dispatched," Rowland said. " 'Twas only the two of them. They did not expect much opposition, it appears."

'Twas said playfully, and Richard took his meaning. "They did not expect a monk to much hinder them in their plans."

"I expect, had they faced a monk, their expectations would have been met. 'Twas their misfortune that they chose to stand against Richard of the Swift Sword."

"As to that," Isabel interrupted, "how did you unhorse Nicholas?"

Richard smiled and shrugged. "I have learned by hard experience that Isabel of Dornei does not relish the realities of combat. Let it be said only that I did unhorse him."

"But—"

"You did not doubt me, did you, Isabel?" he asked, looking askance at her through the gloom of rain and dusk. "You trusted in my ability to best a knight whose fighting style I well understood and whose cause was so wicked?"

What answer could she give? Could she admit that she had thought her husband incapable of armed combat? Could she give public voice to her belief that Richard would pray away his foes? Nay, she could not, not when her own fears so shamed her. How could she have doubted Richard?

"Doubt you?" she said lightly. "I have been warned against doubting you, Richard, and most recently. I believe you capable of anything."

"A belief well founded in fact, Lady," he said.

"How far until we reach Dornei?" William asked. "The boy starts to feel his wound."

"Moments now," Richard answered. "There, the torch is seen through the trees. The plain is before us."

"Do not hurry, Lord William," Isabel instructed. "Better slowly and carefully, his bleeding stilled, than to hurry to escape the rain."

"Ulrich," William called. The squire and Elsbeth, on William's authority, had kept well back during

Richard's battle. Once all was safe, Ulrich had been allowed to return. He had taken his charge most seriously; Elsbeth he had guarded with his life. "Ride on and tell Dornei of our coming. Do not abandon your lady in your race to serve."

"Never, my lord," he answered, only slightly affronted. "Shall I return?"

"Nay, stay and have water heated, the fires stoked," William said. "Your pardon," he said, nodding to Richard. "I did not mean to overstep my place."

"You have not," Richard said. "Your instruction is sound. The boy must be warmed, the cauterizing iron prepared. How does he fare?"

"He trembles," William said. "I fear a fever."

"Nay," Isabel said, drawing her horse near. "It is only the cold and the shock, I think. 'Tis too soon for fever. Ride on, Ulrich, and take Elsbeth with you. Elsbeth, you know what must be done. I will stay with Edmund."

"I have no fever," Edmund protested. "I do not like being carried like a babe. I can ride."

"What you like does not pertain," Richard said. "Lie still and learn the merits of submission."

"I see no merit in being carried," Edmund mumbled.

Richard smiled. "The merits of submission are not easily nor pleasantly learned. That is the first lesson."

They left the wood track and were on the plain. Dornei rose black against the stormy sky, the glow of firelight warm and welcome in a sky wet and cold. Isabel clutched Rowland's cloak about her nakedness. How was she to enter Dornei thus attired? She felt as naked as she was; surely someone would note her lack of aught but cloak, and that cloak not her own.

"Richard," she whispered on a hiss of sound. "Richard!"

Richard turned to her, his face white in the darkness that now enveloped them completely; only Dornei glowed in all that dark night. A moment he paused and then he smiled. She could see it, full and bright; he could not deny that he was laughing at her.

He did not even try.

"Cold, Isabel?" he laughed.

" 'Tis naught to laugh at! What will be thought to see me thus?" The talk had run so wild when Adam had trapped her in the barbican; what would be surmised when it was seen that she rode through the night unclothed?

"What care you what people think? You were never of a mind for that."

"I am Lady of Dornei. I must have a care—"

"Nay, Isabel, you are Richard's woman, and Richard finds you very pleasing in your borrowed cloak. Hold up your head, as is your natural way," he chuckled, "and ride into your holding with all the dignity of your place."

"There is little dignity in a sodden cloak," she mumbled.

"Isabel," he said seriously, "you have all the dignity you shall ever require in your very nature.

Head high, my wife. You do good service. Edmund's need is sharp, and there is not time for you to dress."

'Twas true. Would she imperil Edmund for the sake of her pride? 'Twas not a question worth the time in asking.

The gates of Dornei were open; Ulrich had done his work. She kept her eyes on William, who led them in, and pulled her cloak tight with a clenched fist. All was quiet; no eyes pried to see beneath her cloak. Through the barbican they passed and into the inner bailey. Ulrich waited at the base of the stair tower, Gilbert at his side. The men on the curtain wall kept their eyes to the invisible horizon.

Ulrich had, indeed, done his work.

"My thanks, Ulrich. You have indeed held my reputation in your hands and have guarded it well," she said when she had dismounted. "You are a most efficient, most honorable squire."

"Thank you, Lady," he smiled, ducking his head against her compliment. "Elsbeth has prepared the room she shares with Aelis to cosset Edmund."

Edmund moaned. Isabel was not entirely certain his distress was physical in nature.

Gilbert took the lad and carried him up; Isabel swiftly followed. Richard and his guests remained in the hall, leaving her to her duty. The cauterizing iron awaited.

The men stood by the massive fire in the hall, drinking their ale in silent companionship. The light played against their skin, shadows of yellow and red that displayed the curve of cheek and the line of jaw but left their eyes in shadows of black. The strong smell of wood smoke was especially fragrant after an afternoon in the rain of a cold spring. Their clothing steamed, droplets falling to the rush-covered floor to be quickly absorbed. They were well content.

"She seemed to have some skill with wounds," Rowland remarked placidly, facing the fire.

"She is most skilled," Richard said. "In all of Malton, she was unequaled in her talent. Edmund will recover," he said.

"How bad was it?" William asked.

"Bad," Rowland said. "The wound was straight, but just above the hip. A wound like that can quickly turn foul."

"Isabel has seen worse," Richard said.

"As have I," Rowland said. "She let him bleed out. He will be weak."

"He could be lame," William said, keeping his face to the fire. "Or worse."

Richard said nothing. Edmund was a bright lad, quick to learn and eager to excel; he deserved a kinder end than disfigurement. Isabel would do all she could, and Richard had great trust in her ability, yet there was something more which could be done.

"The chapel awaits," he said to his friends. "The Lord awaits our prayers on Edmund's behalf."

She found him there, kneeling in silent prayer, his warrior comrades by his side. Where else to look for Richard but at the altar of God?

He turned at her approach, read her look, and shrugged. Where else, indeed?

"How is he?" he asked.

"Well," she answered, watching him rise to his feet. "The wound is closed and dry. Tomorrow will tell us more, but he can move his legs, and so that fear is past."

Richard smiled his thanks to God and to his wife.

Had ever such a man knelt before God? His eyes were the blue-black of stormy dusk, his hands heavy with veins and torn with open wounds, the gifts of his knight's training, like Christ's had been upon His cross, signs of His gift of love. As Richard's hands were. He fought for her, always and only for her, for Dornei and for the legacy of her womb; it was all she had dreamed, yet it eclipsed all she had imagined love to be. He gave and gave and gave again, relinquishing whatever dream he had for his life. All for Isabel.

"Does he sleep?" William asked.

Isabel forced her eyes from her husband's face and answered, "Sleep? Nay. I think he would retreat into the silence and solitude of sleep if he had his way, but Aelis and Elsbeth and even Ulrich hover so close about him that he cannot escape. He has made his name among them and must stay awake to hear their praise. They insist."

"You left him to that?" Richard said. "How, when you know that he—"

"He insisted." She smiled. "How often will he be so o'erwashed by praise? Nay, let him have his time. It comes too rarely in this life that we hear such praise."

The men smiled and nodded, and as a body they left the chapel, Father Langfrid with them. The hall was full when they did enter it, full and loud and bright with firelight. It was well that she had changed into a bliaut of palest blue with black embroidery trailing like a vine along the bell of her sleeve. It was good to be warm and so well covered after being wet and cold for so long.

"I would see Edmund," Richard said softly to her, his hand upon her arm. "Enjoy the fire," he directed William and Rowland. "We will return anon and would listen to your tales of walking the Way of the Cross."

"As you will," William replied with a smile which was echoed fully on Rowland's face. "We will await your return."

When Richard and his wife had flown halfway across the hall, William said in an aside to Rowland, "Think you he will return before the Morrow Mass?"

"With Edmund's wounding, we have lost the chance to test our wager against Aelis. Should another wager be struck, I would lay that we will not see Richard until Sext."

"So late? He has impressed you with his stamina," William said thoughtfully, stroking his chin.

"Nay, it is his . . . willingness to pleasure his wife which has impressed me." Rowland grinned.

"Ah." William nodded. "I cannot argue it. But I would lay that he will be among us for Terce. He is a man of monkish habits, a prayerful man."

"A married man, first and last," Rowland argued.

"The same wager as before?"

"Done," Rowland agreed.

And both men smiled, certain of one thing. They would not be telling tales of battle to Richard anytime soon.

Isabel found herself ushered across the hall, her steps hardly able to keep pace with her husband's. "He will not fly off; we need not hurry," she said.

"Does not Isabel always hurry? I but keep pace with you," Richard argued with a grin.

They were up the darkened stair tower, Isabel's breathing labored and sharp to her own ears, and into the chamber that sheltered Edmund. It was as she had said; he was well attended by Elsbeth and Aelis, even Ulrich doing his part.

"I did nothing, I tell you," Edmund protested. "Except to find my way into the path of an arrow."

"You performed your service to your lord," Ulrich stated with staunch authority. "It is the highest honor, and you did not fail."

"He did not have benefit of his shield," Edmund grumbled.

"He did not require it," Richard inserted.

All turned to him upon the words, the girls dropping into graceful curtseys and Ulrich bowing from the waist.

"My Lord Richard," Edmund said, his cheeks flushed in excitement, fever, or embarrassment. "I did not attend you as I should—"

"Be still, boy," Richard said, coming fully into the small chamber. "You did your service and well. There is no censure." When Edmund looked to argue anew, Richard said, "They must have thought you vital, a most important link to their success, or you would not have been felled so quickly. Think on that, Edmund. They feared your involvement."

Edmund's mouth hung agape for the time it took for the words to find a warm and sheltered place within his youthful heart. And then he lifted his chin and surveyed the room, his eyes proud and confident.

'Twas not lost on the women of his confinement. Aelis glowed her favor and her appreciation of a squire so bold. And Elsbeth—why, Elsbeth looked to Richard with all the devotion of a daughter. She smiled her thanks, her smile a gentle and awkward play of emotion on her face, but smile she did. Richard returned her smile . . . and winked.

Isabel missed none of it.

"My lord, are you satisfied?" she asked. "Edmund is well, or will be well if he could but rest. Alone."

"My lady, I will escort Elsbeth from the chamber," Ulrich volunteered.

"I know my way," Elsbeth argued, avoiding Ulrich's touch upon her arm.

" 'Tis dark. You might lose your footing. I will attend," Ulrich said. "Do not deny me the pleasure of your escort, Elsbeth, for, to speak a truth, I will not be denied. I will follow, though you fly from me to heaven itself. I will attend. My heart can do naught else."

Elsbeth's sigh was deep and her answer heard though she and Ulrich were well within the confines of the stair tower. "I only go to find a bench on which to lay my head. I am not for heaven, in flight or otherwise."

"Then my heart can rest, for to lose an earthly life as sweet, as precious as your own to so untimely a departure for heaven . . ." Ulrich's voice trailed off softly as they descended the stair tower.

Isabel was not uncertain that she heard still more exasperated sighs from Elsbeth.

"I fear he will talk her to her death," Richard murmured for her ears alone.

Isabel smothered the laugh that rose up and turned once more to Edmund. "You are content? Your needs and comforts met?" She touched his face; he had no fever.

"I will see to his needs throughout the night, Lady Isabel," Aelis offered, her blue eyes bright with eager intention.

"Very well," Isabel answered, her hesitation only barely masked. "You will come if he has need?"

"Aye, lady," she said demurely.

It did not sit well; Aelis was not demure.

"It is well with you, Edmund? You are content with Aelis as your attendant throughout the night?" Isabel asked.

Edmund managed a look that was both disinterested and confident. "Yea, my lady. She can attend. I am content."

With a slight frown, Isabel let Richard lead her from the chamber into the stair tower.

"He seems very well content," Richard whispered. "How bad is his wound?"

Isabel caught his meaning and smiled, "Bad enough that two upon that bed would cause him pain."

"Intense pain?" Richard asked, his expression playful.

"How intense would pain need be to keep a man from tumbling?" Isabel said softly, her own grin wide.

"Cutting off his leg might do it," Richard answered. "Might. He is young."

They left the stair tower as they spoke, their own chamber before them.

"I thought we were to hear stories of battle and valor before the fire of our hall. Are not William and Rowland awaiting our arrival?" she asked as he led her in and closed the door behind her.

"I would lay a wager that they are not," Richard said with a shrug.

Isabel smiled and shook her head in mock disapproval. "The ways of men are strange to me. You play at words and meanings when to state your intention clear—"

"And who was it who yearned for a seductive game of chess with every beating of her heart?" he interrupted, holding her to him, toying with the laces at her back.

" 'Twas you who taught me to play. I only wanted to test my skill."

The knot was undone and her bliaut loosened.

"You play badly," he said, his mouth at her temple.

"I want practice," she said, turning to his mouth.

"You cheat."

"I like to win," she said, kissing his throat, her arms around his back. He was so strong; he held the world away and sheltered her within.

"You have won," he said, releasing her from the bonds of her bliaut.

"Have I?" she whispered, marking him with her mouth. "And what of Elsbeth? Did you think I did not see the smile you gifted her?"

" 'Twas all in innocence," he protested without alarm. She knew him.

She knew him as he had not known himself. He was all honor, and all his passion was for her. Upon this rock of knowing she rested, her heart at ease.

"Does she know that? You are a man to make a woman dream," Isabel said, rubbing her hips against his arousal.

"Only one woman dreams of Richard," he said, lifting the skirt of her undergown. "And for Richard, there is only one."

He kissed her hard, his mouth hot against hers, his hands urgent and demanding. She met his desire with equal force and equal urgency; ever they had been matched in this.

She pulled back from him, her eyes lit with the knowledge of her own worth and her own attraction, her words teasing. "And does Elsbeth know this? Have you said—"

"All the world knows the truth of this. For Richard there is only Isabel," he growled, grinning, tossing her upon the bed, her skirts above her hips. "Need I prove it?"

Isabel smiled and played with a curl of her hair. He was her world, a dream realized, a prayer answered, a gift divine.

With a smile, she issued her challenge.

"Do you think you can?"

JENNIFER ASHLEY

Egan MacDonald was the one person Princess Zarabeth couldn't read. Yet even without being able hear his thoughts, she knew he was the most honorable, infuriating, and deliciously handsome man she'd ever met. And now her life was in his hands. Chased out of her native country by bitter betrayal and a bevy of assassins, Zarabeth found refuge at the remote MacDonald castle and a haven in Egan's embrace. She also found an ancient curse, a matchmaking nephew, a pair of debutants eager to drag her protector to the altar, and dark secrets in Egan's past. But even amid all the danger raged a desire too powerful to be denied....

Highlander Ever After

ISBN 13: 978-0-8439-6004-4

EMILY BRYAN

"An author to watch."
—Michelle Buonfiglio, LifetimeTV.com

BURIED TREASURE

All it took was a flick of the wrist. A deft touch of his sword point and Drake the Dragon bared her bound breasts. Then with the heat of his hands along her skin, he bared her soul. All the wantonness Jacquelyn had denied herself as a famous courtesan's daughter, all the desire she'd held in her heart while running Lord Gabriel Drake's estate flooded through her at his touch. Not that she could let a bloody pirate know it.

Gabriel may have left his seafaring days behind, but his urge to plunder was stronger than ever. Especially if it involved full, ripe lips and a warm, soft body. Unfortunately, he needed Jacquelyn's help, not her maidenhead, to learn how to behave properly toward a lady so he could marry and produce an heir. Yet Mistress Jack was the only woman he wanted, no matter what her heritage. And everyone knows what a pirate wants, a pirate takes....

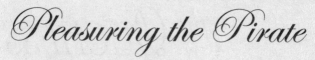

Pleasuring the Pirate

AVAILABLE AUGUST 2008!

ISBN 13: 978-0-8439-6133-1

EMILY BRYAN

BARING IT ALL

From the moment she saw the man on her doorstep, Lady Artemisia, Duchess of Southwycke, wanted him naked. For once, she'd have the perfect model for her latest painting. But as he bared each bit of delicious golden skin from his broad chest down to his—oh, my!—art became the last thing on her mind.

Trevelyn Deveridge was looking for information, not a job. Though if a brash, beautiful widow demanded he strip, he wasn't one to say no. Especially if it meant he could get closer to finding the true identity of an enigmatic international operative with ties to her family. But as the intrigue deepened and the seduction sweetened, Trev found he'd gone well beyond his original mission of...

DISTRACTING the DUCHESS

AVAILABLE MARCH 2008!   ISBN 13: 978-0-8439-5870-6

To order a book or to request a catalog call:
1-800-481-9191

This book is also available at your local bookstore, or you can check out our Web site **www.dorchesterpub.com** where you can look up your favorite authors, read excerpts, or glance at our discussion forum to see what people have to say about your favorite books.

CONNIE MASON

The Black Widow

That was what the desperate prisoners incarcerated in
Devil's Chateau called her. Whatever she did with them, one
thing was certain: Her unfortunate victims were never seen
again. But when she whisked Reed Harwood out of the cell
where he'd been left to die for spying against the French, he
discovered the lady was not all she seemed.

Fleur Fontaine was the most exquisitely sensual woman
he'd ever met, yet there was an innocence about her that
belied her sordid reputation. Only a dead man would fail to
respond. Reed was not
dead yet, but was he
willing to pay...

The Price of Pleasure

ISBN 10: 0-8439-5745-X
ISBN 13: 978-0-8439-5745-7

To order a book or to request a catalog call:
1-800-481-9191
This book is also available at your local bookstore, or you can
check out our Web site **www.dorchesterpub.com** where
you can look up your favorite authors, read excerpts, or
glance at our discussion forum to see what people have to
say about your favorite books.

JOY NASH

THE DRUIDS OF AVALON

Hidden away on a misty isle, steeped in the teachings of The Lady, they used enchantment to stem the tide of the invaders while battling a still darker enemy.

CHALYBS

It was the Roman word for bright iron, and Marcus had long been struggling to forge of it a mighty weapon. Though his workmanship surpassed all others, the right combination of heat and force eluded him...until a familiar silver-haired beauty appeared beside his anvil. Gwendolyn's lithe body aroused in him a white-hot fire, a need fanned ever higher by her nearness. Though he could not help remembering the golden glow of a wolf's eyes when he looked into her hypnotic gaze, he knew he must surrender body and soul to her mysterious powers, for only with Gwen guiding his hammer could they create...

DEEP MAGIC

ISBN 13: 978-0-505-52716-5

DAWN MACTAVISH

Lark at first hoped it was a simple nightmare: If she closed her eyes, she would be back in the mahogany bed of her spacious boudoir at Eddington Hall, and all would be well. Her father, the earl of Roxburgh, would not be dead by his own hand, and she would not be in Marshalsea Debtor's Prison.

Such was not to be. Ere the Marshalsea could do its worst, the earl of Grayshire intervened. But while his touch was electric and his gaze piercing, for what purpose had he bought her freedom? No, this was not a dream. As Lark would soon learn, her dreams had never ended so well.

The Privateer

ISBN 13: 978-0-8439-5981-9